To,
Helen & Ian
With best wishes

John Powell

THE COLONIAL
GENTLEMAN'S SON

THE COLONIAL GENTLEMAN'S SON

The Story of a Young Man in a Young Country

John Powell

Book Guild Publishing
Sussex, England

First published in Great Britain in 2010 by
The Book Guild Ltd
Pavilion View
19 New Road
Brighton, BN1 1UF

Typesetting in Garamond by
Keyboard Services, Luton, Bedfordshire

Printed and bound in Great Britain by
CPI Antony Rowe

A catalogue record for this book is available from
The British Library

ISBN 978 1 84624 496 4

BURKINA FASO

Bolgatanga

Wa

G H A N A

Tamale

Yendi

TOGO

CÔTE
D'IVOIRE

Lake
Volta

Wenchi

Sunyani

Techiman

Kumasi

Konongo

Ho

Obuasi

Akosombo

Oda

Koforidua

Tema

Accra

Tarkwa

Cape Coast

Takoradi

| 0 | Kilometres | 200 |
| 0 | | 150 |

Contents

1

Konongo

Kwame Mainu was four days older than his country – he was born on Saturday 2 March 1957. Four days later the British colony of the Gold Coast became the Dominion of Ghana. On that day the first elected prime minister, Kwame Nkrumah, declared, 'Ghana is free forever!' It was a memorable week for Ghana and for the Mainu family in Konongo.

The baby born at that auspicious time bore the same name as the prime minister. Kwame means 'born on Saturday'. The Akan people of southern Ghana have a special name for boys born on each of the seven days of the week and a corresponding set of seven names for girls. As for Mainu, it originally signified that an ancestor was a second-born child.

The prime minister's surname, Nkrumah, suggests a ninth-born child, but it resulted not from the birth status of his forebears but from a mistake made by his first schoolteacher in recording his name in the class register. He was named at birth, in September 1909, Francis Nwia-Kofi Ngonloma, with Kofi suggesting that he was born on a Friday: the name Kwame Nkrumah was formally adopted in London in 1945. Considering this history of changes, one might suspect that the first leader of modern Ghana had something of an identity problem. It was a trait that some of his successors were to share.

Little Kwame's father was Kwesi Mainu. Kwesi (Sunday) was an Ashanti and a native of Konongo, a town in Ashanti Region situated 50 kilometres east of the regional capital Kumasi, along the road to the national capital Accra. Kwame's mother was Amma Ansah-Twum, a Bono from Wenchi, 155 kilometres to the north-west of Kumasi. At that time, Wenchi was also in Ashanti Region but it was destined later to be part of the new region of Brong-Ahafo.

Kwesi Mainu, like most Ashantis, rejoiced in Ghana's independence but opposed the leadership of the prime minister. He had voted for the opposition party led by Dr J.B. Danquah. Amma, on the other hand, followed her family in Wenchi in supporting Kwame Nkrumah. In times past her people, the Bonos, had been oppressed by the Ashantis, and the creation of the new region of Brong-Ahafo was to bring the Bonos greater freedom at the same time as reducing the power of the Ashanti opposition to the government. However, Amma chose not to let politics intrude in her marriage and kept her secret ballot secret.

Kwesi and Amma raised their son in one room of a typical Ashanti compound house, which consisted of a single-storey concrete block structure with a corrugated metal roof extending along the four sides of a large rectangular courtyard. All the many rooms opened onto this enclosed area. Access from the road outside was through an opening at the centre of one side that may once have been closed by a large gate. The original design was clearly intended to provide security for the residents, there being only one access point to be defended against intruders. The absence of the gate suggested that the perceived danger from outside was less than in former times.

Until Kwame was two years old he spent most of the daylight hours tightly wrapped in a cover cloth on his mother's back. This was the most convenient way for Amma to care for her baby while trading or moving about the compound or the town. Throughout this same period Kwame derived most of his sustenance from Amma's breast, so whenever he demanded feeding, the source was always close at hand. Later, if she chose to leave Kwame behind in the compound, there were always other women, old folk and older children to help watch over him.

All the residents of the house belonged to the same extended family or clan. The room in which Kwame was born had been bequeathed to Kwesi by his widowed mother, who had not lived quite long enough to witness the birth of either her grandson or her new country. Although the space was small it was used only for sleeping and storing the family's few possessions. Most other activities took place in the courtyard.

The compound house, in common with many other houses in the town, gave the impression of never having been completed. The large central courtyard was unpaved except for a few small areas of concrete outside some of the rooms. It was on this hard-trodden and often-swept bare earth floor that Little Kwame learned to crawl and toddle and play with other children while his mother cooked, attended to household chores and conversed with the other women. Constant sweeping kept the compound free of grass and weeds but the courtyard was big enough to accommodate three shade trees under which the men could gather to smoke their pipes and vent their grievances. In addition to the trees, the courtyard was littered with building materials left over from the original construction and later extension projects. These piles of sand and discarded building blocks had gradually become weathered into smooth and familiar contours that nobody thought of removing, either to construct a new facility or to improve the appearance of the compound.

Many of the shade trees in Ashanti towns and villages are mangoes. These were unpopular with the adults because the children made so much mess in May every year when the fruit was ripe and ready to eat. The children's standard technique of harvesting was to throw sticks up into the trees. These fell back accompanied by the fruit and also by copious quantities of foliage. Young Kwame was soon to become familiar with this activity, although his early efforts produced little result. He was dependent on the older children for the delicious treat that left his face and hands stained and dripping with bright yellow-orange juice.

Kwesi Mainu was an important man and regarded as one of the leaders of the compound community. His status was derived from his employment in government service; he was an inspector of sawmills. The Gold Coast had long been a major exporter of tropical hardwoods such as mahogany and iroko, known in Ashanti as *odum*. Much of the timber was exported as felled logs but the government had for some time been encouraging the sawing of logs into planks to add value and increase foreign earnings. Sawmills had been established by European companies and by Lebanese, Syrian and local businessmen. The new government of independent Ghana continued the regulatory system introduced in colonial times.

The operation of large and powerful sawing machines and heavy lifting cranes posed many potential hazards, and accidents were frequent. It was Kwesi's duty to make regular inspections and to shut down and demand the repair of any unsafe equipment. It was not a job to make him popular with the sawmill managers, intent on meeting their production schedules. However, with the authority of the government and the support of the workers, who appreciated his efforts to keep them safe, Kwesi tried to carry out his duty conscientiously. He stoically rejected the bribes offered by Lebanese and Syrian sawmill owners and resisted their efforts to use political influence to undermine his authority.

Qualities of integrity in government service had been nurtured in colonial times and Kwesi was resolved to carry them forward into his new Ghana. However, he came increasingly to realise that the combination of strong inducements and veiled threats employed by large sawmill operators, such as Hanabis of Kumasi, was exploiting the venality and vulnerability of his fellow inspectors. As the years passed his self-imposed mission seemed more and more forlorn and he felt increasingly isolated. He would have been distressed to realise that the shadow of this sense of mission would persist to darken the life of his son.

The sawmills of southern Ghana were scattered over the timber-growing areas of the Central, Western and Ashanti Regions, including the south-western part of the area that was to become Brong-Ahafo Region. Visiting these sawmills involved a great deal of travelling and some nights away from home. There was no ideal centre from which to reach all locations but Konongo was reasonably centrally located. Although specially assigned to the large group of sawmills in and around Kumasi, Kwesi often had to travel farther afield to cover for other inspectors who were sick or on leave. This increased the number of nights he was forced to spend away from his family.

Newly independent Ghana possessed a limited railway system sometimes referred to as the Golden Triangle. It linked the three major cities of Accra, Kumasi and Takoradi and encompassed roughly the land area over which cocoa was grown – hence its name. The railway from Accra to Kumasi passed through Konongo and afforded Kwesi a means of travelling to the port of Takoradi where most of the whole logs were shipped out and where several sawmills had sprung up. Along that same route were dropping-off points, such as Obuasi and Tarkwa, providing access to other sawmills. Apart from this, Kwesi had to rely on road transport. Some sawmills were deep in the forest and could be reached only by dirt feeder roads. He spent many more hours jolting over potholes than inspecting machinery.

Kwesi was not provided with a vehicle – he was reliant on public transport and this usually meant travelling on a *trotro* or mammie wagon. These vehicles had wooden bodies locally constructed on an old lorry chassis, the most popular being a five-ton Bedford. Plying on all roads, and operated by private owner-drivers, *trotros* provided affordable transport for the general population. With hard, wooden plank seating and often overloaded with passengers and their luggage, travelling on a *trotro* was both uncomfortable and unsafe. Large potholes, especially at the road edges, frequently caused badly worn tyres to burst, throwing the *trotro* off the road or into other vehicles. Such events often resulted in the vehicles toppling over, causing the wooden box structure to collapse sideways, ejecting or crushing the unfortunate passengers. Sometimes Kwesi found himself wondering which was safer: riding on a *trotro* or pushing a wooden plank with bare hands through an unguarded circular

4

saw. Life was full of hazards and the roads were no safer than the sawmills.

Pursuing his ambition for complete independence, Kwame Nkrumah declared Ghana a republic on 1 July 1960. Ghana ceased to be a dominion under the British Crown and President Nkrumah replaced Queen Elizabeth II as Head of State. One year later Nkrumah made himself the supreme commander of the armed forces and imprisoned Dr J.B. Danquah, his rival for the presidency. By this time all political opposition had been suppressed and the economy was deteriorating. The country that had inherited foreign exchange reserves of more than £300 million in 1957, and had been the world's leading exporter of cocoa, was now in debt and seeking loans from overseas. Little Kwame was four years old and Kwesi was already wondering if his son would grow up to enjoy what they had all expected to be the fruits of independence.

If Amma had any worries she did not show it. With Kwame off her back and off her breast for more than two years she still rejoiced in her regained freedom. She often wondered why the burden had not been replaced – other women did not enjoy such a respite – but she was content to let nature take its course. Kwesi's salary provided for their basic needs and her small-scale trading supplied a few extras. From a plywood kiosk on the Accra-Kumasi road that ran past their house Amma sold basic commodities such as soap, candles and tins of sardines. Supplies were generally plentiful and prices were affordable, although there were signs of increasing rates of inflation and occasional shortages.

Little Kwame was growing fast and seemed to be quite intelligent. He could chatter fluently in their native Twi language and his parents were encouraging him to pick up more English words in preparation for starting primary school. Kwesi and Amma knew that state schools in Ashanti Region uniquely taught the first year of primary school in the vernacular, but they hoped to be able to send Kwame to a private school where education was in English from the outset. Fortunately Kwesi had fluent English, using it extensively in his work, and he had already started to pass on this essential skill to his son.

Every day Amma would cook the evening meal for her family. Her source of heat was called a coal pot, a welded steel stove that burned charcoal. Those who could not afford charcoal still used the traditional stove, called *bokyea*, which consisted of three large stones to support the cooking pot, with spaces between them to allow wooden poles to be fed to the fire. All the women cooked in the compound at the same time so the air was filled with wood smoke and the acrid scent of burning charcoal. The cooking took several hours and consumed large quantities of fuel. Kwesi, who was widely read, often wondered why poor people had such a wasteful way of preparing food, but Amma only speculated on the quality of the result.

The most popular food in Ashanti was fufu. It was made from yam, unripe plantain or cassava, boiled and then pounded into a firm dough. Traditionally, an Ashanti would not eat cassava fufu, regarding it as the food of slaves. However, as the years passed and the economy continued to decline, more and more proud people were compelled to hide what was in their cooking pot. Fufu was eaten with a meat stew. Three types were popular. One was flavoured with groundnut paste, another with palm oil and the third, called light soup, contained only the basic ingredients of tomato, onion and pepper. All three soups were hot with the flavour of red pepper. Chicken was the most popular meat for those who could afford it and protein content was otherwise provided by the inclusion of large edible snails.

Fufu and soup are eaten with the hand and the technique is to form a small cup out of a ball of fufu and use it to scoop up the soup. The skill takes some time to acquire, and failure to master it can be a source of malnutrition in weaning infants. They succeed in eating the fufu but miss out on the soup, which is the main source of nutrients, especially if the fufu is made from cassava. Fortunately for Kwame, Amma helped him to consume his fair share of soup by letting him use a spoon until his little hand acquired the necessary dexterity. Unfortunately for Kwame he gained an excessive liking for pepper, which later had unwanted consequences.

Whenever Kwesi was at home the family gathered outside their room to share the evening meal. Most of the other families also enjoyed the cool of the compound after six-thirty when the sun had set. When the meal was over, by the light of flickering oil lamps, one of the elders would start to tell the tales of Ananse the Spider and an eager group of children would gather round. These tales, precursors of the Uncle Remus Brer Rabbit stories, relate the adventures of a loveable trickster and his friends. Through these tales the art and craft of living by one's wits was passed from generation to generation. Kwame was born in time and in circumstances to share this experience. Within a few years it would be swept away by the power of television.

With bowls of fufu and tales of Ananse the Spider, Kwame's early years passed peacefully by. At the age of five he began to attend a private primary school and with the active encouragement of his parents his command of English developed apace. Kwame liked school, but what he did not like was being made to attend church with his mother on Sunday. Everyone in Konongo belonged to a church. Most were either Roman Catholics or Seventh Day Adventists but Anglicans, Methodists, Baptists and other denominations had churches or chapels in the town. Kwame found it all very confusing. Every Sunday Amma would drag him unwillingly to one church while most of his playmates were taken off to different churches. Amma usually attended the Catholic church but she sometimes chose one of the other churches for a change. Kwame would have preferred to stay at home with his father.

Kwesi seldom accompanied his family to church as the other fathers did. Sometimes Amma would cajole him into coming, telling him that it was Christmas, Easter or Harvest Festival. Occasionally, if Kwame was ill or had some other valid excuse, Kwesi would take his son's side and persuade Amma to leave the boy at home. Kwame was pleased when his father supported him in this way but he wondered why he did not help him to stay at home every Sunday.

The political and economic outlook in Ghana was becoming ever bleaker and this had an adverse effect on family life in the compound. In 1964 Kwame Nkrumah established a one-party state with himself as Life President. Dr J.B. Danquah was imprisoned again and died, still incarcerated, the following February. Kwesi felt a sense of foreboding and spoke with the other men about his concerns for the restoration of democracy. Corruption was widespread and cadres of Nkrumah's party, the CPP, were bragging that 'Osagyefo has killed a big elephant and there will be plenty for all to eat.' (Osagyefo, the Saviour, was a title given to Nkrumah, from its use in Christian churches for Jesus Christ.)

Amma's concerns were more immediate. Her trading business was not doing well and she had come to realise that Kwesi's salary would never provide her with her own house. She could not face spending the rest of her life in one small room. When she raised these issues with Kwesi he spoke only of better times ahead when democracy was restored. Amma was impatient for a change in her life. She challenged Kwesi to explain why other sawmill inspectors were able to build fine houses for their wives while she was compelled to exist in this hovel. Kwesi, of course, knew the answer, but chose not to give it. Amma's respect for her husband was becoming undermined by his apparent lack of ambition for his family.

Rumours of attempts to remove the President circulated freely. As early as August 1962 a bomb exploded at Kulungugu, narrowly missing Nkrumah on his return from a visit to Upper Volta (the country is now known as Burkina Faso). Other assassination attempts were rumoured and it seemed that his days were numbered. However, his Russian-trained personal bodyguard still afforded him effective protection against all but the most determined and disciplined military force.

It was the most determined and disciplined military force available that finally removed him. A group of Sandhurst-trained senior army officers, includng Major A.A. Afrifa, and the Chief of Police staged a coup on 24 February 1966 while Nkrumah was away on a state visit to North Vietnam and China. The National Liberation Council (NLC), which took over the reins of government, stated its intention to return the country to democracy as soon as possible. Things were looking better for Ghana, and Kwesi was much happier about the future prospects for his country and for his family. It was then that disaster struck, and Little Kwame's world was changed almost as profoundly as Big Kwame's had been.

Unusually, Kwesi had been directed south-eastwards towards Accra. There were not many sawmills in that area but he was instructed to inspect one at Oda in the south of the Eastern Region, near the border with the Central Region. This was outside his normal territory but he was filling in for a colleague on leave. He could have reached Oda by train but he would have had to go to Accra first and take a chance on a connection to Oda, making the journey much longer. He decided to go by road, and boarded a *trotro* to Suhum where a large lorry park provided a transport hub for the region. There he could get a second *trotro* to Oda, although the route was tortuous and some of the roads were very bad.

Kwesi left early in the morning as usual. Planning to spend one night away, he told Amma to expect him the following evening. The evening came, but Kwesi did not. After waiting up late, Amma tried to sleep in expectation of Kwesi's return the next day. However, he did not come on the next day, nor the day after. Amma tried to telephone Kwesi's head office from the post office but the service was poor. When at last she did get through she was told that the *trotro* on which Kwesi had been travelling between Suhum and Oda had had a serious accident. Kwesi had been taken to Korle Bu Hospital in Accra.

8

Amma took Kwame on the train to Accra and hurried to Korle Bu. The news was very bad: Kwesi had been seriously injured and the doctors told Amma he would not walk again. When he was fit enough to travel, Amma brought him back to Konongo. After a few weeks an official letter reached them, informing Kwesi that his government service had been terminated and he was to receive a modest disability pension.

Amma made a brave attempt to manage the new situation but she was soon overwhelmed. Now all her dreams of a better life had flown away. Still an attractive woman with many admirers, she received offers that were difficult to refuse. It would be many years before Kwame could understand his mother's dilemma and forgive her for the decision she took. He was too young to realise how dire economic circumstances can force the head to rule the heart. Amma announced that she was leaving in search of greener pastures. Nine-year-old Kwame was left alone to care for his disabled father. His whole world had been turned upside down.

Kwesi was no longer able to afford the private school and was forced to move Kwame to the state primary school. Even the state school fees were hard to afford. Moving school is always traumatic, but Kwame was lucky to find friends from his home compound among his new classmates. Amma's departure brought Kwame one relief. He was no longer compelled to sit through a long boring church service every Sunday, but this minor benefit in no way compensated for the loss of his mother.

Ghanaian children were expected to give much help with household chores and Amma had insisted on Kwame doing as much as other children. Now he had to do everything. Before leaving for school in the morning Kwame had to help his father wash and dress, and prepare their breakfast. At lunchtime he hurried home to make sure his father had everything he needed, and in the evening he cooked supper and cleaned their room before preparing himself and his father for the night. It is said that children faced with such responsibility grow up quickly. This was certainly the case with Kwame.

Kwesi's immobility and Kwame's need to provide care gave father and son extended opportunity for conversation. Kwesi resolved that although there was little physically that he could do for Kwame he would try to pass on his knowledge and experience of life. Kwesi was a quiet and thoughtful man, largely self-educated and intent on learning from his life experience and the recent history of his country. While deeply conscious of its rich traditional culture, Kwesi believed that Ghana should become a modern state, preserving and developing most of the innovations in democratic government and institutions introduced in the colonial era. To Kwame, Kwesi appeared to possess all wisdom, and he listened attentively to his father and tried to remember what he said. At school he made rapid progress and his teachers were impressed by his general knowledge and by his ability to express himself in English as well as in Twi. A bright academic future was predicted, but this would depend on much more than raw ability.

In 1968, at the age of eleven, Kwame entered Konongo Secondary School. To help with paying the fees he joined a team of boys operating a trolley in Konongo market. Market trolleys were locally made, with a wooden platform and four old car wheels. The two front wheels were steered by a metal bar that could extend in front of the trolley when it was being pulled, and hinge back over the platform when it was ridden downhill. Two or three boys usually made up the team. The leader was responsible for steering, and the assistants helped with loading and unloading and pushing the trolley uphill.

Motor vehicles could not penetrate far into the market because only narrow lanes were left between the stalls. All goods had to be conveyed to the point of sale by head-load or by trolley. A trolley could carry three or four head-loads at a time and many of the stall holders preferred their stock to arrive by trolley because they had fewer deliveries to monitor. For these reasons the boys operating the market trolleys earned a steady income. Some young men saved up their earnings to buy a second trolley and hired a fresh team to operate it. This process of expansion continued in some cases until the accumulated capital was enough to finance a serious business venture like a trading store or repair workshop. Kwame took note of how these budding entrepreneurs were operating but decided that for the time being school studies must take precedence. He allowed his trolley pushing to be determined by his available spare time as well as by his basic financial needs.

In 1969, after a national election had been held, Dr Kofi Busia was installed as prime minister. Kwesi was overjoyed that democracy had been restored and the party he supported was in power. Kwame, now twelve, was old enough to understand the significance of these events so Kwesi took pains to explain the reality of politics in Ghana to his son.

Dr Busia, he told Kwame, was in the political party that opposed Kwame Nkrumah, the long-term president. This party, so long in opposition, was always popularly regarded as the Ashanti party. Dr Busia came from Kwame's mother's hometown, Wenchi, in what was by then Brong-Ahafo Region. However, Kwesi explained, Amma's family continued to support Kwame Nkrumah's party. In this one small town could be found the political divide of the whole country. Ashantis, represented by the Ahafo people, supported Dr Busia, and the Bono, or Brong, people supported the party of Kwame Nkrumah.

Kwame wanted to know how this political divide had come about. So Kwesi explained that in pre-colonial times the Ashantis had been by far the strongest political power in the region, with an empire extending over most of what was now central Ghana and even reaching into the neighbouring states of Togo and Côte d'Ivoire. The Ashantis had conquered and enslaved many of the other tribes, especially those living to the north. The British colonial government had abolished slavery but it still survived in hidden pockets and in the memories of the formerly oppressed people. Prior to independence, Kwame Nkrumah had gained power by forming an alliance of all the non-Ashanti tribes: Ewes from the Volta Region in the east, his own tribe, the Nzimahs, Ahantas and Fantis in the south and west and the many tribes of the north. These two power blocks, Kwesi speculated, would probably continue to dispute the political leadership of Ghana for the whole of Kwame's lifetime.

Kwesi told his son that he now looked forward to better times ahead. Kwame Nkrumah had adopted a top-down approach to economic development, manifested in his great push for industrialisation that had wasted vast sums of money on giant prestige projects that were inadequately planned and badly managed. Kofi Busia, however, proposed to grow the Ghanaian economy upwards from its grassroots. He toured the rural areas encouraging the development of agriculture and post-harvest industries and he visited the urban *kokompes*, informal industrial areas where wayside fitters (mechanics) and self-employed artisans eked out a meagre living. On one of these tours, in March 1971, he came to Konongo and addressed a large gathering in the market square. Kwame took his father along on his market trolley to hear Busia speak and they were encouraged by the sincerity of his vision for his less-fortunate countrymen.

Kofi Busia was known to be a pious man and he called upon the help of God to turn Ghana into the Promised Land. It seemed to Kwame that the prime minister expected to receive some mysterious help in making Ghana a better place. He asked his father about this. Kwesi told his son that Kwame Nkrumah had tried to reduce the power of the churches, especially the Roman Catholic Church, but Dr Busia had

11

restored religious freedom. Kwesi hoped that this would release more human energy for the development of Ghana.

Kwame asked what Kwesi meant by religious freedom and was told that it was the freedom for each person to attend the church of his choice without fear of being ridiculed or treated unfairly. Now Kwame thought he understood why his father used to let Amma take him to church every Sunday.

Kwame asked his father why he did not go to church like most of the other people. 'Is it because you don't want to pay money to the priest?'

Kwesi replied that it was nothing to do with the collection, although there were times when that could be a problem. It was a matter of belief. If you believed in a religion then it was usual to perform its rituals. If, on the other hand, you did not believe, going to church served only to silence the gossip of neighbours. Kwame had to admit that he heard plenty of criticism of his father from other people living in the compound. He wondered how many people went to church just to keep their neighbours quiet.

Kwame asked why his father did not believe in a religion. Kwesi explained that like most other boys he had been sent to Sunday school and taught the rudiments of Christianity. Much of what he heard seemed no more credible than the tales of Ananse the Spider. However, it was not until he read Voltaire's *Candide* that he rejected religion altogether.

Kwesi explained how the great Lisbon earthquake of 1755, an 'act of God' that killed about 100,000 people in Portugal and Morocco, had put doubts about the truth of religion into the minds of many thinkers. He quoted Voltaire, telling Kwame, 'Those who can make you believe absurdities can make you commit atrocities.' Since that time, scientific and historical discoveries had shown more and more religious beliefs to be based only on myth and legend. 'You must examine the evidence for yourself,' he told Kwame, 'but always support leaders, like Dr Busia, who seek to preserve religious freedom and leave everyone free to make up their own minds.'

As time went by, Kwesi began to suspect that Dr Busia had vision but lacked the resources to transmute it into tangible form. The country's once-overflowing coffers were empty. It was widely believed that Nkrumah had neglected the vital cocoa industry because most of the cocoa was produced in opposition territory. He had, after all, made a pre-election promise to take the wealth away from the cocoa farmers and give it to the people. The Busia government tried to revive cocoa growing, but with newly planted trees taking four years to bear fruit it was inevitably a slow process. In its struggle to balance its books the government found little scope for extending the subsidies on healthcare and education that alleviated the poverty of the most disadvantaged people. Kwesi realised that there was to be no immediate help for people like himself and Kwame; no additional funds to help feed an ever-hungry young man now well into his teens.

Kwame was growing hungry in more ways than one. He had always taken a special interest in his female teachers and in some of the women who lived at his compound. From the age of six he had fantasised about being close to one or other of them, even though he didn't know exactly what that closeness could be. He liked it when the women in the compound took off their top cover cloths on hot and humid afternoons. It was a strong feeling that occurred frequently but passed away quickly and did not interfere with his studies. At the age of fourteen, however, his feelings took on a new intensity, focused on girls of his own age. The ache became constant and his interest in studying evaporated.

Some of the boys in Kwame's class were similarly afflicted. They frequently discussed their obsession and teased each other about which boy and which girl would do it first. Those not yet transformed wanted to know the secret, and their curiosity was treated with disdain and ridicule by the initiates. One by one, however, they claimed membership of the club until it included all the boys in the class. Some of the other boys told Kwame that although they talked about it all the time with their classmates they couldn't mention it to their parents at home. However, Kwame's intimacy with his father gave him an exceptional opportunity to discuss his problem.

Kwesi told his son that he understood the strength of his affliction but he must try to resist all wayward thoughts and concentrate on his studies. He assured him that life would present many opportunities in the future for him to enjoy his new powers, and being an attractive young man he would have few problems in getting girlfriends. For the moment, however, it was important to take the opportunity to pursue his education. That was one of the surest ways to gain security in life.

Kwame admired his father and had great respect for his learning. He supposed that Kwesi in his day had taken every advantage of what education was available to him. He felt sure that Kwesi had followed the same advice that he now gave to him. Maybe Kwesi's father had given him this advice or, being so intelligent, he had worked it all out for himself. Either way, Kwame believed that his father must have maintained a celibate existence until he finished school. The more he thought about it the more he marvelled at it. He did not feel that he could do the same. Were the urges dragging on his mind and on his body greater than his father's had been? Was he abnormally charged with passion? How was it possible to keep his mind on mathematics or geography when every bulging blouse could tighten his trousers?

The dilemma of adolescence is that one knows what is needed, but not how to get it. Kwame knew that his need could only be satisfied by a girl, but he didn't know how to ask for it. His desire was opposed by his shyness. He decided to compromise. To subdue all thoughts of girls was impossible, but if he could find one girlfriend on whom to focus his thoughts he might be free during classes to concentrate on his studies. There was one girl who particularly attracted him. If he could befriend her, maybe he could otherwise follow his father's advice. Kwame tried this compromise on his father and was relieved when he raised no strong objection. He took this as tacit approval.

Comfort Opokua was the liveliest girl in the school. She was a natural choice for class captain and was twice voted the most popular student in her year. Perhaps she was not the most beautiful, but her vivacity left the other girls standing in line when comparisons were made. Like most of the boys in his class, Kwame was captivated by Comfort. At the same time he realised that he stood little chance of winning her close friendship. Nevertheless, thinking of Comfort helped to keep other thoughts at bay and calmed his mind for study. They knew each other of course, and her casual greeting as they passed in the street could set Kwame's heart pounding for an hour.

Kwame was worried that Comfort would take another boyfriend. He tried to watch her and asked after her in what he hoped was a casual way. To his great relief it seemed that she treated all boys in the same way, giving each a friendly smile and cheery greeting but avoiding all but casual conversation. Her motto seemed to be 'Safety in Numbers'. To Kwame this was both a relief and a disappointment. Perhaps the relief was the greater, because he was compelled to spend much time with his studies, his father and his trolley. These demands left little time for any serious courting. He regarded Comfort as a pleasure in store that was being kept on ice until he was ready. He knew that this was only a dream, but such a beautiful dream that it sustained him through this turbulent phase of his life.

Kwesi's injuries and the stress of maintaining his impoverished existence without the support of his wife had taken their toll. His health had deteriorated and he was forced to spend more than he could afford on doctor's bills and medicines. Kwesi had placed all his hope in the government of Dr Kofi Busia, and its overthrow by Colonel Ignatius Kutu Acheampong in a military coup on 13 January 1972 came as a great shock. In his weakened condition Kwesi felt that all prospect of a better life had been denied him. He feared for the future of his son and realised there was little left that he could do to help him.

On 27 April the news arrived that Kwame Nkrumah had died of natural causes in Romania. Kwesi gained no solace from the death of his old oppressor. He sensed that his own end was fast approaching and prayed that if there were a life hereafter, Kwame Nkrumah would play no part in the administration. Kwesi Mainu passed away peacefully in his sleep on the night of 29 June 1972. In the morning, all Kwame's efforts to rouse him were in vain.

2

Suame Magazine

Eight days after Kwesi's death, Kwame Nkrumah was buried in Ghana. His body had been brought back from Guinea Conakry where he had been living since his overthrow in 1966 and where his body had been returned after his death in Romania. There was much debate about whether the remains should be brought back to Ghana but in the end traditional sentiment ruled. So on 7 July 1972 a state burial was held for the former president, and in Konongo a more modest gathering paid its last respects to the memory of Kwesi Mainu, former inspector of sawmills.

After the death of his father, Kwame resolved to try to continue his education by extending his market trolley operations. Not having to care for Kwesi allowed more time, and if this was profitably employed he might earn enough to meet the cost of his school fees and other essentials. It was also good to keep himself occupied during those long hours that he used to spend with his father discussing how Ghana was in the past and how it could be in the future. Together they solved all the county's problems. Now Kwame must focus on solving his own.

Kwame soon realised that although his father's pension had been small, and had not kept pace with inflation, it had still been the foundation of their subsistence. Replacing it with extra trolley work was not easy. Sometimes there was no work to be done and at other times the only work available was during school hours. He was forced to make economies wherever he could. Fortunately he paid no rent for his room as it had been owned by his father and now passed to him, although Kwesi's will to that effect might be challenged as it ran against the traditional matrilineal inheritance system of the Akans. He tried to cut down on food but was repeatedly defeated by a raging mid-teen appetite. He resolved not to buy any new clothes or shoes but to make do with what remained of his father's. Unfortunately Kwame, at fifteen, was already bigger than his father and still growing fast. His school uniform was too small and needed to be replaced. It seemed that wherever he turned, economies were difficult to make.

By working whenever he could and borrowing from friends Kwame struggled on for a few months. His target was now to finish the school year. He realised that continuing his education beyond that point would be impossible. Reaching that point would be difficult. Yet reach it he did, with hard work, ingenuity and help from friends. At the age of sixteen Kwame was ready to leave his hometown and set out to seek his fortune. Employment opportunities in Konongo were very limited so he resolved to go to Kumasi, Ghana's second city and the capital of Ashanti Region.

Kwame needed a little capital to pre-finance his new venture but that was not difficult to acquire. Now that he was leaving his room he could rent it to another person. In Ghana it was the custom for landlords to take an advance of, typically, three years' rent. To move into a room it was necessary to hand over what was by local standards a large sum of money. Kwame had some difficulty finding a tenant who could afford the rent advance, but was fortunate to find a government official newly posted to Konongo who was able to take a loan from his employer. It was a relief for Kwame to have the money in his hand because no absent relative challenging his father's will could grab it now. As soon as the money was handed over, all his creditors came quickly to collect their repayments. Realising that the next wave of visitors would be loan seekers, Kwame pocketed the residue of the rent advance and boarded a *trotro* for Kumasi.

Friends in Konongo had told Kwame that he could expect to find cheap accommodation in Ayigya *zongo*. He got down from the *trotro* at Ayigya, a village on the outskirts of the city, located directly across the Accra road from the University of Science and Technology. Kwame knew that the *zongo* was an extension of Ayigya village that had formerly been occupied by slaves. It was still home to the poorest people in the community. Searching for accommodation, he was dismayed to find that as many as ten or more people were sharing a room. They could not all sleep in the room at the same time and so they arranged to sleep in rotation. When he asked how they were able to do this he was told that most of the people of the *zongo* were unemployed and could choose to sleep at any time.

Kwame met an old friend from school who told him that he was now working as an office clerk in the department of social studies of the university. He said that some of the professors had made a survey of Ayigya *zongo*. It had been found that the people lived essentially off the vast expanse of the university campus. They took every available temporary labouring job, rounded up stray goats, chickens and dogs and took them home for the cooking pot, grew corn on every spare patch of land, and helped themselves to the produce of every farm and garden. These activities brought them into frequent conflict with the university's security force and a few people without connections ended up in police cells. In spite of all this effort the people of the *zongo* were sometimes reduced to eating rats and mice. The survey had shown, the friend continued, that in the whole of Kumasi, on average, seven people lived in each room; in Ayigya *zongo* eleven people lived in a room. This last fact Kwame had already discovered for himself.

Kwame had been hoping to find cheap accommodation in Ayigya but he now realised that this meant sharing a room with several strangers. Unused to sharing a room with anyone but family, and accustomed to the comparatively low-density living in Konongo, he was filled with dismay. How could he protect his nest egg if he slept in a room with strangers? Getting accommodation was one priority but finding employment was another. There was clearly little prospect of finding a job in Ayigya, so Kwame decided to move on in search of work. If and when he found a job he would look for a room nearby.

Kwame had been told by his father that apart from the palace of the Asantehene, the King of Ashanti, Kumasi was famous for three great institutions. The first was the University of Science and Technology, the second was Kejetia market, claimed to be the largest in West Africa, and the third was Suame Magazine, claimed to be West Africa's largest informal industrial area. Kwame knew of the reputation of Suame Magazine and its thousand workshops, and felt that it must offer some prospect of employment for an energetic and enterprising youth. So he boarded a second *trotro* to travel on another ten kilometres to the north-western suburbs of the city.

Suame Magazine sprawled over several square kilometres between the road north to Mampong and the road north-west to Techiman. Not much visible from the Mampong road, the Magazine extended along both sides of the Techiman road, with the main Magazine on the northern side and an extension known as New Suame on the southern side. Kwame got down from the *trotro* at Suame roundabout, the junction of the two roads, and walked along the Techiman road. It was jammed with vehicles of all types. About half of them were taxis with bright yellow-painted wings. There were many *trotros* and private cars of every make and type. Cocoa trucks with their high wooden bodies and brightly painted slogans inched forward in the melee and not a few huge articulated trucks blocked the road even more effectively. What Kwame was soon to realise was that Suame Magazine lived off the motor vehicle.

Although many of the vehicles were intent on progressing towards Techiman, or heading into Kumasi, Kwame realised that many others were either coming out of the Magazine or trying to enter it. He found that there were no surfaced roads entering the Magazine. The only access was gained by deeply rutted dirt roads that squeezed between the workshops, often with insufficient width for two vehicles to pass. Not only workshops lined these roads. Abandoned vehicles, machinery and scrap materials were scattered everywhere, some projecting into the road and some actually lying in the road where they had been run over by a thousand vehicles and become embedded as a permanent feature. Kwame wondered who owned all this stuff and whether it would ever be put to any good use.

Kwame soon realised that unlike in the village, where most of the houses were built to the same basic pattern, in the Magazine all the workshops were different. Most of the larger workshops were built with concrete block walls and corrugated metal roofs, and some of the smaller workshops were similarly constructed. Many more of the smaller workshops were built with wooden board walls but the corrugated metal roofs were standard. The roofs differed only in the material, steel or aluminium, and the degree of rusting if they were steel. Kwame noticed that most of the newer workshops had aluminium roofs. Many workshops had open sides and others were little more than a wooden workbench. Some artisans sat on the ground in the shade of a mango or neem tree with only a small toolbox by their side.

The level of activity impressed Kwame. He had never seen so many people, mostly men, busy at work or moving about with obvious purpose. Everywhere there was the noise of hammering, the flash and crackle of electric welders and the hum of drilling and grinding machines mingling with the constant roar and drone of vehicle engines. Kwame also noticed that there were people who seemed to have nothing to do. Some were watching the work of others and some were sitting outside their workshops, apparently waiting for work to come to them. He wondered why these people didn't make greater efforts to keep themselves busy.

Kwame was fascinated by what he saw as he wandered deeper into the Magazine. Most of the workshops seemed to be involved in vehicle repair. Some claimed to be experts in repairing certain makes of vehicle:

Benz, Land Rover, Toyota or Bedford. Some specialised in repairing certain vehicle components: batteries, brakes and clutches, bodywork or diesel engines. A few had special machines for carrying out precision work such as crankshaft regrinding or cylinder reboring. Every workshop had a name-board proudly proclaiming the services it offered. Many of these were brightly painted and some gave lists of services in great detail. The neatness of these name-boards contrasted with the chaos that surrounded the workshops and, in many cases, penetrated inside. Everywhere machine parts, materials and tools lay around in apparent abandon.

A young man of Kwame's age was sitting on the ground beside a bench cleaning a piece of machinery. Kwame asked him what he was doing. He was told that the part was a fuel pump and the job was to clean it thoroughly. For this purpose the young man had been given some petrol in a tin can and an old rag. He told Kwame that he was apprenticed to the master who owned the workshop. Being in his first year, his work was confined to cleaning. This gave him the opportunity to know the parts well in preparation for learning how to repair them in subsequent years. Kwame asked how long the apprenticeship would last and was surprised when he was told five years. He felt that he wouldn't want to wait that long to become a master.

After some time roaming among the workshops Kwame found that, in addition to offering repair services, some workshops made a product to sell. He saw larger workshops constructing the wooden bodies of *trotros* and cocoa trucks. Alongside these bigger businesses were blacksmiths' shops supplying steel bolts and nuts, hinges and brackets to the body builders. Some smaller workshops were producing coal pots: charcoal-burning stoves like he used at home for cooking. Piles of these coal pots stood waiting for collection by market traders.

Kwame was fascinated to find an artisan producing farm cutlasses from old bandsaw blades from the local timber sawmills that his father used to inspect. The artisan was using a steel chisel and a heavy hammer to cut out the cutlass shape from the flat metal sheet. It was very hard work because the bandsaw blade was as hard as the chisel, and after every few blows the chisel was blunted and needed resharpening. An old grinding machine with a worn-out abrasive wheel was used both to resharpen the chisel and to finish and sharpen the cutlass blade. Kwame wondered if any of the bandsaw blades had been condemned by his father. Some of them looked as though they might have been lying around long enough to date from his father's active years.

So much was going on in the Magazine that Kwame couldn't take it all in. There were some activities that he could not understand because he lacked the necessary technical knowledge. He was so fascinated by all he saw that he lost track of time. To his surprise the sun was going down and his thoughts turned to supper and sleep. Where was he going to spend the night? He decided to go back to ask the help of the apprentice he had met. He had some difficulty finding his way, as there were no signposts in the Magazine, and by the time he arrived the workers were leaving for home. However, his new friend was still there.

Kwame found that the apprentice came from a village far away from Kumasi. He had no place to stay but his master allowed him to sleep in the workshop. He invited Kwame to join him. Part of his function was to provide overnight security and for this two men were better than one. In return for this kindness Kwame funded their supper: fufu and groundnut soup purchased from one of the many women food sellers who plied their trade in the Magazine. Kwame's father had often warned him of the dangers of buying food off the street, but on this occasion there was no alternative. The soup was very hot with pepper, perhaps to compensate for the lack of any other flavour, but Kwame liked his soup that way. He slept soundly on his first night in Suame Magazine.

Next morning, after breakfast of roasted plantain and groundnuts, Kwame resumed his tour. He soon came across an artisan making market trolleys. It was not a large workshop but Kwame still wondered how he could have missed it on the previous day. Here was something that he knew much about and he lingered to learn all he could about how the trolleys were made. He soon discovered that although market trolleys were made by many workshops in many different towns, they were all made to a standard pattern that had become traditional.

The platform of the trolley consisted of a welded angle-iron frame about 60 centimetres wide and 150 centimetres long. Inside the angle-iron frame were laid wooden planks, cut exactly to the right size to give a close fit. Under the steel frame were welded-on attachment points for the wheels. All four wheels were from scrapped cars, the rear two fixed and the front two able to pivot to provide steering. Kwame was very familiar with the structure from his days in the market at Konongo. He immediately felt that if he were to do anything in Suame Magazine it would have to be connected with market trolleys.

Kwame noticed that the artisan was sitting outside his workshop doing nothing. One trolley was parked nearby. Kwame asked the man if the trolley was sold and he replied that he only produced to order. If a customer wanted a trolley he would pay a deposit to cover the cost of materials and come back in a few days to pay the balance and collect his order. Kwame asked why the man was not working. The reply was that nobody had come to place an order. 'How do customers know where to come for their trolleys?' asked Kwame.

"Oh they know I am here,' was the reply.

'Would you make a trolley for me if I pay the deposit?' asked Kwame. 'Of course,' said the man.

'There is just one condition,' said Kwame. 'I want to watch the trolley being made.' The man reluctantly agreed.

Kwame knew what he wanted in a market trolley. He insisted that all the wheels should be identical, not taken from different makes of vehicles. The tyres, though inevitably worn, should not be completely treadless or damaged. He insisted that the trolley should run smoothly in a straight line and turn easily. He wanted all the welds to be neat, the wooden boards smoothly planed, and the final painting done to his choice of colour and style. All this was done with much grumbling from the artisan, who did not appreciate the lesson in quality control that Kwame inadvertently provided. However, the finished trolley was noticeably smarter than his standard product and the artisan took much pride in its appearance.

Kwame had not been sure when he placed the order whether he would operate the trolley himself or try to sell it. In either case it would be useful to visit the market and assess the situation. So he trailed his new trolley from Suame down the hill to Kejetia, a distance of about two kilometres. Nobody gave him a second glance. Young men pulling market trolleys were commonplace all over Kumasi.

Few people could be prepared in advance for the impact of Kejetia market, and Kwame was no exception. What Suame was for repair and manufacturing, Kejetia was for trading. However, whereas Suame was muddled and irregular Kejetia was ordered and regular. Long lines of identical market stalls ran for hundreds of metres in straight lines or gentle curves up the hillside. Between the rows of stalls were pathways thronged with people. Underfoot was beaten earth but, unlike Suame, the surface was reasonably flat and clear of obstructions. Some market trolleys were carrying loads through the market but Kwame realised that during the day this was a slow and difficult process because the pathways were very congested. The main goods transport, he surmised, must be undertaken at night, or early in the morning before the start of business.

Standing near the entrance to the market Kwame wondered what to do next. Should he try to enter the market with his trolley and ply for business or would it be better to go away and come back at a quieter time? People were milling all around and he feared that he would be accused of obstructing the flow of shoppers into the market. Then he heard a voice behind him say, 'That's a very fine trolley. Is it for sale?'

Kwame turned to find a short fat man with a shiny bald head smiling up at him. 'Why do you think it's for sale?' asked Kwame.

'Well, it can't be for hire with only you to push it,' said the man. Then he held out his hand. 'I'm Uncle George, or at least that's what everyone calls me around here. I operate more market trolleys than anyone else in Kejetia. I'm looking to smarten up my fleet, replace some of the old wrecks, so I'm really interested in your new model.'

'Well yes, I suppose that I could sell it to you,' said Kwame, 'but I'm afraid that it's a little more expensive than the standard model.' Kwame mentioned a figure that would give him a good margin of profit.

Uncle George frowned. 'I wasn't expecting to pay as much as that,' he said. They haggled over the price for a while but Kwame could not come down below the price he had paid to the artisan and the negotiations became deadlocked. 'OK, young man,' said Uncle George at length. 'Will you give me the trolley at my price if I order another ten?' Kwame's heart leapt; now he was in business!

Kwame didn't know how he was going to produce ten good trolleys at the price Uncle George had offered but he was determined to find a way. Before returning to Suame, however, he decided to explore further in the centre of the city. Not far from Kejetia he found another large market called Asafo and he heard that there were more markets located in each of the main suburbs of the city. On the roads throughout the town centre Kwame observed many trolleys in operation. Some were carrying boxes of market goods and others were laden with building materials, wooden products from carpentry shops, furniture and household equipment like refrigerators and washing machines. There seemed to be no limit to the loads that were carried and no limit to the distance over which they were delivered. Trolleys supplied a low-cost goods transport service that almost everyone could afford. Kwame had thought he knew all about market trolley operations but he had never before envisioned anything on this scale. He felt that he had come to the market trolley capital of the world.

He had decided to continue to sleep in the workshop with his apprentice friend. That night sleep did not come easily because his mind kept returning to the problem of producing trolleys at a lower cost. He was eager to meet the artisan in the morning and explore with him all the possibilities. However, when he reported on his order for ten trolleys the immediate reply was, 'Where's the deposit for the materials?' Uncle George had paid for the single trolley but this only recovered for Kwame what he had paid out. He resolved to use this money, and more from his modest reserves, to pre-finance the purchase of materials, but he decided to handle the purchases himself and to sub-contract the work to more progressive artisans.

Trolley makers, Kwame found, usually bought their materials for one trolley at a time. By negotiating for material for ten trolleys Kwame was able to realise a significant reduction in cost. He kept careful records of what he paid for angle-iron, wooden boards, old car wheels and all the other necessary parts. Then he toured the Magazine looking for trolley makers who worked to the highest standards and offered the most competitive prices. He found that the younger men who had recently completed their apprenticeships were keen to develop their operations and take part in a new joint venture. By bringing in specialist welders and carpenters Kwame was able to make further savings as well as quality improvements.

Over the next few months he supplied Uncle George with the first ten trolleys and with several repeat orders. He negotiated to rent a plot alongside the Techiman road on the New Suame side, and kept a large number of finished trolleys lined up to attract custom and to supply to customers ex-stock. This ensured that his operations became known to the thousands of drivers and passengers who passed slowly by each day. He also ensured that his products were regularly demonstrated at the major markets, and handed out printed leaflets highlighting the qualities of his trolleys. Kwame did none of the manufacturing himself but he controlled quality and costs and handled all the marketing and sales. In business parlance he had become an entrepreneur, but he thought of himself as an heir to Ananse the Spider.

As his sales increased and his small band of sub-contractors grew slowly bigger, Kwame was providing himself with a steady income. There were many in the Magazine who envied him but Kwame was not yet satisfied with his progress. This was not what his father would have wanted. More than anything else Kwame yearned to return to full-time education. He decided to enrol in evening classes and try to gain admission to the engineering diploma course at Kumasi Polytechnic.

* * *

During this time at Suame, Kwame's hormones raged as they had in Konongo. Now, however, he had the means and the maturity to do something about it. There were plenty of young women around Suame in the evenings who were willing to assuage his passion. At first Kwame was surprised that the girls he met seldom asked for money. If he asked them what they wanted they would invariably reply, 'Oh, give me what you like.' He realised that they were surviving as best they could in difficult circumstances, doing what they hoped might lead, if they were lucky, to a long-term relationship.

Kwame was faced with a dilemma. Was he exploiting the girls' poverty or helping them to survive? Should he use their services less often or more often? He decided on a compromise. He would try to see them less often but give them more. He also adopted the habit of giving a small gift to any woman who accosted him, even though in most cases he did not use her services. In this way he felt that he was helping to alleviate the poverty of some whom he judged to be mothers and even grandmothers.

It was also at this time that Kwame achieved reconciliation with his own mother. After Amma's departure from Konongo following Kwesi's accident, Kwame felt that his loyalties should remain with his father. After his father's death, however, he felt a strong need to re-attach himself to his mother and her family. Like all Akans, he believed that it was his mother's blood that flowed in his veins. Akan society is matrilineal and inheritance is usually through the mother. Kwame felt that he belonged to his mother's extended family rather than to his father's. So although Kwame's mother had abandoned him, Kwame still felt a strong pull towards her and regretted that contact had been lost. Now that he had a little money to spare he resolved to set out to find her.

Kwame suspected that his mother was living back in her hometown, Wenchi. So early one Friday morning he set out from Suame in an old Land Rover borrowed from a friend. Wenchi lay beyond Techiman and he was already on the Techiman road. He turned left away from Kumasi and headed to the north-west, passing through the small towns of Ofinso, Nkenkasu and Akumadan before reaching Techiman, about 130 kilometres from Kumasi. Then he continued on to Wenchi, a further 25 kilometres or so. The road throughout was in a poor state of repair, and there were many potholes, some very large. The journey had been long, slow, hot and dusty and Kwame was glad to stop driving.

The procedure to find someone in any Ghanaian town or village is straightforward, although it can be very time consuming. Kwame reported to the chief's palace and asked for an audience with the chief. He was asked to wait in a cool room and given a glass of cold water. It was a relief to have a quiet moment in which to recover his strength and compose his thoughts. He rehearsed in his mind the set procedure for addressing his request to the chief. All had to be conducted in the vernacular and there were standard opening remarks to be made on both sides. If it had been a large town with a chief of high rank, all conversation would have to be addressed through the chief's linguist, the *okyeame*. On such occasions it was necessary to approach the meeting with one's own linguist. Kwame expected that the Wenchi *Omanhene* would not use a linguist on this occasion.

After half an hour or so, Kwame was asked to attend on the chief. The Wenchi *Omanhene*, Abrefa Mbore Bediatuo VI, was sitting in state with two of his elders and the Queen Mother, Nana Atoa Samangyedua III. Kwame was relieved to see that no linguist was present and he could address the chief directly. The chief began by assuring Kwame that there was peace in the town. Then he asked of Kwame's mission. Kwame assured the chief that the journey had been peaceful and he brought no trouble with him. Then he told the chief his mother's name and said that his mission was to find her and re-establish contact with his family. One of the elders whispered something in the chief's ear and Kwame was told that someone would be detailed to take him to her.

The house in which Amma was living with her current husband was not far from the chief's palace. There, Kwame met for the first time his half-sister, Adjoa Ansah, a girl of six years who ran off to fetch Amma from the farm where she had gone to harvest corn. Once more Kwame was asked to wait with a glass of cold water, and when he declined, an immediate offer was made to fetch him a bottle of Coca Cola or Sprite from a kiosk on the main road. Amma soon came, and when she had got over the shock of seeing how Kwame had grown since she last saw him, the pair settled down to filling in the life histories of the past decade. Kwame later met his mother's husband and shared their evening meal. They found him a place to rest for the night, and after breakfast of fried plantain and red bean stew he set out to return to Kumasi.

After his reunion with his mother, Kwame made periodic trips to Wenchi. Socially these trips were very pleasant but economically they became a great drain on his resources. Kwame was now accepted as a full member of his extended family and so he was expected to contribute to its upkeep. Requests were made for the payment of school fees and hospital bills. He was expected to attend all family funerals and make substantial donations. If a relative had poor eyesight, he was expected to pay for spectacles. He tried to extend the period between visits to Wenchi but if he delayed too long a relative would arrive in Suame on a *trotro*. He would then have to bear the cost of bed and board and pay the *trotro* fare home, as well as comply with the request that had been brought to him. On the whole he found it less expensive to revert to regular visits to Wenchi but it still absorbed most of his spare cash.

Three years went by and Kwame was finding it increasingly difficult to maintain his business and meet his family commitments. Under I.K. Acheampong, now a self-promoted general, Ghana's economy continued to decline. Acheampong struggled to restore confidence in his administration by changing his ministers and even changing his nickname. At one time he sought to popularise himself as 'Kutu' and at another as 'Ike', but all was in vain. By 1976 all imported goods were very scarce and the issue of import licences promoted wide-scale corruption. Goods imported with an import licence at the official exchange rate of 1.15 Ghanaian cedis to the US dollar could be sold at a rate equivalent to about 20 cedis to the dollar. This was the scale of profits that were being made. As Ghana was very short of foreign exchange, relatively few import licences could be issued. The demand greatly exceeded the supply. The soldiers gave the import licences to their relatives and girlfriends, and to the traders who paid the highest bribes.

Kwame saw that some Suame artisans were making a lot of money through having established a virtual monopoly in the sale of imported vehicle spare parts and engineering materials. He knew that the government had introduced 'controlled prices' for the sale of all imported goods but, in general, these were being ignored. However, some large stores and motor agencies, owned by British and European companies, observed the law and sold at controlled prices whenever they received a shipment of goods from overseas. The Suame artisans, through their contacts working in these companies, got early warning of these shipments and arranged by various means to purchase whole consignments at controlled prices. When people got to know that the parts and materials were available only in the Magazine, all repair work was diverted there. The artisans not only made large profits from reselling the parts and materials but they also benefited from the increased demand for repairs.

Ghanaians called this period of their history the era of *kalabule*, thought to be an Akan corruption of the Hausa term *kere kabure*, 'keep it quiet'. In this era, goods were resold repeatedly at ever-increasing prices. All essential commodities were scarce and when any came to hand the temptation to resell them was hard to resist. Kwame read in the *Daily Graphic* about one man accused in court of selling tins of sardines that had gone bad. He said in his defence that the fish was intended for trading, not for eating! The slogan 'No Brother in the Army' started to appear on *trotros* as people saw that all soldiers' families seemed to be prospering. The girlfriends of army officers were seen driving new Volkswagen Golf cars, which were soon widely known as 'honey bottoms'. All respect for the military government had evaporated and individuals felt compelled to live by any means available.

Kwame reflected ruefully on the story he had heard the old men telling about the creation of Ghana. God, watched by his angels, was putting so many good things into one place: gold, manganese, diamonds, bauxite, a great river, fertile soils and a warm climate. 'Is it fair to put all the good things into one place?' asked one of the angels. 'Ah,' replied God. 'Just wait until you see the people I will put there.' In the era of *kalabule*, Kwame was forced to admit that the problem really did seem to be the people. So few were strong enough to stand against corruption that it seemed the whole nation was infected.

Now 19, Kwame was still selling market trolleys but the business was only just ticking over. He was sorely tempted to join the whirlpool of *kalabule* and was held back only by the memory of his father and the lack of suitable connections. In his weaker moments he tried to discover if any of his childhood friends and schoolmates had gone into the army. He knew that the army had no friends in the Magazine. When a party of soldiers tried to enter, their way had been blocked by a determined band of artisans armed with cutlasses and iron bars.

Although he had despised those artisans who sat and waited for business to come to them, Kwame felt that he himself had now fallen to that level. However, even sitting and waiting can be done in style. Kwame sat behind his neat row of market trolleys, in a comfortable cane chair in the shade of a neem tree. That was how he was sitting reading the *Pioneer* when a shiny new Mercedes Benz saloon drew up. He was slow to notice, as he had much on his mind, but his mind snapped immediately to attention when he heard a familiar female voice call out, 'Hey Kwame, what are you doing here?' He looked up and was amazed to see the vision that had enchanted his schoolboy dreams: Comfort Opokua!

Comfort had come to buy a market trolley to augment her trading activities. She told Kwame that she now sold ladies' shoes. The business had grown to the point where she sometimes needed a market trolley to transport her stock.

'Do you really need your own trolley?' asked Kwame.

'Well, I suppose not,' she replied, 'but Oboroni is paying for it and I can hire it to other traders when I don't need it for my own work.' *Oboroni* is the term used to denote a European or white person.

'Oboroni?' asked Kwame.

'Yes, my white sugar daddy; the Benz is for him. Look, why don't we meet up later? I'll pay for the trolley now and send Kofi around in the morning to pick it up.'

'Kofi, is that your driver?' asked Kwame. He had not looked carefully at the car but he was vaguely aware of a white face behind the windscreen and had taken it to be the white man himself who was driving. Now he looked more carefully and noticed that Kofi was an albino with African bone structure, curly pale yellow hair and whiter-than-white skin, devoid of pigmentation.

That evening, Kwame met Comfort at a restaurant near Kejetia. He thought she looked even more beautiful than he had remembered her in Konongo. Then she had been in school uniform while now she wore an elegant dress; then she wore no make-up and now she made full use of the bewitching art. After the meal Comfort invited him back to her flat in Nhyiasu.

'Won't Oboroni object?' he blurted out in surprise.

'That's business, this is pleasure,' was her quick reply.

Kwame was surprised to discover that, back in Konongo, Comfort had felt much the same about him as he had about her. At that time both had been too shy to do more than admire from afar. Now they were older and more experienced; it didn't take them long to consummate their friendship. They resolved to meet as often as circumstances allowed.

For Kwame a new excitement had come into his life but his basic economic problem still remained. He told Comfort about his desire to pursue his education. From the earnings from his trolley business he had been able to attend evening classes and had succeeding in gaining the qualification needed to pursue a diploma course in engineering. This was a full-time four-year programme with the first two years at Kumasi Polytechnic and the last two years at the University of Science and Technology. How could he afford to pay the fees and support himself for four years?

29

'Let's see if Mama Kate will help,' said Comfort.

'Who's Mama Kate?' asked Kwame.

'Don't you know Mama Kate?' joked Comfort. 'I thought everyone knew her. She's the Shoe Queen at Kejetia market. All the traders get their shoes from her. She's very rich and likes to help handsome young men.'

'What's the catch?'

'Oh, I expect she will want you to become her toy boy.'

'Won't that make you jealous?'

'No, that's business, this is pleasure,' replied Comfort, putting her arm around his waist.

That was how it worked out for Kwame. When he was introduced by Comfort to Mama Kate, she took an immediate liking to him. He provided the services she needed and in return Mama Kate sponsored him on the engineering diploma course. Kwame knew that he was not Mama Kate's only diversion and he wondered if her interest in him would last for four years. He resolved to do his best to preserve her interest as well as to pursue his studies. With luck, he would succeed with both.

Kwame thought that he was saying a final goodbye to Suame Magazine. He had some regrets. The Magazine had its own mysterious pull on the emotions. It was a monster to be loved and hated at the same time. Much the same, he supposed, could probably be said of the University of Science and Technology. The two benign ogres glared at each other across the wide expanse of the city. He looked forward to the transition, but first he must study for two years at the polytechnic.

3

University

Kwame's two years at Kumasi Polytechnic passed uneventfully. Devoting as much time as possible to his studies, he was able to make steady progress and he had no great difficulty in passing his exams at the end of each year. His romance with Comfort was his greatest joy, and his duty towards Mama Kate also gave him some pleasure. He delighted in the contrast between the two women, one with the nubile form of a Greek goddess and the other with the mature voluptuousness of an ancient Sumerian earth mother. Mama Kate retained her interest and kept her part of the bargain. So Kwame, at the age of 21, was preparing to enter the university.

The year was 1978 and, like too many in the history of Ghana, it was marked by a military coup. In July General Acheampong was moved from his seat of political power, Christiansborg Castle in Accra, to his place of detention near Ghana's main source of electrical power, the great dam on the Volta river at Akosombo. General Akuffo, one of Acheampong's former associates, took his place at the castle in Accra. The new regime promised to prepare Ghana for elections and a return to democracy, but for most people very little changed in their everyday lives.

Everybody was glad to see the back of Acheampong but few expected much different from Akuffo. Kwame heard that an effort was made to try to retrieve some of Ghana's lost foreign exchange reserves. A pistol was held to Acheampong's head in an attempt to persuade him to reveal the number of his Swiss bank account. This failed. He had made his family wealthy for generations and wasn't going to betray this legacy. This time the trigger was not pulled, but he was destined to meet more determined marksmen less than a year later.

Kwame knew that most people wanted a return to democracy but few were certain that they would get it. This was the first change of government since the coup that had seemed to bring about the death of his father. Since that time Kwame had taken little interest in politics.

The main effect of Akuffo's coup on Kwame was to reawaken the sense of loss at his father's passing.

Kwame's university career began in October 1978. He was very proud to have gained admission and he hoped that his father, wherever he was, would be able to share his pride. With his father's great love and respect for learning, Kwame knew that he would rejoice in his son's achievement. So, having tried for six years to put thoughts of his father out of mind, Kwame now drew on his father's memory to sustain and inspire him in his new academic life. He also recalled with pleasure that his father had approved, or at least accepted, his friendship with Comfort.

For the next few months Kwame had the peace of mind to concentrate on his studies. He liked the more relaxed atmosphere of the university campus. The contrast with the noise and bustle of Suame Magazine could not have been greater. Telling his family in Wenchi that he was now a student, he was temporarily relieved of the burden of constant requests for money. He lived with Comfort in a house in Ayigya, near the university campus. The house was in the main village, not the *zongo*. Oboroni, Comfort's boyfriend, had paid the rent advance for the usual period of three years so their tenancy was secure for the duration of Kwame's course.

Oboroni had a new girlfriend and was happy to see Comfort settled in a permanent relationship. Kwame found that he quite liked this older white man now that he had stopped making demands on Comfort. The way he spoke reminded him of his father. Kwame recalled that he had heard his father referred to as 'a colonial gentleman' and now he understood what had been meant. He realised for the first time that people thought his father had adopted the manner and speech of an Englishman.

Kwame had not had a white friend before. He was content to have one now, especially as he derived benefits from the relationship in several ways. Oboroni continued to help Comfort and this also benefited Kwame. He could turn to Oboroni for advice as he had turned to his father long ago. Last, but not least, Oboroni provided Kwame with a drinking partner who paid the larger share of the bill. Up to this time Kwame had been only an occasional drinker but he was happy to increase his indulgence if someone else was paying. Kwame had been weaned on Star beer brewed in Kumasi, but Oboroni preferred Club beer brewed in Accra. Not all their preferences were the same.

Kwame spent several evenings with Oboroni during what proved to be Oboroni's last few weeks in Ghana. After a few beers, inhibitions on both sides fell away and man-to-man talk flowed freely. On one such occasion the conversation turned to women in general and to Comfort and Mama Kate in particular. Oboroni had heard much of the appetite of Mama Kate and had suspected that she had her tentacles on Kwame. He teased Kwame on this relationship but seeing that his friend was embarrassed he sought to ease his mind by saying, 'You know, I have also been of service to her.'

'How did that happen?' asked Kwame.

Oboroni then explained that Mama Kate had found out that Comfort had a white boyfriend. When Comfort admitted that it was true, Mama Kate said that it was something she had always wanted; she had never had the pleasure of tasting the blood of a white man. Comfort was told that if she could negotiate an assignation Mama Kate would give her a pair of top-quality shoes free of charge for her own use. 'So I did it for Comfort and for a laugh,' concluded Oboroni.

'How was it?' asked Kwame, interested to know the other man's experience.

'Well, there's certainly a lot to handle, but she enjoys herself so much it has to be pleasurable.'

Kwame asked Oboroni about his work. 'I'm in business,' he said, 'imports and exports.'

'Where's your office?' asked Kwame. 'I often see you driving on Prempeh Street and around Kejetia.'

'That's right; I have an office at Hanabis, just off Prempeh Street.'

'That's a Lebanese company, isn't it? Isn't Mr Suleiman Hannah the boss?'

'Yes, and Bachir Abizaid and Omar Issah are also directors; that's how they came up with the name Hanabis.'

'Don't they also own a sawmill? I heard my father speak of them.'

'Right again, old boy; they're into everything that makes money: timber, gold, diamonds, you name it, they do it!'

'How is it that they are so successful when the economy is doing so badly?'

'Politics, my boy; not what you know, who you know!'

'So they're in with Acheampong and Akuffo's people, are they?'

'Your guess is as good as mine,' replied Oboroni, touching the side of his nose, and Kwame had the impression his friend was signalling that he had said enough.

Kwame was curious to learn more about Oboroni and his relationship with the Lebanese community. Ghanaians refer to all people of Arabic origin as 'Lebanese' though many of them refer to themselves as Syrians,

Palestinians, Armenians, etc. He knew that there were several thousand people of Lebanese descent living in Ghana. Most of them seemed to be in business and Kwame, like many Ghanaians, wondered how they always seemed to be wealthy even when the economy was doing badly. He remembered his father telling him of the trouble he had inspecting Lebanese-owned sawmills; how the automatic reaction to any request to correct a safety defect was to offer a bribe for turning a blind eye. He resolved to seek an opportunity when Oboroni's tongue was well lubricated to probe deeper into this dark underworld of Kumasi life. In the meantime he could ask Comfort.

He chose his moment carefully to ask casually, 'Oboroni is close to the Lebanese community, isn't he?'

'Close,' replied Comfort. 'He works for Hanabis. That's how I met him. He came to our parties.'

'What parties?'

'Oh, the Lebanese have lots of parties; Lebanese men and Ghanaian girls. You should see the food and drink! They're really wild!'

'And you were involved in all this?'

'It was my first chance to earn some money. They paid us really well, but I stopped when Oboroni asked me to. He got jealous of the others and wanted me to stop before it was my turn with the dog.'

'Oh no! You didn't do it with a dog!'

'That's right, I stopped before that, and most of the girls who did it also stopped soon afterwards because they had enough money to start their own businesses. Oboroni promised to help me start the shoe trading so I didn't need to go on. All the girls left when they had enough money.'

'They let you go, just like that?'

'Oh yes, It's easy for them to recruit new girls and they like fresh talent, as they call it.'

'So, many of the girls who trade with people like Mama Kate get their capital from the Lebanese.'

'That's right.'

'You say that it's easy to recruit new girls,' said Kwame. 'How is it done?'

'In my case I was recommended by a teacher who was paid to be what they call a talent scout. You know many teachers take a girlfriend, and it's an easy way for them to pass them on when they want a new girl from a new class.'

'But you weren't a teacher's girlfriend, were you?'

'No, but I was told I could get a job with Hanabis after I left school.'

'How else is it done?'

'Well, they spot pretty girls who shop at their fashion stores. One of my friends was given several expensive dresses for free before she agreed to go to the parties.'

'Do any girls refuse to go?'

'Oh yes, many of them refuse, especially the *dadabas*, children of rich parents who don't need the money.'

Casual sexual relations were also a feature of academic life. Being more mature than most of the other students, who had come straight from school, Kwame was able to resist the usual distractions which might have included the lure of the female students. His relationships with Comfort and Mama Kate absorbed all his energy in that direction. This was fortunate, because Kwame soon realised that male students were wise to avoid friendships with their female classmates. Some lecturers took a girlfriend from the classes they taught, and a male student who even sat in class beside one of these chosen young women could be destined to fail his exams. Some female students also complained that if they declined the advances of their professors they could expect to be awarded lower grades than those who were more generous with their favours. Success or failure in academic life, it seemed, could be dependent on a number of peripheral factors.

Much to his surprise, Kwame found that African Studies was included as a compulsory subject on every course offered by the university. His immediate response was to wonder why this should be so, as it reduced the time available to pursue the important technical subjects. However, as the course progressed Kwame came to realise that he was provided with a valuable opportunity to relate his technical studies to his country's cultural heritage. He had learned much from his father and from the tales told on long dark evenings during his childhood in Konongo. Now he had a chance to deepen and broaden his understanding. He also came to appreciate the rich store of cultural artefacts and records held in the archives of the university's College of Art, where he spent some time visiting the museum and talking to staff and students in the traditional craft departments: textiles, pottery and metalworking. He was also inspired to visit the National Cultural Centre in Kumasi and attend some of the special events such as the popular proverb-striking competitions.

Kwame's studies impressed upon him ever more deeply how the culture of Ashanti was integrated with its language and ancestral wisdom. Every pattern woven in the beautiful *Kente* cloth had a name and told a story, as did every pattern printed by the *Adinkra* cloth printers and every 'gold weight' figurine cast by the traditional lost-wax bronze casters. The literature of these craft industries, like the many traditional proverbs and spider stories, contained numerous archaic words and expressions. Some of these Kwame recalled from his childhood and some he learned now for the first time. Later, the enhanced vocabulary of his mother tongue engendered by these studies was destined to be exercised in circumstances he could never have anticipated and might have preferred to have avoided. However, for the moment Kwame was forced to put aside his cultural pursuits to prepare for his end-of-year examinations.

The approach of the examinations always caused attendance at churches and chapels on the campus to increase sharply. This puzzled Kwame and he asked some of his friends why they were spending so much time at church and in prayer meetings instead of revising for their exams. They told him that they were praying for success. He was asked which church he attended, and when he replied that he did not go to church, several different churches were recommended to him. One student from Navrongo in the far north suggested that he should go to the Kumasi mosque. Another student, who had failed his exams and was repeating the year, advised Kwame not to follow the religion which had led to failure. This reminded Kwame of what his father had told him. If he chose a church, or a mosque, how could he be sure that it was the right one? He decided to stick to revision.

Just as Kwame was preparing to take his examinations at the end of his first year at university, another upheaval struck Ghana. After a failed attempt on 15 May, on 4 June 1979 yet another military coup swept aside General Akuffo and all that was left of the Acheampong regime that had oppressed the country since 1972. Kwame remembered his father telling him how one military coup inevitably led to another. First came the generals, then the colonels and finally the junior officers. Ghana's coups had roughly followed this sequence. Generals had helped to oust Nkrumah, colonels had overthrown Busia, now it was the turn of two junior officers, Flight Lieutenant Jerry John Rawlings, and an army captain, Osahene Boakye Gjan, to take over the government of the country.

Kwame was surprised to find that there was great enthusiasm among the students for this coup. People had grown tired of the Acheampong era with its hardships and widespread corruption and they were happy to see it swept away. Rawlings, named at birth Jeremiah, owed his eventual name, like Kwame Nkrumah, to a mistake, in this case on enrolment in the Ghana Air Force. A young and charismatic figure with a curiously bright orange complexion, Jerry John Rawlings promised to cleanse Ghana of the corruption that had blighted previous regimes. He announced that he would clean out the corrupt elements and then hold the elections promised by Akuffo to return the country to democratic rule.

Three weeks after the coup, Rawlings confirmed the cleansing process with the summary execution of some twelve individuals, including three former heads of state: Afrifa, Acheampong and Akuffo. Many Ghanaians were horrified by these executions. Kwame was deeply shocked. Ghanaians had formerly claimed that their coups were bloodless. Rawlings' violent behaviour was attributed to his part-foreign ancestry. His mother was from the Ewe tribe of the Volta Region but his father was a Scotsman. Ashantis were particularly shocked at the execution of Afrifa. What had he done to deserve such a fate? He had returned Ghana to democracy in 1969, handed over as head of state to a ceremonial president in August 1970 and vigorously opposed the Acheampong regime from the time of the coup in January 1972.

If many Ghanaians, Kwame included, were already doubting Rawlings' suitability to lead the country, this doubt was not shared by most of the university students. Soon after the executions Rawlings came to Kumasi. Standing on the roof of his vehicle beside a very nervous vice-chancellor on the university sports field, surrounded by two thousand students, Rawlings forcefully declared his aims. He wanted nothing less than a revolution. There was in Ghana, he said, an extensive network of people who manipulated the economy for their own benefit. Included were businessmen in the import-export trade, Ghanaians, Lebanese and Syrians, as well as high officials in government ministries and departments and the heads of many institutions, including schools, colleges and universities. He cast suspicion on all people of professional and managerial status, and said that workers and students should act to expose the guilty people. 'You know who these people are,' he shouted. 'Help us to root them out!'

Much to Kwame's alarm, the students now started to shout for all these people to be executed like the twelve who had just met this fate. Rawlings said that it would be impractical to go that far. The corrupt people should be punished but he could not agree to execute them. The students still insisted on the execution of all their corrupt oppressors

37

and the meeting deteriorated into a state of deadlock. It was late afternoon and the shadows were lengthening across the sports field so the vice-chancellor suggested continuing the debate in the Great Hall of the university. No doubt he was relieved to abandon his precarious perch on the roof of Rawlings' car.

Nothing that Rawlings or the vice-chancellor could say could dowse the students' ardour. They insisted on howling for blood. Eventually, to bring matters to a conclusion, Rawlings issued a challenge. 'You know the corrupt people in this university. Bring them to me here at eight o'clock tomorrow morning and I will have them executed.'

That night many professors, lecturers and administrators did not sleep in their beds on the university campus. Meetings went on in the students' halls of residence throughout the hours of darkness. But the next morning Rawlings waited in vain. Coups and revolutions in Ghana are, or should be, bloodless.

During his first short administration in 1979, Rawlings did succeed in reducing the level of corruption. Many foreign businessmen left the country in haste and Kwame later remarked to Comfort that Oboroni and some of his Lebanese friends must also have gone at this time. Most wealthy people and all those who had been prominent in politics felt that they were under threat from the new regime and many such people also made their departure. Those who remained at home tried to maintain a low profile. Rawlings, under pressure it was rumoured from Captain Boakye Gjan, kept his word, held the elections planned by General Akuffo, and returned the country to democracy by the end of the year. The new president, Limann, was from one of the northern tribes, and his vice-president was a Fanti from the extreme south. Kwame mused that his father would have been disappointed at this outcome: the anti-Ashanti party was back in power, but his mother's family in Wenchi was probably well satisfied.

Kwame discussed the new government with Comfort and asked her opinion. 'I don't know much about President Limann,' she said, 'but I know of the vice-president from his time at the Building Research Institute (BRI).' Kwame knew that the BRI was one of two Council for Scientific and Industrial Research (CSIR) institutes located on the university campus but he knew nothing of the personalities that had been associated with them. Comfort, however, had a cousin whose father worked at BRI and lived on the campus. Sometimes, when the senior officer was entertaining, the girls had been asked to go and help prepare the meal and wait upon the guests.

On one such occasion some visiting professors from the UK and the USA were being entertained. After dinner and several drinks the conversation turned to slavery. The visitors were told that although the British claimed to have abolished slavery it still continued. 'We still have slaves in our houses,' proclaimed the future vice-president of the republic.

Comfort remembered this remark because she felt that it was people like her and her cousin who were being referred to as slaves. When he heard this, Kwame began to wonder if Rawlings might have been right to say that it was necessary to rid Ghana of the people who led its government agencies and public institutions, and to be suspicious of all professionals and managers. Surely, nobody who was prepared to regard his fellow citizens as slaves should hold public office! Such a person could easily turn a blind eye to all forms of corruption, not caring what effect it had on the poorer sections of the population. It seemed to Kwame that Rawlings had not completed the house cleaning he promised. If there were others like this in the Limann government, he might have cause to come back.

In February 1980 Comfort gave birth to a daughter, Akosua. She assured Kwame that there was no doubt about the paternity of the baby; her relationship with Oboroni had ended long before his departure in June 1979, and in any case they had always taken care to avoid a pregnancy. Kwame was delighted to have a daughter. He arranged to marry Comfort in Konongo by traditional ceremony the following month. In this contented state of mind he prepared to take his final examinations.

In July 1980, at the age of 23, Kwame learned that he was to be awarded a Diploma in Mechanical Engineering with Distinction. This meant that he was qualified to continue on the course for an honours degree, Bachelor of Science (BSc). His mind began to focus on this possibility. At some stage, however, he must do a year of National Service.

He discussed the possibilities with Comfort. Did she think Mama Kate would sponsor him for another three years at the university? She was showing much less interest in him these days and it was several weeks since he had seen her. Comfort didn't know what Mama Kate would say. For the last few months her trading had slowed almost to a standstill because of the baby, and she also had not seen Mama Kate for some time. They decided to visit the market queen at her mansion in Manhyia, not far from the palace of the Asantehene. After explaining the position Kwame waited anxiously for the reply. Mama Kate was noncommittal. It was clear that she had new interests and was unlikely to continue her support. Facing this reality, Kwame decided to do his year of National Service right away; that would give him time in which to plan his future. He began to search for an interesting attachment.

In January 1972 the University of Science and Technology (UST) had established a Technology Consultancy Centre (TCC) to offer consultancy services to local industries. Inspired partly by the initiative taken by the government of Kofi Busia, the expatriate director of the TCC, Dr Jones, had taken a particular interest in helping the artisans of Suame Magazine. The aim was to help upgrade the operations of small enterprises in the Magazine by introducing more advanced manufacturing technologies. As early as 1973 some pilot production units had been established on the university campus but the transfer of technology did not take place because the Suame artisans could not be persuaded to make regular visits to the university. So, beginning in 1975, the TCC had made efforts to raise funds to establish an extension centre in the heart of the Magazine. The project was to be called an Industrial Technology Transfer Unit (ITTU).

Funding for two ITTUs had become available in 1978. One was to be in Tamale, the capital of the Northern Region, and the other was to be in Suame Magazine. Tamale was 380 kilometres north of Kumasi, a seven-hour journey on a very bad road, and the logistical problems of establishing the ITTU had ensured that by 1980 very little progress had been made. At Suame, however, a suitable building had been purchased and renovated, machines and equipment had been installed and full operations were to begin in August. When Kwame learned of this project he was filled with excitement. He would love to play a part in bringing the advanced technical knowledge of the university to the grassroots industries of the Magazine. He hurried across to the TCC office to see if there were any openings for National Service personnel.

After his friendship with Oboroni, Kwame felt that he knew how to talk to foreigners. He was confident that he could persuade Dr Jones, the TCC director, to take him on. After all, few other diplomates could have his intimate knowledge of the Magazine. He carefully rehearsed what he would say at the interview. He had heard that the TCC office was an informal place and the director was prepared to see most casual visitors. On arrival, however, he was disappointed to learn that the director was ill with jaundice and was convalescing at home in his bungalow after spending three weeks in the university hospital. With the director away, and the opening of the ITTU drawing near, the Suame ITTU manager, also serving as acting deputy director, was extremely busy. Nevertheless, he agreed to see Kwame the next day.

Sosthenes Battah, a tall, gaunt man from Tsito in the Volta Region, had a reputation for hard work. Although quiet and reserved, he was respected by his colleagues for being approachable and fair. When Kwame described his long experience of working in Suame Magazine and his success in gaining his diploma with distinction, he could see that he was exciting interest. The acting deputy director said that he was impressed by Kwame's enthusiasm and that was a quality much prized at the TCC. He could see the benefit to the project of having him on the ITTU staff. Their greatest challenge, he thought, was convincing the artisans that the academics really understood their problems and could offer them practical solutions. The TCC already had a few technicians who had been recruited from Suame and trained for service in the ITTU but, in his view, more technically qualified people were needed. He promised to discuss Kwame's application with the director when he next visited him at home. If the director agreed, he would apply to the National Service Secretariat in Accra for Kwame to be assigned to the Suame ITTU.

That was how Kwame secured another year attached to the university. He was able to work at the ITTU from its first day of operation. His work involved advising artisans who called with technical problems and arranging for them to receive training and other forms of assistance to develop their businesses. In every possible way he was to help transfer new technologies to private workshops. The method of working was very flexible, innovation was encouraged, and staff members were given the opportunity to try out their own ideas. As this was a new concept, everyone was intent on making the ITTU succeed, and that meant responding to the needs of clients and trying out as many new ideas as possible. Kwame enjoyed being part of this pioneering effort.

At this time the TCC was an international undertaking. It was funded not only by the government of Ghana but also in various ways by the British, Canadian and United States governments, as well as by several non-governmental organisations (NGOs). This broad-based international support provided the TCC with far more disposable resources than any other part of the university. Its annual subvention from the government

41

of Ghana represented less than ten percent of its total revenue. The TCC director was from Britain, and there were several other foreign lecturers acting as part-time technical advisers. British, American and German volunteers were attached to its various projects. Several of these expatriate volunteers were involved in the Suame ITTU. In the past Kwame had made only one foreign friend – he now had the opportunity to make several more.

On 23 February 1981 the Suame ITTU was formally opened by Mr M.P. Ansah, Minister for Industries, Science and Technology. Both the deputy ministers were also present, including Dr Francis Acquah, who was to play a leading part in the future development of the ITTU programme. It was a memorable occasion graced by the presence of many important people. The Ashanti Regional Minister was there, together with the British and Canadian High Commissioners. The proceedings were hosted by the vice-chancellor of the university, Professor E. Bamfo-Kwakye. It was the first time that Kwame had met people of this eminence and he was proud to shake their hands and tell them about his work when they toured the ITTU after the opening ceremony. The occasion reinforced Kwame's awareness of the power and wealth of the advanced countries that were supporting development projects in Ghana like the Suame ITTU.

In March 1981 Kwame was formally awarded his diploma at the Congregation for the Conferment of Degrees. It was a crowded and colourful occasion held in the Great Hall of the university. At the beginning of the ceremony the professors and lecturers paraded across the lawn from the university library to the throb of energetic drumming. The procession entered the back of the Great Hall and walked slowly forward down the central aisle through the assembled throng of proud parents and friends. This splendid parade of vivid academic gowns was greeted by low sonorous blasts from enormous Ashanti horns located in the gallery above. It was the most exciting sound that Kwame had ever heard. He sang the National Anthem with more vigour and pride than ever before and vowed that this was a day he would never forget. He could feel his father smiling down on him!

Kwame enjoyed the work at the ITTU and felt that he was really doing something useful for the people, but he was concerned about his longer-term future and brooded on this problem more and more. The conventional wisdom among university students was that graduation should provide an escape route overseas. The aim of many was to gain a first- or upper-second-class honours degree that would qualify them for post-graduate studies in an advanced country. He saw several of his fellow students leave for the UK and the USA and knew that they intended to stay away for many years. Once armed with an international MSc or PhD the world would be their oyster. However, Kwame was still at least three years away from gaining an honours degree, even if he succeeded in getting funding support.

Kwame realised that the TCC was an effort on the part of the university to spin off benefits for the local community and counter arguments that it was doing nothing directly to assist the development of the country. Back in Wenchi, on visits to his mother, Kwame had often heard the old men complain that the university had never done anything for them. It only took their sons and daughters away and sent them overseas or into government service in Accra. 'The university has done nothing to develop this town' was an often-heard remark. Yet these same grumpy old men would at other times be heard boasting of the success of their young relatives and the large sums of money that they were sending home from overseas.

Almost all of the new houses going up in the town were financed by remittances from overseas. Many a mother proudly showed off the house that her sons or daughters had built for her. Brothers and sisters gained enhanced income, and enhanced status, from a new taxi, tipper truck or trading kiosk financed from Europe or America. These people were the envy of the greater numbers who had no relative overseas and who seemed to grow poorer by the day. Kwame was convinced that the only way he could provide adequately for himself and his family was to travel overseas.

The word used by Ghanaians for the western countries collectively is *aburokyiri*. Getting to *aburokyiri* was the aim of many young people. Kwame was familiar with the escape route through the university but many less-educated people succeeded in escaping by other routes. Analysing the situation he saw that there were two basic problems. The first was the obvious one of funds. Air tickets were expensive and it was almost impossible for an ordinary person to raise the necessary sum of money. The second problem was getting a visa. This could also be obtained if one had enough money but for the ordinary person this too was out of reach. The value of a good university degree was that it eased the problems of getting the visa and gaining sponsorship. Kwame had heard of other ways of getting both necessities, and most of these involved befriending a foreign national. He resolved to find his own *oboroni*.

Kwame turned his attention to the foreign volunteers working with him at the Suame ITTU. Ralph Morgan was an American, a Peace Corps volunteer, an engineer, not much older than Kwame. He was assigned to the ITTU to install and commission an iron foundry. The project was in its early stages and was not scheduled to be ready until 1982. Ralph lived on the UST campus with his wife, Marlene, who was employed on the TCC's apiculture project, teaching farmers and honey hunters modern methods of beekeeping. Both Ralph and Marlene were hard workers and great enthusiasts. Being sociable people they made many friends and all their working colleagues were welcome in their home. Kwame took every opportunity to help Ralph with his work and to seek his advice whenever he encountered a difficult technical problem.

Apart from Ralph and Marlene, the other foreign volunteers attached to the TCC and Suame ITTU were much older than Kwame, and although he tried to be friendly towards them it was more difficult to form a close bond. The year of National Service passed quickly and Kwame had to face the possibility that his opportunities were slipping away. He looked like losing his job and his house in Ayigya at the same time.

He was lucky with the first task of finding a job. Dr Jones, the TCC director, had adopted the policy of using the National Service scheme to find hard-working and enthusiastic staff for his projects. He told Kwame that he was impressed with his contribution to the development of the ITTU and offered him a three-year contract to continue the work. This was unusual for a person who held only a diploma as most senior staff posts in the university went to graduates. Kwame realised that the director must have made a special arrangement to employ him at this level, and suspected that it was only possible because the TCC's foreign funding support allowed greater flexibility.

The problem of the house was more difficult. Oboroni was no longer around to pay another three-year rent advance and Comfort and Kwame failed to find any other adequate source of funding. Comfort's trading business had revived, and Kwame might have been able to get a salary advance from the university, but it would not have been enough. Comfort was forced to move back to her family house in Konongo with Akosua, and Kwame found himself a room with a workmate in boys' quarters on the university campus. It was not satisfactory, but both regarded it as a temporary measure.

On 31 December 1981 disaster struck Ghana once again. In what became known as his 'Second Coming', Jerry Rawlings overthrew the elected government of President Limann and once more assumed the role of head of state. This time the upheaval was even more profound. Calling his return a people's revolution, he declared that all educated and professional people were against the revolution and must be removed from power and authority. Every community was to elect a People's Defence Committee (PDC) and every workplace was to elect a Workers' Defence Committee (WDC). These committees were to take over from the old leadership. Professionals were explicitly excluded from standing for election.

At the university a WDC composed of semi-literate night-watchmen and farm labourers challenged the authority of the vice-chancellor, the university council and the academic board. All routine work on the campus was disrupted and it was not long before the university was forced to close down all its academic programmes and send the students home. It was fortunate for the TCC that most of its activities were off-campus and not directly linked to the regular teaching programmes. At the Suame ITTU work was able to continue with only occasional delays and interruptions.

Ralph Morgan regarded Kwame as one of his most able and willing colleagues and called upon him whenever he needed more hands to help with the work. As the day drew near when the ITTU iron foundry would come into operation, Ralph needed more and more help. He asked for Kwame to be formally transferred to his team and early in 1982 iron was cast in Suame Magazine for the first time. The TCC had succeeded in demonstrating an important industrial process in the midst of the *kokompe* and the challenge was now to transfer the technology to private workshops. Ralph asked Kwame to help plan the manufacture of iron-melting furnaces so that they could be supplied to the first group of potential foundry owners already undergoing training in the ITTU foundry.

It was Ralph Morgan who lent Kwame Dr Fritz Schumacher's famous book, *Small is Beautiful*, and introduced him to the economic philosophy that lay behind what was first known as 'intermediate technology' and later as 'appropriate technology'. Dr Schumacher had founded the Intermediate Technology Development Group (ITDG) in London in 1965 and it was ITDG which had helped the University of Science and Technology to plan the TCC. Now Kwame understood how it was that the TCC had from the outset taken a keen interest in promoting the activities of the small enterprises of Suame Magazine. Although Dr Busia had been overthrown before *Small is Beautiful* was published, Kwame wondered if the future prime minister had heard of Dr Schumacher or read some of his earlier writings while serving as a fellow of St Anthony's College, Oxford, from 1962 to 1969. Whatever his original inspiration, Dr Busia had, during his brief term of office, pursued policies of which Dr Schumacher would have approved.

Kwame, now 25, felt that he was making progress in his engineering career. He had gained the confidence of his bosses and was charged with work of increasing responsibility. However, it was difficult to make ends meet on his meagre salary and he could spare very little money for Comfort and Akosua. He still wanted to further his education and the restless urge to find a way to escape overseas was only partially suppressed. He knew that one day it would resurface.

4

Tamale

With an iron foundry established at the Suame ITTU, it was decided to begin preparing to establish the same facility at the second ITTU slowly coming into being at Tamale. Small-scale aluminium casting had long been undertaken in Tamale as a traditional craft industry, and Kwame was asked to help study this activity and assess the interest of the artisans in moving on to iron casting. It was his first opportunity to see the north of Ghana. Used to the rich green forests and rolling hills of Ashanti, he was surprised to see vast flat expanses of parched straw grassland and only occasional small groups of stunted trees with dark green foliage.

Kwame made his first visit to Tamale in May 1982. He took a liking to the place straight away. The town was much smaller than Kumasi, not really much bigger, it seemed, than his hometown Konongo. The people spoke several languages that he couldn't grasp but most of them knew some Twi or English and he quickly learned the universally used Dagbani greeting: '*Naa.*'

Tamale was laid out on flat land with long straight roads lined with trees that provided much-needed shade. Bicycles were little used in Ashanti Region with its high humidity and many hills, but here on the flat dry lands of the north they were very popular. In these days of scarce fuel, the roads of Tamale were full of bicycles, ridden by people of all ages and often carrying two or more people and large amounts of cargo of every shape and size. Kwame found Tamale in a very run-down condition with broken roads and neglected buildings but it still retained a unique character.

The man in charge of the ITTU, Frank Johnson, was an African-American engineer in his sixties with a pale brown complexion and short curly white hair. He had been seconded to the project by the United States Agency for International Development (USAID). Kwame took an immediate liking to this older man and sensed that the feeling was

47

mutual. Frank lived alone in a large bungalow assigned to the project by the regional administration. With two or three rooms usually vacant, Frank could accommodate TCC staff sent to Tamale on short assignments. Kwame was invited to stay with Frank on most of his visits.

Kwame liked to stay with Frank and spend the evenings in conversation. He listened with much interest to stories of Frank's exploits as a gunner on a US battleship in the Pacific in the Second World War, and his experiences since coming to Ghana in the 1960s. He had come at the indirect invitation of Kwame Nkrumah who had encouraged black Americans to come home to Africa. Frank had made a permanent home in Ghana and bought a small house in Accra where he lived with his Ghanaian girlfriend. He had run an engineering business in Accra before falling out with his senior partner and being hired by USAID to work for the TCC in Tamale.

Life in Tamale at this time was much more difficult than in Kumasi. Fuel was always scarce and the electricity and water supplies were off more often than they were on. Running a project was almost impossible, but Frank found a way to surmount most problems. Always casually dressed in oil-stained T-shirt and faded baggy jeans, and with a sailor's bowlegged gait, Frank could walk into the office of the regional minister at any time if he felt that he was not being helped effectively by officials at lower levels in the administration. Not that the regional minister could solve all their problems, but at least Frank could be assured that they had done as much as possible. Often Frank would suggest a solution to a problem that the minister was able to implement.

Kwame was impressed with Frank's easy way of talking to the minister. It contrasted markedly with the demeanour of other petitioners, like village chiefs and businessmen seeking favours for their villages or businesses. He realised that Frank's easy manner was based on the sure knowledge that he could help the minister as much as the minister could help him. He heard the minister ask Frank to move permanently to Tamale with an offer to find him a plot of land on which to build a house. Kwame resolved to try to develop a similar relaxed approach to people in authority, based on confidence in his own ability. He realised that he still had much to learn, but life was providing many opportunities to remedy that defect.

Relaxing together one evening on Kwame's second trip to Tamale, Frank mentioned that Sally would be coming into Tamale the next morning.

'Who's Sally?' Kwame asked.

'She's a British VSO who runs our project at Yendi,' Frank replied.

Kwame had not heard of the project at Yendi and was anxious to learn more. Yendi was a small town some 80 kilometres east of Tamale, not far from the border with the Republic of Togo. A mission station in Yendi, linked to a foreign NGO, had asked the TCC to transfer some of its rural technologies to the local farmers and artisans. Regarding such an effort as a natural extension of the Tamale ITTU, it had been decided to locate a foreign volunteer in Yendi with the support of Frank's small team in Tamale.

Sally Green had been sent to Ghana by the British Voluntary Service Overseas (VSO). Kwame had already met other VSOs in Kumasi, some working with the TCC and some with other departments of the university. Many VSOs were employed as teachers in secondary schools but some worked on development projects of various kinds.

Kwame knew that the TCC had projects to help rural farmers involved with beekeeping, fish farming and minimum tillage crop production. It was also introducing training programmes for upgrading the skills of rural blacksmiths to enable them to supply a wider range of better tools to farmers and rural craftsmen. In preparing for the Tamale ITTU, Frank had introduced the manufacture of cotton-spinning wheels and weaving looms. Now he was setting up training programmes to teach village women to spin cotton and weave cloth much faster than by traditional methods. Frank's plan was for Sally to extend some of this activity to Yendi.

Next morning Sally rode into the compound of Frank's bungalow on her motorcycle. Kwame knew that VSOs were supplied with motorcycles but he had not expected that a frail white girl would make this long and difficult journey alone. He suspected that the road from Yendi was even worse than the road he had travelled on from Kumasi. He also knew from reading the newspapers that Yendi was notorious for tribal conflicts that could turn to violence. His immediate impression of Sally was of a woman of strong independent spirit.

Sally was short and slim with straight fair hair. Kwame had never before seen anyone so white, except perhaps Oboroni's albino driver in Kumasi. Most *aborofo* (white people) acquired some degree of tan after a few weeks in Ghana but this had not happened to Sally. With crash helmet in hand, she came quickly into the shade of the veranda and with obvious relief slumped into the soft cushions of one of Frank's comfortable cane chairs that reminded Kwame of the one he had sat on under the neem tree in Suame. Frank further assisted Sally's recovery with a bottle of Coca Cola straight from the refrigerator.

For Kwame's benefit, Frank and Sally briefly summarised what had happened so far. After some orientation training in Accra, which included instruction in a local language, Sally had been sent to Kumasi for briefing and then on to Tamale. Frank had shown Sally what he was doing in Tamale and what he expected to be able to do to support her work in Yendi. Then he had taken Sally on to Yendi with her motorcycle in the back of his Chevrolet pick-up truck to introduce her to the mission station that was to be her new home. Sally now reported that she had settled into her new accommodation and got to know the local girl assigned by the mission to serve as her counterpart and help her in the work. She had hoped to bring the girl with her to Tamale but she had refused to make the journey on the back of a motorcycle.

On his next visit to Tamale, Kwame was surprised to find Sally working with Frank in Tamale. Tribal conflict had again flared up in Yendi and the Ghana Army had cordoned off the town until peace could be restored. Sally had been forced to leave her post but Frank was able to find plenty for her to do in Tamale. Even as they spoke four elderly ladies in long dresses and headscarves were sitting on high stools on the veranda learning how to spin cotton on Frank's new spinning wheels. From time to time Frank would kneel down in front of one of his students and gently guide her shrunken foot on the treadle of the machine. No doubt he was hoping that Sally could soon take over such duties.

At that time in Tamale, before the permanent ITTU building was ready, much of the project activity took place in the compound of Frank's bungalow. Frank had established a workshop in the garage with a workbench, a small metalworking lathe, a blacksmith's forge and an electric welding set. Carpenters were at work at a bench in the shade of a neem tree, making beehives, weaving looms and cotton-spinning wheels. Cotton spinning was in progress on the veranda and in the lounge a young woman was at work weaving cloth on a broadloom. In the garden behind the bungalow a beehive had been installed to provide an opportunity for training beekeepers. Almost everything that Frank was doing was new to Sally but she had taken a special interest in helping to promote cotton spinning, weaving and beekeeping. She hoped to introduce these crafts to the women in Yendi when she was able to return there. In the meantime she had much to learn in connection with all three crafts.

Young men helping out with metalworking and carpentry told Kwame that they were members of an Appropriate Technology Club. Frank had formed the club to help them develop ideas for starting their own small businesses. They were allowed to try out their own ideas and given help to bring them to practical reality. Frank hoped that some of these young men would become clients of the ITTU and benefit from its full range of services when it was in operation. One young man of special interest to Kwame, Abu Musah, already operated his own aluminium foundry making large spherical cooking pots. His interest in moving on to iron casting had prompted Frank to suggest to the TCC director that Abu be offered the chance to train at the Suame ITTU foundry until the facilities were ready in Tamale.

Kwame often visited the site where the ITTU building was under construction. The Americans had brought a prefabricated metal structure from the USA and it lay on the site waiting to be erected. The work of laying the foundations was going forward painfully slowly. Everything was in short supply and the project was held up for months while the TCC and the Ministry of Industries tried to organise the delivery of the necessary cement and reinforcing rods. Kwame wondered at times if he would ever see the building erected. He understood why Frank was trying to promote activity by other means, not just waiting for the completion of the ITTU building.

One day, after the close of work, Sally asked Kwame if he would like to go with her to buy guineafowl for their supper. They walked through the town in the brief half-light of dusk to the central market where several women were roasting portions of guineafowl for sale to passers-by. They bought three portions, and some roast plantain to take back to share with Frank.

It was now dark and, as usual in Tamale at this time, the power was off, so there were no streetlights. Under these conditions pedestrians took advantage of the headlights of passing vehicles to light their way. A continual stream of passing traffic can maintain almost constant illumination and make the sidewalks relatively safe. Unfortunately fuel was in short supply and most vehicles were parked in long queues at the filling stations, waiting for a tanker to arrive from the south. So the passing traffic was intermittent, bringing rare swathes of light followed by long intervals of blackness. Each vehicle allowed a safe path to be gauged over only the next few metres. It was essential to see the path ahead because all pavements were badly broken and some roads had no pavements. Most road edges had deep storm drains that could easily turn a missed step into a broken leg. Walking in the roadway exposed pedestrians to the dual hazards of deep potholes and passing vehicles. Drivers tried to weave a path between the potholes and this led to vehicles swerving without warning. The walk home promised to be less than straightforward.

Frank had lent them his torch but it needed fresh batteries. They enquired in the market at several kiosks selling electrical goods but could find no batteries to buy. So they set out for home in some trepidation. Waiting for each vehicle to pass, they were able to move forward a few metres at a time. It helped their progress that the bad roads slowed the traffic and extended the periods of illumination. When they came to a smoother stretch they could risk moving further in the darkness with Kwame walking carefully ahead and warning of any obstacles. At one point they were able to cut across an open expanse of grass, trying to keep to the well-trodden path and hoping that no poisonous snakes were lurking nearby. Kwame knew all about night adders that didn't get out of your way – he didn't want Sally to learn about them the hard way. He felt responsible for the safety of this stranger in his land and was determined to get her home safely. He wondered if she had anticipated this hazardous return when she proposed the expedition. After all, he reasoned, this was almost certainly not the first time she had fetched Frank's supper.

Although nothing more intimate occurred on the way home than catching Sally once or twice when she stumbled, Kwame felt that the shared experience had created a bond between them. It was then that he realised the foreign friend he sought could be Sally. He decided that on his return to Kumasi he would ask for a permanent transfer to Tamale.

Kwame started his attachment to the Tamale ITTU in October 1982. One year of his contract was already completed and he had two more remaining. He continued to enjoy working with Frank and learning from him the practical engineering skills that solved technical problems with minimal resources. He came to appreciate that Frank was a natural appropriate technologist, able to achieve his objective using what-ever tools and materials were at hand. From his experience at Suame Magazine, as well as in Tamale, Kwame could see that Frank's approach was exactly right for Ghana. However, he doubted if many of his former fellow students would understand this. It had not been included in the theory taught at the university. He wondered if these practical skills he was learning were as important overseas as they were in Ghana.

Kwame's friendship with Sally grew closer as days and weeks went by. They spent much of their off-duty time together. Nightlife in Tamale was almost non-existent, but films were shown weekly at the Catering Rest House and occasional discos were held at a private hotel on the other side of town. Both these venues, and a few smaller bars, could provide an acceptable ambience for a quiet drink on a quiet night. After the long hot dusty working days, however, they were often content to spend the evening at Frank's bungalow. Frank usually retired to his room early, either to sleep or to catch up on his paperwork, and so Kwame found that he had plenty of opportunity to talk to Sally on a one-to-one basis.

Kwame was an experienced lover but he had never had cause to develop powers of seduction. The women in his life had all been willing. He knew that he was attractive to Ghanaian girls – he had often been told so – but he was less sure where foreign women were concerned. He felt that Sally liked him as a friend but he had no idea if the feelings ran any deeper. Then there was the problem that he did not really find Sally sexually attractive. She was rather too slim for his taste. He sensed that she could never satisfy him in the way that Comfort did. He knew that the main compulsion that he felt to take the relationship further was the opportunity it presented of escaping from poverty. Sally was his target more because she was there than because he wanted her. He wrestled with these thoughts for some weeks while he kept the friendship at a purely platonic level.

After a few months, Sally was able to go back to Yendi. In discussion with Frank it was decided that she should divide her time between Yendi and Tamale, recruiting farmers and artisans in Yendi and arranging for them to receive training in Tamale. Sally told Frank and Kwame that she was happy with this arrangement because it broke the monotony of life in Yendi while still letting her feel that she was discharging her responsibilities. For Kwame, it afforded more time to think through his options.

Kwame returned to Kumasi at the first opportunity. He was able to travel in a TCC vehicle bringing staff to Tamale and taking others back to Kumasi. He took a *trotro* to Konongo to see Comfort and Akosua. The next day he went back to the campus to talk to his old friends at the university. He found the campus alive with speculation that Major, formerly Captain, Boakye Gjan was raising an army in the Ivory Coast to invade Ghana and rid the country of Jerry Rawlings. By this route, Boakye Gjan would pass through Kumasi on his way to Accra. Many people in Kumasi, Kwame was told, were arming themselves to rise up and march with him.

Kwame knew that Boakye Gjan was popularly held to be the person who had persuaded Rawlings to hand over power to President Limann in 1979, but he did not feel that the newly promoted major could do much to improve the situation now. Knowing that Rawlings was popular in Tamale, he suspected that this popularity was widespread in all those areas of Ghana that had supported Kwame Nkrumah. Rawlings was trying to link his regime to that of Nkrumah by promising to restore Ghana to the true path from which it had been diverted since the coup of 1966. He had also sought reconciliation with Nkrumah's old enemies to the extent of marrying an Ashanti wife, Nana Konadu Agyeman. Kwame feared that bringing an army into Ghana with the support of the Ashantis would start a civil war. He hoped that it would not happen.

Kwame was relieved to find on a subsequent visit to Kumasi that the excitement had subsided and Boakye Gjan was in London editing an African economics journal. He heard that Dr Jones, the TCC director, had met Boakye Gjan on a visit to Britain and he was publishing an article in his journal about the ITTUs. Kwame was happy that peace had been preserved and proud that his project was receiving international recognition. He could not have hoped for a more satisfactory outcome.

Another year passed and Kwame had only one year left of his contract. He thought that he could get an extension, there was still much to do to establish the Tamale ITTU, but he had set himself the target of escaping before his contract finished in 1984. The experiences of 1983 were enough to force the most patriotic of Ghanaians to scheme to get away. There was a severe drought and forest fires sent dense clouds of black smoke over Kumasi. The economy was in perpetual doldrums with the cost of everything in the market going up much faster than wages and salaries.

The Ghanaian cedi had been devalued in June 1978 to 2.75 to the US dollar. This was still the official exchange rate in January 1983. In April, the official value of the cedi fell to 24.69 to the dollar, and in October to 35. With this almost thirteen-fold fall in the value of the currency within only six months Kwame felt a new sense of urgency to escape. Time was slipping away and the pressures were building up. He decided at last to try to take his friendship with Sally to a higher level. However, it was Sally who took the initiative.

'We've known each other for some time,' she said, 'but just how serious is our relationship?' While Kwame groped for an appropriate response she continued, 'At the last meeting of VSOs in Koforidua, we went to see the film *Love Brewed in an African Pot* and afterwards the girls got together in the dormitory to discuss their love lives. Several were bragging about their Ghanaian boyfriends and those who didn't have one were so jealous – and I wasn't sure which group I was in.' It was widely believed, Kwame was surprised to learn, that white women thought that Ghanaian men were considerate and sensitive lovers. He hoped that he could live up to expectations. He wouldn't want to be responsible for damaging a hard-earned corporate reputation.

Kwame felt that he had taken a significant step forward but he realised that he had much more to do. He knew that Sally would soon go back to England and he was desperate to be going too. He raised the subject with her, and although they discussed it at great length, she could suggest no practical way of helping him. He suspected that her attitude might become more positive if he proposed marriage, but something held him back from taking this step. He believed that his customary marriage to Comfort was not legally binding, but that was not all that concerned him. He knew that, in the last analysis, Sally was in the right place at the right time, but she was not the right woman.

Kwame knew who the right woman was but he doubted if she could do anything to help him. Nevertheless, on his next visit to Kumasi he asked Comfort again if she was sure that she didn't have Oboroni's address in England. Although she had denied it in the past it was possible that she had come across it in an old diary or letter. He explained that maybe if he wrote him a letter explaining his dilemma, Oboroni would be able to send him an air ticket and an invitation letter to help him get a visa to travel overseas. Comfort's reply was to tell Kwame that if she had found the address she would have given it to him at once. This wasn't the first time that they had discussed the issue. 'You wouldn't like to find another foreign boyfriend, I suppose,' he joked, but Comfort failed to laugh.

Then help came from an unexpected direction. He was asked to see the TCC director. Somebody was needed to take charge of the iron foundry at the Tamale ITTU. So far Kwame had assisted the two American engineers, Ralph Morgan in Kumasi and Frank Johnson in Tamale, with the installation of equipment, but he had not been much involved with operations. Ralph had already left Ghana, and Frank was responsible for the whole of ITTU operations in Tamale and couldn't be spared to look after the foundry as his full-time concern. The Tamale ITTU needed a full-time foundry manager and Frank had recommended Kwame for the job. Kwame had gained much of the necessary practical knowledge at Suame but the director wanted to be sure that he possessed all the necessary operational skills. He was proposing to send him on a three-month course at a foundry training centre in England.

The TCC sent many staff overseas for training. Opportunities ranged from a few weeks or months to acquire a specific skill to one-year MSc programmes at universities such as Bradford and Cranfield. Kwame knew about these opportunities but never expected to be included, at least not this early in his service. The people he saw being sent overseas were almost all graduates and all had been with the TCC for several years. His turn had come much sooner than expected. The prospect filled him with excitement. It wasn't permanent emigration but it was a good chance to see *aburokyiri*, make more contacts and open up new possibilities.

When he told Comfort about his good fortune she made it clear to him that she had mixed feelings. She wanted him to succeed in his career but it was bad enough having him in Tamale; England was much further away. 'But I'm only going for three months,' protested Kwame, 'and I'll bring back lots of pretty clothes for you and Akosua.'

After the excitement of knowing that he was going to travel abroad, Kwame suffered the anticlimax of waiting for the time to come. The course wouldn't begin until the middle of March 1984. Before he could fly away he would have to collect his passport in Kumasi and then travel to Accra to get an entry visa from the British High Commission. In the meantime he had to return to Tamale and resume his duties until the time was right for making these final preparations.

On his return to Tamale, Kwame was congratulated by Frank and Sally. Frank was pleased that his recommendation had been acted upon, and Sally was excited to think that Kwame would be visiting England and might be able to meet her parents. Best of all, she would herself be back in England before Kwame finished his training in June. Kwame wasn't sure if this was all good news but he decided to treat it as such.

It was shortly after this that Frank told Kwame he was planning to return to the USA. Kwame was surprised because he had believed from what Frank had told him earlier that the black Texan had come to Ghana intending to make it his permanent home. However, he knew that many of the African-Americans who had come to Ghana at the invitation of Kwame Nkrumah had either returned to the USA or died in Ghana, and their children had returned. Frank explained that it was becoming a family man that had finally changed his perspective on sharing the deprivations of life in Ghana.

For several years Frank had lived in his small house in Accra with his Ghanaian girlfriend, a Ga native of Accra. He had trained her as a photographer and provided her with all the necessary equipment to take, develop and print good-quality photographs. With much natural ability she had built up a successful business which had held her in Accra when Frank moved to Tamale. She had known Jerry Rawlings from their schooldays together at Achimota. After the Flight Lieutenant's second coup she had become an enthusiastic supporter of the revolution and had travelled the length and breadth of Ghana with a military bodyguard, documenting the birth of the new era. Now, nearly two years later, disillusioned like most of her fellow revolutionaries and newly pregnant, she had decided that Ghana was not a suitable place in which to raise her child. So she had persuaded Frank to take his family home to Texas. Kwame couldn't help wishing that he too had a Texas to go back to, but he limited himself to asking when Frank proposed to leave.

'I'll work until the end of my contract,' replied Frank. 'That will take us to August, so I should still be here when you come back from England.' Kwame was not sure that this would be so. Maybe he would have effected his own escape by then. In any case, working in Tamale without Frank's inspirational and relaxed leadership was not a prospect likely to draw him back. Tamale without Frank and without Sally now held little attraction for him. He doubled his resolve to seize the opportunity that fate had placed in his hands.

A few weeks before he was due to travel, Kwame returned to Kumasi to obtain his passport and a letter from the director to support his application for the UK visa. He enjoyed a short period of leave with Comfort and Akosua in Konongo. Collecting the passport involved several visits to the passport office in what he recognised as the 'go and come treatment', a system devised to create maximum opportunity for gratuities. On one such visit Kwame met a young man whom he recognised as one of Mama Kate's boys and they fell into conversation. Kwame mentioned to Bra Yaw his good fortune in gaining an opportunity to travel to *aburokyiri*. He was surprised to be told, 'Mama Kate will be very pleased to hear your news. She has several of us going and coming these days but she's always keen to add more.'

On Kwame's next visit to the passport office Bra Yaw was waiting for him. 'Mama Kate has been complaining that you don't come to see her these days. Why don't we go round to her place when you've finished here?' So as soon as Kwame had satisfied himself that he could do no more that day to push his passport forward, they took a taxi down Prempeh II Street to Kejetia market. Then Bra Yaw led the way through the dense crowds between the rows of market stalls to where the shoe queen held her court.

Mama Kate was still engaged in allocating stock to the numerous younger women who retailed her imports. The problem was always the same. The retailers wanted stock supplied on credit and Mama Kate needed to devise ever more intricate ways of securing her cash return. She justified her large profit margin by the costs she incurred in giving credit and sustaining losses. As a last resort she could use her boys as debt collectors, but she was never quite sure where their loyalty lay; some of the shoe retailers were young women in full bloom.

Kwame didn't mind waiting until the morning's allocations were completed. Then Mama Kate beckoned for him to come into her office. She asked why she did not see Comfort so often these days and Kwame explained that since the birth of their daughter her business had slowed down. Then after enquiring about Akosua, Mama Kate said that she had heard that Kwame would soon be travelling to the UK.

'That's an expensive undertaking. Will you need any help from me?' she asked. Kwame explained about the support that he was getting from his employer. He had not liked to trouble Mama Kate because she had not been able to help him continue his studies.

'You will need a little more spending money to take full advantage of your trip,' insisted Mama Kate. 'I'm sure we can find you something nice.' She rummaged in her tight waist cloth and then handed Kwame a roll of bank notes held together by an elastic band.

When Kwame showed Comfort what Mama Kate had given him she took off the elastic band and unrolled the paper. 'English pounds!' she exclaimed. 'I've seen them at Mama Kate's before.'

'Oboroni showed me some once,' said Kwame, 'but they were crisp and clean. These are as creased and dirty and torn as Ghanaian cedis! Are you sure that I will be able to spend them in *aburokyiri*?'

'They're the same as the ones Mama Kate sends to the UK to purchase her supplies,' replied Comfort.

On the next visit to the passport office Kwame came home proudly clasping his new green passport. Comfort and Akosua insisted on inspecting it thoroughly. After that it didn't look quite so new and Kwame put it away safely until he needed to take it to Accra for the visa. When the TCC director heard that Kwame had his passport he arranged for him to travel the next day. He was advised to be at the British High Commission very early in the morning because by the official opening time there would be a long queue and he might not be served that day. Following this advice, and assisted by the official letter from his employer, Kwame was given the visa and returned to Konongo for the last few days before travelling.

Comfort and Akosua didn't want Kwame to go and he had mixed feelings about leaving. Their last few days together were flavoured with forced cheerfulness and the rehearsal of parting words. The ultimate evening quickly arrived and they sat together to enjoy Kwame's last supper before his three-month fufu fast. They had just finished eating when there was a knock on the door. Bra Yaw was there with a small parcel.

'Can you please take this to Mama Kate's sister in London?' he asked. 'You can post it when you get to England.'

'What is it?' asked Kwame.

'Oh, just some *kenke*, I guess,' replied Bra Yaw.

As soon as Bra Yaw had departed Comfort said, 'You won't take the parcel will you?'

'Why not?' asked Kwame.

'I think it might get you into trouble. I'll send it back to Mama Kate after you've gone.'

'Then you'd better send the money back too,' replied Kwame regretfully.

The next morning he left for Accra to begin his journey.

5

Aburokyiri

Kwame, at the age of 27, was in many ways quite mature. His experience of caring for his father and his early business experience, together with the perpetual hardships of life in Ghana, had forced him to face the reality of life's economic challenge. His romantic liaisons had given him confidence in his relationships with women. Knowledge gained and knowledge glimpsed from his father and from Frank, as well as from his studies at the polytechnic and university, had produced in Kwame the feeling of relative inadequacy and thirst for more that higher education and mature reflection brings. In all these areas Kwame was at least as developed as most of his contemporaries. Where he remained a boy, however, was in the presence of the technology and global organisation of the modern world.

Kwame knew that there were many chop bars in Kumasi that sold a strong local spirit or *akpeteshie* called VC10. He also knew from the newspapers that the original VC10 was a big aeroplane proudly owned by Ghana Airways. Now, sitting in just such a great machine, but this one a DC10 owned by British Caledonian Airways, six miles above the Volta lake, Kwame could hardly contain his excitement. At last he had achieved his long-held ambition to fly away from poverty to a land where the streets were paved with gold. He had left Accra behind and in six hours he would be arriving in London!

Kwame recalled from his geography classes that the road in the sky between Accra and London lies northwards along the Greenwich meridian, through roughly one eighth of the earth's circumference. He would soon be passing over Tamale and he strained to see the ground far below. It was strange to think of Frank and Sally down there. He reasoned that even in daylight they would be too small to be seen, even if they were outside waving up at him. Now it was night, and he tried in vain to see the lights of the town. It was probably experiencing one of its frequent power-cuts. Either that or he was looking in the wrong place.

In spite of the novelty of the situation, he soon grew tired of staring into blackness and settled back to sleep away the journey as most of the other passengers were doing.

Unusually for Kwame, sleep did not come easily. His mind wrestled with the challenge that lay ahead of him in England. He tried to imagine how it would be. He had retained a picture imprinted by his father in the conversations of his boyhood. England was the embodiment of all perfection: a place of order and prosperity. Kwame wondered how his father had formed this view. Kwesi had never visited England and knew it only from the education provided by Ghana's former colonial masters. Perhaps it was wiser to trust the reports and letters from those who had flown off in more recent years: the ones who sent back the money that financed so many businesses and buildings. Could their accounts be trusted? Kwame knew that back in Ghana they only heard from the ones who were successful. There were others who disappeared overseas and were never heard of again. What had happened to them? What would happen to him? Soon he would know.

The British Caledonian Airways DC10 landed at Gatwick Airport at 06.00 on a Monday morning in March 1984. Kwame followed the stream of passengers to the large hall in which long lines of travellers waited for their passports to be inspected. There was a line of Ghanaians queuing at a desk below a sign reading 'Commonwealth Citizens'. When Kwame's turn came he waited anxiously while a stern-faced official scrutinised his passport and visa but he was only asked how long he expected to stay and was soon allowed through. Then he followed the passenger stream to the hall where the baggage could be collected and waited for his suitcase to arrive on the carousel.

Kwame collected his suitcase, loaded it onto a trolley and then looked for the way out. There were two possibilities. One way was labelled with red signs reading 'Something to Declare'. The other was labelled with green signs saying 'Nothing to Declare'. Most people were heading for the green exit, so Kwame followed. They came into a smaller room with a row of tables and uniformed officers standing behind. Most people were walking straight through but a few people had been stopped and the officials were looking into their suitcases open on the tables. Kwame thought that he had slipped through unnoticed but at the last table a young officer called him over and asked him what he had in his case. After rummaging among his socks and shirts for a few moments the official told him he could close the lid and continue on his way. 'I should get some warmer clothes if I were you,' was his parting remark.

Kwame gave thanks that Comfort had dissuaded him from bringing Mama Kate's parcel.

He followed the passenger stream out of the customs room into a much larger hall filled with people hurrying to and fro dragging suitcases and pushing trolleys. It was surrounded by brightly lit kiosks offering information, foreign exchange, cars for hire, hotel accommodation and other services. In front of the bustling crowd, lined up behind a steel barrier was a group of people holding hand-written signs. On one of them Kwame was surprised to read his own name. He walked towards it and was greeted by a middle-aged *oboroni* who introduced himself as Robert Earl. 'Welcome to England,' he said. 'I arranged your training programme on behalf of the TCC and I'll see you safely to Coventry.' Kwame was relieved to be met and helped in this way. Now he would not have to worry about making his own travel arrangements.

Kwame thought that he could drive. Like most youths in Ghana he had taught himself by trial and error in cars borrowed from family or friends. He had taken full advantage of the fact that when a father or older brother brings a car into the family it is difficult for him to prevent sons, brothers and close friends using it whenever it is not immediately required by the owner. In such instances not holding a driving licence was not usually considered a valid reason for withholding the keys. Kwame had had many friends in Suame Magazine who owned old vehicles of various types and he had taken many opportunities to practise his skills. He had usually borrowed one of these vehicles when he wanted to visit his mother in Wenchi. Yes, he thought that he could drive, but as soon as Robert Earl turned the car onto the M23 motorway Kwame realised that here was a whole new world to conquer. He made a mental note to get some driving lessons before buying a car in England.

Buying a car was for Kwame, as for most of his fellow migrants, a number one priority. Everyone escaping even for a limited period was expected to return with a car. Many used cars were imported into Ghana but Kwame knew that the prices were highly inflated and that cars were much cheaper in *aburokyiri*. So coming home with a vehicle was obligatory. It was unlikely that he would be able to afford to run it as a private car but he would operate a taxi service if he could find a reliable driver. He had no plans to become a taxi driver himself. In the last resort he could sell the vehicle at a profit and claim that he was testing the market as a car importer. However, if he were going to use the car in England before shipping it to Ghana, he would first have to take some driving lessons.

Kwame knew that many of his mates would not have been concerned about this issue. Their approach to driving in England would be the same as in Ghana. Kwame, however, wanted to maintain a low profile in this foreign land. He suspected that being caught by the police without a driving licence would land him in much more trouble than back home where most problems could be solved by a few cedis. He had no intention of drawing attention to himself or getting his name on any official record. So as Robert Earl steered the car smoothly off the M25 onto the M1, Kwame pulled his thoughts back to the here and now with the remark, 'I never saw such roads before. In Ghana we have only one small motorway, from Accra to Tema.'

'It doesn't matter how many you have,' replied Robert. 'You will soon find that there are enough vehicles to jam them up.'

Kwame brooded on the contrast between the roads in Ghana and those he was now riding on. He considered himself to be an expert at negotiating potholes: those you steered around and those you passed between the wheels, those you slowed down for and those that brought you to a virtual halt. Here, this skill would be redundant. He recalled the remark of a friend who was asked how he enjoyed his holiday in Britain. 'I hired a car and drove for 1,500 miles and never saw a pothole,' he had said. At the time this had seemed to be an incredible statement but now Kwame suspected that it might have been true. He mentioned it to Robert Earl who replied that potholes might not be a problem but the constant resurfacing of roads caused obstructions, long tailbacks and delayed journeys. Kwame was startled to discover that not having potholes could also have its downside.

Another thing that impressed Kwame was the road signs. Everywhere there was written information helping you to find your way. It had been the same at the airport. He remembered Oboroni telling him years ago that finding your way about in England was very easy if only you could read and understand English. He now saw the value of this advice and resolved to follow it. However, he was still not sure of Oboroni's second recommendation: 'If you are lost and all else fails, ask a policeman.'

Kwame recalled his father telling him that British policemen were unarmed and always ready to help the public. According to Kwesi, this was also the case in the Gold Coast in colonial times. Anyone attempting to bribe a policeman was met with the standard reply, 'I like my pay!' However, in Ghana, almost two decades of military rule and increasing poverty had led the public to view all policemen as predators, more intent on taxing the citizen than helping him. It would take Kwame some time to see policemen anywhere in a different light.

Kwame found the traffic on the motorway very confusing. Robert had told him that there was a legal speed limit of 70 miles per hour. There were three lanes of traffic. The inside lane was dominated by heavy trucks moving at a slower speed of perhaps 50 or 60 mph. For long stretches between the trucks, Robert Earl also drove in the inside lane, but when he came up behind one of these slower vehicles he moved out into the middle lane to overtake. Many drivers were following this pattern of using the inner two lanes and seemed to be driving not much above the 70 mph limit. However, all the time a third stream of vehicles was passing at a much greater speed in the outer lane, flashing their lights at any vehicle that strayed into their path.

'Who are these privileged motorists?' Kwame asked. 'Are they police or members of the government?'

'Nobody knows. It's a mystery,' replied Robert. 'We say we have two legal lanes on the motorway and one illegal one!'

'Why do you call the outer lane illegal?' asked Kwame.

'Well, either the cars in that lane are travelling at an illegal speed, or you must have some special permission to use the lane and it is illegal for ordinary motorists to enter it.'

Kwame had read about Britain's traditional class system but this was his first encounter with it. He wondered how it would affect him personally and watched carefully to see if he could spot any black faces racing past. He soon relaxed. A good proportion of the speeding drivers appeared to have origins in Africa. He felt sure that one day he too would drive in the fast lane.

With such musings and intermittent conversation the journey passed quickly and the car turned into the yard of what seemed to be an old and grimy factory. Kwame recalled his father reading to him the books of Charles Dickens set in Victorian England. This place is just like what Dickens described, he thought. 'Here's the foundry training school,' announced Robert. Kwame's heart sank. Had he come all this way to spend three months in this dark and dirty place? Getting out of the warm car under a grey overcast sky the cold hit him with vigour for the first time. It froze his spirits. It was only with a great effort that he managed to greet his new instructor with a wide white Ghanaian grin. The warmth of Fred Brown's greeting produced only a partial thaw.

After introducing him to Fred Brown, Robert Earl took his leave, saying that he would come back in the afternoon to take Kwame to his digs. After explaining the meaning of digs, Fred took Kwame into a small office and said that they would discuss his training needs and work out a programme of work experience. Kwame described the small foundries that he had helped to install at Suame and Tamale and said that he had come to learn more about how these foundries could be used. So far they had installed crucible lift-out furnaces, but they hoped later to introduce tilting furnaces and perhaps cupola furnaces. Kwame also knew that there was much to learn about pattern making and mould making.

'Hold on,' said Fred, 'let's take things one at a time. We could be trying to do too much in the time available. What are your first priorities?'

'Let's stick to crucible furnaces, lift-out and tilting, together with some basic mould and pattern making,' replied Kwame.

'Right,' said Fred. 'That we can do.'

Fred took Kwame on a tour of the foundry. All foundries are coated in black dust and this was no exception. The workshops and laboratories were well equipped, however, and Kwame saw much that he had never seen before. When Fred showed him some of the metal castings produced in the foundry Kwame's interest really perked up. He looked in vain for blow holes, inclusions and cracks, and finding none he asked Fred, 'How do you get them this good?'

'That's what you've come here to learn,' replied Fred. Now Kwame's wide white grin was genuine. In spite of the cold and the dirt he felt that he had come to the right place. It can't be cold when the furnaces are operating, he reflected, and as for the dirt, one can always take a shower before the evening's social activities get underway.

Kwame experienced a similar roller-coaster ride of emotions when Robert took him to his accommodation. At first he found the house and the room small, dark, cold and alien, but after a friendly chat with his landlady, Mrs Chichester, and a hot roast dinner, he felt more philosophical about his prospects. It might not be too bad. The rent seemed very high when converted into Ghanaian cedis but it was only a small part of the monthly allowance he was to receive. He tried to work out how much he would need to spend and how much he could save to spend on things to take home. He would try to economise as much as possible on daily expenditure. If only he could meet some local Ghanaians he was sure that they would give him much useful advice in this respect.

Kwame wondered if he could negotiate a reduction in his room rent. Should he broach the subject right away or wait until he got to know Mrs Chichester better? Would Mrs Chichester, a portly middle-aged divorcee who in a curious way reminded Kwame of Mama Kate, appreciate his special attentions as Mama Kate had done? He decided that any approach in that direction had better wait. A premature move might get him thrown out of his digs and that would cause embarrassment with Robert Earl and Fred Brown.

Next morning Kwame was introduced to the traditional English breakfast. He was presented with a large plate supporting two fried eggs, four rashers of bacon, two fat sausages, fried tomatoes and mushrooms. Mrs Chichester also brought him a rack of hot toast, butter, marmalade and a pot of tea. He was asked if he also wanted fried mashed potato and baked beans. There was also a choice of breakfast cereals and fruit juices. 'Why have you given me so much?' asked Kwame.

'When I saw what a big fellow you were,' replied Mrs Chichester, 'I thought: how am I going to fill you up in the morning before you go for a whole day's work at the foundry? A man needs a good breakfast if he's to do a good day's work.'

Kwame was familiar with eggs, tomatoes and mushrooms. He decided that he liked bacon but the sausages tasted strange to him and he asked Mrs Chichester not to give him sausages again. He also asked if he could have some pepper sauce to add to his meals. He missed roast plantain, bean stew and gari, but on the whole he was happy to start the day with an ample English breakfast. Having experienced more hungry mornings than he cared to remember he agreed with his landlady that it was good to set out for work on a full stomach.

The foundry was within walking distance. It was a bright morning and Kwame saw the English sun for the first time. Also for the first time he was happy to walk on the sunny side of the street; under the tropical sun in Ghana, Kwame would certainly have crossed to the shaded side. Although it was early, there was plenty of traffic and people hurrying to work on foot and by bicycle. With some relief, Kwame noted that a sizeable minority of people had black and coloured faces. He felt that there must be some Ghanaians or Nigerians that he could befriend to lessen his feelings of isolation.

Kwame found the work very interesting from the outset. Fred had planned the training well and Kwame felt that he was learning much that was relevant to the needs of the ITTU foundries in Kumasi and Tamale. Fred and the other instructors and foundry hands worked just like Ralph Morgan and Frank Johnson. They took much care and paid attention to detail in a way that indicated a deep sense of vocation. Kwame recalled the old man in charge of the university mechanical engineering workshops in Kumasi, Mr Essilfie, telling the students about

66

his apprenticeship in England in colonial days. 'What I saw,' he said, 'was that the English technicians did the work as though it was for themselves.' Kwame now sensed this too and felt that he had discovered the true secret of craftsmanship.

Kwame mentioned his discovery to Fred over lunch in the works canteen. 'I'm glad you appreciate what you saw,' said Fred, 'but I'm afraid craftsmanship is dying fast in British industry. There are not many places like this where we try to preserve the old practical skills and pass them on to the younger generation.'

'Why is that?' asked Kwame.

'It's the pressure to make everything faster and cheaper,' replied Fred. 'Craftsmanship is too expensive. They want to make everything on automatic machines to avoid paying wages to human beings.'

'Are there many automatic machines?' asked Kwame.

'Not too many so far,' said Fred, 'but we hear that the Japanese and Americans are using more and more, and I guess it will soon be the same here.'

Kwame returned to the afternoon's work in a thoughtful mood. What was the value of craftsmanship to Ghana? He knew that the Ashantis and the Ewes had a reputation for craftsmanship in traditional rural industries such as narrow loom weaving, the famous *kente* cloth, but how far should they go in promoting craftsmanship in the engineering field? Should they work through what might be termed a 'Victorian era' of engineering progress based on craftsmanship to reach the modern era of technology, or could they leap straight to the modern era by introducing the latest automatic machines? Kwame Nkrumah had advocated a 'big push' to industrialisation that involved importing the latest large-scale technology from advanced countries. Kofi Busia, on the other hand, had tried to develop Ghana upwards from the grassroots by helping farmers and small enterprises to advance step by step. Busia's approach would have involved an era of craftsmanship in engineering and this was what the ITTUs in Ghana were trying to promote.

Kwame felt that neither Nkrumah's nor Busia's approach had been given a fair chance to succeed and it was difficult to form a judgement based only on Ghana's experience. He suspected that in Nkrumah's time Busia's approach might have been better, but now that progress was being made in developing flexible small-scale automatic machines with computer control, the argument was more finely balanced. He resolved to suspend judgement until he had learned much more about both craftsmanship and modern technical advances.

Mrs Chichester was providing Kwame with bed, breakfast and an evening meal. That evening, after eating, Kwame decided to go out looking for other Ghanaians. He had come to England armed with a list of names and addresses supplied by friends in Ghana, but he was disappointed to find that none of these was in easy reach of Coventry. They were scattered about London and the major cities of the midlands and the north. The nearest was in Birmingham and he decided to delay until the weekend before venturing so far from base. Tonight he would look in bars, dancehalls, night clubs and discos, whatever he could find.

Kwame took a bus to the centre of the city. He was heading for the bright lights and he found them. What a contrast with Tamale, he thought, but I doubt if there is any roast guineafowl to be had. The nearest that he could see was Kentucky Fried Chicken. McDonalds and Burger King offered hamburgers and Pizza Hut offered pizzas, but having already eaten Kwame was not looking for more food. Neither was he ready for a drink so he decided to look around the city centre. There were plenty of people about and a number of them appeared to be from Africa. He mingled with the crowds drifting along the pedestrian precinct and listened out for words in his mother tongue, Twi.

Kwesi had told Kwame that in England a city was defined by the presence of a cathedral. So Kwame was not surprised to find a cathedral near the city centre. He had thought from what his father had told him that all cathedrals in England were old. He was surprised to find that this one was new. He also remembered his father saying that all cathedrals were beautiful. This one was not. Was his father wrong about all this? Then Kwame caught sight of the floodlit ruins of an old cathedral standing behind the new structure and his faith in his father was restored. He read from a plaque that the original cathedral, built in the fourteenth century, had been destroyed by German bombs in the Second World War. It had been replaced by the new one in 1962. Kwame wondered why the old building had not been restored to its former glory.

Knowing how interested Ghanaians were in religion Kwame loitered near the cathedral hoping to run into some of his compatriots. Sure enough, a few moments later, Kwame saw a black couple with two children. The young boy was complaining in English, 'Oh Mother, you like church too much! Let's go and eat. I'm hungry.' Then he heard the mother remark to the father in Twi, 'They are always hungry and trouble our minds.' The parents were staring up at the floodlit ruins of the old cathedral, bracing themselves against the pull of their offspring intent on answering the call of their stomachs. The children prevailed in the tug of war and the two adults turned reluctantly away and allowed themselves to be towed towards the scent of hamburgers.

Having found some compatriots Kwame was uncertain how best to approach them. So he followed them towards the commercial area until they became separated from the general throng. 'Are you from Ghana?' he asked in his vernacular. The family turned round in some surprise. Kwame continued in Twi, 'I beg you, there is nothing bad, I heard you speak Twi and wanted to greet you.'

'We are happy to meet you,' replied the father in English. 'It is always good to meet someone from Ghana. Come and join us at McDonalds and we'll have a chat. The kids can't wait to get to grips with double cheeseburgers.'

'You must have been in England a long time if the children like cheese,' said Kwame when they were all seated in the restaurant, 'They say it takes a Ghanaian as long to like cheese as it takes a European to like *kenke*.'

'That is probably true,' replied Isaac, the father, 'but the kids were born here and they developed the taste from an early age. Amma,' he added, indicating his wife, 'is still not very keen on cheese, especially the more potent varieties.'

'I can appreciate that,' said Kwame. 'The smell puts me off. I haven't been able to give it a serious try.'

'Your mention of *kenke*,' interjected Amma, 'makes me feel quite homesick. Can't we go home for a visit this year, Isaac?'

'It's the cost,' replied her husband. 'Not the airfares, but the presents you are expected to carry home. It will wipe out all our savings.'

'I should leave it for a year or two before going home,' said Kwame. Isaac looked relieved, but Amma wanted to know what he meant. So Kwame explained the difficult conditions he had left behind in Ghana only a few days before. 'When were you last in Ghana?' he asked.

'We left soon after the Acheampong coup in '72,' said Isaac, 'that's twelve years since we sat in the shade of a mango tree.'

'What's a mango tree?' asked Kofi, aged eleven.

'You know mangoes,' chided Amma. 'We get them at the supermarket.'

'Yes, but we didn't know they grew on a tree,' complained Little Amma, aged nine.

During this conversation Kwame learned that the Owusu family lived in Birmingham. Isaac and Amma had brought the children on a day trip to visit Warwick and Coventry. They had spent much of the day at Warwick Castle and had come on to Coventry to see the cathedral.

Such trips were still a novelty. For several years after coming to England the Owusus had regarded outings and holidays as something that only the native English did. The children, however, clamoured to do the same as their schoolmates and so Isaac and Amma were cajoled into adopting this local custom. They now admitted that they had grown to enjoy such visits and were eager to see more of the towns, countryside and seashores of their adopted country.

Isaac told Kwame that all the family now held British passports. He and Amma had naturalised, and the children, being born in the UK, had citizenship from birth. The adults retained their Ghanaian passports, of course, having renewed them at the Ghana High Commission in London. 'Can you do that?' asked Kwame. 'I thought dual nationality was not allowed.'

'It isn't allowed officially by Ghana,' said Isaac, 'but everybody does it. It makes getting into Ghana much easier when you go home because you don't need to apply in advance for a visa and you can stay as long as you like.'

'It hasn't helped us much,' reflected Amma ruefully.

Isaac told Kwame that he worked in a bicycle factory in Birmingham. It had provided him with steady employment for most of the past twelve years but he was concerned about how much longer the work would last. The industry was in decline, factories were closing and many jobs were being lost. Isaac's factory had been taken over by a company based in Nottingham and there were rumours that all the production was to be transferred there. 'I may have to move to Nottingham or find another job,' said Isaac. Amma interjected that she didn't want to move because the children were doing well in school in Birmingham and she didn't want to leave her job in a local supermarket.

By now the children had finished their double cheeseburgers and Coca Colas and were clamouring to go to Kentucky Fried Chicken for a second round. 'Don't you think you've had enough?' said Amma, knowing that she wasn't to be let off that lightly. Isaac made a resigned gesture to Kwame and followed Amma out into the brightly lit street. The children pushed past and ran ahead, trying to hurry the adults.

'You see what happens when you have your children in England,' observed Isaac. 'You lose all control over them. In Ghana the kids behave themselves and work hard at school. Here there is no discipline and the kids do just what they like.'

Kwame parted from the Owusus, promising to visit them in Birmingham one weekend, and looked for a bar where he could buy something stronger than Fanta Orange. He soon found one. After ascertaining that neither Star nor Club beer was available he settled for a cold Stella and looked around for a black face. He wouldn't mind if it were a female one. From what Sally had told him he thought that his libido might subside in cold grey England but he was not surprised to find that a hysteresis effect apparently caused a few days delay. 'It seems a long time since I last slaked my thirst,' he thought, as he gazed into the half-drained glass.

There was no luck for Kwame that night. After three or four bars and more glasses of lager than he cared to remember, he reluctantly turned his steps towards his lodgings. As usual the alcohol had given him some relief from both his thirsts. The possibility of making an offer to Mrs Chichester flitted only briefly through his thoughts before he consigned himself to bed and sleep.

The work at the foundry continued to be both interesting and practical. Kwame could see the relevance of what he was learning to the work that was planned for the ITTU in Tamale. It would certainly help the local engineering industry to achieve an important advance. He applied himself diligently and took every opportunity to learn all he could from Fred and the other instructors and skilled workmen.

As the weeks passed, Kwame found his mind wrestling more and more with the question of what he would do at the end of the three months. Should he return to his duties in Ghana, or should he take what seemed like a once in a lifetime opportunity to stay on in England? Perhaps he would settle down with Sally for a limited period. She would return soon at the end of her service in Ghana. How was he to handle that? He found it hard to focus on this aspect of his future prospects.

At a fundamental level Kwame knew that he was facing the dilemma that confronted every educated citizen of a developing country. He knew a good deal about the theories of economic development. If governments pursued the right policies it was possible for national economies to grow by a few percentage points every year. If the new wealth was fairly distributed, each citizen could expect his lot to improve gradually in line with the growth in the economy. However, experience had shown that fair distribution was rarely achieved. A few prospered spectacularly at the expense of the masses. In many cases any advances for the masses were nullified by population growth. In this way he had seen Ghana's economy steadily decline over almost three decades.

Projects like the one that Kwame was helping in Tamale aimed at introducing new industrial activities to increase employment prospects. He knew that some people were benefiting from this effort. He also knew that such projects depended heavily on foreign support and that the benefits could be largely swept away by a downward trend in the economy at large. New small enterprises that prospered for a few years often went out of business because they could no longer get the imported tools or materials to continue in operation. His work in Ghana was swimming against the tide and there was no certainty that the tide could be turned within the foreseeable future.

But the personal issue went deeper than that. Even if the efforts of the government and development agencies achieved growth in the economy, was a rate of, say, five per cent a year attractive to an ambitious young person? Didn't one need annual growth rates measured in hundreds and thousands of percentage points if one was ever to have all one wanted: a big house, a Mercedes Benz, a BMW, plenty of girlfriends and enough spare cash to keep the extended family happy? Individuals could achieve these high growth rates, not by waiting for economic development, but by taking a bigger share of what already belonged to others. That is, it was more profitable for the individual to help himself to a bigger share of the existing national cake than to wait for the cake to grow. From his experience at Suame Magazine Kwame realised that this was what motivated most would-be entrepreneurs.

Yes, human life was too short to wait for economic development. Kwame knew that this was understood instinctively even by the bushmen and illiterates back home. They were all intent on seeking ways to escape to a better life. Hundreds of thousands had run off to Nigeria during the 1970s, attracted by the oil wealth, and had recently been returned *en masse* by the Nigerian government. It was only intellectuals like himself who worried about rationalising the situation and spelling it out as his father would have done. Painfully, with this rationalisation came a desire to leave behind something more tangible than wealth. Shouldn't an educated man also leave his mark on the history of his country? Could he do something that would make his name remembered for generations to come? Could he be like Tetteh-Quarshie, whose name was still honoured after almost a hundred years as the man who brought cocoa to Ghana?

Kwame felt that the quest for lasting fame was the path of honour. He must put avarice aside and sacrifice his personal wellbeing in order to serve his country in the field in which he was best qualified. He would need to pursue his education much further. The monetary rewards would be modest, he might even struggle to survive, but he felt that he could forgo material comforts for the promise of lasting fame. Would he succeed, however, even if he made the sacrifices? He had already seen that the work was hard and did not always achieve its objectives. Lasting fame could not be guaranteed. Could he bring himself to condemn Comfort and Akosua to share his deprivations? He felt they deserved the good things in life as much as he did.

Was consideration of his family merely an excuse to justify the pursuit of wealth? Was that what he really wanted? Couldn't wealth, if used philanthropically, also bring fame? After all, it was the wealth of overseas Ghanaians that was building houses in Ghana and helping to establish new businesses. Couldn't such a programme be devised to help far more of the poor by building larger numbers of small dwellings and creating industries with high employment potential? Couldn't wealth used in this way possibly lead to an appointment as a government minister or a chief executive of a state corporation? Surely the pursuit of wealth did not automatically close the door to the pursuit of fame.

Would staying on in England lead to the acquisition of a personal fortune? It certainly hadn't for Isaac Owusu. Kwame had been shocked when he first met the Owusus in Coventry. They were still riding in a small Ford, not the obligatory Mercedes Benz or BMW. How could they have made so little progress after twelve long years in England? When he visited them in Birmingham he had found them in a three-bedroom semi-detached house that would belong to Isaac in another fifteen years when the mortgage was paid off. If Isaac succeeded in keeping in employment for that long he could retire to Ghana in comfort but certainly not in affluence. Amma would be eager to accompany him but would the children leave their double cheeseburgers for the gastronomic pleasures of red-red? Their Twi was not nearly good enough to pass as natives in Ghana. Isaac and Amma would have to leave their children behind in England to the life they had known from birth.

These were the thoughts that were endlessly recycled in Kwame's mind as the days and weeks ticked away. He knew what his father would have advised, and what Comfort would want him to do, but where could he get realistic objective advice here and now to reconcile these opposing views? The *abrofo*, Robert and Fred, were no use. They could never understand his dilemma. Isaac might have helped, but Kwame regarded him as unlikely to give objective advice. The other Ghanaians he had met in Birmingham, mostly friends of Isaac and Amma, all seemed to be compromised in a similar way. How could he meet a compatriot who had grown wealthy in Britain to learn more about that side of the issue?

The end of Kwame's training period was approaching and Sally had returned to her home in Croydon. She had started telephoning him at work and at his lodgings, eager to come to visit him in Coventry. Kwame was running out of gentle excuses for delaying her visit. While he would like to have a friend around and he would enjoy her company, he was not sure what he would say to her about his future plans and whether or not she would feature in them. He knew, too, that Sally would want him to visit her parents and he certainly wasn't ready for that.

Then, once again, help came to Kwame from an unexpected direction. Chatting to Fred over lunch one day at the foundry, Fred asked him about his future plans. Kwame told his instructor about his desire to go further with his education. He explained that his diploma with distinction from the university in Kumasi qualified him to enter the honours degree course but he had not been able to gain sponsorship.

'Would it qualify you to enter a British university?' asked Fred.

'It probably would,' replied Kwame, 'because our courses were established by the British on the same lines as at London University.'

'Let's go to visit my friend Dr Arthur at Warwick University,' said Fred. 'He will know what's possible and what's not.'

The next day Fred drove Kwame to visit Dr Arthur at the University of Warwick on the southern outskirts of Coventry. Dr Arthur, a metallurgist, was a senior lecturer in the faculty of engineering. Kwame was surprised to find a man of only about 30 years of age in such a responsible position. Fred introduced Kwame as one of his students at the foundry training school. He mentioned how Kwame had impressed him with his keen interest, his practical skills and good basic understanding of the work. Kwame had not heard himself described in such glowing terms before and was very happy that Fred had formed this high opinion of him. Dr Arthur was clearly impressed and said that the university was always looking for overseas students of such calibre. Funds were available for scholarships but it was always difficult to be sure that the candidates from overseas were suitably qualified and motivated to succeed. With an evaluation from someone of Fred's standing, the university would look favourably on Kwame's application to join the BSc (Eng) honours course.

Dr Arthur took Kwame to the registrar's office to obtain an application form. 'You will need to send us your original certificates and a reference from your employer in Ghana,' Kwame was told. 'You are rather late to apply for this year's entry, so you should apply to start next year, October 1985. Fill in the form and send us all the documents we need from Ghana after you return there. We will return original documents to you after we have seen them. Please don't send us photocopies.' Then Dr Arthur turned to Fred. 'We will need a written reference from you as well.'

'That will be no problem,' said Fred.

Suddenly, it seemed, Kwame's future was clear before him. He could return to Ghana on schedule and work for one more year in Tamale or Kumasi. He was confident that Dr Jones, the British director of the TCC, would give him a good reference and he would be able to return to England for three more years to take the engineering degree course. Then, who knows, maybe he could stay on for his master's or doctorate degree! Best of all, this course of action kept his options open. He could defer his vital decision for a few more years.

That evening he telephoned Sally to tell her that he would be returning to Ghana as planned. He pleaded pressure of work for his failure to see her earlier and suggested that she meet him at Gatwick Airport to see him off. Then he made a thorough examination of his finances in preparation for a last-minute shopping expedition. He had promised to take pretty things home for Comfort and Akosua, now four years old, and this became his first priority.

Kwame realised that he had little money to spend. The cash available was only what he had been able to save from his subsistence allowance. He realised that he would have to face the indignity of returning home without wheels but who could buy a vehicle within three months on a student grant? So he turned his attention to the needs of his womenfolk, and these included his mother and half-sister in Wenchi as well as his family in Konongo. He discussed the problem with Mrs Chichester who immediately offered to accompany him on a shopping trip at the weekend. With this help he was able to pack his suitcase with some confidence in receiving an enthusiastic welcome home.

At least he didn't need to fill his suitcase with toilet rolls, he mused as he struggled to close the lid. He recalled with a smile how Ghanaians returning home in the 1970s would travel with their cases full of toilet rolls and with bulky hand luggage filled from the toilets at the airport. Toilet rolls were no longer a priority item but there were many other basic commodities still in short supply in Ghana. He had bought as many as he could afford. His resources were exhausted and he was lucky, he reflected, that Robert was driving him back to the airport.

75

During his stay in Coventry Kwame had received several letters from Comfort. He read that Mama Kate had not been happy about his refusal to take her parcel to England. She had complained to Comfort that now she would have to bear the cost of sending Bra Yaw. Comfort reported that she had given Mama Kate Kwame's address in Coventry and he could expect Bra Yaw to pay him a visit. Kwame had wanted to meet more Ghanaians in England, but long-term residents, not visitors newly arrived in the country. He had no special interest in seeing Bra Yaw. Now, on the eve of his departure, Kwame reflected that his visitor did not seem to have made it in time.

Robert and Kwame arrived at the airport early and Kwame was able to check in quickly and get rid of his heavy suitcase. After thanking Robert and bidding him farewell he was startled to hear his name called on the public address system. He was summoned to meet someone at the information desk. He realised that it must be Sally. She saw him approaching and ran to embrace him. 'Why are you off so soon?' she asked. 'Couldn't you have stayed longer for a short holiday?'

'That would have been nice,' said Kwame, 'but they gave me the ticket to return as soon as the training was over.'

'You could have easily delayed your return flight,' said Sally.

Kwame was reduced to concluding lamely, 'Oh well, it's too late now.'

The rest of their conversation while they waited for the flight to be called was punctuated with long pauses while they thought of things that must be said. Promises were made to keep in touch but Kwame said nothing about returning to study next year. The call for boarding brought bitter relief and Kwame walked through passport control looking back for a last brief glimpse of a waving tearful Sally. Then he turned his thoughts ahead, anticipating his arrival back in Ghana.

6

Home Again

Kwame marvelled at his achievement of remaining celibate during three months in England. He would never have believed that it was possible, but after the first few days the time had flown by painlessly. Maybe Sally was right after all. Nevertheless, on the flight southwards he couldn't drag his mind away from the thought of Comfort and the welcome he would get once Akosua was tucked up for the night.

Kwame was delighted to be home. From the airport Comfort took him to the house of one of her relatives, newly constructed at Medina, north of Accra near the University of Ghana at Achimota. The house owner was resident overseas and another relative was acting as caretaker. Comfort and Kwame were allocated one of several en-suite bedrooms set aside for guests. After supper of chicken and jollof rice, Kwame carried a sleeping Akosua to their room. His mind was narrowly focused on renewing his relationship with Comfort but he was also aware of a dread of what was uppermost in her mind. 'When are you going to build a house like this for me?' she said with grim predictability. 'Is that the best welcome home you can manage?' Kwame blurted out before he could formulate a more measured response. The magic moment had passed and his passion evaporated. He lay awake for some time wrestling with his demons.

Next day, they travelled to Konongo by a one-pound, one-pound, a large saloon car, usually at this time a Peugeot 504, travelling between Accra, Kumasi and other towns. Originally, in colonial times, the fare was one pound each way, hence the name.

Comfort now occupied the same room in the compound house in which Kwame had passed his early years. Kwame's thoughts inevitably alternated between childhood memories, bitter and sweet, and the realisation that he had achieved nothing in providing better conditions for his family. Here he was, a married man, less than three years from his thirtieth birthday, and his family was living in virtually the same conditions that he had met on his entry to the world. His story, he reflected ruefully, was the story of Ghana. After eight political eras – Nkrumah, NLC, Busia, Acheampong, Akuffo, Rawlings, Limann and Rawlings again – the life of most of the people was no better than it had been at the start. When would he, and Ghana, break out of this economic torpor?

When Kwame reported to the TCC director in Kumasi he was pleased to hear that reports of his hard work and good progress in Coventry had reached base ahead of him. After congratulations were given and received, Dr Jones asked him how soon he could return to Tamale. Kwame said that there was nothing preventing an early return to his duty post but he would like to discuss one other issue first. Then he told the director about the possibility of pursuing the course at Warwick University and asked for his support with a referee's report. Dr Jones agreed to provide the reference, and promised his support in applying for leave of absence from the university, but expressed regret at the prospect of losing Kwame's services for three years. 'I'll be able to put in more than a year before I go,' said Kwame happily.

Returning to Tamale without Sally, and with Frank soon to leave, was not an inviting prospect. Frank would be a great loss but why was he going to miss Sally? He had avoided her company in England. In Tamale, however, Kwame realised with surprise, she had been an essential part of the social environment. Without her, Tamale would be quite different. He resolved to write and express his feelings; this would please her. When he had left Tamale, he hadn't been sure that he would see Frank again, but now he was heading north to share the last two months of his friend's twenty years in Ghana.

'What will happen after you go?' asked Kwame.

'Well, Dr Jones has asked USAID to provide another engineer to replace me,' replied Frank.

'It'll be different here without you,' said Kwame, 'We will all miss you.'

'I wish I could stay,' said Frank sadly. 'I never intended to return to Texas but family responsibilities must come first.' Kwame realised that his friend was right.

When the day came for Frank's departure it seemed that the whole of Tamale was there to express their regrets and their thanks. From the regional minister to many humble citizens there was great appreciation of what Frank had achieved and the way in which he had achieved it. After Frank was gone, Tamale seemed empty. Kwame had never known the city without his friend in residence. He wandered around the deserted bungalow and its large compound filled with relics of Frank's industry, wondering if the project could ever succeed without the black Texan's guiding hand and wise counsel.

The new manager had not yet arrived in Tamale and Kwame was asked to serve as acting manager during the interval. He now had the bungalow to himself and decided to ask Comfort and Akosua to join him. If the new manager needed the space later on, his family could return to the south. So he arranged for his wife and daughter to travel to Tamale on the next project vehicle. This brought some domestic compensation for Frank's absence but did nothing to lessen the challenge of the work.

Kwame felt stretched to the limit in his new role. Only now did he fully realise all that Frank had been doing. The budget was tight and it was very difficult to find funds to pay the staff salaries and meet all the bills as they fell due. Kwame soon realised that Frank had often paid out of his own pocket when official funds ran out or came late. He learned this from a report that the university's internal auditor submitted to the finance officer. He heard of a note from the finance officer to the TCC director requesting that Frank should be reimbursed. Frank, being an ex-patriot on a hard currency salary, could afford to subsidise or pre-finance the work. Kwame, on a local salary, certainly could not.

Kwame called all the staff together to review the new situation. 'We all know what a wonderful job Frank was doing,' he told them, 'but now that he is gone it is up to us Ghanaians to show that we can keep the work going in the same spirit.' With words such as these Kwame hoped to inspire his colleagues to maintain progress until the new manager arrived. However, with salaries so low and living conditions so hard it was difficult to keep minds focused on the work in hand. Every worker felt compelled to seek ways of getting additional funds on which to survive. The employees of the project considered themselves to be in government service and they knew that government employees spent little time on the job and far more time on their private business activities. Frank had been able to counter this tendency by providing various extra perks from his own pocket and from the flexibility that the TCC as a whole enjoyed. Kwame knew that he couldn't do so much and he feared that the work output would slump.

As always in Tamale progress was slow, but Kwame managed to keep things moving forward for several weeks until the new manager arrived. USAID must have had great difficulty in finding a replacement for Frank

Johnson because from the outset it was obvious that the new man was not of the same calibre. A white American in late middle age, Jim Connell was betrayed by his speech. Hardly able to form a grammatical sentence and using expletives for punctuation he seemed to see his mission as persuading the natives that there were also bushmen in America (a derogatory term used in Ghana for an uneducated person with bad manners). Kwame was shocked. All the foreign advisers and volunteers he had previously met had impressed him with their good manners and correct speech. Now here was a representative of God's Own Country who expressed in his demeanour all the frustration of an unemployed school drop-out.

Kwame found it difficult to work with Jim Connell from the outset. For one thing, Jim made it very clear that on his inadequate salary he intended to do as little as possible. He left most of the work in Kwame's hands but was quick to criticise when anything went wrong. Jim possessed few of the practical skills that Frank had brought to the work and refused to improvise when the correct tool or material was unavailable. His manner soon exhausted the fund of goodwill built up by Frank at the regional administration and official support was in danger of drying up. Kwame found himself constantly having to make excuses for his new *oboroni* boss. The workers, who would have walked across the Volta lake for Frank, began acting as though they would like to throw Jim into it.

One thing that particularly upset Kwame was Jim's attitude towards women, especially those working on the project or numbered among its clients. Young and attractive women were often described in crude language as exhibiting provocative behaviour inviting instant rape, which Jim would have administered personally but for his advanced age and marital status. Kwame was warned that if younger male Peace Corps volunteers were assigned to the project they would surely execute this sentence. Yet in Kwame's experience the Peace Corps volunteers that he had worked with would not have behaved any differently from himself. They might have taken a girlfriend but rapists they most certainly were not. He could only ascribe Jim's remarks to some form of sexual frustration. He was glad that Comfort and Akosua had returned to Konongo and were not exposed to the foul language and crude innuendos.

It was with some relief that Kwame received a call to Kumasi to help with a special foundry training programme at Suame Magazine. It was an opportunity for him to pass on some of the skills he had learned in Coventry to the staff and mature clients of the Suame ITTU foundry. After arriving at the university campus in a project vehicle he took a *trotro* to Konongo to rejoin Comfort and Akosua.

That evening after fufu followed by pawpaw and pineapple Comfort asked Kwame if he had heard about Bra Yaw. 'What about Bra Yaw?' he asked.

'Well, I saw Mama Kate a few days ago to get more shoes to sell and one of the other traders told me that Bra Yaw had not returned from his last trip to the UK. Mama Kate seemed to be very worried about him.'

'Bra Yaw isn't one of her new boys,' said Kwame. 'She normally only worries about the new ones.'

'Oh no, he's been around for years, maybe as long as you.'

'Then why is she worried? Does she think he's run away?'

'It's more likely that he's been arrested,' said Comfort.

'What do you mean, arrested?' asked Kwame, but he suspected that he already knew the answer. 'Was it that parcel? What was in it?'

'Well it's only a rumour, but it's been going around among the shoe sellers for some time,' replied Comfort. 'We all wonder where Mama Kate's great wealth comes from. It's seems unlikely that it all comes from importing shoes.'

'You mean she does a bit of exporting as well?'

'That's what we think.'

Kwame enjoyed passing on his new skills at the Suame ITTU. He tried to instruct his associates as Frank Johnson and Fred Brown had instructed him, in a confident, friendly and relaxed manner inviting feedback and sharing a joke. Good results were achieved and the time passed quickly. He was reminded how much faster it was possible to move in Kumasi than in Tamale. In his report to the TCC director he recommended that the management team in Tamale should be strengthened, perhaps by secondments from the Suame ITTU. He did not relish returning single-handed to bear the burden of Jim Connell.

Although he returned reluctantly to Tamale, good news awaited him on his arrival. Jim, who had never ceased to complain bitterly about his terms of employment, saying that USAID had hired him on the cheap, announced that he had secured a better job and would be leaving as soon as he could be released from his contract. USAID asked the university if the usual three months' notice could be waived and Dr Jones, equally tired of Jim's laziness, bad language and sexual innuendos, agreed without hesitation. So by the end of the month Jim was gone, and Kwame was once more acting manager. This time it was a relief to take on the full responsibility without a back-seat driver.

The episode with Jim had given Kwame much food for thought. He had never met Jim's sort before, even in England where he had met many *abrofo*. Most of the Europeans and Americans he had come to know had been friendly and hard-working people. Some were reserved and seemingly cold at first but all had responded eventually to his wide white grin. They demonstrated in their approach to work, to a greater or lesser degree, what his father had sometimes referred to as a 'sense of vocation' and at other times as the 'Protestant work ethic'. They put their work first and seemed to pay little attention to material reward. Frank Johnson, for example, had paid from his own pocket to keep the work moving forward. Jim was the first *oboroni* colleague that Kwame had ever heard broadcasting complaints about his salary and terms of employment.

Until getting to know Jim, Kwame had held the largely unquestioned view that, with the notable exception of his father, all Ghanaians were materialistic. He regarded this as a symptom of their poverty. The matter of money, how to get it and the cost of desired objects, seemed to dominate most conversations. On the other hand, *abrofo* seldom mentioned money and Kwame attributed this to their relative affluence. In Jim, however, Kwame had met a relatively rich man who was obsessed with getting richer and did only as much work as he could not avoid.

Kwame's stereotypes were challenged. If some *abrofo* behaved like Jim, how was it that he had not met such people in Coventry? Robert Earl, Fred Brown and even Mrs Chichester had not behaved in this way. Kwame remembered overhearing some of the foundry workers discussing their pay and complaining about income tax but they had changed the topic as soon as he approached. He also recalled reading in the *Guardian* newspaper that England was becoming increasingly materialistic under the rule of Prime Minister Margaret Thatcher. So there must be some materialistic *abrofo*, he concluded, and materialism is not only caused by poverty. He filed this new-found insight for future reference and review.

It was decided that no more expatriate managers would be employed on the project in Tamale. The TCC sent one of its young graduate engineers to work with Kwame and prepare to take over when Kwame left for his studies at Warwick University. Dan Baffour-Opoku had known Kwame during his student days. They got on well together. Dan, who hailed from Kumasi, had never thought that he would enjoy working in the north. However, the challenge of the work and Kwame's enthusiastic support made it a pleasant experience for him.

Dan became as dedicated as Kwame to making the Tamale ITTU every bit as successful as the Suame ITTU was proving to be. He soon understood that the Tamale project served an essentially rural clientele whereas the Suame ITTU operated in an urban setting. The approach must be different although the impact could be equally profound. Frank Johnson had realised this and it was essential that the Tamale ITTU continued to follow the course that the American sailor had charted. As the months passed Kwame grew more and more confident that he would be leaving the project in good hands.

Kwame and Dan worked out a schedule that allowed each of them to make frequent visits to Kumasi. This gave Kwame more opportunities to be with his family in Konongo. On one such visit Comfort told Kwame that she had heard more news of Bra Yaw. It appeared that he had been arrested by customs officials at Gatwick Airport when it was found that he was carrying cannabis, known in Ghana as *wee*, hidden inside balls of *kenke*. 'So it was *kenke* after all,' exclaimed Kwame.

'Yes, *kenke* plus.'

'When will he be coming home?'

'It seems that he was given three years but they say that with good behaviour he could be sent home in eighteen months.'

'No wonder Mama Kate was worried. This must have seriously disturbed her export business.'

Kwame recalled reading in the *Daily Graphic* about a Ghanaian arrested at London Airport for carrying cannabis concealed inside a coconut. The author of the article had marvelled at the ingenuity of the smuggler in devising this clever method of concealing his contraband. Kwame, however, took more note of the fact that in spite of this expertise the cannabis had been detected. He felt that it might have been more appropriate for the journalist to have highlighted the skill and resources of the customs officials but that, he supposed, would have been unpatriotic.

'Why are they so much concerned about *wee* in *aburokyiri*?' Kwame mused aloud, 'So many people smoke it here, even Jerry Rawlings, the Head of State.'

'You're not supposed to say that,' joked Comfort.

'But it's written in the newspapers.'

'Only in the *Kumasi Pioneer*, not on the Accra papers: the *Daily Graphic* or the *Ghanaian Times*.'

'Well, everyone knows that it's true. They say he started when he was at school in Achimota.'

'Everyone also knows the state that people get in when they've been smoking *wee*. We see it all the time. I guess the *abrofo* don't want their people getting in the same state.'

Kwame was still not convinced. 'I don't see that it does much harm and it's tough on poor Bra Yaw.' Kwame saw the look of concern on Comfort's face and added hastily, 'Oh, don't think that I'll be taking his place as Mama Kate's courier. I know you want me to grow rich but I hope I can find a safer way to do it. My father told me that according to Pascal, "Behind every great fortune there lies a crime," but I've always hoped that wasn't always true.'

'It seems that it's true of Mama Kate's fortune,' observed Comfort, 'but I'd rather you spent three years at university than three years in prison.'

'Well, I've refused once and I'll refuse again if she ever asks me.'

Kwame was happy that Comfort was against him getting involved in Mama Kate's shady activities and much relieved that she had warned him when Bra Yaw had first asked him to carry the parcel to England. However, she continued to complain about their poor living conditions and pointed out that time was passing with no perceptible improvement in their situation. She often urged him to give more thought to the problem of making money and this reminded Kwame of his mother's haranguing of his father which eventually resulted in her departure. Comfort ardently wanted him to acquire wealth but thankfully not to the point of him risking his freedom.

Kwame told Comfort that things would be better when he gained his degree, but to Comfort this meant another wait of more than three years. Couldn't he do something in England to earn money at the same time as studying? He promised to pursue this possibility. Although Comfort's frequent nagging annoyed him, Kwame was equally annoyed with himself. He craved material progress as much as she did, but with the constant stimulus of interesting and challenging work he was prepared to be more patient. The desire for wealth was imbedded deep in his mind but days, weeks and months passed without it rising to the surface. When it did surface it was usually due to prompting from Comfort. Kwame had no desire to let this difference in priorities spoil their otherwise satisfactory relationship. For both of them, much of the magic of their initial encounter still remained.

With pleasant working conditions in Tamale and frequent happy breaks at home in Konongo the year rolled around much quicker than Kwame had expected. He passed his twenty-eighth birthday in March 1985 and the time for his return to England was fast approaching. His passport was valid for five years, and nearly four years still remained before it would need to be renewed. It would cover the whole three years of his course. The grant of the visa to attend Warwick University was a formality. This time Kwame knew the routine and he experienced none of the anxiety that had preceded his first overseas venture.

Kwame was delighted to find that his visa was valid for three years with multiple entries. This would allow him to make as many trips home as he could afford. He resolved to find some part-time work to keep his promise to Comfort and allow him to save up the air fare. He told Comfort and Akosua of this plan and they were much happier to know that they would be seeing him for a few weeks at least once each year. Comfort was greatly relieved. She told Kwame that she believed he had remained celibate for three months in Coventry but she doubted very much that he could hold out for three years. She hoped that the anticipation of a home visit each year would keep his mind focused on home comforts. With renewed vigour, she made these as sweet as possible to stock his memory. Kwame knew what she was doing and was content to enjoy in silence.

During his last few months in Tamale Kwame noticed that Dr Jones no longer made his regular short visits to the project. Instead it was the Suame ITTU manager who came. Kwame asked if the director was ill and was surprised to learn that he had been interdicted for insubordination to the vice-chancellor. He was suspended from duty while the case was investigated by the university's disciplinary committee.

'How did that come about?' Kwame asked.

'The director had a problem with the new deputy director who is an old friend of the vice-chancellor. It seems the director wrote directly over the head of the V-C to complain to the chairman of the University Council. Now both directors are suspended from duty pending the outcome of the enquiry.'

'How will that affect our work?' asked Kwame.

'Well, we are all hoping for a speedy solution,' said the ITTU manager, 'Dr Acquah, the minister of industries, has written to the vice-chancellor expressing his concern. The government wants the matter resolved quickly because they are planning a big expansion of the project. They want ITTUs to be established in all ten regions of Ghana and they want Dr Jones to be in charge.'

Kwame was surprised to hear this news. He had always regarded the TCC director as typical of the hard-working *abrofo* who were helping with the project. However, unlike most other expatriates who served as volunteers or advisers, the director had managerial responsibility and had to work strictly within the university's disciplinary structure. It was very unusual for an expatriate to be treated in this way but it was now unusual for an expatriate to be in a line management position. Back in the 1960s it had been the norm, and even in the early 1970s it was not uncommon, but by 1985 there were very few expatriate heads of department or deans of faculty left in the system. The British government's salary supplementation scheme for university staff had ended in 1983. The director had managed to stay on with European Economic Community (EEC) support. He was one of the last of a species soon to be extinct and it was clear that his post would soon be vacant. The new deputy director would be in line for the directorship and the vice-chancellor must have seen an opportunity for one of his friends. It was Kwame's first encounter with nepotism.

Kwame believed that Dr Jones had always treated him fairly. He had employed him for his National Service, given him a permanent post, sent him to Coventry for the foundry training and supported his application to Warwick University. Kwame felt that he owed his director a debt of loyalty and he hoped that his troubles would soon be over. Kwame had not met the new deputy director, and learning that he was a Ga man from Accra did not inspire sympathy in an Ashanti heart. When he returned to Kumasi in August to prepare for his departure Kwame again enquired how the matter stood. 'The director has gone to England on home leave,' he was told. 'He will return to post when he hears that the matter is resolved.'

This time on the eve of his departure there was no Bra Yaw to come calling. Kwame had not seen Mama Kate since his return from Coventry but Comfort had continued to see her occasionally to obtain supplies of shoes. The big lady did not let the defection of her ex-toy-boy spoil a good business relationship. Comfort was a ready cash customer and these were increasingly hard to find. However, Comfort reported that their dealings were decidedly cooler than before and strictly limited to the shoe trade. Mama Kate was clearly anxious to conceal her other business activities from those who had chosen not to be involved. Kwame wondered if he could be considered a security risk but decided that as he possessed no real facts he would not be seen as a serious threat to Mama Kate's operations. She had more obvious and immediate problems to worry about.

Comfort and Akosua travelled with Kwame to Accra and saw him off at Kotoka International Airport. This time Kwame had few concerns about what lay ahead and slept soundly through the night as he winged his way northwards.

7

Warwick University – First Year

Kwame walked confidently through the airport and came out of the baggage reclaim through the customs hall unaccosted. He was expecting to be met by Fred Brown. Instead he was surprised to find Dr Arthur waiting for him behind the barrier. After warm greetings Dr Arthur explained that he had suggested to Fred that if he provided the transport it would give him a chance to brief Kwame on the return journey to Warwick. Fred had agreed readily as he had no special desire to get up at 4 am to drive from Coventry to Heathrow.

'But I don't suppose you did either,' interjected Kwame.

'Oh, I'm always up early,' was the cheerful reply.

Tom Arthur was only three years older than Kwame and Kwame sensed that they could become good friends. It soon became apparent that Dr Arthur had a keen interest in Third World development and wanted to quiz Kwame on his experience with the ITTUs in Ghana. He wanted to explore the possibility of starting some form of collaboration between Warwick University and Kwame Nkrumah University in Kumasi. Kwame soon realised that this was the real reason for Dr Arthur's interest in meeting him at the airport. Dr Arthur had read Fritz Schumacher's *Small is Beautiful* when it came out in 1972. Since then he had read all he could find on appropriate technology. He expressed the view that the approach the TCC was taking in Ghana could usefully be extended to other developing countries, especially in Africa. He was surprised when Kwame voiced some doubts.

Kwame told Tom he felt that neither Dr Nkrumah's top-down approach nor Dr Busia's bottom-up strategy had been given a fair trial. He believed that Dr Busia's approach would have worked well in Dr Nkrumah's time when large-scale western technologies had been badly matched to Ghana's skills, raw materials base and small market size. At that time it would have been good to adopt and adapt older smaller-scale technologies and train the craftsmen to make and operate them. This would have encouraged the promotion of small private enterprises and created much more employment. However, the situation was changing. The west was now developing computer-controlled small-scale flexible technologies and this promised to supply small enterprises with means of production that were technologically advanced yet still affordable. All entrepreneurs wanted to minimise their labour costs and so would welcome the new technology.

Tom Arthur was impressed by this argument, which he had certainly not expected, but he thought that Kwame was looking far ahead. It could be another decade or two before the appropriate small-scale technology might be available. In the meantime, what was the best approach to follow? Here Kwame was uncertain. He related how he had discussed the role of craftsmanship in engineering with Fred Brown. He greatly admired the craftsmen he had met in Coventry and felt an urge to train such craftsmen in Ghana. However, Fred had said that craftsmanship was dying in England. If they trained engineering craftsmen in Ghana, for how long would they be needed? Would they be out of work in a decade or so? Neither young engineer had an answer to that question.

Tom and Kwame agreed to keep this issue under periodic review. They would work towards a close collaboration between their two universities. Tom expressed the wish to accompany Kwame back to Kumasi on one of his home leave visits and Kwame agreed that that would be interesting for both of them. On that basis they turned to discussing Kwame's orientation onto his engineering degree course, and soon they arrived at their destination.

On this second visit to England Kwame settled in very quickly. He decided to lodge once more with Mrs Chichester rather than occupy a room in a university hall of residence. Realising that at 28 he was much older than most undergraduates, Kwame felt that he would have more peace and quiet for studying if he lodged away from his classmates. He had experienced student life on campus in Kumasi and he knew that there were many distractions to interfere with studies. He suspected that there were relatively more sports, social and religious clubs and societies at Warwick than in Kumasi and he wanted to be able to distance himself from campus life whenever he felt the need.

Although Warwick University was new to Kwame he was already familiar with university life. He soon found his way around the campus and located the lecture rooms, laboratories and workshops where he would pursue his studies. After a few classes Kwame realised that he had covered much of the first-year work on his diploma course in Kumasi. He consulted his tutor and was told that if he already knew what was being taught he need not attend those lectures but he would need to attend the practical laboratory sessions and hand in reports. Kwame was surprised by this degree of flexibility; in Ghana attendance at lectures had been compulsory. Now he had some free time to do some work and earn some money.

He began his search by consulting Fred Brown. Fred said that the foundry school was taking more students from overseas developing countries and he would like Kwame to join his team as a part-time instructor on the practical aspects of foundry work.

'You will encourage the African students when they see what you can do,' said Fred.

'But your English technicians know much more than I do,' protested Kwame.

'Not that much more, and I want you to show your people what can be achieved by hard work and serious study,' replied Fred.

Kwame smiled to himself at all Africans being seen as 'his people' but Fred was too good a friend for this remark to be contested. Kwame owed much to the older man and gratefully accepted this latest helping hand.

From that time onwards Kwame worked at the foundry every week on two afternoon and evening shifts on weekdays, and a full day on Saturdays. This left him enough time to study and brought him an income of roughly half the full-time salary. Together with his student's grant this income seemed more than adequate for his everyday needs and he was able to begin saving for a car and the other things that he wanted to send home to Ghana. However, Christmas 1985, especially sending presents to his family back home, consumed his modest savings, and Kwame began to realise that he needed to generate a somewhat larger income.

On his first visit to Coventry Kwame had always suspected that if he could befriend other West Africans he would get practical help with his economic problems. Now, at the university, he came to meet Ghanaians and Nigerians studying on various undergraduate and post-graduate courses. Some had been at the university for several years, having completed a first degree course and stayed on to study for a master's degree or doctorate. In some cases the aim seemed to be to stay on as long as possible irrespective of the outcome. Kwame heard of one man in his late forties who had researched for five years for his doctorate before being compelled to return home empty-handed. He had been compensated by an appointment as chief director in a government ministry. Kwame had heard of Indians who put 'BSc failed' after their names. It seemed to him that 'PhD failed' could be even more valuable.

Kwame was surprised to meet someone he knew. He had only met Peter Sarpong once, at the home of Uncle George in Kumasi. It had been during the time that Kwame was supplying Uncle George with market trolleys. Peter was Uncle George's nephew, the son of his younger sister. According to Akan custom this was a close blood relationship and Uncle George had met his family responsibilities by taking a special interest in his nephew's education. A successful businessman, and having no children of his own, Uncle George had been able to meet the high expense of sending Peter overseas for his tertiary studies. After secondary school at Prempeh College in Kumasi he had sent Peter to Warwick University. The young man was now in his second year reading economics.

Kwame would not naturally have expected to be befriended by a *dadaba*, the child of a wealthy family. Now they were brought together by their common status as Ashanti exiles in Academe. Kwame was the older and more experienced man, but Peter had been longer at the university and had more local knowledge and personal contacts. It was largely through Peter that Kwame came to meet the other Ghanaian and Nigerian students.

The West African students constituted an informal club, sharing the same tables at lunch in the refectory, and accumulating at the same end of the bar at the students' union in the evenings. Kwame had promised himself that he would not be distracted from his studies by excessive socialising but he found it harder to resist peer pressures than he had expected. On the days when he could not plead that he had work to do at the foundry he found himself joining his fellow continentals in their evening gatherings at bars, parties and discos.

Most of the West Africans were male and the two female students who frequented their gatherings could not nearly meet the demand for their company. This was the main factor compelling many of the men to socialise in a broader community and several had formed long-lasting relationships with white girls who usually attended the more important evening functions. Kwame wondered if he should invite Sally to accompany him to the engineers' ball, one of the major social events of the academic year.

As Kwame suspected, the major topic of conversation among the African students was money; how to get it and how to spend as little as possible on necessities to leave ample funds for desirables. He was surprised to learn that there was much that could be obtained for free, or at very little cost, if one knew how to go about getting it. He suspected that much of what he was told was strictly illegal and he was reluctant to get into trouble with the authorities. The safest tactics seemed to be those employed on final departure, like shipping home the luxury saloon car on which one had paid only the minimum deposit, or returning home bankrupt with all the borrowed funds safely invested in a house in Accra or Abuja. These were fine as long as you did not intend to return to *aburokyiri*. Kwame preferred not to burn his boats and to keep open the option of commuting along the Greenwich meridian. In the short term at least the West African group had no acceptable suggestions for enhancing Kwame's income.

Kwame renewed his resolve to keep socialising to a minimum and leave more time for studies and part-time working. His work at the foundry was interesting but did not fully satisfy his economic needs. He felt that he could do more, and set out to find some additional employment. Fred had done all he could to help, so Kwame turned to Mrs Chichester. After dinner one evening he raised the issue with his landlady as she was clearing the table and he was helping to carry dishes to the kitchen. 'So you need to earn a bit more in your spare time, do you?' she mused aloud. 'How much time could you spare?'

'Well, I work at the foundry on two evenings a week but I could work somewhere else on the other evenings,' replied Kwame.

'Leave it with me for a few days,' said Mrs Chichester, 'and I will see if I can come up with something.' Kwame suspected that she already had something in mind.

It was only two days later that Mrs Chichester returned to the matter. 'I belong to a ladies' social club and there's a vacancy for a barman. Would you be interested?'

'I've never served in a bar before; would I be qualified?' asked Kwame.

'Our members are more interested in looks than work experience,' she replied. 'I told them what a big handsome young man you were and the committee members were very interested, even if some of them tried to hide it. They will interview you tomorrow evening if you want to apply.'

The next evening Kwame walked to the social club with Mrs Chichester. He was interviewed by six ladies who composed the executive committee. Mrs Chichester was a committee member but clearly junior to the big women who were introduced as chairwoman, secretary and treasurer. Kwame had been a little concerned that the committee might not have been expecting a black man but it seemed that they had been well briefed. He received a warm reception from the matrons and after a few questions he was told that if he could work in the evenings on Fridays, Saturdays and Sundays the job was his. Kwame accepted this commitment and apart from on Saturdays, when he would be tired from a whole day in the foundry, it suited him well enough. In addition to the weekend duty Kwame agreed to do one more evening each week on a rota to be agreed with the committee member acting as bar manager.

Walking back to his lodgings Kwame thanked Mrs Chichester for her help. 'It's the committee that should be thanking me,' she said. 'The secretary told me how lucky I was to have you all to myself in the house. They're jealous of me already. You'd better be nice to all of them or I might be voted off the committee.' Kwame was slowly learning to appreciate English humour but he was never quite sure when his landlady was joking.

The work in the bar at the ladies' club was not difficult. Kwame started at 7 pm when the bar opened and finished around 11.30 pm, after clearing up after last orders. Kwame was surprised at how much his customers could drink and how often some of them drank far too much. Most of the women were much older than Kwame. Some of the heavier drinkers would sit at the bar and try to engage him in conversation. When things were quiet it was hard to avoid these overtures. He did his best to answer politely without leading on to a new topic, aware that he was expected to remain alert to the needs of other members. He was often offered drinks for himself but refused anything stronger than beer. He soon learned the bartender's standard retort, saying that he would take it later and pocketing the cash. In this way he augmented his earnings and boosted his savings.

One lady, Ethel Banks, became a constant feature at the bar when Kwame was on duty. On quiet nights she did her best to tell him her life story. Divorced fifteen years ago she had raised two children until they were established on their own. Now, she said, she was footloose and fancy free, with her own home and car and independent means. 'All I have to do is enjoy myself,' she declared, but Kwame could not detect much happiness in her words or demeanour. She seemed to be able to afford to drink till she dropped, and he saw her drop more than once, but what was the enjoyment in that? Kwame could not help measuring in his mind what he could do with Ethel's wealth back in Ghana. He felt that she was wasting what she had but he couldn't help admiring her determined search for gratification.

One day Ethel asked Kwame if he could get her a smoke. He immediately reached for the cigarettes packed behind the bar but she stopped him with the interjection, 'I don't mean a fag but a smoke – you know, what all the kids are smoking at school.'

'If you mean cannabis, then I don't have any. It's illegal here, isn't it?'

'It might be, but the last black barman here could always get us some. I'm sure that you could get some if you wanted to.'

'Maybe, but I'm not doing anything to get myself into trouble. I don't want to be thrown out of the country before I finish my studies.' Then, in answer to her questions he told her a little about the course he was taking at Warwick University and the work he had been doing in Ghana.

A few weeks later a special night of entertainment was organised by the ladies' club. Some of the ladies were especially excited by the promised highlight of an act by a well-known group of male strippers. Kwame had heard of men's clubs where there was entertainment by female strippers but this was the first time that he realised that men were involved in entertaining women in this way. He was curious to see how it would be and how the ladies would react. He asked Mrs Chichester about it and she told him that special evenings were organised every three months and were very popular with the members.

'Do their husbands allow them to see other men naked?'

'Some of them bring their husbands along, and others don't tell their husbands. The unattached ladies, like me, don't have to tell anybody, do they?'

Kwame was on duty on the special evening. Not having much time for social life he was happy to watch the entertainment. It began with a small group playing music that he enjoyed and a comedian telling jokes that he could not understand, but who got a lot of laughs from the ladies. Then everyone settled down for the act that topped the bill. Kwame watched with curiosity as three young white men danced and took off their clothes in slow approximate synchronism. He felt that the dancing was stiff, self-conscious and devoid of any real sense of rhythm. It wasn't the sort of dancing that they did in Africa. The ladies called out encouragement and tried to speed up the inevitable climax which they greeted with much acclaim. They crowded around the performers to get a closer look and feel flexed muscles. Kwame was not surprised to see Ethel in the centre of this activity.

As soon as the show was over Ethel came over to the bar and ordered a drink. Then she asked Kwame what he thought of the strippers. 'I don't know how they get the courage to do it,' he said. 'I couldn't do anything like that.'

'Oh, what a pity,' said Ethel. 'We were hoping you would put on the next show for us. I'm sure that you're a much better dancer, your skin is as smooth as silk; and I'm equally sure that's not the end of your attractions.'

'Then I'm sorry to have to disappointment you a second time,' said Kwame.

'But do you realise how much you could earn?' persisted Ethel, and she mentioned a sum that was equal to all he could earn in two or three months.

'Maybe I'll do it just for you,' he joked, with immediate regret because he suspected that Ethel took it as a serious offer.

'I'll take you home with me after we close next Friday,' she said happily.

Kwame walked home with Mrs Chichester as he often did if she had to stay behind for an unscheduled committee meeting that delayed her until he had finished clearing up. They usually chatted all the way but tonight his landlady walked in silence. Halfway home Kwame could bear it no longer and asked if anything was wrong.

'I overheard you talking to Ethel Banks,' she said quietly. 'I don't think you should get involved with her.'

'She took my joke seriously; I really don't intend to get involved with her.'

'Has she asked you to get her drugs?'

'Yes, but I told her I couldn't help.'

'I would prefer that you didn't supply her with anything else.'

'Why is that?' asked Kwame, somewhat surprised that his landlady should seek to constrain his social life.

'I feel responsible for you while you're so far away from your wife and family,' she confided.

Kwame's life was now full of scheduled activity. He had little time to relax with his friends. He tried to keep one evening free each week to be with Peter Sarpong and the West Africa club but it did not always work out. He was never free at the weekends so he avoided the really wild parties and more serious drinking sessions. During the first year of his course Kwame had little difficulty keeping up with his studies. He knew that things would get more difficult in the second and third years and so he resolved to save as much money as he could while the going was good. The time passed quickly and he soon found himself revising for his end-of-year examinations. Once they were over he could turn his mind to a holiday back home in Ghana.

Tom Arthur was also thinking about spending part of the long vacation in Ghana. After his chat with Kwame on the way back from the airport he had tried to keep in touch on the matter of establishing a link between the two universities. They had had several brief discussions after lectures but Tom found it difficult to arrange a meeting where they could discuss at length what they should do. However, once the examinations were over and Tom Arthur was free from his heavy marking load he telephoned Kwame at his digs and they arranged to meet. Tom told Kwame that he had cleared an approach to Kumasi University with his bosses in Warwick, and the dean of engineering in Kumasi was willing to meet him during the long vacation. He proposed to visit Kumasi during the time that Kwame was home so that they could both take up the matter in detail with the university authorities.

'Why don't we fly down together?' suggested Kwame. 'I haven't booked my flights yet and I could fit in with your plans. I could help you with accommodation in Accra and transport to Kumasi.'

'That would be fine,' said Tom. So they arranged to fly together in July and to send letters ahead to warn all concerned of their intentions.

'Do we need to see anyone at a ministry in Accra?' asked Tom.

'It would be good if we could see Dr Acquah,' replied Kwame. 'He's back in charge of the Ministry of Industries, Science and Technology (MIST), although they call him the secretary now, not the minister. I hear he's planning to start the GRID project to establish ITTUs in every region.'

'It would be good to get his support for our link-up,' said Tom.

8

With Tom in Accra and Kumasi

They flew south together on a Wednesday afternoon in July 1986 and were met at the airport by Comfort and Akosua. Kwame and Tom were taken to the house of Comfort's relative in Medina where they stayed for three nights. Tom was surprised at the comfort and elegance of his room and of the house generally, and formed the impression that Comfort hailed from a wealthy family. As soon as Kwame noticed this he hastened to clarify the situation. Such houses are being built by Ghanaians who have good jobs overseas, he explained. 'When will they come home to enjoy their new residences?' asked Tom.

'Some never do,' said Kwame, 'It's often the relatives who stay behind who benefit most, but they don't feel it because they don't have the pride of ownership.'

Next morning, Kwame telephoned to try to arrange a meeting with Dr Acquah but was told that the Secretary of State was in Cape Coast and would be back in his office on the next day, Friday. So Kwame proposed that they visit Tema, the port of Accra, where MIST had an engineering training workshop. They motored from Medina to Tema along Ghana's only motorway and found the workshop located in the industrial area directly across the road from a group of enormous concrete structures. 'What on earth is that?' said Tom pointing skywards.

'Cocoa silos,' replied Kwame. 'They were intended to control the global market price. Nkrumah had the idea of storing cocoa when there was a glut and the price was low, and releasing it onto the market when there was a shortage and the price was high. So he built these huge silos to hold the raw cocoa.'

'Is there any cocoa in them now?'

'No, and there never has been. They say they are full of rain water.'

They were welcomed by the manager of the workshop, John Assuah, like Kwame Nkrumah a native of the Western Region. He explained that the workshops were rather neglected by the ministry but he tried to do his best on a modest budget.

'We hear that we may be taken over by the GRID project and operated as the Tema ITTU,' he said. 'Then we will get some new investment in machines and facilities.'

'What is GRID?' asked Tom.

'It's an acronym for Ghana Regional Industrial Development,' John Assuah replied. 'The aim is to establish an ITTU in each of Ghana's ten regions. We will be the third, after Kumasi and Tamale.'

'That will be a big project,' said Tom, 'Who's funding it?'

'We hear that the EEC, the Canadian International Development Agency (CIDA) and USAID are all involved.' said Kwame. Then he added proudly, 'The idea came from my outfit in Kumasi, the TCC.'

The next day all of this was confirmed by Dr Acquah. They saw the Secretary of State in his office in Accra. It was the first time that Kwame had seen him since the formal opening of the Suame ITTU in January 1981. Kwame had already told Tom how, after the overthrow of Dr Limann's government on 31 December 1981, the new government of Flight Lieutenant Jerry Rawlings had asked Francis Acquah to stay on at the Ministry of Industries. The offer was declined on the grounds that Dr Limann, the democratically elected president, was under house arrest. However, three years later, after the release of Dr Limann and the former vice-president, Francis Acquah agreed to take up his responsibilities once again. In Kwame's view, apart from Dr Kwesi Botchwey, the Secretary for Finance and Economic Planning, Dr Acquah was the only widely respected member of the Rawlings administration. Now he was in the midst of a broad programme to revitalise the industrial sector.

Dr Acquah's efforts had come into the glare of publicity with the Indutech Exhibition, held at the National Trade Fair site in Accra in March that year, 1986. This was an international event aimed at publicising Ghana's recent progress in industry, science and technology. The TCC mounted a major exhibit on behalf of the Kwame Nkrumah University of Science and Technology. This showed not only what the university was doing but also what was being done by its numerous small-scale client industries in Kumasi and Tamale. Dr Acquah had ensured that Jerry Rawlings visited the KNUST stand to be shown around by the TCC director. His aim was to get the head of state to approve the GRID project, the second of his new initiatives.

Francis Acquah told Tom and Kwame how he had asked Dr Jones to draw up a plan to establish ITTUs in all ten regions of Ghana. The

TCC had been operating the Suame ITTU in Kumasi for nearly six years and the Tamale ITTU was coming into operation after a long delay in constructing the building. He explained that the Tamale ITTU was a collaborative project implemented by the TCC in partnership with the DAPIT project under his ministry. In answer to Tom's questions, Dr Acquah explained that DAPIT stood for Development and Application of Intermediate Technology, and the project was supported by the United States Agency for International Development (USAID).

Dr Acquah went on to say that the third ITTU, and the headquarters of the GRID project, would be in Tema. He would allocate the MIST training centre in Tema to accommodate both the ITTU for Greater Accra Region and the head office of GRID. He also had some machine tools donated by the Indian government that could be assigned to an ITTU for the Central Region in his home town of Cape Coast. 'Beyond that, we shall have to rely on further foreign support,' said the Secretary of State, 'but I am happy to say that the Canadians, Europeans and Americans are all interested in extending their support for the ITTU concept. All I need now is the approval of the cabinet.'

'When are you expecting to get the go-ahead?' asked Tom.

'It could be soon but I'm prepared for a long delay because the cabinet hasn't given the project a high priority. My hope is that we can get started early in 1987.'

Tom was impressed by Dr Acquah's enthusiasm and his willingness to speak openly about his plans and hopes for the future. He guessed that here was less a politician than a technocrat doing what he loved best. When he mentioned this to Kwame after the meeting, Kwame confirmed that people did not consider Dr Acquah to be a government supporter in the political sense but a patriot trying to do all he could to help his country grow in prosperity. Tom's instant respect and admiration for Francis Acquah made Kwame think again about his own ambitions. Was the wide-scale acclaim now accorded to Francis Acquah, a fellow engineer, what he would like to achieve for himself?

After meeting Dr Acquah, Tom was keener than ever to try to establish a link with KNUST and get involved with the programme of extending ITTUs to all corners of Ghana. So early the next morning the two engineers, together with Comfort and Akosua, set off on the long road to Kumasi. It was Saturday, the day when the whole of Ghana travels to attend funerals, so the traffic was heavy. The journey seemed longer than it should because long stretches of road were under reconstruction and the diversions were even worse than the old road that was being replaced. Kwame was pleased to see that at last the road was being improved after many years of neglect. Tom was thinking that if this was the road between Ghana's two greatest cities, what were the other roads like?

In spite of the bone-jarring ride, the drama of driving into the tropical forest was not lost on Tom. He had never seen trees of such height: massive towering columns rising from great buttress roots to a 'British-standard' tree perched on top. Kwame explained that most of the trees left standing were of little commercial value. The exportable timber had long been removed from this easily accessed part of the forest. The *odum* (iroko) and mahogany were gone and only trees like the *onyinaa* (kapok) remained. Kwame told Tom about his father's activities as an inspector of sawmills. He said that most of the sawmills his father visited were further up the road, around Kumasi and beyond in the Western and Brong-Ahafo Regions. He didn't mention that his father's accident had occurred in the Eastern Region through which they were passing, although the exact location was many miles off to the south.

For Tom, the further they went the more dramatic the scenery seemed. The trees grew even bigger and closer to the road. He bathed his eyes in a greenness he had never imagined existed and which he found gently soothing. It was a greenness enlivened by frequent flashes of bright scarlet or gold as they motored past trees in glorious full flower. However, not all the sights were pleasant. Tom was disturbed by the sad procession of animal corpses displayed along the roadside. Held aloft by the tail by boys and youths, recently executed mammals and reptiles of great variety were offered for sale to passing motorists. When Tom expressed his disgust Kwame explained that bush meat was highly sought after in Ghana and many drivers would stop and buy. The most common bush meat on offer was forest snails, as big as tennis balls, sold alive and strung together in bunches with tough braded strings of elephant grass. Their abundance was testimony to their near universal popularity.

After they entered Ashanti Region and pressed on towards Kwame's home town of Konongo the road rose and fell with a regularity that bred monotony in frequent commuters but fascinated Tom. It was like riding on a low-frequency radio wave cast in red laterite, he mused. The roadside wares became more attractive with each undulation. Masses of tomatoes, oranges and bananas came into view, piled high on wooden tables at strategic selling points. Lay-bys provided easy parking off the main carriageway and numerous cars were stopped at each location. Also on offer were farm products less familiar to the Englishman: yams, plantains, pawpaws and avocados. As the car came to rest at one such location, Tom was alarmed to find the vehicle immediately surrounded by a crowd of women and children, all shouting the supremacy of their wares. Each vendor balanced a round tray of produce on her head while she held out a sample specimen for instant trial. Tom tasted an orange. He was equally surprised by the greenness of its exterior and the sweet juiciness of its interior. He had previously supposed that all oranges were orange in colour. Now he knew that some of the sweetest were green. The downside was that they were also full of pips.

Comfort took the opportunity to stock her larder for the week ahead. The staple items were yams and green plantain. Tomatoes, onions and peppers took next priority and then smaller quantities of most other commodities on offer. Tom was amazed at the ferocity of her bargaining. He couldn't hear what she was saying but he thought he caught the sentiment. Every price, it seemed, was grossly exploitative and only affordable by a rich foreigner. Were they playing Rule Britannia? Through a long discourse of declining volume every price was beaten down to a fraction of the initial asking. Then, most amazing of all, an extra quantity of produce was invariably added when the deal was done. No offence was taken on either side. Both parties seemed to enjoy the confrontation. At the end, buyer and vendor parted the best of friends, promising to do business in the future at every opportunity.

They drove on towards Konongo with the car filled with the produce of the forest farms. Tom hoped that no forest wildlife in the form of snakes, scorpions or spiders had accidentally hitched a ride, concealed in the voluminous bunches of plantain. Comfort assured him that she had checked everything carefully before loading it into the car. There was some bush meat that even Ghanaians didn't relish, she joked. In answer to his question she assured him that the snails too were unable to escape from their binding.

At Konongo, Comfort and Kwame had come home. It was still 50 kilometres to Kumasi but they could not pass through without welcoming Tom to their modest abode. So they parked the car in a side turning and showed Tom into the Ashanti compound house where Kwame had been born 29 years before. At last, Tom thought, he was in the real Africa of real people. He entered an expansive yard of bare orange/red laterite soil, beaten hard by generations of footfalls, littered with piles of sand and long neglected concrete blocks and the plastic detritus of the modern world. The surrounding walls might once have been white but now they had taken on the colour of the soil beneath. The broken wooden doors sagged on their hinges and the louvred windows had cracked and missing glass, some replaced by plywood strips.

As they entered, a crowd of children and a few women came to greet them. Tom was overwhelmed by the warmth of their welcome. Somebody fetched a wooden chair and a wooden bench and indicated a place of shade beneath a mango tree. Two or three old men sitting there greeted Tom with dignity and moved aside to let the children place the chair in the favoured spot of densest shade. No sooner was he seated than he was offered a glass of water. He looked anxiously at Kwame who immediately assured him that the water was safe to drink. So he drank readily to slake the thirst generated by the long hot dusty journey. Next, he was offered a bottle of Coca Cola by a small boy who had clearly run back from a nearby store to which he had been dispatched by his mother. 'You must stay for fufu,' he was told.

Looking around Tom noticed that food preparation was under way at several points around the compound. Large aluminium pots were boiling on charcoal and wood-burning stoves. 'How long will it be before the food is ready?' asked Tom.

'Oh, not long; I will hurry them up,' said Comfort reassuringly.

Two hours later Tom was wondering how long it might have taken without Comfort's intervention. By now the compound was reverberating to the sound of fufu pounding. 'This is the last stage before we eat,' said Comfort, striving to stem the flow of her fast-draining credibility.

'Come to Africa to learn patience,' thought Tom, but he answered reassuringly that the wait had sharpened his appetite. When it came at last, Tom found that fufu was not nearly as bad as he had feared and the groundnut soup and chicken were delicious, even if red pepper made it hotter than anything he had ever tasted before. Kwame had mounted an expedition to find a bottle of Star beer and the two friends drank to the health of the community, sharing as much as possible with the old men and women in attendance.

Tom asked Kwame about the availability of beer. 'It's true that we have to import barley and hops to feed Ghana's four breweries,' said Kwame, 'but however short we are of foreign exchange the government cannot afford to cut back on beer production. Sometimes we can find no soap in the market but beer is always available. We say that soap politics is one thing but beer politics is another.'

Tom laughed. 'I guess it's the same everywhere but are there never any shortages?'

'It's often not available at the government's controlled price,' said Kwame, 'but you can usually get it if you pay the *kalabule* price.' Then Kwame explained to Tom how the term *kalabule* had grown up during the Acheampong era to signify the black market.

Kwame left Comfort and Akosua in Konongo and drove on with Tom to Kumasi. It was early evening before they reached the university campus so Kwame took Tom straight to the guest house. Tom was delighted to find his temporary home surrounded by grassy lawns, tall trees and flowering shrubs. 'What's that beautiful house over there?' he asked.

'That's the new vice-chancellor's residence. The old one has been converted into this guest house,' explained Kwame. 'You are staying in the house where Dr Baffour entertained Kwame Nkrumah with the most beautiful girl students. There was a swimming pool that's now concealed under the floor of the dining room.' Then he called the man who had carried Tom's suitcase to his room and told him to take good care of his friend. Tom was assured, with eager words and a broad smile, that he was in good hands.

'Tomorrow is Sunday and I will leave you to cool off and have a rest,' said Kwame 'Take your lunch at the Senior Staff Club, just down the road there, and meet some of the expatriate lecturers. Talk yourself into a game of tennis or snooker. I'll call for you on Monday morning and we can see the TCC director and book some appointments with the V-C and deans.' Kwame was then free to drive back to Konongo.

'Have you been a good boy all this time?' asked Comfort after Akosua had fallen asleep and they were left to themselves in their tiny room.

'My landlady has taken on the role of chaperone,' laughed Kwame, recalling Mrs Chichester's intervention with Ethel Banks.

'Then you deserve a proper welcome,' said Comfort, knowing that Kwame was never really relaxed in the Medina house and would only feel at home now he was back in Konongo. She carefully avoided the touchy question of getting her own house, knowing that she must postpone the issue if she wanted to enjoy her husband's homecoming to the full. For Kwame it was much better than the dreams he had dreamed on cold nights in Coventry.

On Monday morning Kwame took Tom to meet the TCC director. The two English PhD engineers greeted each other warmly. 'I've heard and read so much about the TCC,' said Tom, 'that I'm really happy to be here to see for myself.'

'It's good to have you here to help us,' replied Dr Jones, 'How long are you planning to stay? I hope that it will be long enough for Kwame to show you what he's been doing in Tamale.'

'Oh yes, I wouldn't want to miss that,' said Tom enthusiastically. 'My people at Warwick are particularly keen to be involved with problems in the rural areas.'

'Well, they certainly need all the help they can get,' replied the director, 'but our grassroots engineers in the urban areas need our help just as much and, if they get it, they can provide much of the help that the rural folk need.'

'That's exactly what I wanted to ask you about,' said Tom.

This was a central theme of the work of the TCC and Kwame had heard Dr Jones expand upon it several times. Nevertheless, he was more than content to sit back and hear it run through one more time for the benefit of his English friend. He felt that Tom could not fail to be impressed with the logic and practicality of the approach. So the director launched into his pet theme by explaining that the small-scale engineering industry in a developing country like Ghana was essentially focused on repair and maintenance. The rural blacksmiths, who for centuries had made all the tools the farmers needed, were now engaged in trying to repair imported tools and machinery. In the towns, the wayside welders and fitters spent most of their time repairing imported motor vehicles, industrial plant and domestic equipment.

The big urban *kokompes*, like Suame Magazine here in Kumasi, were almost totally devoted to the repair of motor vehicles. However, some manufacturing started through the recycling of parts. 'Young Kwame here has probably told you how he became a leading entrepreneur in the market trolley business,' continued the director. 'That's the sort of initiative we want to encourage, but we want to get beyond the recycling of auto parts and building trolleys, *trotros* and trailers on a one-off basis.' He went on to explain that in a survey of Suame Magazine, undertaken by the university in 1971 for the Busia government, only six centre lathes had been found and all were engaged on repair work like resurfacing worn brake drums. 'So when we started our work in that same year we decided to make our main thrust the introduction of machine tools of all types and the demonstration of quantity production techniques.'

'Did you have to train the machinists or were there some already trained?' asked Tom.

'That's an important issue,' replied Dr Jones, who went on to explain that there were many centre lathe turners and other machinists already trained by the polytechnics, technical colleges, large companies and self-employed machine owners. A few of these machinists found work in government workshops or big enterprises but many found that there were no opportunities for them to practise their skills.

'Because there were so few machines around?' interjected Tom.

'Exactly,' replied the director. He noticed that Tom looked disappointed. 'Universities are in the business of training people but at this point training is not the first priority,' explained Dr Jones. 'One sometimes feels that in the past every well-meaning project set up a training programme but gave little thought to employment after the training was finished. The market was over-supplied.'

The director continued to explain that many of the trained machinists would have liked to set up their own businesses, especially the young men who graduated from an apprenticeship with a self-employed lathe turner. 'We realised at once that the first need was for machine tools to supply to self-employed artisans and small workshops.'

'How can a university supply machine tools?' asked Tom.

'With difficulty,' replied the director. 'We realised that used machine tools were available in the UK at low prices that the artisans might be able to afford but our problem was how to persuade agencies to give us funds to buy used machines.'

Dr Jones went on to explain that most governments and international aid agencies had rigid policies against the supply of used machines to developing countries. So the TCC turned to the NGOs and after much fast talking, backed up with extensive writing, some modest funds began to trickle in. 'The people who helped us first were organisations like Oxfam, World Council of Churches, Rockerfeller Brothers Fund and Barclays Bank International Development Fund. By 1973 we were able to set up some production units on the university campus and invite the grassroots engineers to come and see for themselves.'

'What were you producing?' asked Tom.

'We had two main engineering production units at the TCC and a few more that we supported in the faculty of engineering,' was the reply. 'The first TCC production unit produced steel bolts and nuts using semi-automatic capstan lathes. There was a big demand for coach bolts in Suame Magazine for use in the construction of the wooden bodies on *trotros* and cocoa trucks. There was also a good market for hexagon-headed bolts for the roof trusses of buildings and, a little later, for fishing boat construction. It was the demand of the boat-building industry in

Accra that eventually persuaded a private workshop to take up the technology.'

'What was the other production unit making?' asked Tom.

'That was the most significant of all our early projects,' reflected the director. 'We began by making small-scale plants for grassroots soap producers. In the Acheampong years of the mid 1970s, soap was in very short supply. So when the TCC demonstrated a small-scale technology for soap making many people came forward for training and wanted to buy a plant. The second TCC production unit was set up to meet this need. Called the Plant Construction Unit (PCU), it was involved with welding and steel fabrication and produced more than fifty soap plants between 1973 and 1975. The soap was made from palm oil and caustic soda so the PCU was soon producing palm oil extraction plants and plants to produce caustic soda from slaked lime, until that time an industrial waste product. The output of the PCU quickly brought into existence hundreds of small enterprises employing thousands of people scattered in towns and villages all over the southern half of Ghana.'

'Now I see why you want to support urban engineering manufacturing,' said Tom, 'The engineers in the town can promote much economic activity and employment in the rural areas.'

'That's it exactly,' affirmed the director.

'Now tell me about the ITTUs and Kwame's foundries,' requested Tom, eager to bring the story forward to the present.

'That's a big leap forward,' replied Dr Jones, 'but I will try to be brief.'

Tom listened intently to how the TCC had come to the conclusion that the best way to transfer technology to grassroots artisans was to establish the university's production units in the middle of Suame Magazine. The ITTU was a group of production units under one roof operating where they could easily be seen and studied by any interested craftsman or entrepreneur. The emphasis was still on manufacturing, and especially on making plants and tools that were needed in rural industries. As technologies transferred to private workshops the university introduced new technologies. That is how it had become involved with non-ferrous, and then ferrous, foundries and the local manufacture of various types of foundry furnaces.

'We now have several private foundries in Suame Magazine making grinding plates and bearing shells for corn-milling machines,' interjected Kwame.

'Dr Acquah told us he wants to establish ITTUs in all ten regional centres,' reflected Tom. 'Does that mean that the university will hand the project over to the Ministry of Industries?'

'We have in mind a project under the ministry,' replied the director. 'We call it GRID. It will have a finite lifespan of perhaps ten years. Its objective will be to put the eight remaining ITTUs in place, and when that is done it will be wound up. The university will remain the essential technical resource supporting the ITTU network and providing a constant stream of new technologies and new ideas for productive activities. Has Kwame told you any of the stories of Ananse the Spider? The GRID project will build a technology transfer web across Ghana but the university will remain Ananse at the centre.'

'How do you see the University of Warwick helping you?' asked Tom.

'Well, we would see you as a partner in identifying new ideas and developing new technologies. In particular, we would like to think of you as a high-tech back-up with the expertise and facilities to do more advanced research and longer-term projects in support of our technology transfer programme. We would like to refer to you technical problems that we do not have the resources to tackle here in Kumasi. We would welcome your involvement through visits and staff secondments and we would like you to be involved in training our staff as you are training Kwame. We particularly need to train some graduate extension officers on MSc courses in production management and Master of Business Administration (MBA) courses.'

'Can we draw up a project proposal while I'm here?' asked Tom.

'Yes, why not begin the drafting with Kwame as you go around, then bring it to me for my input?' replied the director. 'I would also want my deputy director to be involved. He will be taking over here soon when I go to Accra to help Dr Acquah. He's at Suame today, so please see him there or make an appointment to see him here tomorrow.'

'When we have a project proposal, where should we go to seek funding?' asked Tom.

'We would suggest the Overseas Development Administration (ODA) or the EEC,' replied the director. 'You could call in at the British High Commission and the EEC Delegation when you go back to Accra. But doesn't Warwick have its own contacts in the UK?'

'We have some, but we're still new to this field of work,' concluded Tom.

'How do you find the director?' asked Kwame after they had left the office.

'He's certainly very enthusiastic about the work and his enthusiasm is

107

infectious,' replied Tom. 'I hope that I can remember half of what he told us.'

'Don't worry about remembering things,' said Kwame, 'He writes everything down and makes us do the same. We have quarterly newsletters, annual reviews and dozens of reports on every project. Just let me know what you need and I will see that you get it.

'Shall we go to Suame today?' he asked. 'It will give us an early chance to meet the deputy director.'

'How about some lunch first?' enquired Tom.

Kwame was startled, he had not thought about lunch. 'Most of us don't stop for lunch,' he said, 'We just grab some groundnuts and roast plantain. Would you like to go to the Senior Staff Club?'

'Oh, I'm happy to join you with the local fare,' said Tom. 'When in Rome and all that.'

So Kwame found his favourite purveyor and with the food wrapped in yesterday's *Daily Graphic* they drove across the city to the great Magazine.

'Isn't Kumasi known as the Garden City?' asked Tom as they navigated slowly around potholes far bigger than he had ever imagined possible on a city street. 'Doesn't anyone ever repair the roads?'

'This part of the country is not very popular with the government,' observed Kwame. 'They say that a contract has been awarded to an East German company but the Ashantis don't want communists building the roads in Kumasi.'

'Well, I don't see much that could be called a garden,' persisted Tom.

'The gardens are all in Nhyiasu where the big men live. They even have a golf course there,' said Kwame.

'What's this area called? I can't see any big men's houses.'

'This is Ashanti New Town or Ash Town for short. We'll soon reach the Magazine.'

Tom found Suame Magazine difficult to relate to anything he had known before. The nearest he got was to see some resemblance to cities as portrayed in Hollywood films some years after a nuclear war, with the surviving residents living in shacks among the wreckage. However, the wreckage was not from fallen buildings but the remains of vehicles that had crawled into the Magazine in terminal decline. He found the scale of the apparent devastation hard to encompass. The Magazine extended over several square kilometres and was home to about 45,000 craftsmen.

Tom asked Kwame if he could take some photographs and was told that it would be all right as long as they asked permission first. Kwame told Tom a story about Frank Johnson's girlfriend, the photographer and friend of Flight Lieutenant Jerry John Rawlings. Shortly after the revolution, early in 1982, the lady had come to the TCC with a military escort to take photographs of Suame Magazine. Dr Jones had told her that he could arrange for her to take any photographs she might want but she had better leave her bodyguard behind. So she took her tour of the Magazine with the Suame ITTU chief technician as her sole guide and protector.

'She was quite safe then,' observed Tom.

'Oh yes, I guess the fitters assumed she was taking photographs for the ITTU.'

'How would the fitters have reacted to the military?'

'With cutlasses and iron bars, I guess.'

Tom was relieved to find that the ITTU building and compound was a haven of order in the midst of chaos. Kwame explained that the TCC insisted that the ITTU should always present a neat and ordered appearance. This was an essential element in what was called its 'demonstration effect'. The ITTU was intended at all times to present an impression of efficiency and modernity. At the same time there was no gate to the compound and the surrounding artisans were free to walk in at all times. This traffic was further encouraged by a small retail store that became popular in the early 1980s for selling soap produced at the TCC's pilot plant at Kwamo village. The retail store also sold the products of the ITTU and of its clients. At various times it carried on a steady trade in steel bolts and nuts and corn-mill grinding plates. Many a client of the ITTU had first called at the retail store before later enrolling for training and the supply of the essential tools of his chosen trade.

'Isn't there a risk in providing such easy access to the ITTU?' asked Tom.

'Well, we certainly lose a lot of small tools, in spite of having a security man on duty at all times.'

'How does the director view these losses?'

'He says we are working in the informal sector and as such we must accept some informal transfer of technology. Some losses are hard to replace, but at least the stolen tools contribute to the efficiency of the grassroots workshops we are trying to help. As long as the losses do not seriously cripple our operations, our open door policy will not be changed.'

'That's a very enlightened view to take,' observed Tom.

Kwame enquired about the ITTU manager who was also serving as acting deputy director of the TCC. 'He's tied up with a visitor at the moment,' was the reply, 'but we told him that you were here and he will see you as soon as he's free. He suggested that you show Dr Arthur around in the meantime.' Kwame was happy to show his English friend the place he knew so well.

After showing Tom the ITTU's own workshops – machine shop, welding and fabrication shop, foundry and woodworking shop – Kwame explained that four client workshops also operated within the ITTU. One of these produced gear wheels and chain sprocket wheels by milling, shaping and hobbing. It was the first workshop in Kumasi to possess this capability. Most of the production of gear wheels and sprocket wheels was going to the nearby Yugoslavian Tomos motorcycle assembly plant. All the other parts of the motorcycles were imported. 'This is the ITTU's first successful effort in promoting sub-contracting to the Magazine from a large international company,' said Kwame proudly as he showed Tom around a neat but somewhat congested workshop, full of activity and piled high with finished products awaiting transport to the assembly plant.

Tom was impressed. In just six years the ITTU had raised the level of technology from simple jobbing repair work on basic centre lathes to quantity production of precision engineering products by advanced machining operations, and to a level of quality acceptable to an international company. Outside of the modern precincts of the ITTU the Magazine still sprawled in its aboriginal condition. The history was cast in the geography. But the ITTU was no ivory tower. It welcomed all comers to step from the past into the present, from the grassroots to the mainstream.

Kwame led the way to a second client tenant of the ITTU who operated an iron foundry.

'Apart from your famous corn-mill grinding plates, what else do your foundries produce?' asked Tom.

'We recycle a lot of scrap material and supply it in reusable form,' explained the proprietor. 'For example, the fitters need the cast iron from cam shafts to replace burned-out engine exhaust valve seatings. So we melt down worn-out cam shafts and supply lathe turners with bars of cast iron of suitable size.'

'And I suppose some foundries recycle a lot of non-ferrous materials, brass and bronze,' observed Tom.

'I'm telling you,' interjected Kwame, 'and some traditional aluminium cooking pot makers have adopted our modern furnaces and extended their range of products.'

'What are your other two tenant clients doing?' asked Tom.

'They are both essentially machine shops,' explained Kwame. 'One proprietor was trained in England. He is a specialist in engine repair machining and has introduced several new techniques into the Magazine.' Kwame led Tom to the third client workshop and introduced the proprietor. 'Frank Awuah here is famous for repairing Volkswagen engines by replacing the main crankshaft bearings.'

'Yes, using this lathe, the biggest that the TCC has brought to Suame, we devised this special jig to hold the crankcase while the bearing seating is machined,' said Frank.

'So you do get involved in some vehicle repair work,' observed Tom.

'Yes, but only when it introduces a new technique that makes possible a repair that wasn't done in the Magazine before,' replied Kwame.

'And the fourth workshop?' prompted Tom.

'That one is a little disappointing,' admitted Kwame. 'It is run just like a typical *kokompe* machine shop with materials, tools and work-in-progress scattered about everywhere. The proprietor has made a few machines for rural industries but he always complains that he has no orders and is forced to do jobbing repair work most of the time.'

'Does he do any sales promotion?' asked Tom.

'No, I'm afraid not,' said Kwame, 'He waits for the ITTU to bring him an order when we are asked to supply a rural development project by the government or a development agency.'

'Do you get many such opportunities?' asked Tom.

'Not too many, but they are often for large numbers of products and we need to spread the work among several clients.'

'Were all these four enterprises created with used machine tools imported by the project?' asked Tom.

'Oh yes, and many others around the Magazine and in other parts of Kumasi,' replied Kwame. 'The others all found their own accommodation. These four were lucky to be given space in the ITTU when they failed to find any other workshop to start in.'

'They must benefit from on-site advice and shared facilities,' observed Tom.

'That's true, but they also help us to show visitors like you what the ITTU is doing, and they attract many new clients to the ITTU.'

When Tom asked about training, Kwame told him that the ITTU did not train beginners. All clients were expected to possess the basic skills of their trade. However, training was given wherever it was needed for a new technology or the manufacture of a new product. The training was tailored to suit the needs of the client. It could be full-time or part-time and the client decided when he had learned enough to transfer the activity to his own workshop. For an interim period, perhaps before his own machines arrived, the newly trained client was allowed to hire time on an ITTU machine. In this way the ITTU was maintained as a hive of activity with a constant interchange of people with the community it served. Tom was impressed by what he had seen and congratulated the manager as soon as he met him in his office.

Sosthenes Battah was soft spoken but it was soon clear to Tom that he was armed with a deep understanding of the work and fired with an earnest enthusiasm. Tom wondered how they could all be like this; the director, deputy director, Kwame, all spoke of their work with a pride and zeal that contrasted sharply with the grim reality of the grinding poverty they had set themselves to alleviate. Could they really spread the impact of the ITTU over the vast expanse of the Magazine? Could they promote similar changes in all the regions of the country? Could they really find enough people who were similarly motivated? He resolved to probe more deeply with Kwame on these issues.

'Have you seen all parts of the ITTU?' It was the manager who was speaking.

Tom brought himself back from his musings with the thought that it must be the tropical heat that induced this unexpected lethargy. 'Yes, thank you,' he blurted, 'Kwame is a good guide and has told me much that I wanted to know.'

'Then would you like to visit client workshops in other parts of the Magazine or look around the Magazine generally?' asked Mr Battah.

'Whatever you recommend,' said Tom.

The rest of the afternoon was spent walking around the extensive maze of dirt roads that wound irregularly between the thousands of concrete-block workshops and wooden shacks that composed this greatest of Ghana's industrial assets. Walking was difficult, as the ground underfoot was rendered irregular by potholes, stony outcrops and half-buried vehicle parts. Vehicles in all states of disrepair lurched past in clouds of black smoke and choking red dust. Everywhere was red earth, rusting iron and black oil stains, with an occasional stunted tree to remind the stumbling adventurers that they were in the heart of a tropical forest. Through a haze induced by heat, humidity and dust beyond his past experience, the Magazine became for Tom a kaleidoscope of half-focused images of men hammering, sawing, watching and waiting, accompanied by ringing blows, violet flashes and the roar of tortured engines.

Seeing Tom's apparent distress, Sosthenes Battah stopped at a wayside kiosk and purchased three cold bottles of Coca Cola, one of which he handed to Tom and another to Kwame. 'I'm sorry not to be able to offer you a choice,' he said to Tom, 'but we rarely find more than one soft drink on sale at a time.'

'It's a case of Henry Ford syndrome, is it?' joked Tom, but he was not sure that he was understood. So he added hastily, 'You know, you can have a car of any colour you like as long as it's black.' The look on his companions' faces suggested that they feared he was suffering from heatstroke.

'It's Dr Arthur's first working day in Kumasi,' Kwame explained to the ITTU manager. 'Maybe we have done enough for today and I should take him back to the campus.'

'Are you staying in a university guest house?' asked Sosthenes.

'Yes, I'm in the old vice-chancellor's lodge.'

'I also stay on the campus in a staff bungalow. I'll call round for a chat one evening, if that's all right with you.'

'Yes, please do. I would like that.'

Tom was relieved to reach the cool and quiet of his guest house. He invited Kwame to stay for another cold drink in a more relaxed setting. As his head cleared he remembered the questions that teemed in his mind as he half-listened to the manager at the Suame ITTU. However, it was Kwame who spoke first. 'How did you find Suame Magazine?'

'It's vast, much bigger than I imagined. How big an impact do you feel the ITTU can have on the lives of so many people?'

'It's a big challenge. So far, at Suame, we're judged to have done rather well but our critics insist that Suame is a special case.'

'How do you mean?'

'Well, Suame Magazine has long been famous for its dynamism. People say that any project can succeed there and the success of the ITTU at Suame does not mean that it can succeed elsewhere.'

'What do you think?'

'I've also seen the concept succeed in Tamale, but that was largely due to one man, Frank Johnson, the first manager.'

'That's my big worry,' said Tom. 'You seem to have some good people who can make the concept work, but do you have enough of them?'

Kwame realised that Tom had focused on an important aspect of his own dilemma. He knew that people like himself, who understood the concept and had faith in it as a means of transforming Ghana, also knew that it was a task that would last more than one lifespan. Many were attracted to the call of such a project but they were also acutely aware that life was too short to indulge such long-term interests. The needs of self and family were much too urgent. So he said, 'Our type of work attracts a lot of good people but we work with foreign agencies and many take the first opportunity to seek their fortune overseas. There are few like Mr Battah who are prepared to devote their lives to the work here in Ghana. Some of Mr Battah's peers make jokes about him driving an old car and not having built a house but I respect him for the good work he has done and is still doing. He will shortly take over as TCC director and we all expect him to keep the work on track.'

'I can see that Mr Battah is a fine man, a perfect exemplar for you younger chaps, but I still doubt that there are enough of you to fulfil the expansion plans that Dr Acquah and the director have drawn up,' insisted Tom.

'Yes,' said Kwame, 'there are not enough people willing to put the interest of the community before their own self-interest.' He went on to explain that in some ways self-interest, greed, helped the work. The TCC worked with entrepreneurs who all wanted to make a fortune. A few of them succeeded in making a great deal of money. That was good for the project, but it made some of the university people jealous. They said, 'Why should we work to make someone else rich?' This led some to leave the work and start their own businesses, which the director actually encouraged, but a few stayed in the job and started taking bribes, diverting supplies and embezzling project funds. 'The director didn't mention this, but he spends a lot of time setting up committees to investigate things that go wrong.'

'Can you give me an example?' asked Tom.

'Yes,' said Kwame. 'We had a project to help a traditional craft industry making glass beads. The craftsmen asked the TCC to improve the colour of their beads. They were using crushed coloured glass, beer bottles for amber and green and Milk of Magnesia bottles for blue, but the resulting colours were rather dull. The director started importing ceramic pigments from England and supplied them directly to the craftsmen at a fair price. The new beads were more brightly coloured and started to sell rapidly. Soon, with our encouragement, traders started importing the pigments but they sold them at much higher prices. We thought that in time the price would stabilise at an affordable level. However, the craftsmen came to the TCC to complain that the only pigments that were available were the highly priced ones from the traders. The TCC was still bringing in large quantities of pigments but our officers were selling it in bulk to the traders, not direct to the bead makers. The director was forced to sack one of our best rural industry consultants.'

'I can see how such temptations can divert effort when people are poorly paid,' said Tom, 'and that there are many faster ways to a fortune than working on a university salary, but will there be enough honest and well-motivated people left to see the ITTU programme succeed?'

'I don't know,' replied Kwame, acutely conscious that he was questioning himself, 'but if I don't go home soon Comfort will lock me out!'

'Yes, you must go,' said Tom. 'Please tell Comfort that it's all my fault.' Then, much to his surprise, the thought of vivacious and curvaceous Comfort waiting at home for Kwame filled him with envy. This place certainly stimulates the hormones, he observed to himself as he made his way to the dining room for his evening meal. He recalled that when Kwame Nkrumah stayed here girls were supplied to order. Maybe he should ask Kwame if Comfort had an unattached sister.

9

With Tom in Tamale

Kwame was eager to show Tom the work that he had been doing in Tamale. He was also keen to see how the project had fared since he had left the year before. So the next day they took advantage of the offer of a TCC vehicle and, with Kwame at the wheel, they headed north.

'How will the weather be in Tamale?' asked Tom.

Kwame sensed the concern in his voice. 'It is usually hotter than in Kumasi but much less humid. Most *abrofo* prefer it.'

'That's a relief,' said Tom. 'It was getting on top of me yesterday.'

'We could see that,' said Kwame, 'that's why Mr Battah bought you the cold Coke.'

'How far is it to Tamale?' asked Tom.

'Nearly 400 kilometres,' replied Kwame, 'but the road is bad and it usually takes about seven hours to reach there.'

'What about fuel?' asked Tom, who knew that it was in short supply.

'We carry it with us,' said Kwame. 'Our vehicles run on diesel and have double fuel tanks. The TCC buys the fuel in bulk and stores it on the campus in Kumasi. Then our vehicles can do return journeys to any part of Ghana without needing to buy more fuel. It has been essential to operate this way since fuel became scarce. Diesel is always more plentiful than petrol and it also gives more miles per gallon.'

'Do all your vehicles run on diesel?' asked Tom.

'Yes, ever since we adopted this policy in 1979,' said Kwame. 'USAID sent three vehicles for the Tamale ITTU but they ran on petrol and the director sent them back. This caused quite a stir. The Americans said that nobody had ever returned vehicles before.'

They reached Tamale in the late afternoon and went straight to the project bungalow where Kwame's old colleague, Dan Baffour-Opoku, greeted them and showed them to their rooms. Tom was pleased. The bungalow was comfortable enough but still provided the feeling of living in the community. He had both Kwame and Dan as companions for the next few days. Both young men spoke excellent English and he looked forward to interesting conversations on the long dark evenings.

It started on that first night. Dan had already purchased the guineafowl and roast plantain that he knew Kwame liked and he had even managed to save a few bottles of Star beer that he had brought with him from Kumasi. So the three men settled down to a modest meal that would probably have been regarded as a feast by most of their neighbours. 'I can't wait to hear how things are going with the ITTU,' said Kwame. 'I hope you haven't ruined everything since I've been away.'

'Then you'll be pleased to know that we have finally erected the main workshop structure,' said Dan. 'People here are very impressed with it. They say that it beautifies their town.'

'Were all the parts found to be intact?' asked Kwame, recalling that the prefabricated building had lain on-site waiting to be erected for more than two years.

'Yes, it was a miracle,' exclaimed Dan. 'Frank did a very good job to keep the parts safe all that time.'

'I'm keen to hear how operations in Tamale differ from those in Kumasi,' said Tom. 'I hear that it's a whole new world up here.'

'We have a different climate, different terrain and different people, but the biggest difference is that Tamale is really a large village and the ITTU serves an essentially rural community,' explained Dan.

'I thought from what the director told us that the TCC focuses mainly on promoting urban engineering manufacturing,' said Tom. 'How did you come to choose Tamale for the second ITTU?'

'The short answer is that USAID was prepared to finance a project in Bolgatanga or Tamale and nowhere else,' said Dan. 'Bolgatanga is even further north, smaller and more isolated, so we took the dollars and settled on Tamale.'

'How much is the project costing?' asked Tom.

'About $980,000,' was the reply. 'That includes the building, vehicles, machinery and equipment, technical assistance from USAID experts and a supporting project in the Ministry of Industries. Now we have what Frank Johnson always said would be the best engineering workshop in Ghana north of the Volta River,' said Dan proudly.

'But is it a good project in the wrong place?' persisted Tom.

'At times over the past six or seven years we were tempted to think so,' replied Kwame.

Tom turned to Dan. 'What do you think now that you are getting into operation?'

'I think we are all pleased to find that the Tamale ITTU can achieve a similar impact to that achieved in Kumasi, although in many ways the impact will be different,' Dan replied.

'Then I can't wait to see it in the morning,' said Tom yawning, as he excused himself and made his way to his room, hoping that the electric power supply would sustain the air conditioning through the night. It didn't, but by the time it went off he was sound asleep, and the nights are cooler in the north.

The next morning was bright, clear and cool although it showed every sign of heating up quickly. The three engineers arrived at the ITTU at 7.30 just as the workers were reporting for duty. Tom observed that most of them arrived in project vehicles that brought them in from various parts of the town. A few arrived by bicycle and others came on foot. Tom could not fail to be impressed by the large, modern, brand new building, filled with new machines and equipment. It had been purpose built to specifications developed by the TCC and the university's faculty of architecture. Unlike Suame, where use was made of an existing building with much adaptation and compromise, here was the ITTU as conceived by its originators in a building designed from the outset with every need in mind.

The mains electricity supply in Tamale had long been unreliable and so the Tamale ITTU was equipped with its own 60KVA diesel-powered generator which started automatically whenever the mains power went off. It had now run for several months and Dan told Tom that it was needed during about 60 per cent of working hours. The ITTU workshops could not operate effectively without this in-house back-up.

'Do you only supply the ITTU workshops or do nearby client workshops also benefit?' asked Tom.

'Yes, we are in process of extending power to a few client workshops,' said Dan, 'but we have to be careful because illegal connections are very common here and we don't have too much power to spare over and above our own requirements.'

After a tour of the workshops Tom realised that the technical facilities were much the same as in Suame only laid out in better order in more spacious accommodation. There was a machine shop, a welding and steel fabrication shop, a ferrous and non-ferrous foundry and a woodworking shop. However, the level of relative activity was very different. In Suame, the ITTU woodworking shop produced mainly patterns for the foundry and as such it was small and in only intermittent use. The manufacture of wooden products such as beehives and weaving looms was farmed out to client workshops. In Tamale, with such client workshops still to be promoted, the ITTU's woodworking shop was piled high with beehives, weaving looms and cotton-spinning wheels. 'This is our busiest section,' said Dan.

'Where do the orders come from?' asked Tom.

'Mostly from central and regional government rural development programmes and foreign aid agencies,' replied Dan. Then he explained that most agencies, governmental and NGO, had much more interest in promoting development projects in the north where they felt that the people were poorer and in greater need. These agencies had welcomed the ITTU with open arms and rushed to place their orders for hundreds of items to use on their projects. Instead of needing to go to Kumasi or Accra, or order from abroad, they could now get much of what they wanted in Tamale. It obviously suited them very well.

'Is that altogether good for them?' asked Tom.

'Well, we often think that they order too much or the wrong items,' replied Dan. 'They are always in a rush and sometimes won't wait until the fully developed and tested product is ready. They are all under pressure to spend their budgets within the allotted time-span, and we find it hard to turn business away. There are always willing workers needing employment.'

'What is needed to transfer this production to private workshops?' asked Tom.

'We are teaching trained carpenters how to use the powered tools and soon they will be able to take the work away and complete it in their own workshops,' said Dan, 'but they won't be able to do it all in their own workshops until we can supply them with their own powered tools.'

'When will that be?' asked Tom.

'Some of the powered tools, like bench saws and wood-turning lathes, are already made by engineering firms in Kumasi and could be made here in the ITTU. We can supply these fairly soon, but imported machines will not be available until the GRID project starts up, hopefully early next year. Until then, we either do the machining in the ITTU ourselves or we let clients hire time on our machines.'

'I can see that the woodworking shop is achieving the main aim of the ITTU, that is: promoting manufacturing to sustain rural industries,' said Tom. 'Are the other sections doing the same?'

'To some extent,' replied Dan, 'but the machine and welding shops tend to be overwhelmed with repair work.'

'Why is that?' asked Tom.

'Well, formerly, any vehicle or machine that had a serious breakdown needed to be sent to Suame Magazine in Kumasi to be repaired. Now the people feel that this repair work can be done here. You see, Suame Magazine is an enormous repair facility and the Suame ITTU did not need to get involved in repair work, except to introduce a few new ideas and techniques. Here, the available repair facilities are very basic and the ITTU is expected to get much more involved in providing a local repair capability.'

'It's a key feature of the ITTU concept that it's very flexible, so the new ITTUs in the regions must adapt to the local situation,' interjected Kwame.

'Have you any plans to develop the local vehicle repair industry?' asked Tom.

'Oh yes,' said Dan, 'with the help of a client in Kumasi we have started engine cylinder re-boring and training local people to do that work. Then we have ordered a crankshaft-grinding machine. There are several privately owned crankshaft-grinding machines at Suame, so the ITTU never got involved in that technology, but there are none of these machines in Tamale. So the ITTU must introduce the service. Also, we are already doing all the engine repair machining operations that can be done on a centre lathe, surface grinder or shaping machine. I guess you're familiar with all that.'

'Yes,' said Tom confidently, 'after my tour of Suame Magazine. Do you have any plans to do manufacturing in the engineering sections?'

'Of course,' replied Dan. 'We want to introduce the production of a wide range of machines already made in private workshops in Kumasi such as corn mills, cassava graters, oil presses, bench saws and wood-turning lathes. We also want to look out for opportunities to make machines for northern industries that don't exist in the south.'

'What sort of machines?' asked Tom.

'Well, there's the machine for producing shea butter for a start,' said Dan.

'What's shea butter?' asked Tom.

"You've seen it in the market,' laughed Kwame, 'That bright yellow paste you asked me about.'

'Yes,' said Dan, 'but the bright yellow is an added dye. Raw shea butter, as extracted from the nut of the shea tree, is pale cream, almost white. The process of extraction is very labour intensive and done by groups of women. It takes a whole week to produce even a small quantity. We are hoping that with a few simple machines which we can make locally, the process can be scaled up and made faster. The TCC has been working on the problem with chemists and engineers at the university in Kumasi, and we expect to get some prototypes to test soon.'

'What is shea butter used for?' asked Tom.

'Here we use it for cooking, as a body cream and for making a local traditional soap called *amonkye samena*,' said Dan, 'but I believe it has important uses in the cosmetics and food industries in Western countries. If we could produce enough, it could be exported.'

The Tamale ITTU had its own workers' canteen and so at lunchtime they joined the ITTU staff for the break. A woman had been hired to cook the food and run the canteen under contract. Tom found the food basic but edible and much better than going hungry. He took the chance to talk to some of the individual workers and was pleased to find that most of them had enough English to answer his questions. They were all happy to have employment and training opportunities although all felt that the government could afford to pay them much higher wages. He was amused that the workers assumed that all development projects belonged to the government and blamed the government for their poverty. He was relieved to find that most of the workers did not smoke but his questions revealed that more would smoke if they thought they could afford it.

A young lady with a friendly golden smile reminded Tom that she was Lydia whom he had already met briefly as the chief weaving instructor in the textiles unit. She had been sent to the TCC in Kumasi for training before being appointed to her present post. Tom was flattered by her attention, especially when she proposed visiting him at home in the evening with a few of her trainees, nubile sirens who had already distracted him on his tour of the workshops. However, the plan was abandoned when Lydia learned that he was staying with the ITTU manager. She told Tom that her husband was in the army and they occupied a bungalow at Tamale's Gonja barracks. Tom had already asked Kwame about the slogan sometimes seen painted on *trotros*, 'No brother in the army', excusing the poverty of the vehicle operator. So now he understood how Lydia could afford gold teeth in a community where most people never saw a dentist in their lifetime.

Tom surmised that Lydia hardly needed her job for the money and that her interest in the work was quite genuine. She spoke of what she did with great pride and enthusiasm and told Tom that many young women could earn a living as self-employed weavers. As her trainees left the ITTU, each with a shiny new loom, she was enrolling them into a Northern Region Weavers Association. The Association was planning to open a small store in the town where all their products would be on sale. Lydia hoped that the ITTU would help her find suitable premises in which to set up the store.

Kwame laughed when he saw that Tom had been waylaid by Lydia. 'She is keen to practise her English on all our European visitors.'

'Well, her English is certainly very good,' said Tom.

'Did she offer to find you a girlfriend?'

'She seemed to be on the point of offering me the pick of her trainees,' replied Tom, surprising himself at his lack of reserve.

'But you didn't fancy any of them?' continued Kwame. 'Don't worry, I'll ask Comfort to find you someone really special in Kumasi.'

For once, Tom was lost for words, and turned away wiping his face in his handkerchief, but Kwame had already observed his burning cheeks, and did not attribute them only to the heat of the tropical sun.

When Tom had recovered his composure, he asked Dan if there were any client workshops near enough to be visited on foot.

'Yes,' replied Dan, 'this whole area is designated for light industrial development. The ITTU is at the centre and eventually it will be surrounded by small workshops, like a miniature Suame Magazine. So far, only a few clients have been able to put up permanent buildings or even temporary wooden structures but these few places we can visit.'

On the approach to the ITTU, Tom had not taken in its surroundings as he had not realised he was near until they turned into the compound. Now standing just outside the main entrance he saw that the land was flat and open with some patches of tall grass, red gravel tracks and a few small trees. He could see a few small structures scattered here and there with much open space in between. 'There's certainly plenty of room for expansion,' he observed.

'Not necessarily for the individual workshop owners,' replied Kwame. 'It will depend on the size of the plot they are renting.'

'I was thinking of the community as a whole,' said Tom.

'It will be a wonderful thing if we can fill the whole area with thriving small industries,' agreed Dan, already anticipating the pride of achievement.

The first workshop they visited could not have been smaller. It contained one of the smallest bench-mounted centre lathes Tom had ever seen and there was just room for the owner to stand and operate it. 'Frank Johnson found this man some time ago and promised him that one day he would have a full-size machine,' said Kwame.

'Yes,' added Dan, 'and since we have been operating the ITTU he has been attending every morning to study the operations of our large machines. In the afternoons, he returns here to do his own work.'

'What can he do?' asked Tom.

'Not much,' said Dan. 'There are very few repair jobs that he can do on such a small machine. He's mostly helping out with the repair of small electric motors on domestic equipment, skimming commutators and making bearing bushes.'

'Are there no larger engineering businesses in Tamale?' asked Tom.

'We can go from the smallest to the biggest,' said Kwame. 'Over there is Alhajji Issah Masters.'

The tall man strolling towards them in long flowing white robes was an impressive figure. He greeted the three engineers with '*Salaam aleikum*', to which Dan replied '*Aleikum as salaam.*'

Tom hoped that not all the conversation would be in Arabic or Dagbani and was relieved when a large brown hand gripped his hand firmly in synchronism with the greeting, 'You are welcome Dr Arthur. When did you come to Tamale?'

'He is reporting to you on his first day in Tamale,' Kwame cut in quickly before Tom could reply.

'I'm delighted to meet you, Mr Masters,' said Tom. 'Kwame has told me much about your good work here and I'm looking forward to seeing your workshop.'

'We do what we can but it's very difficult,' replied Issah Masters. 'My workshop is just over there,' he added, pointing across an open space to some permanent buildings about 200 metres away.

The group walked slowly across to Issah Masters' workshop, following the red gravel path between patches of tall grass. For Tom, the short walk was a marathon as the early afternoon sun beat down unrelentingly. He would have preferred to walk faster to gain some shade as quickly as possible but their pace was set by the slow measured stride of the man who had followed his prophet to Mecca. Much to Tom's relief, on reaching the compound they were taken into a cool office and invited to sit in comfortable chairs while cold soft drinks were quickly pulled from a refrigerator and offered to the guests. An oscillating desk fan rhythmically ventilated Tom's sodden shirt with a cold shock that was almost painful. By the time the drinks were finished and a visit to the workshops was proposed Tom's shirt was dry and he was ready to face the heat again.

Issah Masters' main activity was welding and steel fabrication and his two best-selling products were bed frames and steel trunks. 'These items are always in demand,' he told his visitors.

'Do any other workshops in Tamale make these items?' asked Tom.

'Oh yes, about six and they are all my ex-apprentices.'

'How did you start in this business?'

'I was trained as a blacksmith and developed the business by adding other skills in metal working.'

'What other products do you make?'

'I produce a bullock plough for farmers converting to animal traction, and I plan to take up some products from the ITTU, like corn mills and cassava graters.'

'How have you benefited from the ITTU?'

'In many ways; the TCC loaned me a lathe for two years until the ITTU building was ready and I produced steel bolts and nuts in my workshop, they trained my people in Kumasi and now here in Tamale, and I hope to benefit from orders sub-contracted to my workshop. I am also hoping that when the GRID project starts I will be able to buy more machines on credit.'

'You should ask Alhajji what he has done to help the ITTU,' said Kwame. 'He has been our strongest supporter since we first came to Tamale.'

'We need the ITTU very badly,' said Issah Masters, 'and we must all help the TCC to bring it here.'

'Alhajji is too modest to tell me himself so you must tell me,' said Tom.

'Well, he started by organising an artisans' association and lobbying the regional administration to support the ITTU project,' said Kwame. 'I heard Frank Johnson say that without Issah Masters' support he could not have started the Appropriate Technology Centre that served for several years as a pilot project for the ITTU.'

'As soon as GRID gets under way,' added Dan, 'they will form regional advisory boards and Alhajji will be a member of the board for the Tamale ITTU.'

Later, as the three engineers walked back to the ITTU, Kwame and Dan explained to Tom that Issah Masters was a key political figure for the project. In addition to being a leader of the artisans he was also a chief of one of the several villages that made up the town of Tamale.

'When you visit a place for the first time you are expected to first call on the chief,' explained Kwame. 'That's why I broke in just now

124

to emphasise that you were calling on Issah Masters on your first day in Tamale.'

'I see,' said Tom. 'It's important to follow local custom wherever you mount a project. That must be difficult.'

'The university is fortunate to draw staff and students from all parts of Ghana,' explained Dan, 'so we can usually find one of our own people to brief us even before we visit an area for the first time.'

'How profitable is Issah Masters' business?' asked Tom.

'The business probably makes a profit,' said Dan, 'but Issah is always in financial straits. Our society with its extended family system does not help people in business. Most entrepreneurs find it very difficult to separate their business from their private finances and for a chief like Issah Masters it is doubly difficult. There are so many demands on his resources, and as a chief and a businessman he must play the part of a rich man. Poor Alhajji, he owes money to every bank in Tamale, he has taken loans from numerous development programmes and has exhausted all possible credit facilities in the Northern Region. He is now trying to get credit in Kumasi and Accra. That's one reason why he's so keen on the GRID project with its plans for a machine tool hire purchase scheme and working capital loans.'

'How will it affect the project if Issah Masters goes under?' asked Tom.

'Oh there's no fear of that,' said Kwame. 'He's survived this long and I'm sure that he will continue to find a way through all his problems. After all we don't, any of us, regard cash loans in the same way that you do in England. In the end, most of them get written off, or that's the general expectation.' Tom made a mental note not to lend any money to a Ghanaian that he could not afford to lose.

That evening Tom asked if the next day they could visit a village where some of the rural projects were located. Dan agreed to brief Kwame on the locations where beekeeping and cotton spinning had been introduced using inputs from the ITTU. Kwame knew one village north-east of Tamale where these projects had been established some years before. He was eager to see what progress had been made since he, Frank and Sally had visited regularly in the days when they had been together. He now learned from Dan that travelling in that direction it would be possible to visit at least three villages where the ITTU had made some impact.

*   *   *

125

Next morning, according to his usual practice, Kwame set out early while the air was still cool and some progress could be made in comparative comfort. He realised that his English friend was feeling the heat more than he admitted, and wanted to lighten the burden as much as possible. Tom was pleased to be pressing on to the north into what was for him uncharted territory. They followed the main road towards Bolgatanga and then turned off onto a dirt track heading east. Tom had got used to the main trunk roads being tree lined but he was surprised to find that even these rural tracks were also planted on both sides with trees, especially in and near the villages. In broad flat grasslands with few trees in the general landscape it seemed that a great effort must have been made at some time in the past to provide shade along so many of the roads. Tom asked about the trees and Kwame said that most of the trees were neem, planted in the colonial era after the pattern introduced by the French in surrounding territories.

When they reached the village Kwame drove to the chief's palace. Tom saw a discarded cotton-spinning wheel on the veranda of a nearby house. 'This one doesn't seem to have been used very much,' he observed.

'Oh that's the queen mother's gift,' said Kwame. 'We don't expect that one to get much use.'

'How do you mean?' asked Tom.

'When we introduce a women's project into a village we must first get the approval of the queen mother,' explained Kwame. 'The big lady usually insists that she be given a spinning wheel to beautify her palace. We know that she won't use it but we can't refuse if we want to help the women in that village.'

'Is that why we are here?' asked Tom.

'Yes, we must let the queen mother know that we are visiting her women.'

Kwame went inside the queen mother's palace for a few moments and then returned to tell Tom that it was all right for them to see the women spinning cotton. 'At least we're not asking to see them winning clay,' said Kwame with a big grin.

'Would that be allowed?'

'Definitely not! No man is allowed to be there because the women do it naked.'

'I guess that it saves a lot of clothes washing,' observed Tom.

They found a group of old ladies busy on their spinning wheels in the compound of a nearby house. 'How did they do it before they had Frank Johnson's wheel?' asked Tom.

Kwame asked one of the ladies to show him her traditional technology that consisted of a thin stick about 25 centimetres long with a ball of clay near one end. Then he explained that both methods only spin a single thread of cotton but the wheel is four times faster and makes a stronger thread with fewer weak points. The ladies were trained at the ITTU or in their village and when they were competent they were supplied with a spinning wheel on credit terms. In some villages, various donor agencies were supplying the spinning wheels free of charge provided that the ladies attended the training provided by the ITTU. In other villages the women were supposed to pay for their machines on easy terms, but in practice collecting the small periodical payments proved very difficult, costing much more than it yielded, and so was often neglected.

Kwame reminisced about his time with Frank. 'One day we were visiting the regional minister and he asked us to teach cotton spinning to the witches.'

'Did you say witches?' asked Tom. 'Are there such people?'

'We were told that four villages had been established for the witches,' said Kwame, 'but the women needed help to generate more income to feed themselves.'

'Wait a minute,' said Tom. 'Where did the witches come from?'

'They are old women who are accused of witchcraft by enemies, usually enemies of their sons or daughters,' explained Kwame. 'They are driven from their home villages and cannot go back, and no other village will take them in. They used to wander about in solitude until they died, often from starvation. So the regional administration established four sanctuaries for them. Some time before, we had been asked by the Catholic Church to train some witches in Burkina Faso. It was when we told the regional minister about them that he asked us to train our own witches here in the Northern Region.'

'Charity begins at home,' murmured Tom, lost in thought for some time.

Tom emerged from his contemplation of man's inhumanity to woman by asking about beekeeping. Kwame said that there were beekeepers in the village and asked the cotton spinners where they might be found. They were told that some people kept bees in hives supplied by the ITTU but they were located some way away from the village. They showed Kwame which trail to take to lead him to the apiary. Tom saw that it led to an area where there was a clump of small trees and Kwame said that the hives would be located in the shade under the trees. After a longer walk than Tom had expected, for the path was neither smooth nor direct, they arrived at where two men dressed in beekeepers' protective overalls, hats, boots and gloves, and armed with smokers, were busy among a group of five or six Kenyan top-bar beehives.

'I've heard of the African killer bees,' said Tom, 'but are they really as dangerous as that looks?'

'We teach the beekeepers to take every precaution and supply all the essential protective clothing and equipment but we don't have many accounts of aggressive bees,' replied Kwame. 'Still, it would be wise not to go too close, at least until they've finished opening the hives.' One of the men in a beekeeping suit waved to Kwame but he couldn't recognise the man behind his veil. Maybe he was just greeting them as strangers. They watched until the men finished what they were doing and walked over to them, lifting off their hats and removing their gloves for the customary handshakes. It was then that Kwame recognised one of the beekeepers as a trainee during the days of Frank and Sally. 'It's good to see you, Simon,' he said. 'How's the beekeeping going?'

Tom learned at first hand that the introduction of beekeeping had provided a small additional cash income for subsistence farmers as well as honey for their families. The beekeepers told them that they were reinvesting their profits in more beehives to build up the size of their apiary to a commercial level. Although they had far to go in this village, Kwame encouraged the beekeepers by telling them of other villages in Brong-Ahafo Region where some apiaries now had hundreds of hives and the owners were selling their honey to traders from the Ivory Coast. 'Who knows?' he said. 'Soon you may be exporting your honey to Togo!' The beekeepers liked that idea because the CFA franc was still regarded as a hard currency, immune from the rapid inflation of the Ghanaian cedi.

As the beekeepers returned to their work Tom said, 'Listen! Is that a diesel engine I can hear?'

'It certainly sounds like it,' replied Kwame, heading off in the direction of the sound. After walking several hundred metres they came upon a small hut in which was installed an ancient Lister single-cylinder diesel engine driving a corn mill. Tom marvelled at the fact that this machine must have operated for decades at this remote spot with what he assumed would have been minimum attention to maintenance and lubrication. Kwame confirmed that usually in these rural locations little attention was paid to machinery until it breaks down. After greeting the operator Kwame asked how long the corn mill had been in operation. He learned that it had been at its present location for about five years but it had operated for many years before that in a bigger village on the Tamale-Bolgatanga road.

Kwame told Tom that the northerners greatly appreciated the British products that they had come to know and trust in colonial times. The Lister diesel engine was much used for corn milling, water pumping and generating electricity and there were many old installations like the one they had found, scattered across the Northern and Upper Regions. Similarly, the northerners loved the Raleigh bicycle and the original Land Rover four-wheel-drive vehicle. They called these products 'original' and always asked for them. However, these days they could not be purchased new because almost all current imports were from China and India. These countries produced copies of the Lister engine and the Raleigh bicycle but the northerners soon came to discover the difference in quality. That's how the constant demands for the 'original' began.

Tom said that he feared that if the British products were imported into Ghana these days the rural people would not be able to afford to buy them, and in any case, the quality was not as good as before. 'The quality of the Asian products can be expected to improve,' he said. 'That may be some consolation.'

'I think that the people would try to pay more for better quality,' replied Kwame. 'The problem is that they are not offered a choice. The traders import what will earn them most profit. Recently, the Cotton Development Company imported some bicycles for sale to their workers on easy payment terms by deductions from their salaries. Most of the bicycles were from China but they added a few Raleighs from the UK and sold them at higher prices. It was the Raleighs that were spoken for first, in spite of the higher cost.

'This has puzzled me a lot,' added Kwame. 'I thought that the free market is supposed to be controlled by the law of supply and demand.'

'That's the theory,' agreed Tom.

'But what if the market does not supply what the people demand?' complained Kwame. 'With this system that the IMF and the World Bank has forced on Ghana, what we are supplied with is determined by the importers. We are forced to buy the stuff because there's no alternative, but we are not happy with it. One of my friends bought three Chinese padlocks for his house and in six months only one was still working. Such products are not cheap. That's not a free market! It's more like a slaves' market.'

'I've not heard these things before,' said Tom. 'Let me think about them and we'll discuss them later.'

Kwame wasn't quite ready to let go of the bone. 'Take the machine tools in the ITTU,' he said. 'We always tell the donor agencies that we want used machine tools from England or Germany but they tell us that it is their policy to supply new machines. Then they tell us that the new British or German machines are too expensive, or the model we want is no longer produced, and they want to supply new Indian or Chinese machines. We've argued this point so many times over the years but none of the politicians can understand. In the end, for the Tamale ITTU, we were fortunate, because the Americans supplied mostly new machines from the USA and a few used machines from the UK. However, I fear that when the GRID project starts negotiating for really big orders for the other ITTUs they will be forced to accept Asian machines.'

'It will be interesting to see if that's what happens,' said Tom.

On the way back to Tamale they made detours to two other villages where the ITTU had projects. In the first one, some women were being introduced to broadloom weaving at the request of a donor agency with a development programme in the village. A short training course had been arranged in the primary school during the long summer vacation and Lydia was there with one of her assistants. Six looms and a warping mill had been brought from the ITTU and set up in the school assembly hall. A young woman was busy at each loom and many more women and children crowded around to see what was going on.

Lydia told Tom and Kwame that to meet the demand the course might need to be repeated several times in this one village alone and she had been told by the sponsors that there were more villages waiting their turn. Kwame told her not to worry because the would-be trainees had, as yet, no real understanding of the work or the level of reward it could yield. When a few serious women set up in business they would all see how hard it was to earn a modest living. After that, only a determined few would persist in their interest. 'Everyone will stand in line for a handout,' he said to Tom, 'and with projects like this people think they can get something for nothing. The white man's pockets are bottomless,' he added with a grin.

'Do you mean that many people start training, and even acquire equipment, but do not seriously pursue a business venture?' asked Tom.

'That's for certain,' replied Kwame, 'especially where donor agencies are too generous in introducing new projects. Sometimes, for instance, they pay the trainees a living allowance while under training. That's always a mistake. We advise against it, not because we are mean, but because it attracts people who only want the allowance, not the training. We have found that it is always necessary to ask the trainees to make some contribution or sacrifice to supplement our input. This is essential to finding people with a genuine interest in developing a new business.'

'How do you determine genuine interest?' asked Tom.

'It's best if you can attract people who are already in the business and want to improve their operations,' said Kwame. 'Most of the older ladies who show an interest in our cotton spinning wheel are in that category. They know the business well, do not have inflated expectations and just expect to do a little better than before. Except for the queen mothers,' he added, grinning at Tom, 'we have few problems with recruiting serious cotton spinners. However, there are very few people who already earn a living by weaving and it is much more difficult to select serious people for training. Lydia here is facing a big challenge, but I'm pleased to see that she has found enough serious weavers to form her association.'

'Some of our people were cloth traders before becoming weavers,' said Lydia, 'so they know something about the market, the type of cloth in demand, its uses and its selling price. Others were cotton spinners who know something about the yarn supply situation. So we look for these kinds of business links in selecting our trainees.'

Once again Tom was impressed with Lydia. The TCC seemed to find people who could not only do their job but had the imagination to overcome problems and suggest new areas of activity. They could both do the work and improve the work. He admired the system that gave technical staff the freedom and opportunity to try out their own ideas. Lydia, for example, did not only teach basic broadloom weaving but designed new patterns of cloth and sewed them into new products to test the local market. Some of her ideas had been taken up by trainees when they started their own work, and seeing how she worked inspired others to devise their own new products.

Lydia told Tom that currently various items with a name woven into the cloth were very popular with church groups and clubs. Hand-woven cloth could never compete directly with cheap imported cloth for everyday use but there were niche markets for quality items with special features such as woven-in names, emblems and logos, and the colours could usually be supplied to the customer's requirements. There were times when a village chief or a queen mother would be attracted by a new design of cloth or style of garment and wear it at a festival or funeral. This often led to many other local dignitaries also seeking to be similarly adorned. As always, it was an intimate knowledge of the local market that led to success in business.

Lydia asked Kwame for a lift back to Tamale. She was commuting to the village each day during the course but her assistant had opted to stay overnight in the village and she would supervise the trainees until the close of work. Kwame was pleased to have Lydia's help because he wanted someone to introduce them to the third village where a group of women was extracting shea butter. It was this village where the ITTU was planning to test the new machines, but Kwame had yet to visit there and did not know the people. So they drove on in the general direction of Tamale with Lydia as their guide.

Kwame had not been much aware of the TCC's interest in shea butter and he had only just heard from Dan that a research fellow had been at work in Kumasi for several years. Much had been learned about the chemical and physical characteristics of the extraction process but it needed a practical engineer to envisage a machine to put the theory into practice. It was then that one of the TCC's oldest engineering clients, SRS Engineering of Kumasi, took up the matter and its inventive managing director, Solomon Djokoto, designed the machine that promised a breakthrough to much higher productivity. The machine had been tested in Kumasi but the shea trees grew only in the northern grasslands and that was where the traditional industry was located.

The TCC wanted the new technology to be available to the women's groups that traditionally produced shea butter. They wanted to avoid for as long as possible the new machines falling into the hands of relatively wealthy male entrepreneurs who would drive the women out of business. Such gender shifts had occurred in other women's industries when a machine came along to lessen the physical burden.

It seemed socially desirable to see if the existing women's groups could be mechanised and kept in operation in the villages rather than the work migrating to larger plants in urban centres. The concept was aided by the fact that the shea trees grew wild and were scattered over all of the Northern and Upper Regions. Collecting the nuts and transporting them to an urban centre would present logistical problems and be costly. Until commercial plantations became available the raw material supply situation favoured decentralised production. Here was an opportunity to protect social benefit from the death's hand of economies of scale.

When he heard all this from Kwame, Tom felt that the approach was idealistic and unrealistic. If the machine worked well, would SRS Engineering refuse to take orders from entrepreneurs? Could the women be trained to operate and maintain the machines? If not, would a man not be hired to run the machine and wouldn't he eventually take over the business? Tom felt that it would require a strong project to provide the necessary support to the women's groups. Kwame said that the TCC planned a project with funding from GTZ of Germany to build four sets of equipment at the Tamale ITTU for supply to four women's groups in the Northern Region. The managing director of SRS Engineering had agreed to visit Tamale and show the ITTU engineers how to produce the machines. The village they were visiting would be the first of the four pilot projects.

When Tom saw how the women were working at the long and arduous task of extracting the shea butter he was more than ever convinced that they would never master the mechanised system. Here were some of the poorest and frailest creatures working with a few metal pots and wood-burning stoves for a whole week to produce little more than a handful of product. 'Don't be misled,' said Kwame, 'they may be illiterate, but from the research done in Kumasi it appears that they have a great deal of hands-on scientific knowledge about the process. For example, the shea butter separates from the aqueous solution only over a very narrow temperature band and they know exactly how to control the process within these fine limits. They are much cleverer than they look. I think we will be surprised how well they master the machine.'

'You are ever the optimist,' laughed Tom. 'I hope you are right.'

In the late afternoon they dropped Lydia at the gate of Gonja army barracks and drove on into Tamale. They were both very hungry, having lunched lightly on bananas and groundnuts. They hoped that Dan had remembered to buy in the guineafowl and they were not disappointed, only tonight it was perched on a pile of rice. They were intending to head back south in the morning and Tom was contemplating an early night when Kwame said that he was planning to visit his family in Wenchi on the return journey and would Tom mind? Tom said that he would not mind at all and asked how long was Kwame planning to stay in Wenchi. 'Only two nights, just over the weekend,' was the cheery reply.

Then Tom said 'Tell me again about your family in Wenchi. Your mother is there, isn't she?'

'Yes,' said Kwame, 'she is living there with her husband and my half-sister Adjoa.'

'How old is Adjoa?' asked Tom.

'Oh, you have me there, I guess she'll be nineteen this year,' said Kwame. 'She's ten years younger than me.'

133

'What does she do?' asked Tom.

'I really don't know,' replied Kwame. 'She wanted to do some trading like Comfort but I don't know if she ever got started. You'll be able to ask her tomorrow.'

Tom yawned. 'Let's get some sleep. I guess you'll want to make your usual early start in the morning.'

10

To Wenchi

They drove from Tamale west and then south, back down the road they had taken from Kumasi. After about four hours they reached the town of Techiman. Kwame always thought of Techiman as the last town of the south driving north, and the first town of the south driving south. South of Techiman the land seemed to be densely populated with many towns and villages, but north of Techiman the country stretched for long distances with only widely scattered small settlements. So Techiman stood like a sentinel on the frontier of the land of the Akans. For Kwame, even though he loved the north, it represented the door to his homeland.

At Techiman, Kwame turned right to travel the 25 kilometres north-west to Wenchi.

'Does Wenchi have a meaning?' asked Tom.

'Well, my mother always says it is derived from *wan akyi* meaning the light behind,' said Kwame. 'It signifies a clearing in the forest. You can see the light shining through the trees before you reach the clearing.'

'That's a very poetic derivation. Are there other names like that? What about Kumasi, what does that mean?'

'That's a longer story.'

'I'm still interested to hear.'

'Well, we are told that in the distant past the great Asantehene, Osei Tutu, was not sure where to establish the capital of Ashanti. Two places were under consideration. His fetish priest Okomfo Anokye instructed that kum trees should be planted, one at each location. At one place the kum tree died, that is now the small town of Kumawu; but at the other place the kum tree flourished, that is now the great city of Kumasi.'

'What does Kumasi mean – literally?'

'It means the kum tree has stood.'

'Your language seems to contain a rich culture.'

'I'm telling you,' said Kwame, 'with our famous *anansesem*, or spider

135

stories, and our thousands of *mmebusem,* or proverbs, our language has many different and poetic ways of expressing most concepts. The old people can say almost everything in proverbs and they even hold proverb-striking competitions to see who can remember the most.'

'Where could we see such a competition?' asked Tom.

'They hold them at the National Cultural Centre in Kumasi,' laughed Kwame, 'but I don't think you would understand very much.'

'Couldn't you translate for me?'

'No chance; for one thing they speak far too quickly, and for another each proverb would require a long explanation. If you're really interested I will buy you a book that has about 1,000 proverbs translated into English, with explanations in both English and Twi.'

'Why do you need explanations in Twi?'

'For modern people who were educated in English and had little chance to delve deeply into our traditional culture. I was lucky that my father took the trouble to fill in this part of my education and the university included African Studies in its curriculum.'

'Doesn't the TCC have a Twi proverb as a motto?' asked Tom.

'Not a proverb,' said Kwame, 'but the name of a traditional symbol used in *Adinkra* cloth printing. It means "I must change myself and play many parts".'

'Sounds very appropriate,' said Tom, 'but I want to be able to say it in Twi.'

'Then you really will need a girlfriend in Kumasi.' laughed Kwame.

When they were still several kilometres from their destination, Kwame pointed ahead to the crest of a broad hill in the distance and said to Tom, 'There's Wenchi.'

Tom could just make out some low buildings extending along the line of the road. 'It doesn't look like a clearing in the forest any more,' he observed.

'No, the trees are much fewer and smaller these days,' explained Kwame. 'There is dense forest still to the south but Wenchi itself is rather exposed. It lies now in the transitional zone between the forest and the grasslands.'

Like many towns in that part of the world Wenchi lay strung out along a trunk road, in this case the road leading from Techiman to the ferry on the Black Volta at Bamboi and onwards to Wa in the Upper West Region. Kwame kept going so far through the town that Tom thought they were driving out again on the other side but just before the houses stopped he drew off the road to the left and parked the vehicle. 'Now we go on foot,' he joked, but Tom guessed from his manner that the walk under a blazing midday sun would not be too long. Kwame strode towards one of the houses and called out what sounded to Tom like '*Kawkaawkaw*' to which came the immediate reply '*Memeeme*'. Then as they turned the corner into the compound Kwame was engulfed in the voluminous embrace of a tall handsome woman who Tom assumed was his mother. An almost equally enthusiastic embrace greeted Tom as Kwame hurried the introductions.

'Did you see your sister's kiosk as you drove through town?' asked Amma.

'No,' replied Kwame, 'what is she selling?'

'Shoes,' said Amma, 'don't you remember? Comfort helped her to get them at Kejetia market.' Then Kwame recalled that Adjoa had asked Comfort to help her buy shoes in Kumasi for sale in Wenchi. He guessed that Comfort had introduced Adjoa to Mama Kate. He wasn't sure that he was happy with this arrangement.

Amma suggested that after they had rested a while with a cold drink they should walk back to visit Adjoa in her kiosk on the main road. Tom asked after Adjoa's father and Amma looked puzzled. She hadn't seen him for a several years. Kwame spoke to his mother briefly in Twi and then said to Tom, 'Mum's husband will be back later and he will be happy to meet you.'

As they walked to Adjoa's kiosk Kwame said to Tom with some embarrassment, 'My Mum has moved on from Adjoa's father, she likes to change her man from time to time. Sometimes I think she still dreams of meeting the rich man who will sweep her off to a life of ease and luxury.'

'She's certainly an attractive woman,' said Tom.

'Yes,' replied Kwame, 'but she will soon have to face the reality that her dreams of a better life are fading.' Then he demanded of his friend almost in anger, 'Why do African souls live so long? Why don't they die younger like Europeans?'

'Ah, you've been reading T.E. Lawrence, *The Seven Pillars of Wisdom*,' observed Tom. 'I've wondered about that myself when I see students from Africa at Warwick still studying for a first degree in their forties and fifties.'

'I'm just the same really, aren't I?' persisted Kwame. 'I'll be over thirty when I graduate.'

'That's not so old,' said Tom. 'You've done a lot already, and you still have plenty of time for a full professional career.' But he sensed that that was not Kwame's primary concern.

Kwame greeted his sister warmly with the Ga call of '*Ayeekoo*' to which she replied dutifully '*Ya Ayee*'.

Tom waited patiently while the demi-siblings embraced and expressed their mutual astonishment at each other's growth since their last meeting. He didn't know how long it had been but looking at Adjoa he could guess that there had been startling developments in the interim. Adjoa had inherited all the alluring attributes of her mother. When she eventually turned to him her smile intensified the heat of the afternoon sun.

'Kwame has told us so much about you in his letters. I've been looking forward to meeting the famous Dr Arthur.'

'Please call me Tom, and may I call you Adjoa?'

'That's fine with me.'

Adjoa showed them her new kiosk. Close beside the main road, it was constructed of wood with a corrugated aluminium roof. It was brightly painted in primary colours and sported a name board announcing 'Adjoa's Fashion Shoes' in large letters. The inside was less impressive. The stock for sale was modest in the extreme. Only two or three pairs of dusty shoes set wide apart on otherwise barren shelves. 'Why haven't you gone to Kumasi for more stock, Sis?' asked Kwame.

'The money was finished,' she stated in a flat voice.

'How did that happen?'

'I got fever and then we had to pay Kofi's school fees...'

'I've told you that your business money must not be used for house expenses. Do you mean that all your trading money is gone?'

'We've been waiting for you to send us more. Now that you're here it will be all right.'

Tom saw Kwame groan inwardly. Now he knows he's home, he thought to himself.

After all three returned to Amma's house, Kwame had a long conversation with his mother in Twi. Their frequent glances in his direction persuaded Tom that it was his overnight accommodation that concerned them. He did not mind this temporary neglect as it gave him an opportunity to talk to Adjoa. He asked where she had been to school and if she had any ambition to continue her education. Adjoa said that she had never done well at school and was happy to leave. She wanted to be a trader, a market queen. Most of all she wanted to travel overseas, buying beautiful things to sell in Ghana. 'That's what Mama Kate does,' she said. 'She lives in a big house in Kumasi with three Mercedes Benz cars. I want to be like her. Do you know Mama Kate?'

'I've heard a bit about her from Kwame,' said Tom, 'but I don't know her personally.'

'Then you must come with us to meet her,' Adjoa replied.

Tom was surprised, 'Are you coming to Kumasi?'

Adjoa smiled, 'Kwame doesn't know, but I will ask him to take me to Kumasi when he gives me more money for trading.'

The long conversation was over and Kwame had something to tell Tom. 'My mother doesn't have accommodation for you here,' he explained, 'but we have a relative overseas who has built a house near here and we can get the keys for you to put up there for two nights. You will have all your meals here with us, of course.'

'That sounds fine,' said Tom. 'I guess you'll take me there with my things when we're ready to turn in.'

'First, you must take fufu with us,' teased Adjoa. 'Do you know how to eat fufu?'

'I'm not very good with my fingers,' confessed Tom, 'but I'm fine if you can find me a spoon.'

'Where have you had fufu before?'

'In Konongo with Kwame and Comfort.'

Adjoa looked disappointed.

Before Kwame could take Tom to his sleeping quarters he spent some time with his mother gathering supplies. He eventually emerged with a large cardboard box and a bucket of water. 'There's no running water and no mains electricity,' he explained, 'but we can give you this bucket of water, sheets and pillows, an oil lamp, mosquito coils, matches, etc. Do you need soap and towels?'

'I have some,' said Tom. 'What you have there will do fine.'

When they reached the house Tom was surprised to find that if it had had running water and mains electricity it would have been similar to the mansion he had stayed in with Kwame and Comfort in Madina. It seemed a great waste of money to sink this large investment in a lifeless dusty pile in the bush, but Tom was glad that it was here. It was strange to be the only person in such a large building. He couldn't help thinking of the people Kwame had told him about in Kumasi who were sleeping eleven to a room, and a much smaller room than the one he now occupied. He guessed from what Kwame had told him that there were empty houses like this one scattered in most small towns and maybe even in villages.

The bed was comfortable enough and getting to sleep was never a problem for Tom. As he descended smoothly into oblivion, the vision of Adjoa and Amma drifted in and out of focus.

When he slowly surfaced the next morning, Tom could have been forgiven for thinking that his dreams had not ended. There stood Adjoa holding his breakfast tray. 'Did you sleep well?' she asked.

'Very well, thank you,' he said, 'and how about you?'

'Oh, the mosquitoes were biting but it wasn't bad,' she replied. 'Do you like pawpaw?'

'Very much,' said Tom. 'Your pawpaws in Ghana are truly delicious.'

'Then enjoy your breakfast,' she said, and stood looking down at him.

Tom drew himself up to a sitting position and noticed that the morning was cool. He was pleased to see that beside the pawpaw was a mug of cocoa, as well as some fried eggs and slices of bread. 'It's very kind of you to bring me breakfast,' said Tom. 'Did you have to get up early?'

'I'm always the first up,' she replied as she leaned forward to place the tray across Tom's knees, bewitching him with a glimpse of her breasts as her towelling bathrobe parted. She seemed to notice his interest and asked, 'Are they like pawpaw? Cameron Dodoo says they are.'

'Who's Cameron Dodoo?' asked Tom.

'He writes books and things in the newspapers; we read one of his books in school,' said Adjoa. 'Well, do they?'

'I think they're much more beautiful than pawpaw,' said Tom, rather weakly, wondering where the conversation was leading, but she had already lost interest and was striding out of the room.

'I must get ready for the funeral,' she called back. 'You are invited.'

Tom was left in some confusion. What did she want? Was she opening a door or only teasing him? He suspected the latter because he had been in Ghana long enough to know that attractive young women often liked to tease white men. He had learned not to respond if they spoke as he passed in the street, knowing that he would only to be rebuffed by a word or gesture indicating that they were addressing someone else, farther off in the same direction.

But Adjoa was different. Her question about pawpaw might have been quite innocent. Africans didn't see female breasts in quite the erotic way that Westerners did. He also remembered Kwame telling him about the traditional puberty rights ceremonies at which each candidate exposed her breasts to confirm her transition to womanhood. He admitted however that the ceremony was now rarely performed in urban communities but was popular with the young men when revived occasionally on a cultural pretext for the benefit of tourists.

Tom was still meditating on this diverting theme, and had almost finished his breakfast, when Kwame came in. 'What's this about a funeral today?' asked Tom.

'Oh, we have funerals every Saturday,' replied Kwame. 'Which one are you interested in?'

'Adjoa told me I was invited,' said Tom. 'Which one is she attending?'

'I'll have to ask her,' said Kwame. 'I've not been informed yet, but I guess that we'll be expected to put in an appearance at several before the day is over.'

'It sounds as though we'll have plenty to do then,' said Tom. 'Is it like this every Saturday?'

Kwame explained that on whatever day a person dies, the funeral is almost always held on a Saturday, often several weeks later. Funerals are the biggest and most important social events and all family members, however distant, are expected to attend. Also invited are workmates and members of the deceased's church, clubs and associations. In towns and cities the funerals are announced in the newspapers and fill several columns every Friday. People scan the columns to see which funerals must take priority in compelling their attendance. Family ties are paramount, then levels of acquaintance in hierarchical order from close friendship down to not knowing the deceased but only a relative of the deceased. Other criteria of selection include the social standing of the deceased, the wealth of the family and the expected quality of food, drink and entertainment. The bottom line is that everyone hopes to show a profit on their funeral donation.

'So we have to pay to attend a funeral,' observed Tom.

'Mounting a funeral is very expensive,' explained Kwame, 'and many poor families risk going into serious debt when a death occurs. So people make a donation to help defray the cost. Even so, most funerals make a loss.'

'Why do poor people spend so much on funerals?' asked Tom.

'You should have asked my father,' said Kwame. 'He was always telling people we should have modest funerals like the *abrofo*. We should spend our money on the living, not on the dead. We should send our money forward into the future, by investing in our children, not back into the past by burying it with our ancestors. He deplored the fact that much of the money was wasted, as he saw it, on beer and spirits.'

'But you don't follow your father's advice,' cut in Tom.

'Personally, I think that Dad was probably right but nobody listened to him. Most people are still wedded to tradition and families compete with one another to mount ever more impressive funerals. Occasionally, one sees an article in a newspaper that restarts the argument but nothing has changed as yet.'

After Tom had attempted to bathe in his bucket of water, and dressed as formally as his limited travelling wardrobe allowed, they walked over to Amma's house to find out about the day's programme. Amma had decided that there were three funerals that required their presence. One was for an aged distant relative, another was for a neighbour's child taken by malaria, and the third was for a farmer killed on his farm by snakebite. 'We must attend the burial service for our relative,' Amma said, 'and spend most of our time over there, but we will look in on the other two funerals during the afternoon.' Then she turned to Tom, 'How did you like your breakfast, did you enjoy the pawpaw?'

'Very nice, thank you,' said Tom. 'Adjoa brought just what I needed.'

Tom and Kwame waited patiently while the ladies prepared themselves for the funeral. At length Tom looked at his watch and said to Kwame, 'Doesn't the service start at 10?'

'That's the time in the announcement but we always assume it will be 10.30,' replied Kwame. At 10.30, the two women had still not emerged from the inner sanctum.

'Is it far from here?' asked Tom.

'Not far at all,' answered Kwame. 'Calm down, nobody minds the time here, we won't be late.'

When Amma and Adjoa finally emerged Tom was both relieved and surprised. They wore identical full length Victorian-style dresses with matching head scarves and waist cloths in black and reddish-orange cloth. 'Is this traditional funeral wear?' asked Tom.

'Yes, do you like it?' asked Adjoa. 'I know Kwame doesn't like it much.'

'I'll need to get used to it,' said Tom diplomatically, and Kwame forced a laugh.

'I guess I've had long enough to get used to it, but it still fills me with dark thoughts.' He didn't want to mention his father in Amma's presence.

When they reached the church it was almost an hour past the announced starting time but mourners were still making their way slowly in that direction from all points of the compass. The priest showed some signs of agitation, he probably had another funeral service scheduled later, and the chief mourners agreed that the proceedings should begin. Tom was relieved that the printed programme was in both English and Twi although most of the hymns and prayers were voiced in the vernacular. The priest decided to repeat his long address in English, apparently for only Tom's benefit because everyone else had understood the first time through. Kwame whispered to Tom that the priest didn't often get a chance to show off his English. Tom made a mental note to thank the priest and compliment him on his erudition.

After the burial the crowd moved to the church hall for the next stage of the celebration. They stood around chatting in small groups until a truck arrived with a load of plastic stacking chairs and volunteers were called forward to help with the unloading. At length the hall was ringed with chairs and the guests were invited to be seated. Then a pick-up truck arrived, piled high with beer crates and a few crates of soft drinks. This time the band of volunteers was over-subscribed and drinks began to be handed around.

Tom observed that most of the women were dressed as Amma and Adjoa in traditional funeral clothes. Many of the men wore a simple black cloth wrapped around the left shoulder and held under the right arm. Other men, perhaps the more affluent, wore locally woven *Kente* cloths, mostly in black and red but with intricate patterns. Rich and poor were equally afflicted by the constantly recurring need to replace the cloth over the left shoulder from which it fell with monotonous regularity. As the heat and alcohol took hold, many cloths were left where they had fallen, exposing manly chests and shoulders to general view. Tom was forced to admit to himself that the spectacle was far less offensive than if the exposed flesh had been of paler hue.

Above the general babble of animated conversation, some voices could be heard raised in speculation about the fate of the food and entertainment. This information was relayed to Tom by Kwame who added that a band of musicians to entertain the guests had been hired from Kintampo and food had been ordered from a restaurant in Techiman. The food came first, with repeated apologies from the caterers that they had to supply five other funerals that day and they had had a puncture on the way. Kwame explained to Tom that very few of the older vehicles plying for trade in the rural areas carried a spare wheel and the search for a wayside vulcaniser could cause a long delay. Tom observed that many of the tyres he had seen on taxis and *trotros* would be illegal in Europe and so he suspected that punctures must be a frequent occurrence.
– Adjoa agreed that the *trotros* she took into Techiman often had

punctures on the way. 'And they often break down for other reasons,' she added.

They were all balancing plates of food on their knees when the band arrived. After moving a number of chairs and relocating the displaced persons and their impedimenta in other parts of the hall, space was made for the musical equipment. It was then that the absence of electrical power was noted and the musicians were informed that they must manage without the benefit of electronic amplification. They looked disappointed but not surprised because electrical power was rarely available at that time. They were soon in action and the dancing began.

All the women wanted to dance with Tom and he was kept on his feet for the next hour or so. His pleading that he was unaccustomed to the highlife fell on deaf ears and he found that whatever movements he made were greeted with general approval. He soon realised that his initial effort was far too vigorous and he quickly adopted the minimalist technique of the other dancers which was clearly more appropriate for endurance dancing on a congested floor in the heat of the tropics. Kwame, Amma and Adjoa were all in action and Tom began to enjoy meeting other members of their extended family and friends from the town. Every face was smiling broadly, every woman, young and old, was friendly and flirtatious and he was soon enjoying himself in a way that he had never previously experienced. This is really how we should enjoy a funeral; life must go on, he thought to himself as he moved slowly in incremental shuffles, approximately in time with the beat of the music.

At length, pleading that he was not used to dancing in tropical heat, Tom managed to escape to his seat and his cold drink. Kwame came over with Amma and Adjoa to say that it was time to move on to the second funeral. However, before they could go they must listen to the announcement of the donations. A master of ceremonies called for silence and began to read out the amounts contributed by each guest. He had a style of presentation that Kwame explained was almost universally adopted. 'Mr Kofi Opoku of Sunyani has donated not one thousand cedis – not three thousand cedis – but FIVE THOUSAND CEDIS!' There were significant pauses between the announcement of each intermediate amount, and the loudly shouted final result was greeted by applause and cries of astonishment.

Kwame groaned and Tom asked him if he had eaten too many chicken kebabs. 'No,' replied Kwame, 'it's just that mother will insist on making the biggest contribution, and it's my money.'

Sure enough, a few minutes later they all heard, 'Madam Amma

Ansah-Twum of Wenchi has donated not two thousand cedis – not five thousand cedis – not eight thousand cedis – but TEN THOUSAND CEDIS!'

'That's it,' said Kwame, 'she's had her moment of glory, but I'll not let her donate more than five thousand at the other funerals.'

'How much has she donated?' asked Tom.

'More than a hundred dollars,' moaned Kwame. 'I gave her the money to spend on herself and Adjoa.'

'You're beginning to sound like your father,' joked Tom, and Kwame realised that he was right.

The next funeral was in full swing when they arrived. It was being held in the open air. Chairs and wooden benches were lined up in rows as for a theatrical performance. Tom was seated prominently in the first row facing the front of a building with wide steps leading up to a veranda from where the master of ceremonies made his announcements. There was a constant flow of people to and fro between Tom's row of chairs and the steps. Immediately in front of Tom was a rock about the size of a football, big enough to obstruct the path but not so big that it couldn't have been easily removed by two adults. Tom watched in fascination as guest after guest dutifully lifted up his or her skirts to step carefully over the rock. He speculated how many people would pass the rock before someone suggested moving it. Then he recalled the debris left abandoned in the yard of Kwame's house in Konongo and the scrap metal similarly scattered around Suame Magazine and realised that unless someone wanted the rock for a specific purpose it would never be moved. Here is a principle of conservation of energy, he thought. Don't expend more energy than is needed to solve the immediate problem.

Kwame asked what he was thinking about and Tom told him about the rock. 'Let's move it,' said Kwame. 'Let's promote environmental awareness.'

'OK,' said Tom, and watched in fascination as Kwame stopped the next big lady with an elegant gesture and beckoned to him. The two men lifted the rock and carried it away, leaving the pathway clear. Then Kwame invited the lady to resume her passage to the applause of the assembled guests. The master of ceremonies said something to Kwame who translated for Tom.

'He said this will be remembered as the funeral at which *oboroni* lifted the rock.'

'What about you? You lifted it too.'

'*Abibifo* don't lift rocks,' replied Kwame with a grin.

145

Amma allowed herself to be constrained in her donation, but suggested that they move on before it was announced. By the time they reached the third funeral it was late afternoon. Some of the guests were beginning to slip away.

'You said this man died of snakebite,' said Tom, 'how common is that?'

'Many people get bitten on their farms,' replied Kwame, 'but only a few of them die.'

'Why is that?' asked Tom.

'Well, first of all, according to George Cansdale of the London Zoo, who made a survey of the snakes in Ghana in the 1950s, we have 70 different snakes but only 14 are venomous. So, many people are bitten by non-venomous snakes, and if they can be convinced of that fact, they don't die. Some people who are bitten by venomous snakes are saved by being given an antitoxin at a local clinic. Then there are people who believe that they have been vaccinated against snakebite by a traditional healer and others who have faith in local herbal remedies.'

'How do you know what type of snake has bitten you?' asked Tom.

'If you are bitten, you are advised to kill the snake and bring it with you to the clinic.'

'I bet that's not as easy as it sounds. How do you kill the snake?'

'Most farmers will be carrying a cutlass or a hoe, so they have a chance to strike back. If you can't kill the snake you must try to get a good look at it so that you can describe it to an expert.'

'What types of poisonous snakes do you have?'

'There are so many: black mambas, green mambas, cobras, vipers, they say the deadliest is the Gabon viper. Perhaps the most common snakebite is from the night adder because it doesn't move away as you approach but lies still in your path. It's often trodden on in the dark. It's not usually fatal for an adult, but a small child can be killed and I have known of dogs dying from a night adder bite.'

'I think I've heard enough,' said Tom. 'If you tell me any more I'll have to emigrate to Ireland.'

They sat with the remaining mourners for some time, took the obligatory drink, expressed their sympathy with the bereaved and made their donation. By that time everyone was tired and looking forward to the evening fufu so they made their excuses and walked slowly back to Amma's house. Tom would have liked to walk back at his natural pace but he was compelled to dawdle at the snail's pace set by Amma, which for him was doubly tiring. Kwame appeared not to notice the speed of progression, he was equally at home rushing like *oboroni* or sauntering beside his mother who stopped to greet every passing neighbour and often backtracked when hailed from behind. Adjoa, however, had been sent on ahead to prepare the evening meal.

Tom told Kwame that he had enjoyed his short time in Wenchi. He felt that he had learned a lot about life in rural Ghana. Together with his time in Kumasi and Tamale, he had been through a crash course in getting to know the country he had chosen to try to help through the link between the universities. He was not interested in joining together two ivory towers, but the TCC had forged strong links with the grassroots and this, he was certain, would interest his colleagues back in Warwick. Ultimately, he reasoned, the people who would benefit would be people like these in Wenchi. Their development programme would be channelled through an ITTU to be established in the regional centre, Sunyani. Kwame had suggested that they return to Kumasi through Sunyani, where they could stop to see what an interest group of local people was already doing to prepare for the coming of the ITTU.

Adjoa had asked Kwame to take her to Kumasi so that she could purchase a fresh stock of shoes from Mama Kate. So she joined the two men in the Land Rover early the next morning. The rest of the vehicle was filled with large bunches of plantain, yams and other farm produce to be carried to Comfort in Konongo. They headed back down the road towards Techiman but after about seven kilometres turned off to the right to head towards Sunyani.

Kwame told Tom about Kwesi Ansah, an oil palm farmer who had learned beekeeping from the TCC and was now Ghana's largest honey producer with more than 300 beehives. Kwesi had organised a group of local people to lobby the regional administration to make all necessary preparations for the coming of the ITTU. Kwame had invited Kwesi to have lunch with them at a restaurant in Sunyani, but first they would be able to visit Kwesi at his mini industrial complex near the market.

They found Kwesi at his workplace. His bald head reflecting the morning sun was outshone by his broad smile and warm greeting. Tom sensed at once that here was a man of outstanding ability, a natural leader. He was eager to show the visitors all he had accomplished in the short time since he had made contact with the TCC. 'I started with beekeeping,' he began, 'then I decided to make my own beehives and set up a wood-working shop. Now I supply beehives to my neighbours in Brong-Ahafo Region and I also train them in beekeeping at my apiary and help them in any way I can to get started. At the TCC in Kumasi I also saw some machines for milling corn and making gari from cassava so I brought some of these machines here to demonstrate these activities and sell the services. My main business was growing oil palms so I got presses and boiling tanks from the TCC to produce my own palm oil. Now I have plans to buy a soap plant and use the palm oil to produce soap.'

Tom marvelled at this entrepreneurial zeal. This one man had transferred several significant rural industrial technologies from Kumasi to Sunyani, some 130 kilometres, provided important new services for the community and created work for numerous people. With such people scattered about the country the ITTU programme could not fail in its quest to generate grassroots industries in all the regions. Tom was impressed by the fact that local progressive entrepreneurs like Kwesi Ansah in Sunyani and Alhajji Issah Masters in Tamale had been drawn into the programme and persuaded to support the introduction of the ITTU in their region. It was clear that these people were convinced that the University of Science and Technology could provide direct help to grassroots industries in their locality.

Kwesi Ansah joined them in the Land Rover to visit his apiary in the oil palm plantation. They drove off in a north-westerly direction towards Bechem on the road to the border with Côte d'Ivoire. Near Nsuatre, Kwesi's home village, they turned off to the left and were soon in the plantation. Kwesi told Kwame to park the vehicle and they got out for what was forewarned to be a long walk.

Adjoa said that she had no interest in long walks and had seen oil palms before. Tom looked with relief at the overarching palm trees, realising that they would be walking in the shade. With a wide sweep of his arm Kwesi indicated the broad extent of his land, all covered in oil palms. Leaving Adjoa sitting besides the vehicle, the three men plunged into the dark shadows that filled the avenues between the trees. Tom tried to steer his thoughts away from the reptilian fauna that might inhabit these shady tracks and grassy verges. He concentrated on following closely where Kwesi had trodden as he enthusiastically led his visitors further and further into the heart of his domain.

They did not attempt to count how many beehives they saw scattered about under the oil palms over a wide area. They hailed occasional pairs of workers dutifully undertaking various aspects of hive management, including the all-important harvesting of honey. Kwesi explained that, unlike in England where honey could be produced only in the summer, here the bees were active all the year round. There were no cold winter months during which the bees needed to be fed. Tom asked about the honey yield and Kwesi said that some hives could produce up to 15 litres a year, although the average was nearer 5 litres. He showed Tom his honey store currently stocked with three full 200-litre oil drums. Beeswax, cast in cylinders about 20 centimetres in diameter and 8 centimetres thick, was stacked to the roof of the shed. 'Can you help us find markets for beeswax?' asked Kwesi. 'I've read that it has more than one hundred industrial uses.'

Tom asked about the local uses of beeswax and Kwame told him that there was a small demand from the traditional lost-wax bronze casting industry and from people doing screen printing but the beekeepers were now producing well in excess of local demand. Part of the problem was the Kenyan top-bar hive that produced more wax and less honey than a modern European framed hive would. The Kenyan hive had been introduced as an easily managed hive for beginner beekeepers but experienced beekeepers like Kwesi should be moving on to a new framed hive now being introduced by the TCC. When the bees produced honey in a framed comb they wasted very little honey in producing wax. The comb in its frame was replaced in the hive after the honey had been extracted and the only wax made by the bees was to cap the cells. With the introduction of framed hives, honey production would increase and wax production would reduce.

Tom asked Kwame why the framed hive had not been introduced earlier. He was told that they were waiting for the introduction of the centrifuge that was needed to extract the honey from the frames. It was only recently that locally manufactured centrifuges had become available. Kwesi said that he would order a centrifuge from SRS Engineering next time he went to Kumasi.

Then Tom asked about the export prospects for beeswax. Kwame told him that the TCC had enquired about the international market and there was scope to supply industrialised countries but the real benefit would come if the beeswax could be processed to remove its colour and scent. This had been demonstrated experimentally by Professor Kuffuor at the chemistry department of the university. In this condition it could serve as a raw material for the cosmetics and pharmaceutical industries for making products as diverse as lipsticks and suppositories. Kwame had also heard that the Roman Catholic Church required that all its candles should be made of pure beeswax. At the present time all beekeepers were being advised to store their beeswax in anticipation of markets being found in the not-too-distant future.

They returned to Sunyani for lunch, although they arrived later than had been expected. The deep interest and wide expanse of Kwesi Ansah's activities had absorbed more time than Kwame had expected. The three men were hungry from their exertions and Adjoa's appetite had been nurtured in sleep. She drifted off again soon after the meal as the men continued their discussion of all that Kwesi had done and was planning to do. Kwame promised to follow up several matters in Kumasi and Tom promised to look further into the possible export and uses of beeswax.

It was late afternoon before they clambered back into the Land Rover and Adjoa finished her slumbers on the road to Kumasi. It was Sunday evening, traffic was light and they arrived in good time. Kwame dropped Tom at the university guest house and continued with Adjoa to Konongo where Comfort and Akosua were waiting with the fufu.

11

Back to Kumasi

Tom had finished his evening meal and returned to his room when he was surprised by a knock on the door. His surprise increased by a further order of magnitude when he opened the door to find two young women standing in the corridor.

'Opokua said you might need some company,' said the taller of the two.

Tom did not recognise Comfort's maiden name and seeing his hesitation the other added quickly, 'Kwame Mainu's wife.'

Now Tom realised that Kwame had kept his promise made in Tamale but he marvelled at the promptness of the action. He could only surmise that Kwame had telephoned Comfort from Tamale or Wenchi.

Realising that he was keeping the two visitors standing in the corridor waiting for a reply he said, 'Come in, have a seat.' They looked at each other as though this was not what they expected and then followed him into the room and took the proffered seats, one in the only easy chair and one perched on a desk chair. Tom was confined to sitting on the edge of the bed. He struggled to adjust the oscillating electric table fan so that its arc of ventilation encompassed all three of them, switching it to its highest speed in a forlorn attempt to offset the dampness spreading from his armpits. He gave a silent prayer of thanks that the power was on.

The taller of the two girls was sitting relaxed and confident in the easy chair with long legs stretched out before her. She wore Western-style clothes, a T-shirt and tight-fitting jeans. Her beauty was cast in a classical mould. Her face could have been any colour from white coffee to ebony through every intermediate shade without the need for any modification of bone structure. Her actual skin colour was light brown and Tom suspected that there could be some European blood in her ancestry. She wore her hair in long Rasta plaits falling over her shoulders. Her figure was slim but curvaceous. She said her name was Akos Mary.

The second girl, sitting stiffly upright on the desk chair, was much darker in colour. With the archetypal West African round happy face ringed by a generous halo of curly black hair, she was of plumper build with Cameron Dodoo pawpaw breasts that reminded Tom of Adjoa. She wore a traditional-style dress which he suspected might be her Sunday best, reserved for church and special occasions. Perhaps she had worn it to church earlier in the day. She told Tom her name was Afriyie.

Tom found both girls attractive in their own way. Akos Mary would be considered potential for most beauty contests. However, Tom found himself wondering if she relied on her looks to substitute for personality. Total compliance with quality standards was essential in engineering but a little boring in women. He turned his attention to the second of Comfort's offerings. Afriyie would have been of no interest to Tom as recently as two weeks ago. However, having studied West African female beauty assiduously since arriving in Ghana, his sense of appreciation had broadened remarkably. He admired both Comfort and Adjoa, and both had dark complexions and fuller figures. He liked Afriyie's modest but elegant dress and natural hairstyle, and her bulging bodice enslaved his gaze while liberating his imagination.

Tom tried to maintain small talk while his mind raced through the possibilities of the situation. What did they expect of him? How had his visitors been briefed by Comfort? Did they expect him to select one girl and send the other away? How could he do that without causing offence or disappointment? Would the reject be content with a generous present? What would be generous in this context? He wished he had Kwame or Comfort to turn to for advice.

Leaving this mongrel to chase its tail, Tom gained some time by asking his visitors about themselves. He learned that Akos Mary came originally from Cape Coast in the Central Region but she had been raised in Accra by her mother's sister who worked as a nurse in Ghana's largest hospital, Korle Bu. Coming to Kumasi to live with another relative who was employed as a lecturer at the university, she had served as a house-girl in return for a room in the boys' quarters of his senior staff residence. She had been able to complete an apprenticeship and now worked as a hairdresser in a wooden kiosk at Tech Junction, Ayigya, just across the Accra road from the main entrance of the university. She had met Comfort when she called at the kiosk to try a new hairstyle. Comfort had been pleased with her hair and had sold Akos Mary a pair of fashionable shoes at a special price.

Afriyie told Tom that she came from a village near Koforidua in the

Eastern Region and had come to Kumasi with her parents when her father got a job on one of the university farms. The family now lived in junior staff quarters on the campus. She was currently employed as an apprentice seamstress and hoped one day to have her own business. In answer to Tom's question she confirmed that she made all her own dresses including the one she was wearing. Tom marvelled at her skill and asked if she also made dresses for Comfort.

'Yes, Comfort is my best customer. She orders dresses and pays for them.'

'How do you mean?'

'Many people order dresses but when they are ready they don't want to pay for them.'

'What happens then?'

'Sometimes my boss keeps the dress at the store and sometimes she lets people take them away on credit, but the credit customers don't pay.'

Both Tom's visitors had mentioned how they came to know Comfort, but Tom wanted to know what Comfort had said to them about this evening's mission. He asked them what Comfort had told them about him. 'She told us you had come from England with Kwame Mainu,' said Akos Mary. 'She said that you were both at the same university in England.'

'That's right,' said Tom. 'We want to make a partnership with the university here.'

'Will you be sending more Ghanaians to England?' asked Akos Mary.

'I expect that will be part of the scheme.'

'Will you help us to go to England?'

'I'm afraid we will only be able to help staff and students of the university.'

'I told you the only way we will get there is to swallow the condom!' said Akos Mary roughly to Afriyie. Afriyie looked down in embarrassment and Tom was unsure what to say.

'Whatever that is, I can't say that I recommend it,' he said at length.

Something had upset Akos Mary. She yawned and looked at her wristwatch in studied slow motion and then spoke to her companion in the vernacular. Tom guessed that she was suggesting they should go. He who hesitates is lost, he said to himself but hesitate was all he could do. Akos Mary stood up and Afriyie followed with obvious reluctance. 'We have to get up very early in the morning to do our housework before we go to business,' said Afriyie, 'and it's a long walk to our houses.'

'Can I go with you?' asked Tom, reduced to clutching at straws. 'The exercise will do me good.'

'You will have to walk all the way back,' said Akos Mary. 'It's much too far.'

'Then let me take you in a taxi,' said Tom. 'There are always taxis running across the campus.'

They had not walked far when a taxi came by and Tom hailed the driver. Akos Mary said that her house was the nearest as it was in the area reserved for senior staff accommodation. She told the driver in Twi where to put her down. Before she left the vehicle Tom pressed a ten-pound note into her hand and thanked her for her visit.

It was another two kilometres to the junior staff quarters where Afriyie was staying. Tom asked the taxi driver to wait and got out with Afriyie. It was a very dark night and the few feeble street lights were widely spaced and partly obscured by the foliage of roadside trees.

They walked a short distance in the general direction indicated by Afriyie while Tom prayed that all night adders and other reptilian fauna were taking the night off. He took a deep breath and seized his opportunity to tell Afriyie that he liked her very much and would like to see her again. She seemed a little surprised but offered no resistance to his kiss. 'Shall I come there tomorrow evening?' she asked. Tom thought that was a splendid idea.

The next morning Kwame called for Tom and they had meetings with the TCC director and the dean of the faculty of engineering. Having finalised the draft of an agreement between the two universities they were ready to call on the vice-chancellor to brief him on their proposal and gain his approval. Everything went off smoothly, there was much enthusiasm for the proposed link with Warwick University, so the two friends were in the best of spirits when they called at the restaurant at the university swimming pool to take their lunch.

When the first Ghanaian Vice-Chancellor, Dr R.P. Baffour, had talked his friend Kwame Nkrumah into financing the construction of modern buildings on the university campus in the 1960s, the university had been heavily dependent upon expatriate teaching staff. To attract enough foreign staff of the right calibre it was decided that there should be a swimming pool in which they could cool off after duty. So the university was endowed with a splendid Olympic-size pool. During the *kalabule* era of the 1970s it became very difficult to maintain the pool in operation but a largely expatriate management committee somehow managed to keep the pool going for most of the decade. By the early 1980s the number of expatriate staff had fallen to a very low level and there was little demand for the use of the pool. When the stock of spare parts and chemicals was exhausted, it fell into disuse. However, the restaurant was kept in operation by the Nigerian wife of Roger Dodoo, the engineering drawing instructor of the department of mechanical engineering.

Mrs Dodoo gained local fame for the quality of her cooking. Business people drove out from Kumasi to sample her fare. On the campus, most senior staff lunched at the pool restaurant if they had a special visitor or a special occasion. Tom exclaimed in surprise when he saw the wide expanse of the pool and expressed his dismay at not being able to plunge into its cool water. 'I envy the expatriates who were here when the pool was in use,' he told Kwame.

'Never mind,' replied Kwame, 'you can have a cold beer and a good lunch.'

Their order was taken by an attractive young woman in uniform and Tom looked around to see several others similarly attired. Kwame observed his friend's interest and said, 'Mrs Dodoo certainly knows how to promote her business. She recruits these young women and trains them strictly in what she says are international standards of service. They appreciate the training and several have left to run their own chop bars.'

'So she competes with her ex-apprentices like Alhajji Issah Masters in Tamale,' observed Tom.

'Yes, but Mrs Dodoo has a big advantage in being able to run her restaurant here,' said Kwame.

'She certainly knows how to pick her helpers,' said Tom, 'or does her husband pick them for her?'

'Speaking of picking girls, how did you get on with Akos and Afriyie?'

'You certainly moved quickly on that one. Did you telephone Comfort from Tamale?'

'No, I couldn't get through from Tamale, but I got a message to her from the post office in Wenchi. Comfort has a friend working in the post office in Konongo.'

'Comfort seems to have a lot of friends.'

'Yes, but which one did you choose, or did you have them both?'

'We don't all have your stamina. After that long day, I wasn't planning on entertaining.'

'So what do I tell Comfort? Should she send you some more to try?'

'You posed me a difficult choice,' said Tom. 'I wanted to ask your advice on how I should handle the situation.'

'What was the problem?'

'Well, how could I have possibly sent one of them away? And how much should I have given them, the one who went and the one who stayed?'

'You certainly are sensitive to other people's feelings. I like that, and I guess the girls appreciated it.'

'I'm not sure about that. Akos Mary seemed to get angry and suggested that they both went home. I took them home in a taxi and gave her ten pounds. Was that all right?'

'That's more than 2,000 cedis. She will have been very pleased. How much did you give Afriyie?'

'Oh, I didn't give her anything. I'm seeing her tonight. She seems very nice.'

'I'm telling you!' said Kwame. 'We must get back to work. Tomorrow will be your last day here. On Wednesday you will be going to Accra to catch the overnight flight back to London. Is there anything special that you would like to do tomorrow?'

'I would like to spend more time at the faculty of engineering,' replied Tom. 'I want to learn more about the special interests of the lecturers and how they see the development of workshop and laboratory facilities to support the technology transfer programme. This is an area where I feel that Warwick could be of real help.'

'I agree with you,' said Kwame, 'but I fear you may be disappointed; only a few of the lecturers have any interest beyond their teaching duties.'

'Perhaps we can motivate a few more,' said Tom, 'especially if we hint at visits to the UK for coordination and training purposes.'

They drove from the pool restaurant along the Accra road into Kumasi but turned off after two or three kilometres to negotiate by far the worst dirt road Tom had ever seen. Here was another grassroots industrial scene, a *kokompe*, but entirely dominated by wood-working. Along both sides of the road were wooden shacks in which carpenters laboured. The road was wide but the narrow navigable track wound its way between piles of sawn timber and wooden products, parked vehicles and huge potholes, some filled with water. Tom noticed that the wooden shacks were arranged in ragged rows stretching three or four deep back from the road side, with narrow tracks giving limited access to those behind. People swarmed everywhere, many carrying head-loads and others pushing and pulling trolleys. The acrid stench of charcoal burning was almost intolerable to the nose and eyes, and Kwame explained that this industry operated incessantly in the valley behind the carpenters' workshops, consuming all the waste material.

Tom asked Kwame where they were and was told this area was known as Carpenters' Row. As most of the carpenters had come originally from Anloga in the south of the Volta Region, it was also known as Anloga. Kwame told Tom that he wanted to show him one of the TCC's oldest engineering clients, SRS Engineering Ltd, the company mentioned in Tamale as designing the shea butter processing machines. Stopping the Land Rover, Kwame led Tom between the inevitable obstructions to a larger than average workshop and into a small office. Here he was introduced to two brothers, Solomon and Ben Djokoto. They were greeted warmly and soon seated with cold Coca Cola bottles in their hands.

Tom couldn't contain his curiosity for long, 'This whole area is dominated by wood-working so how did you come to be doing engineering here?' he asked Solomon, who was clearly the senior partner in the enterprise.

'I was a technician at the physics department of the university but I wanted to start my own business,' explained Solomon. 'I began making physics instruments to sell to secondary schools. An English lecturer was helping me and for a time I did my work in his garage on the campus. As the business expanded and I acquired a few machines we decided to find a workshop here at Anloga where we had family connections. Wood was not the only material we used but it featured in most of our products. Then we developed more wooden products like primary school teaching aids, drawing boards and tee squares.'

'Why did you move away from wooden products?' asked Tom.

'Well,' said Solomon, 'our first customers were private schools run by the churches which paid their bills promptly, but soon we were forced to seek orders from the state schools. We were told to collect payment from the Ministry of Education but we were paid either very late or not at all. We couldn't go on like that.'

'So what happened?' asked Tom.

'It was then that the TCC gave a hand,' cut in Kwame.

'Yes,' said Solomon, 'We heard that the TCC was producing bolts and nuts for the local market and offering training and machine tools so we decided to try that work. However, we soon found that constructing machines was much more profitable and began making bench saws and wood-turning lathes.'

'You had a good market on your doorstep,' said Tom.

'That's right,' said Solomon, 'and now almost every workshop around here has one of our bench saws and I could take you to workshops with four or more of our wood-turning lathes.'

'But you make much more than wood-working machines now, don't you?' interjected Kwame.

'Oh yes,' said Solomon. 'Let's take a look around the workshop.'

Solomon led the way out of the office, leaving his brother Ben to return to his books of accounts. The workshop was bigger than Tom had first thought. To begin with there were five or six centre lathes, some quite large, as well as milling machines, drills and powered saws. Several electric welding sets were in operation, though this activity was suspended temporarily in deference to the visitors. Solomon said that most of the machine tools had been supplied by the TCC. At various stages of construction were bench saws, corn-milling machines and cassava graters, palm oil presses and boiling tanks, feed mills for poultry farms and steam distillation plants for producing perfume from lemon grass and citronella.

Tom marvelled at the great variety of products and was told by Solomon that he tried to supply whatever the customer demanded. He liked the challenge of designing a new machine. 'Yes,' said Tom, 'they've challenged you to make a shea butter extraction plant for testing in Tamale, haven't they?'

'I'm working on a few ideas,' said Solomon.

They returned to the relative quiet of the office where Tom could pursue his questioning of Solomon.

'How do you organise your production?'

'For standard products like the bench saw or corn mill we make batches of ten machines. We may not have orders for all ten when we start but they are usually all sold by the time we finish. If not, we keep the remainder in stock.'

'And what about new products; do you just produce a prototype?'

'That's right. We make one machine for the first customer and if it works well we usually get a second order from the same customer or from one of his friends or competitors. After we've produced several machines of the same design we may produce it in batches of ten if it becomes popular.'

'How many machines have you sold?'

'That's difficult to say, but we've certainly sold more than a hundred bench saws and even more corn mills and gari plants.'

'Gari? Is that made from cassava?'

'Don't you remember trying some in Wenchi?' laughed Kwame.

Solomon explained that traditionally gari was made from cassava by groups of women using simple hand tools and charcoal stoves. When he was asked to produce a mechanical plant for a male entrepreneur he was worried that the women might be driven out of business. However, the TCC, working with the National Council on Women and Development (NCWD), had alerted aid agencies to the danger and it had been possible to supply many of the women's groups with the new technology. 'In fact these days,' said Solomon, 'many of our orders come directly from development agencies promoting rural and women's industries.'

'Did the TCC introduce these people to you?' asked Tom.

'At first,' said Solomon, 'but these days the agencies know we are here and come to us direct.'

'That's true,' agreed Kwame. 'These days it seems SRS helps the TCC more than the TCC helps SRS.'

'How do you mean?' asked Tom.

'Well, they help in developing new machines, training apprentices and contributing to teaching workshops and short courses held at the university.' Solomon added that SRS still relied on the TCC for good used machine tools and they hoped that the new GRID project would continue this invaluable service.

'Could you have achieved what you have achieved without help in acquiring machine tools?' asked Tom.

'No way,' said Solomon. 'Without the machine tools supplied on easy payment terms by the TCC none of this would have been possible.'

'Are there no other ways to purchase machine tools?'

'Well, sometimes we can buy good used machines from a government workshop that closes down or re-equips, but usually the price is inflated by middle men who buy the machines for resale, and occasionally one of the big stores in town might import a new lathe or drilling machine but the machines are usually small and the prices are very high. We don't need new machines and we can't afford them. What we want are the old English machines that we know from our apprentice training. We know that they will last for many years and the price is reasonable but we rely on someone like the TCC to bring them here for us. As an engineering businessman I would say that that is the biggest help we could ever have.'

Tom turned to Kwame, 'What does Dr Jones say about machine tool supplies?'

'When we started importing machine tools in 1972 the price of used machines in England was very low, and with the cedi pegged at a low official exchange rate the machines could be sold here at low prices. However, as the 1970s passed, the demand for used machine tools rose sharply because far eastern countries like Singapore and Malaysia took advantage of this short cut to industrialisation. Now many countries have established purchasing agencies in England, demand is high and the price of used machine tools has risen dramatically. Also, because of the more realistic exchange rate of the cedi, the local price here has risen even higher.'

'Some of us can afford to pay the higher prices,' said Solomon, 'but we still need someone to bring us the machines.'

On the way back to the university Tom told Kwame that once again he had been very impressed by the quality of the entrepreneurs that were working with the TCC. 'Wherever you take me in Ghana,' he said, 'you introduce me to people like Issah Masters, Kwesi Ansah and Solomon Djokoto, not to mention many more at Suame Magazine. There seems to be a tremendous store of entrepreneurial energy just waiting to be released and the secret of your work seems to be that you've identified the constraints and released this energy in many people.'

'I hope you're right,' said Kwame, 'and I hope we can work with such people in every region where an ITTU will be established.'

For Tom it had been a good day and he was hoping that it was going to get even better. He took his evening meal in the guest house at the usual time and returned to his room to await the knock that could open the portals of a new paradise. He tried to read but could not concentrate; he paced about the room and sat repeatedly on every available perch, but still the knock did not come. He opened the door and looked along the corridor. Then he walked to the entrance of the building and roamed outside in an atmosphere that was still hot and humid. Repeatedly consulting his wristwatch he learned anew how slowly its hands progressed. One of the waiters saw him and asked if he could help, then said something to a colleague in Twi that evoked laughter. Tom felt that he was exposing himself to ridicule and returned reluctantly to his room, where he lay on the bed letting the swaying fan rustle his shirt while winds of doubt disturbed the folds of his mind.

Next morning Kwame could not wait to ask Tom how the night had gone. When Tom confessed that Afriyie had disappointed him, Kwame suggested that they call at her workplace in the lunch break to find out what had gone wrong. In defence of his wife's friend, he explained that local people did not have the same sense of time and obligation as someone like himself had gained from working with Europeans. 'She'll probably come tonight,' he said, 'but we can call in to remind her.'

160

'I'm not sure that I want to do that,' said Tom. 'She may have another reason for not wanting to come and I don't want to cause embarrassment.'

'Then I'll call on her on my own,' said Kwame, 'and nobody will be embarrassed.'

The morning passed quickly with Tom meeting new friends and exploring new possibilities for cooperation with the faculty of engineering. As Kwame had expected, the main interest was in the opportunities that might arise to visit the UK. Tom found himself walking a thin line between using the possibility to excite interest and not promising more than he expected could be delivered. He found much to interest him that could be supported by Warwick. In particular, a solar energy project offered opportunities to use electronic equipment at rural locations remote from the mains power supply. He liked a proposal to set up a solar-powered battery recharging centre to enable villagers to use radios and other domestic appliances without recourse to long journeys to town to buy replacement batteries. He also appreciated the value of a unit set up to train local artisans in the repair of all types of electric motors.

After lunch, Kwame left Tom at the swimming pool restaurant and drove off to Tech Junction to visit Afriyie's workplace. Seeing him alone Mrs Dodoo came over to sit with him and make light conversation. After explaining his mission, Tom complimented the plump fair-skinned Nigerian caterer on the good food and pleasant environment of her restaurant. Mrs Dodoo was used to praise of this nature but never tired of hearing it. She explained how difficult it was to maintain standards in the face of shortages of every kind. Then she complained that the young women had no idea how to present food or wait at table but she did her best to keep a few of them off the streets. Tom said that the young ladies who had served him seemed to be well trained and Mrs Dodoo replied that they needed constant supervision and couldn't be trusted to run the restaurant in her absence. Tom said that he was sure that her presence was essential to the smooth running of the business.

Tom saw the Land Rover return to park under the shade trees that ringed the car park and excused himself to walk over to meet Kwame. As he drew near he was surprised to find Afriyie sitting in the vehicle.

After brief greetings, Kwame jumped down and led Tom over to where some workmen had left low wooden stools in the deepest shade. Gesturing to Tom to sit down he asked him what he had done to upset Akos Mary.

'She was the cause of the problem,' he said. 'Afriyie told me that Akos wouldn't let her come to you last night but insisted they go together to a disco in town instead.'

'I didn't upset her intentionally,' said Tom, 'but I could see that she was upset by something.'

'Well, you needn't worry about her any more,' said Kwame. 'I'll drive you and Afriyie back to the guest house to keep your appointment.'

'But it's too early to close from work,' protested Tom. 'It's still early afternoon.'

'And I've heard white men say that Ghanaian girls are best in the afternoon,' laughed Kwame, 'You deserve a little time off after all the hard work of the past two weeks.'

Later, as Tom lay with Afriyie under the pulsing breeze of the lurching fan, with a dazzling sunbeam penetrating the narrow slit between the drawn curtains, he knew that Kwame was right.

Tom's brief visit to Ghana had come to an end. Kwame planned to take him to Kotoka International Airport in Accra and return the same day. Tom would catch the late evening British Airways flight that would get him to London at 6.00 the next morning. Reflecting on Tom's visit to Ghana, Kwame felt that it had been successful in every way. They had drafted a proposal for a cooperation agreement between the two universities and it was now up to Warwick to raise funding to make possible the implementation. Kwame knew that Tom had enjoyed his visit and appreciated the hospitality he had received at all locations. It had been hard work and he was tired but he had gained much from seeing his work through the eyes of the intelligent and knowledgeable English engineer. He now valued even more highly what he and his colleagues were doing for their country's economic development.

At the airport, Kwame set Tom down with his luggage at the entrance to the departures hall. It was with some sadness as well as genuine affection that the two friends embraced beside the vehicle. They knew they would be meeting again in less than two months, but not in Ghana. Tom was determined to come back but he knew that it would not be before next year. Then Kwame drove away, his long arm extending from the open window of the Land Rover in an exaggerated long distance wave. He kept it going, watching in the wing mirror as Tom's image rapidly diminished in size and disappeared in the throng of travellers. It was then that Kwame allowed himself the luxury of dwelling on the happy thought that in a little over three hours he would be back in Konongo with Comfort and Akosua at the start of a well-earned rest.

12

On Leave in Konongo

Kwame had looked forward to a rest but he soon realised that he would have to make do with the proverbial 'change' which was supposed to be just as good. It was now that he must turn his mind to family business. While Tom was around his needs had dominated all Kwame's thoughts and it was not until he was gone that Kwame was free to take some time to attend to the needs of his wife and daughter. He also had his half-sister, Adjoa, staying with him in Konongo. Adjoa had come to Kumasi to see if she could obtain a fresh stock of shoes from Mama Kate to sell at her kiosk in Wenchi. To accomplish this she needed money from Kwame and help from Comfort in approaching the Kejetia shoe queen.

Kwame had come to Ghana with money he had saved from his work in Coventry. He had felt that it was quite a useful sum but his visit to his mother in Wenchi had depleted it severely and now Adjoa wanted more. He discussed the matter with Comfort whose first priority was to buy a plot of land on which to start building a house. She had learned of plots for sale at Old Ahensan, on a gently sloping hill behind the university campus in Kumasi. Only four years earlier, large plots were being sold for 30,000 cedis but by mid-1986 the price had risen to 180,000 cedis, or about $2000 at the official rate of exchange. 'You see what delay is costing us,' complained Comfort, 'the longer we delay the higher will be the cost.'

'If I give money to Adjoa I won't have enough money left to buy the plot,' said Kwame, 'but I can't disappoint Adjoa and mother.'

'What exchange rate are you using to convert the cedi?' asked Comfort.

'The official exchange rate since January has been US$1 = 90 cedis,' said Kwame.

'But we can get a much higher rate than that,' said Comfort. 'I'll ask Mama Kate when we go to see her about Adjoa's shoes.'

Kwame was not sure that he was happy with this arrangement but he didn't want to start a quarrel with Comfort this early in his home leave period.

'You should pay for Adjoa's shoes in foreign exchange,' insisted Comfort. 'That way you will save more money.'

'I want to talk to you about Adjoa's business,' said Kwame. 'She has used up all the money I gave her to start the trading. I want you to teach her how you keep your trading money separate from your house money so that it is replaced as the shoes are sold.'

'So many of the traders have a problem with that,' said Comfort. 'They spoil the money by spending it on family expenses and soon it is all gone and the business collapses. It was Oboroni who taught me how to write accounts and hold on to my trading money. He even showed me how to open a savings account at the bank to keep some of my profit for what he called a rainy day. Not many of the traders buying from Mama Kate know these things. Many of them fail after only a few months. There are always new people coming in whose hands have caught money from relatives overseas or from foreign boyfriends.'

'Well, I don't want to be replacing Adjoa's working capital every time I come to Ghana,' said Kwame. 'So if you want more money to spend on the house, please help to train Adjoa in good business practice.'

They decided to make a social call on Mama Kate and to arrange for Adjoa and Comfort to make a business call later. Kwame didn't have access to a TCC vehicle after Tom's departure so they took a *trotro* to Kumasi and a taxi to Mama Kate's residence. As they entered the compound on foot Kwame recognised a familiar figure coming towards them down the long driveway. It might have been ten years since he had seen Uncle George but he hadn't changed much; he had had no more hair to lose, and if there were a few more lines around his eyes they were hidden behind dark glasses. He might have added a few kilograms but his figure had always been rotund. Much to Kwame's surprise, Uncle George greeted him with 'Just the man I need to see. How are you?'

Kwame returned the greeting and quickly introduced Comfort and Adjoa. He then asked Uncle George if his nephew, Peter Sarpong, was home for the long vacation. 'Oh yes,' replied Uncle George, 'he comes down for every break, Christmas, Easter and in the *aburokyiri* summer.'

'That must be very expensive,' exclaimed Comfort.

'Not when you know the system,' replied Uncle George, removing his dark glasses to give Kwame a knowing look.

'Why did you say that you wanted to see me?' asked Kwame.

'The market trolleys I buy these days don't last like yours used to,' said Uncle George. 'I was wondering if you could tell me who makes the best trolleys now you've retired.'

'You should go to the Suame ITTU and talk to the chief technician, Edward Opare. He will know who's working to the highest quality standards,' advised Kwame.

'I've heard that you're building a house for Peter,' said Comfort. Kwame could not conceal his surprise but Uncle George seemed not to notice.

'Yes,' he said. 'It's coming along very well. Would you like to see it?'

'I certainly would,' replied Comfort. 'We are also planning a project and it would be useful to see what others are doing.'

'The boy has big ideas. I've been trying to advise him to scale things down, but you know how young men are these days, they don't want to listen to old fogies like me.' He laughed, 'There was a time when the youth respected their elders but send them to England and they soon forget all that.' Comfort asked when they could go to see the house. 'Come to my house this afternoon at about five o'clock. It's not far from there,' he said. 'Oh, and thanks, Kwame, I will certainly follow your advice.' Then he waddled on down the driveway to where his driver waited outside the gates with a new BMW.

'He seems to be doing very well,' observed Comfort as the car drew away.

'Yes, he's come a long way since I first sold him market trolleys at Suame.'

'Does he only do business in market trolleys?'

'I don't know, but I find it hard to believe that all his money comes that way.'

'Is he paying for Peter's house?'

'I've no idea, Peter is a student like me and as far as I know he has no income of his own. I've noticed him spending money but I've never seen him earning any. He doesn't seem to have an evening or weekend job in Coventry like I do.

'By the way,' said Kwame to Comfort, 'how did you know that Peter Sarpong was building a house?'

'I've met him a few times here at Mama Kate's,' replied Comfort, 'and he mentioned that his uncle was building a house for him. When I heard you ask Uncle George about Peter I realised he must be the uncle.'

'Do you know about every house under construction in Kumasi?' teased Kwame.

'Not all of them, only the good ones,' she replied in the same vein.

'Do you think that Peter is one of Mama Kate's boys?' asked Kwame, continuing the banter.

'I shouldn't think so,' chuckled Comfort, 'Not with such a rich uncle. *Dadabas* don't usually need that sort of help.'

Kwame was saved from further embarrassment by their arrival at the steps of the mansion where they were greeted by a house-girl. She showed them into a room to wait in comfortable chairs with cold drinks until the market queen was free to see them. At length, they were asked to attend upon the big lady.

Mama Kate was sitting in state surrounded by her courtiers, an assortment of young men and women who sat and stood around ready to act promptly on any instruction. The visitors filed past the throne, shaking the limp damp royal hand in turn, and then accepted the proffered seats. Mama Kate asked to be excused for not standing up to greet her visitors and Kwame could easily see what a mighty effort that would entail. The big lady had used the time since Kwame had last seen her in growing even bigger. He couldn't help reflecting that he was glad to be relieved of his former duties. He feared that the current generation of Ashanti warriors were putting their lives at risk.

Comfort did most of the talking. She explained that Kwame had returned from his studies overseas to spend the vacation in Kumasi. It was their duty to their benefactor to report their presence in town. Mama Kate formally welcomed Kwame and asked when he had come from London. He hastened to explain that he had been responsible for conducting a foreign visitor around the country and this had delayed his house call until today. Mama Kate asked when he would be returning to London and which airline he was using. Kwame was surprised to find that the market queen seemed to be fully informed about the schedules of all the airlines flying to and from Accra. Then he remembered the incident with the suspect *kenke* and the fate of poor Bra Yaw. Was this the true source of her wealth? How many other young people had she sent to their doom?

Comfort made excuses for not taking up too much of Mama Kate's valuable time and asked if she and Adjoa could call back soon for a business discussion. A suitable time was agreed and the trio took their leave. On the way out Kwame took a quick look around outside the house. He noted two Mercedes Benz saloon cars and a Toyota Land Cruiser parked under shade trees. A man was slowly polishing the windscreen of one of the cars. 'Mama Kate is so wealthy she can employ an *oboroni* driver,' said Kwame casually.

'That's not an *oboroni*, it's Kofi Adjare, Oboroni's old driver,' cried Comfort. 'I must go over and greet him.'

During the time that she had been Oboroni's girlfriend, Comfort had spent a lot of time being driven around by Kofi Adjare, Oboroni's albino driver. She had come to respect the old man's wisdom and to appreciate his advice. He spoke only when he had something significant to say and he spoke in the pure language of the ancestors, not the modern Twi of Ghanaian youth culture which had become corrupted with English words and American slang. Kwame always thought that Kofi spoke Twi like his father. Kwesi Mainu had told his son to try to speak perfect English and perfect Twi but never to mix them. Kwame tried to follow this advice, but it was only when he met someone like Kofi Adjare that he could refresh his memory of how his native tongue should be used. So he listened in admiration as the old man greeted Comfort and told her in proverbs how he had missed her company after she had left. 'It's when the frog has died that we see how long it is,' he reflected. Comfort assured Kofi that the feeling was mutual as she had always greatly appreciated his fatherly advice.

On their way back down the long driveway Comfort said to Kwame, 'It appears that no visitors' cars are allowed inside the compound.'

'Yes,' said Kwame, 'even Uncle George had to be met by his driver at the gate. It seems that the security guards in the small office at the entrance have instructions to keep the main gates closed and to allow in only pedestrians.'

Nominally at the appointed time, Kwame and Comfort arrived at Uncle George's house. Only Kwame noticed that it was 5.30 and he made a mental note to try to get into local synchronism for the rest of his stay with Comfort. Uncle George was pleased to see them but suggested they should delay having a cool drink in the house until after visiting the building site because by 6.15 pm the light would be failing. So they trailed in his wide wake for a few hundred metres until they arrived at the current front line of urban expansion.

Over a wide area they could see houses at all stages of construction, scattered about in random distribution on plots of about a half hectare. One or two appeared to be finished and occupied because lights could be seen coming on in the spreading dusk. Some structures had walls up to roof height but no roofs, while a few others had roofs but no doors or windows. Many consisted only of open trenches dug to accommodate foundations and some of these had lain exposed to wind and rain for so long that the trenches had partly refilled. Other potential residences were little more than thick concrete floor slabs. Still others remained as piles of concrete blocks standing as silent sentinels of their owners' intent.

Uncle George led the way to a large structure that consisted of walls surmounted by a freshly cast ring beam, the wooden shuttering still in place. 'Here we are,' he said, 'this is Peter's cottage.'

'Some cottage!' said Kwame. 'It's almost as big as your own house.'

'I think the plan is to make it even bigger at a later stage,' said Uncle George. 'He keeps saying that this is only the first phase of the project.'

'Well, he certainly has plenty of land for expansion,' observed Kwame.

'Is Peter's house the biggest around here?' asked Comfort.

'No, it's the second biggest,' said Uncle George.

'Is that one over there the biggest?' persisted Comfort. 'Who is that for?'

'Yes, that's the big one,' said Uncle George. 'Peter says it's for one of his friends called Bra Yaw.'

'Bra Yaw?' said Kwame. 'I thought that he was being detained at Her Majesty's pleasure.'

'He did have a spot of bother with UK customs but I hear that he's back now. Anyway, there was no interruption in the building work while he was away.'

'Which is more than can be said about most of these building projects,' said Kwame. 'They seem to have been neglected for months or even years.'

'You know how our people are,' said Uncle George. 'We buy a plot, put a few concrete blocks on it, and enjoy the prestige of having a house under construction for the rest of our days.'

'That's being rather hard on us,' protested Comfort. 'People have to start somewhere and they invest in the project as funds come to hand. Sometimes there may be a long time during which no money comes in. That's when nothing may be done for several months. However, by God's grace, the house will be finished one day.'

'That day could come a lot sooner if only we could be satisfied with smaller houses,' said Uncle George. 'With our grandiose aspirations many of us occupy a wooden box before we live in our own home.'

'I understand what you're saying,' said Kwame, 'but does that apply to those houses funded from overseas?'

'The escapees certainly seem to have a lot more money,' said Uncle George, 'but much of it is wasted by their relatives here. I think they could all benefit from investing in more modest projects. After all, a small house can be designed to be expanded later if more funds become available, just as easily as Peter's big house can.'

Night had fallen while they conversed so Uncle George led them back to his home. The conversation continued as they walked. 'Are all the plots here taken?' asked Comfort.

'They were all snapped up long ago,' said Uncle George. 'Land in good residential areas doesn't stay on offer long these days with all the foreign money coming in. Chiefs can sell their land several times over, and sometimes they do. That is the cause of so much litigation. I told Peter that he should study law. The more trouble there is, the more money the lawyers get.'

'But Peter is reading economics,' interjected Kwame.

'Yes,' said Uncle George. 'I told you this morning that he takes no notice of old fogies like me.'

'But shouldn't he pay more respect to his sponsor?' asked Kwame.

'There was a time when he did, but now he has his own money he's dropped the pretence,' said Uncle George with a wry smile.

They travelled back to Konongo by taxi and *trotro* and it was not until they reached home and Adjoa and Akosua were sleeping that they had a chance to review all they had heard that day. 'Are you wondering what I'm wondering?' asked Kwame.

'Yes, where is Peter Sarpong getting his money to build that big house if Uncle George isn't paying the bills?'

'And how is Bra Yaw doing the same?'

'Well, we know roughly what Bra Yaw was up to before he was arrested.'

'Can cannabis smuggling be that lucrative or are they up to something new?'

'Whatever it is, Mama Kate seems to be involved, and I wouldn't be surprised if Uncle George isn't in it too.'

'I'm not sure about that,' said Kwame. 'What do you think we should do?' he asked. 'Leave them well alone or try to find out more about what is going on?'

'That's difficult,' said Comfort. 'We need Mama Kate to supply us with shoes, and perhaps to change some foreign money, but I fear that to learn too much about their other activities could be dangerous.'

'Can you deal with Mama Kate for shoes and forex but turn a blind eye to anything else you see?' asked Kwame.

'If we want to buy a plot of land and make a start on our house, I can't see any alternative.'

'If you want a plot near the campus at Old Ahensan I'll go to see Dr Bilson. He's the chief's brother and handles all the land sales.'

'How do you know that?'

'Our director recently purchased a plot for some of our senior staff at the TCC,' replied Kwame with a grin. 'You're not the only one with inside information.'

The next day Kwame went to Kumasi to see Dr Bilson, and Comfort and Adjoa went to Kumasi for their business meeting with Mama Kate. When they returned to Konongo in the evening they were all in high spirits. 'Who's going to report first?' asked Kwame.

'You go first,' said Comfort. 'You will be quicker.'

'We can have a building plot for 180,000 cedis, as you expected, and Dr Bilson will hold it for us for a few days. He told me that the TCC director had bought two plots and he was pleased with the rate of development so he was happy to help another person from the TCC.'

'We were also successful,' said Comfort.

'Yes, you can see that I got my shoes,' said Adjoa, pointing to two bulging corn sacks filling one corner of Comfort's tiny room.

'The exchange rate offered by Mama Kate was over twice the official rate,' explained Comfort, 'so we were able to buy twice as many shoes for Adjoa and I changed the rest of the pounds into cedis for the land.'

'How much did we get?'

'More than 250,000 cedis. Can we spend the balance of the money on building materials?'

'We had better get an architect to draw up some plans first,' said Kwame. 'That can also be expensive.'

Kwame knew that the lecturers employed in the faculty of architecture took on private commissions. One of these, Sam Larbi, had worked with the TCC on several projects including its biggest building project to date, the Tamale ITTU. So Kwame resolved to ask Sam to prepare drawings for his building project at Old Ahensan, but this business would have to wait until after the weekend. Tomorrow would be Saturday again and Comfort and Adjoa were engrossed in finalising their funeral programme. For Adjoa it was a difficult choice between accompanying Comfort in Konongo and hurrying back to accompany her mother on her weekly round in Wenchi. Kwame calculated that the cost to him would be less if Adjoa went back to Wenchi but Comfort had grown used to Adjoa's company and suggested that she should delay her journey until the next day.

In Wenchi, for the sake of Tom as much as for his mother, Kwame had made a show of involvement in the funerals as the central theme of their extended-family culture. In reality, however, he agreed with his father that the funeral society was backward looking and economically unjustifiable. He also regretted the hole the funeral donations had made in the funds he had brought with him from England. He reluctantly agreed to lead his family to the funerals on Comfort's list but tried to negotiate a maximum budget for the donations. In this he failed miserably, as Comfort insisted he uphold the honour of the family by observing the standards set by those who return from *aburokyiri* with their pockets stuffed with dollars and pounds. So the day's activities bit deeply into the funds remaining after provision had been made for the land purchase. Kwame feared that he would be trying to borrow money before his holiday was over.

Kwame knew that Comfort, like most of her countrywomen, wanted to build a house more than anything else in the world. Logically, he thought, this should entail making sacrifices in other directions to maximise the funds available to be expended on the number one priority. However, he also realised that house ownership was desired as much as a status symbol as a comfort or convenience. Other equally important status symbols, such as funeral donations and fashionable clothes, could not be sacrificed along the way. It was as if one's future wealthy status must be signalled in advance. Yet the more it was signalled the longer the reality would be delayed. The result must be the familiar pile of concrete blocks on a barren plot, the symbolic home ownership that endures to the end, spoken of by Uncle George.

With such social constraints, there seemed to be no way that by hard work and prudence Kwame could achieve the goal of home ownership within any reasonable period of time. He could see no compromise solution that would combine his realistic economic prospects with Comfort's customary aspirations. Only a greatly swollen flood of income could effect the breakthrough. Peter Sarpong and Bra Yaw seemed to have released such a flood and were reaping the benefits, but the route they had chosen could be fraught with danger. Bra Yaw had already been imprisoned and was presumably now a marked man. Kwame was not insensitive to the pull of temptation but prudence, as much as ethical considerations, held him back.

On the Sunday morning he accompanied Adjoa on a *trotro* to Kejetia lorry park in Kumasi where she could board a second *trotro* to Wenchi.

He bore the whole cost of her journey, including the extra charge for the two sacks of shoes. He hoped that this would be the last expense he would bear in Wenchi before his return to England, but he could never be sure.

Before returning to Konongo he called in at the university to try to arrange to see the architect during the coming week. Sam Larbi had a house on the campus in the senior staff residential area. A keen churchgoer, he was still out with his wife Patience when Kwame arrived, but when he came in, attired in his traditional cloth, he greeted Kwame warmly and showed much interest in his project. Kwame explained that his wife had very clear ideas about what she wanted and he would like her to attend their serious working meetings. Sam readily agreed.

Kwame thought that it would be a good idea to agree with Comfort the general specification of their house before the meeting with the architect. He wanted to avoid any confusion and especially any open disagreement. So in the evening when Akosua was sleeping he broached the subject with some trepidation. 'I've been thinking about our house,' he began. 'If we begin with a modest structure we will be able to move in sooner.'

'What do you mean by a modest structure?' asked Comfort. 'I'm not moving my daughter into a boy's quarters.'

'That's not what I mean,' said Kwame. 'It must be big enough for our immediate needs but not necessarily in its final state. For example, how many bedrooms do we need?'

Comfort thought for a moment, 'There's yours and mine and Askosua's, then one for your mother and a guest room, let's say five, or six.'

'Aren't we going to share a room? We do now.'

'We only have one room now, we have no choice.'

'So given a choice, you would choose to sleep on your own?'

'That's not what I meant,' protested Comfort, 'but don't you need your own room for a study or something?'

Kwame tried desperately to cut through the undergrowth of sprouting digressions, 'Don't you think that we could manage with three bedrooms initially, one for us, one for Akosua and a guest room?'

'Don't you want to build me a proper house?' said Comfort. 'Peter and Bra Yaw are building proper houses for their girlfriends.'

Kwame groaned. 'Peter and Bra Yaw aren't building the houses for their girlfriends,' he protested, 'They're building them for themselves.'

'How do you know?' countered Comfort. 'Would you build a bigger house if you were building it for yourself?'

'No,' replied Kwame. 'If I were building only for myself I would build a small house, just big enough to be comfortable and meet my immediate needs. Later, if I had money, I would extend it. I only want to apply the same approach to building our family house.'

'Well, I don't,' said Comfort. 'If I told my friends what you are saying they would laugh at me.'

Kwame tried one last time. 'Comfort,' he said, 'if we plan a house on the scale of Peter and Bra Yaw's houses we will spend most of our lives trying to get enough money to finish the project. Maybe we will never be able to move in.'

'Then it will be there for Akosua,' said Comfort. 'If you can't earn enough to complete it for us maybe *her* boyfriend will be more successful.' Kwame realised that this was an argument he could not win so he resigned himself to going along with whatever plans Comfort demanded. At the same time he decided to consult Sam Larbi to see if there could be an intermediate stage at which they could move in and occupy the completed part of the house while construction continued on the remainder.

At the meeting with the architect, Kwame let Comfort do most of the talking. He was amazed at the detailed specification that she dictated to the largely passive listener, who confined himself to making copious notes, punctuated by only an occasional question. Kwame could detect no element of surprise in Sam Larbi's demeanour. Was he so used to taking instructions from such female clients? The meeting was much shorter than he had expected because there was little discussion. The architect was clearly willing to supply whatever the lady wanted. It is true that he queried if she really needed a two-car garage built into the main structure, pointing out that a separate garage structure could be built later, but he soon gave in when he sensed that Comfort had resolved all such issues in advance.

At the end of the meeting Sam Larbi said that their next meeting should be on the site at Old Ahensan. They would need the plot to be surveyed and he would recommend Kwame Agyei for that task. He also told Comfort and Kwame that as it would be a two-storeyed structure he would like to work with a structural engineer to make sure that the design and construction complied with national and international standards. He recommended Fred Akwaboah of the university's civil engineering department. Kwame smiled inwardly because he knew that Sam always worked on every project with his close friend Fred. He said nothing because he knew that the two men were competent and used to working as a team.

A few days later, Kwame and Comfort met Sam with Kwame Agyei and Fred Akwaboah on their building plot. Comfort was in high spirits. Sam asked her to show him how she wanted the house positioned on the plot. Her main concern was to take advantage of the long view across the shallow valley to the distant hills beyond the town. Then he asked her to indicate the position of the boy's quarters. This was more difficult because it proved impossible to fix a position that didn't involve the felling of at least one mature mango tree. After some discussion it was agreed which tree must be sacrificed in the path of progress and the surveyor was given his detailed instructions. He promised to begin work the next day and to complete it during the university vacation.

After the professional team had left, Kwame and Comfort walked around their estate. The plot measured 58 by 55 metres, or just under one third of a hectare. The land sloped gently towards the south. In addition to the five or six mango trees there were three medium-sized forest trees, the tallest about 15 metres in height. As they gazed up at its high branches, a flock of African grey parrots descended upon it with a flurry of red breasts. Kwame was alerted to look out for other birds and over the next ten minutes he observed several species that he knew only by local names and others that he did not recognise at all. Two that favoured perching on swaying elephant grass were bright scarlet in colour, while another that preferred the trees was bright yellow. He resolved to get a book to help him properly identify his avian visitors. He hoped that they would continue to visit his garden when the house was built and he was in residence.

Kwame sensed that Comfort was also dreaming of the day when she would move into her new home. That day may be years away but he knew that she was consoled by the fact that she could come here at any time and stroll around enjoying the pride of ownership and the vision of her completed residence. She might consider boosting her shoe-trading business so that from time to time she could help speed up the building construction, though not, he suspected, at the expense of her rainy-day savings. After years of waiting, Kwame had at last gathered the money to buy the plot. That was the first step. Comfort squeezed his hand tightly in gratitude. It was the happiest moment they had shared for several years.

For a few days, Kwame enjoyed Comfort's high spirits. She seemed to him quite like she had been in the early days of their friendship. He saw again briefly that bright personality that had characterised her at school and which she still displayed to the outside world. It was the personality she had displayed in front of Tom and which Tom had so much admired, making Kwame yearn for the girl he had lost. He wondered if it was always like this in marriage. Did everyday cares cause every husband and wife to change towards each other while maintaining their former personalities as masks to wear for the world outside? If so, it was not surprising that marriages broke down, with both partners appearing much more attractive to outsiders than they appeared to each other.

Kwame wondered if he had changed as much as Comfort. He felt that if he had changed, it was only in response to the changes he saw in her. Yet he was intelligent enough to suppose that she too saw it the same way. An outside observer would probably say that the blame was equally shared. It seemed obvious to Kwame that it was poverty that brought about this personality change. He felt that if he had had enough money to provide Comfort with all she wanted their relationship could have remained in its honeymoon condition. Even now, he thought, when I can do something to please her, it restores her good humour towards me. If only I had the wealth of Peter Sarpong or Bra Yaw everything would be fine.

He knew that the troubles would return before he departed again to resume his studies at Warwick. The little money that he had left over after buying the land would soon disappear as deposits on fees were paid to the architect and his helpers. Comfort would soon remind him of the need to pay Akosua's school fees and at any time further demands could arrive from Wenchi. He dreaded the thought of anyone falling ill or a close family funeral arising. He was tempted to bring forward his departure to cut his losses, but he wanted to be there for Akosua for as long as possible. She was six years old and already he had missed far too much of her childhood.

Once again in Kwame's life, help came from an unexpected direction. A letter arrived from Tom thanking Kwame and Comfort for their friendship and hospitality during his visit. Kwame had warned Tom never to enclose cash in a letter posted to Ghana but his friend had ignored the advice and enclosed two £50 notes as a contribution towards the cost of hospitality. By a miracle the letter came through safely.

Kwame had no intention of accepting this money as a gift but it constituted a most timely loan. He resolved to pay it back from future earnings in Coventry. In the meantime he asked Comfort to exchange the foreign money for cedis at Mama Kate's. Used prudently, it could tide him over until his planned departure.

Tom also enclosed a letter to Afriyie with a note to Comfort to please forward. Kwame suspected that there could also be a banknote inside that envelope but he said nothing and the letter was delivered the next time that they went to Kumasi. Kwame took the opportunity to celebrate his good fortune by asking Afriyie to sew new dresses for his wife and daughter. Afriyie was delighted to receive Tom's letter and promised to reply at once. Comfort said that she and Akosua must have their hair done to go with their new dresses so they all went on to see Akos Mary.

Kwame, Comfort and Akosua found Akos Mary and two of her apprentices sitting idle at their kiosk at Tech Junction. They told the visitors that the others had taken advantage of the lull in business to catch up on their shopping. Comfort knew that business was very slack generally but she made no comment. She soon had the three girls running round in attention to her needs. Akosua loved to have her hair done by proper hairdressers and was soon perched on a high chair with four hands busily unpicking her plaits. Comfort perused the photographs that adorned the walls of the kiosk to select her preferred style for Akosua's hair. 'What are the latest styles from Accra?' she asked Akos Mary, and the ladies were soon lost in a detailed technical discussion.

Kwame decided to leave the ladies to their fun and walked across the Accra road to the university campus. He strolled past the university hospital and soon reached the TCC office where he was greeted warmly by his colleagues. 'What have you been doing since Dr Arthur left?' he was asked by Stephen Adjapong, the technical officer in charge of the beekeeping project.

'Resting,' said Kwame, 'The two weeks that Tom Arthur was here were very interesting but also very tiring.'

'I hope you're not too tired to give me a hand with the beekeeping workshop next week,' said Stephen. 'I need you to give a talk on beekeeping in Tamale.'

'I can do more than that,' replied Kwame. 'I'll also bring you up to date with what Kwesi Ansah is doing in Sunyani.'

'Is he still producing honey by the oil barrel?' asked Stephen with a wide grin.

'I'm telling you,' said Kwame.

That evening back in Konongo Comfort told Kwame that Akos Mary had spoken about the evening she visited Tom with Afriyie.

'Why did she get upset?'

'Well, it appears that she thought Tom could help them get to the UK, but it appears that he said only university people could go.'

'Tom was probably referring to our cooperation agreement, and I'm sure he said it in a gentle way.'

'I guess she was annoyed that Tom didn't favour her. She's very proud of her looks and probably got frustrated when Tom took more interest in Afriyie.'

'Why did you send her to Tom?'

'I thought he might prefer light-skinned girls.'

'Did Afriyie speak about the incident?' asked Kwame.

'Afriyie never says much. I'm afraid she is easily dominated by Akos Mary.'

'Yes, Akos Mary tried to prevent Afriyie seeing Tom again. By the way, did she tell you that Tom gave her ten pounds?'

'Akos Mary? Yes, she was very pleased about that, especially when she learned that Afriyie got nothing that night.'

'I'm sure that Afriyie has had a nice present now that Tom has sent her a letter.'

'I hope so; she needed a confidence boost, but your order for our new dresses also helped to raise her spirits.'

With a string of pleasant domestic interludes and the occasional special duty to help colleagues at work, Kwame's time on leave slipped by and the day of his return to Warwick drew near. He was fortunate to avoid any family crisis involving unbudgeted expenditure and so his money held out as he had hoped. Comfort remained cheerful and they continued to enjoy each other's company, especially after Akosua resumed school. Kwame reflected happily that it was not only white men who enjoyed lively entertainment in the afternoon. He was glad that their shared house-building project had rejuvenated their relationship and he resolved to try to continue his part-time work in England to keep the project moving. Hopefully, slow but steady progress would convince Comfort that he was doing all he could to secure the family's future. In this contented frame of mind he set out once more for Accra and the flight north to London.

13

Warwick University – Second Year

This was Kwame's third flight to London and he was now quite familiar with the routine. He had expected to take a coach at Heathrow and make his own way to Coventry, so it was with some surprise that he found Tom Arthur waiting in the arrivals hall once again. The two friends greeted each other in Twi with broad smiles on both faces. Tom almost managed all the complex moves of the Ashanti male-bonding handshake. 'Are we going on in Twi or shall we speak English?' joked Kwame, and Tom had to admit that his vocabulary of the Ghanaian vernacular was already exhausted, and, in any case, they were now in England. 'When in Rome, eh?' grinned Kwame. 'Well, it's certainly good to see you. Your red face ended up tanned after all.'

'I couldn't make it to your colour in just two weeks,' laughed Tom, 'but wait until you see what I can do in six months!'

They were soon on the motorway reminiscing on their recently shared experiences in Ghana. 'There's one question I kept meaning to ask you but always missed the chance,' said Tom. 'What happened to all the soap plants that the TCC helped establish in the 1970s?'

'They were all swept away by the International Monetary Fund (IMF),' replied Kwame. Then he explained that when Jerry Rawlings came back at the end of 1981, he said that he would never let the IMF interfere in the affairs of Ghana. However, by 1983 the economy was on its knees. Rawlings had to go begging to the World Bank and the IMF and Ghana was forced to open its domestic market to world trade. By 1985 all the small soap plants were in serious trouble competing with imports and with a reinvigorated Lever Brothers Ghana Ltd. Now they were all gone.

'You sound rather bitter about it,' said Tom.

'You would be bitter too if so much of your work was destroyed and hundreds of your countrymen were thrown out of work,' retorted Kwame. 'And it wasn't only soap plants; countless other small industries have disappeared over the past two or three years.'

178

'Has free trade brought any benefits?' asked Tom.

'Well, our markets are full of the cheap Chinese goods that we talked about in Tamale,' replied Kwame, 'and our people can get plenty of dead men's clothes to wear, but we will be repaying the loans for years after the goods and clothes have been consumed or worn out.'

'So you think that your fledgling industries should be protected?' prompted Tom.

'I do. No other country developed its manufacturing industries without protection, so why are we being forced to open our markets before our industries are strong enough to compete?'

'It does seem very unfair. What happened to the industrial entrepreneurs, did they all become traders?'

'Most of them.'

'Speaking of traders,' said Tom, 'how are Comfort and Adjoa getting on since I left?'

'Comfort seems content with what she's doing but I haven't seen Adjoa since she went back to Wenchi,' replied Kwame. 'Afriyie was happy when I ordered new dresses for Comfort and Akosua, and your letter seemed to cheer her up.' Kwame glanced at his friend to observe his reaction to the mention of Afriyie and found Tom lost in thought behind a shadow of a smile. 'He's back in Kumasi on a hot afternoon,' thought Kwame, so he remained silent, recalling his own post-meridian experiences, until Tom startled him with, 'Do you think she likes me?'

'Why do you ask, didn't she tell you herself?'

'Of course she said something like that but I guess she says that to all the men.'

'All what men?' asked Kwame, wondering what was troubling his friend.

'All the men that Comfort sends her to,' said Tom.

Now Kwame understood. 'There are no other men as far as I know,' he said. 'Girls like Afriyie may seem to be free with their favours but they are really looking and hoping for a long-term relationship. I'm sure that she likes you and is hoping that you like her.'

Tom brooded for a while and Kwame waited patiently for the next question. At length Tom asked, 'Why was she so ready to come to my room, the room of a stranger?'

'Ah! Many Ghanaian girls find it hard to resist the temptation to befriend a white man,' said Kwame, 'Comfort once told me that some *abrofo* refer to it as the Holy Ghost syndrome.'

'That's a new syndrome on me,' said Tom. 'What does it signify?'

179

'It's from the Bible, I think,' said Kwame. 'Even the Virgin Mary couldn't refuse the Holy Ghost.'

Tom laughed, 'I guess it works the other way round as well.'

'You could be right,' said Kwame, remembering what Sally had told him. He felt his friend relax.

'So you think that Afriyie made a big exception for me, do you? Do you think she will wait for me until I can arrange for us to be together?'

Kwame was surprised at Tom's earnestness and hastened to reassure him. 'I'm sure she'll wait for you if you write and ask her.'

Kwame soon settled back into his practised routine but the coursework was more difficult. There was more that he had not covered before and he was forced to devote more time to his studies. He continued to work at the foundry where an increasing number of overseas students were coming for training. Fred Brown would have liked Kwame to put in more hours but he resisted the pressure. With the evening work at the ladies' club he had no time to spare. As usual with Kwame it was his social life that suffered. He felt guilty at not seeing more of Peter Sarpong and the other members of the West Africa club and suffered their reproaches on the special occasions that he could not avoid. He felt a strong bond with Tom and the two met whenever their occasional opportunities could be synchronised, which was not as often as either of them would have wished.

Lodging with Mrs Chichester had long become a home from home for Kwame who was content to suffer a degree of mothering in return for home comforts and a diet now well adjusted to his taste. At the ladies' club, Ethel Banks had stopped pursuing him and the work at the bar taxed his energy much less as he became more familiar with the routine and the preferences of his customers. Kwame focused intently on his two goals: to gain his degree and to earn money to send home to Comfort. He was content with his day-to-day life even if to an outsider it might seem dull, monotonous and devoid of any interest outside of work. It was not to remain like that for long.

One evening, on returning home from the foundry, Kwame was startled to be told by Mrs Chichester that his wife had come from Ghana. Hurrying to his room he was further surprised to find not Comfort but Afriyie waiting for him asleep on the bed. He explained to Mrs Chichester that his visitor was not his wife but one of Comfort's friends and he would wait until she woke up to question her on her mission. Mrs

Chichester said that she could make a small room available if the young lady wanted to stay for a few days. Kwame's first instinct was to telephone Tom to tell him that his girlfriend was in town but he hesitated until he knew what had brought Afriyie to Coventry. So he had his evening meal and read the local newspaper until he heard movements in his room and the door opened.

The friends greeted each other warmly and Kwame welcomed Afriyie to Coventry. He asked after Comfort and Akosua and was relieved that they were well and not in any way the reason for Afriyie's visit. Afriyie assured Kwame that there was no trouble on the road but Kwame knew that this was only the customary report of the traveller. He had to provide Afriyie with water, offer other refreshment and wait for all formalities to be exhausted before he could ask her about the real reason for her visit. What she told him filled him with dismay.

After their first meeting with Tom in Kumasi, Akos Mary kept telling Afriyie that the only way they could visit *aburokyiri* was to accept Mama Kate's offer. Afriyie felt that she might get a chance later, helped by Tom, but realised that this opportunity might not include Akos Mary. So she was persuaded to go along with her friend to see Mama Kate. The two young women were told that they would be helped to make a visit to Britain. They would be given passports and air tickets and money to meet their living expenses. Bra Yaw would travel with them to guide them through all the various procedures.

'How did you get passports and visas so quickly?' asked Kwame.

'They weren't our passports,' explained Afriyie, 'they were for some other girls and we were told to pretend that they were for us. Mine was for someone called Yekuba Williams.'

'What about the photograph, did it look like you?' asked Kwame.

'Not much,' said Afriyie, 'but Bra Yaw said that we all look the same to *abrofo*. He told us that he had travelled with four or five different passports and so far none has been questioned.'

'Can I see the passport?' asked Kwame. Afriyie rummaged in her handbag, pulled out a crumpled green Ghanaian passport and passed it to Kwame. 'You're right, it's not much like you. I'm surprised you were allowed through at the airport.

'Were you asked to carry anything?' asked Kwame, remembering his own experience with Bra Yaw and Mama Kate.

'Yes, we were each given a small packet to carry. We were told to give them to Bra Yaw in London.'

'Did they tell you what was in the packets?'

'No, they wouldn't tell us, but we thought it might be *wee*.'

'Did you give it to Bra Yaw?'

'No, I was afraid it might be something bad and I might get into trouble so I threw it away before we reached London.'

'How did you throw it away?'

'I flushed it down the toilet in the plane,' said Afriyie.

'What did Bra Yaw say when you didn't give him the packet?' asked Kwame.

'I didn't see Bra Yaw after we landed,' explained Afriyie. 'I told the stewardess that I was feeling unwell and she let me off the plane ahead of the other passengers. Bra Yaw wasn't sitting with us, he was several rows behind, so he couldn't stop me. After leaving the plane I ran along the corridors until I found a toilet where I hid for a long time. When I came out I went on through the airport. As I hoped, Akos Mary and Bra Yaw had gone.' Maybe, thought Kwame, Bra Yaw left quickly out of fear that Afriyie might have been detained by the customs or immigration authorities. 'I asked some people how I could get to Coventry,' continued Afriyie, 'and they showed me where to get on a coach to come here.'

'Comfort gave you my address, I suppose.'

'Yes, she gave it to both of us when we told her we wanted to write to you.'

'So Comfort doesn't know you have come here.'

'No.'

Kwame realised that Afriyie could be in danger and Bra Yaw would probably come looking for her. He would know where to come because Akos Mary had Kwame's address and she knew that Afriyie had it too. The first thing to do was to get Afriyie away to a safer location. Kwame telephoned Tom who said that he would come over right away.

Tom was alarmed to hear of Afriyie's predicament and immediately offered his assistance. 'I don't think Afriyie will be safe in my digs in Coventry,' he said, 'but I could take her to my parents' place in the country.' So Tom left with Afriyie in his car to make an unscheduled visit to his parents.

Less than half an hour later Kwame had more unexpected visitors. Mrs Chichester ushered in Peter Sarpong and Bra Yaw. 'Look who's just blown in from Kumasi,' said Peter. Kwame switched immediately to Ashanti welcoming kinsmen mode and hoped that he showed no visible concern relating to his earlier visitor. The boisterous greetings and rapid Twi exchanges sent Mrs Chichester scuttling to the safety of her kitchen, her muttered excuses lost to all but her own ears. Soon the three Ashanti exiles were draped around Kwame's room, beer bottles in hand, hearing Bra Yaw's account of all that was happening at home.

Although Kwame saw relatively little of Peter Sarpong, and Peter was a rare visitor at his home, it was quite natural for him to call when a mutual acquaintance came unexpectedly from Ghana. Yet Kwame suspected from the start that the real purpose of the visit was to find out if Afriyie was there. Bra Yaw said nothing about his travelling companions and Peter restricted himself to asking if Kwame had had any other visitors from Kumasi. He told Kwame that all visitors from Kumasi should be reported to him so that the community could keep in touch for their mutual benefit. Kwame smiled inwardly at Peter's self-promotion to head of the Ashanti community in Coventry but said nothing about Afriyie's visit. He hoped that Peter and Yaw had no means of knowing that she had been there. After their departure he made a careful inspection of his room to reassure himself that Afriyie had left no sign of her visit that the two men might have noticed.

The next day Kwame sent a message to Tom suggesting that they should meet Afriyie in her country hideout to discuss what should happen next. Tom, realising the urgency of the situation, suggested that they drive out to his parents' home that afternoon. Alone with Afriyie, the two men discussed her situation. It seemed to be desperate. She was in the UK illegally on a false passport. She held only a short-term visa and should soon return to Ghana; but was it safe for her to do so? If it was very unsafe, could she apply for asylum in the UK? Would she be any safer here? Could she supply enough information about the drug smuggling to enable the police to apprehend those who were a danger to her? Alternatively, should she return to Kumasi, accept whatever punishment may be meted out to her and then keep well away from Mama Kate and her associates?

Kwame questioned Afriyie in their vernacular, as in this stressful situation her limited English was fragmenting. He soon decided that she really knew almost nothing about the organisation that had brought her to the UK. What she could tell the authorities was little more than suspicions. She did not know for certain what was in the package she had disposed of in the aircraft. She did not know what was in Akos Mary's package or if Bra Yaw had also carried a similar package. She knew nothing to connect Peter Sarpong or anyone else in Coventry to the activity. They discussed these questions at length and repeatedly without reaching any firm conclusion. After realising the circularity of their deliberations they decided to delay a decision until they knew more about what Bra Yaw and Peter Sarpong were doing. Kwame had a bad feeling that this was only passing the initiative to the other side.

It was a few days later that Akos Mary called on Kwame. Ever since Afriyie's visit he had been expecting that Comfort's other friend would not be far behind. He was resolved to use the opportunity to try to find out more about the purpose of their trip to the UK, but he also realised that Akos Mary would be equally interested in questioning him and that she would have been well briefed by Bra Yaw and Peter Sarpong. He welcomed her as a friend of Comfort and acted as hospitably as custom demanded but he soon found himself engaged in a battle of wits in which Akos Mary's feminine allure heavily weighted the odds in her favour.

Kwame realised that Akos Mary had long grown used to being the most attractive woman in any company and Tom's rejection had come as a shock. She might still be jealous of Afriyie and for this reason she might willingly have agreed to help Bra Yaw and Peter find her former friend and now fugitive rival. Kwame doubted if she felt any great sense of loyalty to her sponsors; until recently she would naturally have sided with himself and Comfort, but for the moment her mind might well be focused on getting even with Afriyie.

She began by asking Kwame why he did not spend more time with Peter Sarpong and other friends from Ghana. Kwame found himself making excuses about all his spare time being taken up by his duties at the foundry and the ladies' club. 'Why do you do so much extra work?' she asked, to which Kwame was forced to admit that he needed the money. 'I'm sure that if you discussed your problems with Peter he would be able to help you earn much more,' said Akos Mary. I'm sure he would, thought Kwame, but he said aloud only that he must talk to Peter about it. 'And what about Tom, can't he help you?' continued Akos Mary.

'He helps me all he can,' replied Kwame, 'but as one of my teachers with many other students in a similar situation he can't be seen to be favouring me unduly.'

Kwame realised that he had lost the advantage in the exchange. Akos Mary was setting the agenda. He tried to question her on the purpose of her journey to the UK and her experiences so far but she evaded his questions with more of her own. She expressed much interest in meeting Tom again and asked Kwame for his address and telephone number. In avoiding divulging this information Kwame only succeeded in appearing clumsy and impolite. At the same time he realised that Peter Sarpong could easily find it for her. Akos Mary took the opportunity to take offence. 'I thought that we were all friends,' she said. 'We are alone in a foreign land and we need each other's help but you don't want to be friends with me any more.' After a brief interlude with a handkerchief she continued, 'When you and Comfort wanted me to be kind to your English friend in Kumasi I didn't refuse, but now you refuse to help me see him in Coventry. Has he got enough girlfriends here already?' Kwame started to make faltering excuses but was relieved when Akos Mary decided to leave before her passion subsided or her dramatic skills were found wanting.

Kwame repeated to himself all that had been said. He had failed to gain any explicit information that could help Afriyie. On the other hand, Akos Mary had learned a good deal about Kwame's life and circumstances that would, no doubt, be reported to Peter and Bra Yaw. Yet Kwame did not feel entirely defeated by the encounter. He suspected that Akos Mary knew rather more about Bra Yaw and Peter Sarpong's activities than had been told to Afriyie. He was not sure how this might help him and Tom to help Afriyie but he resolved to bear it in mind.

After Akos Mary had left, Kwame lost no time in telephoning Tom and warning him that Akos Mary was trying to find him. The two friends realised that Akos Mary and Peter Sarpong were sharing information. If he didn't know already, Peter would soon learn of Kwame's friendship with Tom and would soon find Tom's contact details. It would not be long before Peter and Bra Yaw would be trying to trace Afriyie through Tom. Alarmed by this realisation, Tom suggested coming over to Kwame's right away for a full discussion of the revised situation.

They went over the facts concerning Afriyie one more time. It was clear that time was running out and it would only be a few days before Afriyie was traced. Tom was growing nervous for the safety of his parents as well as Afriyie. They must decide to act quickly. They both agreed that Afriyie had very little information of use to the British authorities and only a very weak claim to asylum. So they concluded that the lesser of two evils was for Afriyie to return to Kumasi on schedule and accept whatever sanction was imposed for losing the package. They surmised that even the most ruthless gang of drug smugglers would probably refrain from inflicting actual physical harm in return for recovering their costs. After all, they knew that Afriyie had no real knowledge of their activities and thus no means of incriminating them. Tom and Kwame

185

agreed that they would contribute to the reimbursement of Afriyie's airfare and other expenses, although how this would be negotiated and paid remained an open question.

The next evening, when Kwame was on duty at the ladies' club, he was informed that a friend was waiting for him to go off duty. Before he could excuse himself to greet his visitor, he was surprised to see Ethel Banks ushering in Peter Sarpong and seating him at a table in the shadows at the back of the room. Ethel came to the bar to order drinks and told Kwame not to worry, 'I'll look after your friend, Peter, until you finish up here. If any of the committee members ask, I'll say that he's my guest.'

'Are you sure it's no trouble?' said Kwame weakly.

'Are you kidding?' grinned Ethel, 'He's almost as handsome as you.'

When the bar was closed and Kwame had finished cleaning up, Ethel handed over her charge with obvious reluctance. Peter asked where they could talk and Kwame suggested that the best place was back at his digs. The two young men walked the few hundred metres making small talk with Mrs Chichester who had stayed on for a committee meeting. It was not until they were closeted in Kwame's room that any serious conversation could begin.

Peter asked Kwame about his job at the ladies' club. He expressed the view that the pay could not be very generous. Wouldn't Kwame like to earn more? 'That place could be a goldmine if you sold the right things,' said Peter. 'Don't the members ask for something stronger than cigarettes and alcohol?' Suspecting that the matter might already have been discussed with Ethel Banks, Kwame was forced to admit that occasionally they did. 'I could help you supply them,' said Peter. 'Just let me know and I'll arrange it.' Not wishing to antagonise Peter, Kwame said that he would think about it.

Peter then asked, 'Do you know that Comfort's friend Afriyie has been in the UK?' Kwame, caught off-guard, shook his head in disbelief. 'I'm really surprised,' said Peter, 'because she's been staying with the parents of your good friend, Dr Tom Arthur.'

Kwame couldn't hide his feelings of shock and dismay. 'Where is she now, can I see her?' he blurted out.

'I'm afraid that isn't possible because she's already on her way home with Bra Yaw,' said Peter.

Peter's mood changed. He now appeared more threatening. 'Don't get too close to the *abrofo*,' he warned Kwame. 'Stick to your old friends from home. Think of your Kumasi people. You want Comfort and Akosua to be well looked after, don't you?'

After Peter was gone, Kwame sat for a long time brooding on the veiled threat to his family. He realised for the first time that while he was almost alone in *aburokyiri* his loved ones were alone in Ashanti and he could do nothing to protect them. Even with Tom's help he had been unable to protect Afriyie in England. Was Peter right in implying that the safety of his family and friends in both places depended on working closely with his own people? Kwame usually slept soundly at night, but not that night.

The next morning before breakfast Mrs Chichester called him to the telephone. 'I've just had a call from Dad,' said Tom. 'It appears that your two friends collected Afriyie yesterday.'

'Yes, I know,' groaned Kwame, 'Peter Sarpong was here to tell me. He said that she was already on her way home with Bra Yaw.'

'What will happen to her now?' asked Tom.

'It's like we discussed the other day,' said Kwame. 'I don't think they will harm her but they will want to recover the cost of her trip.'

'Then we must send her money right away,' said Tom. 'I'll see to it immediately. We can discuss the details later.'

Now that the situation had resolved itself, Kwame realised that the outcome was much as they had planned. He and Tom had agreed that the safest course for Afriyie was to return home and weather whatever storm was raised by her erstwhile sponsors. They had been outwitted by Peter Sarpong and Bra Yaw, with help from Akos Mary, but the result was not much different from what they had hoped to achieve. On the positive side, the urgency had gone out of the situation. Kwame was able to return to his normal routine and begin repairing the damage to his studies that had resulted from the pressure of recent events. It was Tom who was to feel the longer-lasting effect.

Afriyie was gone but Akos Mary had not been mentioned as her travelling companion. Had she stayed behind and, if so, for what reason? Tom had asked himself these questions repeatedly as he sat in his bachelor's flat trying to concentrate on setting an examination paper to ambush Kwame and his classmates at the end of their second year of studies. The end-of-year examinations were still some way off but Tom liked to be prepared well in advance of the official deadline. It was always a challenge to come up with some original questions to wring a few words of reluctant commendation from the external examiner who would review his efforts before the papers were printed. Tom relished this intellectual jousting but preferred to undertake the task in the quiet of his own room in the evening, rather than between delivering lectures and supervising laboratory classes.

Did he want to see Akos Mary again? Tom wasn't sure, but he couldn't banish the question from his mind. He had chosen Afriyie and he was happy with his choice. At the same time he felt that it was only natural to wonder what the alternative might have been like. He must force himself to remember, that however beautiful she may be, the lady was now a friend of his enemy, and a friend of his enemy was his enemy, wasn't she? He couldn't be quite sure. Afriyie had been told almost nothing about the purpose of her journey, maybe Akos Mary had been treated in just the same way. Perhaps they were both innocent of any real involvement in Mama Kate's enterprise. Kwame seemed to think that Akos Mary was more deeply involved than Afriyie but how could he be sure?

Thoughts such as these interfered with progress on the examination paper for two or three evenings but they had begun to recede into the shadows of irrelevance when the knock on his door finally came. He opened the door to find a surprisingly contrite-looking Akos Mary standing outside. He invited her in with the words 'I've been expecting you; what kept you?'

'I wasn't sure that you wanted to see me,' was her blunt reply.

'*Akwaaba*,' said Tom, remembering just in time the Ashanti word for welcome.

'*Ya agya*,' she replied, politely acknowledging him as her elder. They shook hands in the usual Ghanaian manner and he invited her to take a seat.

'Would you like a cup of tea?' asked Tom.

'You should offer me water first,' laughed Akos Mary.

'You're in England now,' Tom reminded her, 'but if you'd prefer water I'll give you some.'

'I'll have both,' she decided.

'How do you like England?' Tom called from the kitchen above the whistle of the kettle.

'It's very cold.' she replied, 'but otherwise it's not bad. I like the shops; there are so many beautiful things to buy.'

'If you have money.'

'There seems to be plenty of that about. It's only Kwame who seems not to have much.'

'Is that what he told you? Well he's still a student, isn't he? Things should get better for him when he has his degree.'

'How long will that be?'

'Oh, he has about eighteen months to go before he graduates.'

'I couldn't wait that long to be rich.'

'Is that why you got involved with Mama Kate and Bra Yaw?' asked Tom.

'Tell me another way to get quick money,' she replied. 'There aren't many other options for a young person in Kumasi.'

'So you don't make enough money as a hairdresser?' teased Tom, but Akos Mary showed by her look that she considered the question rhetorical. 'How do you like the tea?' he prompted.

'I prefer it with tinned milk,' she said, 'That's how we make it in Ghana.'

'I'm sorry,' said Tom, 'I should have known, but I only have fresh milk here.' He was tempted to add that he would get in some evaporated milk, but he didn't know if he wanted to hold out the promise of a second visit, so he asked, 'How long do you expect to stay in England?'

Akos Mary sat in silence sipping the hot tea; she seemed uncertain how to respond. Tom mused that this was not the confident interrogator who had called earlier on Kwame.

'I'll stay as long as I can,' she said at last. 'Maybe I can get work as a hairdresser.'

'That should be possible,' said Tom. 'Have you made any enquiries?'

'I asked Peter if he could help, but he said there were better things to do.'

'What did he suggest?'

'I'd rather not say, but I was hoping that you could help me.'

'It's not really my line, I've no contact with ladies' hairdressers – and very little contact with men's hairdressers,' he reflected, sweeping his dangling forelock away from his eyes and wondering when his mother would next complain that he needed a haircut.

'I wish I had hair like yours,' said Akos Mary, 'I would let it grow down to my feet.'

'There's nothing wrong with your hair. It looks very nice.'

'Thanks, but it's not my own hair; most of it is just weave-on,' she replied with a pout. 'You know, many of us feel that we were accidentally born in the wrong place, especially when we think about our hair. We would love to have long soft hair like *abrofo*.'

'I still like your hair the way it is,' insisted Tom gallantly.

Tom was beginning to wonder why she had come. He had originally been expecting a visit prompted by Peter Sarpong and aimed at finding Afriyie's place of refuge, but now that Afriyie had been abducted Tom assumed that Peter had no further interest in him. So if it wasn't for Peter, had Akos Mary come on her own initiative? That could explain the delay in the visit. Had she had to wait for a suitable opportunity when Peter was distracted? He decided to try to find out. 'Does Peter Sarpong know that you are here?' he asked.

'No, he does not,' came her swift reply, 'and I don't want him to know.'

'He won't hear from me,' said Tom. 'I have no dealings with him in the normal course of my work. I only know him as a friend of Kwame's.'

'I don't think that he's a friend of Kwame's, not a real friend,' she said.

Tom tried to hide his surprise at this remark. 'How do you mean?' he asked.

'I don't know if I can trust you,' said Akos Mary. 'I don't know if you like me. I don't know about *abrofo*. Peter Sarpong keeps telling us all to trust only one another, but I don't trust him. I trust Kwame, but I have offended him doing Peter's dirty work. I don't know what to do.'

'Please don't worry about Kwame; I'm sure he's not offended,' said Tom. 'I'm sure that he will try to help you if you confide in him.'

'And what about you, will you be my friend?'

'Of course,' said Tom, putting a protective arm around her shoulders. It was then that he noticed she was wearing no lipstick. There was no reason not to kiss her; but as he did, Tom couldn't help suspecting that Akos Mary and Peter Sarpong might have outwitted them once again.

When Kwame heard of Akos Mary's visit to Tom he felt confused. Was she still acting as Peter Sarpong's agent or was she trying to escape from his clutches? He was sure that Mrs Chichester, through her contacts at the ladies' club, could help Akos Mary get a job as a hairdresser, but should he risk crossing Peter Sarpong once again? Even if he helped her, Akos Mary would probably be sent back to Kumasi by Peter and his associates. Perhaps they had let her stay only until Bra Yaw came back on his next visit. Once again Kwame decided to delay any decision until he could see which way the other side was reacting.

Kwame had looked forward to the end of term as an opportunity to catch up on his studies. He was finding the going more difficult in his second year as his curriculum included fewer of the topics he had covered already in Kumasi. His teaching duties at the foundry were suspended during the Christmas vacation but he was asked to put in more time at the ladies' club in support of the various seasonal festivities. He developed a schedule of studying during the morning and afternoon and working most evenings in the bar. This routine was interrupted only by an invitation to spend Christmas Day and Boxing Day with Tom at his parents' country home.

Kwame was fascinated to discover how *abrofo* celebrated Christmas. He reflected that the experience was probably as novel to him as attending funerals in Ghana had been to Tom. He had not met Tom's parents since the departure of Afriyie and he was not sure how to react to their almost inevitable questions about her abrupt removal. So it was with some surprise that he heard Tom's mother ask Tom why he had not also invited that nice young gentleman Peter to share their Christmas festivities. 'I am becoming quite enamoured of Ghanaian men,' she confided. 'They are as polite and gentle mannered as they are handsome.'

'Careful,' said Dr Arthur senior to his wife. 'You'd better go easy on the sherry or Kwame won't want to come again.'

'I've only had one glass and it's true,' she insisted. 'Look, he's not at all embarrassed.'

Kwame thanked her for her compliment, relieved that he would not face an interrogation about Afriyie.

Tom arranged a quiet hour for the two friends to discuss their concerns in private. Akos Mary had not reappeared and Kwame had had no further one-to-one contact with Peter Sarpong, seeing him only in passing at the West Africa club. 'Things seem to have quietened down,' observed Tom. 'Do you think they will leave us alone?'

'I can't say,' said Kwame. 'It may depend upon whether Akos Mary has gone home. If she's still around and looking for another opportunity to evade Peter's supervision, we may see her again.'

'If she's been sent back, do you think she will come again?' asked Tom.

'Yes, I think she will,' said Kwame.

Kwame wrote regularly to Comfort, usually also enclosing a note for Akosua. Now he decided to write at length explaining all that had happened and warning Comfort to continue to distance herself as far as possible from Mama Kate and Bra Yaw and to treat Akos Mary as a possible collaborator. He advised Comfort to continue being friendly with Afriyie but to try not to do anything to excite the hostility of the others. Comfort wrote back in due course agreeing to follow his advice and confirming that Afriyie had come back to Kumasi. 'She says that you and Tom were kind to her in Coventry,' wrote Comfort, 'but she was forced to come back with Bra Yaw. She doesn't want to come there again and as far as I can see they are not putting any pressure on her.'

* * *

In the New Year of 1987, Kwame settled down to the second term of his second year at Warwick University. He was glad to get back to something approaching his established routine, but he couldn't completely banish thoughts about the safety of his family in Konongo. He looked forward to Comfort's letters with renewed interest and was relieved each time she reported that all was well. He was not altogether surprised to read in one of her letters that Akos Mary had reappeared at the hairdressers' kiosk at Ayigya. It seemed that Peter Sarpong had succeeded in sending her home in spite of her interest in staying and working in England. No doubt the conspirators were hoping that she would carry another parcel to London once she had spent her earnings from the first trip.

Tom Arthur, pursuing his project to link up with Kumasi University, was pleased to hear that the government of Ghana had approved the GRID project on 3 February. He discussed the news with Kwame who immediately regretted that he had not finished his BSc programme in time to apply for one of the technical officer's posts that were now being advertised. He decided to write to Dr Jones, who was now leading GRID, to express his interest in working for the project as soon as he graduated in 1988. He felt that with his track record at the TCC and the Suame and Tamale ITTUs he would be well qualified to play a key role in this nationwide expansion of the technology transfer network. He was delighted to get a letter back from his old boss inviting him to call in at the Tema headquarters during his next long vacation in Ghana.

On 2 March, Kwame reached his thirtieth birthday. He reflected on the milestone with mixed feelings. He was making good progress towards his degree but he was acutely aware that most of the British students on his course were nearly a decade younger. He had achieved his ambition of living and studying in *aburokyiri* but he seemed as far as ever from earning his fortune. He had started to build a house in Kumasi but his contemporaries were much further advanced and building on a far grander scale. He had a happy family back home in Konongo but he feared that Comfort might react as his mother had done if he could not provide her with greater wealth and social status. His work in Ghana was fulfilling

192

his heart's desire to serve his country as his father had wished but he couldn't see how it could help him solve his personal economic problem. Above all he felt that he was too much inclined to wait upon events, to let time pass him by without seizing fleeting opportunities to make faster progress. Should he, after all, talk to Peter Sarpong about the wider opportunities that were arising in this affluent corner of a ballooning world economy?

True to form, Kwame decided to wait until the Easter vacation before taking action. He decided to work out the spring term according to his set routine. This would enable him to stabilise his position in relation to his studies and his revenues, both of which had been adversely affected by recent events. He was determined to pass his end-of-year examinations with the university and with his spouse. By the time he flew to Accra in July, Kwame was intent on accumulating enough money to raise the walls of Comfort's house at Old Ahensan. His plan had been boosted by a generous Christmas bonus from the ladies' club and increased demand for his services at the foundry. According to Fred Brown, Kwame's good work was attracting increasing numbers of African trainees and he had been able to persuade his board to increase Kwame's hourly rate and his hours of work. Now there was no possibility of doing more; every waking hour was fully occupied.

14

The Cartel

With the Easter vacation fast approaching, Kwame decided to contact Peter Sarpong and invite him home for a few beers. He found him on his next visit to the West Africa club and was relieved that Peter reciprocated his cheerful greeting in full measure. Whatever their differences may have been over Afriyie's visit it seemed that their personal relationship had suffered no lasting damage.

This impression was confirmed later when they were closeted in Kwame's room. Kwame welcomed Peter and they went through the full Ashanti male-bonding ritual. Then, bottles of beer in hand, they got down to business. 'I don't think that we should let the little affair with Afriyie spoil our relationship,' said Peter. 'I am sure that she will continue to make her little dresses in peace.'

'I'm glad to hear that,' said Kwame. 'Afriyie is a close friend of Comfort and the main source of her special clothes.'

'In which she always looks so lovely,' added Peter. 'You're a lucky man, Kwame Mainu.'

The first bottle of beer was soon finished. Both young men missed the Star and Club beers of their homeland, besides which English beers tasted like non-alcoholic substitutes. As Kwame opened a second round Peter asked, 'Now, what prompted you to invite me over today?'

'I've been thinking about what you said about the ladies' club,' said Kwame, 'about supplying something more interesting.'

'You think you could pass on a bit of weed, do you?' prompted Peter.

'Weed, is that what we call *wee*?' asked Kwame, realising for the first time that the Ghanaian term was probably derived from the English. 'I know that one lady is keen to get some.'

'Your good friend Ethel Banks, eh?' said Peter with a smile. 'She's not slow in telling you what she wants. How many others do you think we could interest?'

'I'm not sure,' said Kwame, 'but I could begin by asking Ethel. She probably has friends with similar appetites.'

'How about your people at the foundry school?' asked Peter. 'Any chance of pulling in a few helpers there?'

'How do you mean?' asked Kwame.

'Well, you get students from Ghana and Nigeria, don't you? They might like to help extend distribution and sales. Then there's your local students, they must have links with local schools, youth clubs and discos. That's a special interest of ours, integrating with the youth culture and catching them as young as possible.'

'You sound like a Jesuit missionary,' laughed Kwame, but the joke was lost on Peter whose namesake was the Catholic Bishop of Kumasi.

'So you can provide the *wee*, er weed,' prompted Kwame.

'It's good to start with that,' said Peter, 'but we should soon move on to coke and smack, that's what really brings in the big bucks.'

'Can you supply all that?' gasped Kwame, unable to contain his surprise at this unguarded statement, 'Where does it all come from?'

'Need to know, I'm afraid, old boy,' said Peter, tapping the side of his nose.

This remark and gesture set an alarm bell ringing in Kwame's head. It was completely out of character for Peter. Where had he picked it up? Where had Kwame heard someone speaking like that before? He searched his memory in vain. Peter was asking him to confirm his interest; maybe he feared that he had said too much. In his confusion Kwame wanted time to sort through all he had learned. 'I'll let you know by the end of the vacation,' he said.

After Peter left, Kwame went over all that had been said. He had learned that Peter could supply cannabis, cocaine and heroin and was interested in Kwame helping to expand the local market with particular emphasis on recruiting more West African helpers and promoting sales to the youth. Helping with the marketing in Coventry would not involve carrying contraband through customs at the airport and appeared to be less risky than acting as a courier. It could also be done without Comfort being aware of his involvement and so she would raise no objection. Now he had to decide if he wanted to build his house in Kumasi on this activity, as Peter and Bra Yaw seemed to be doing, or whether to leave it well alone as he knew his father would wish.

This was a big enough issue to ponder yet something else kept intruding on his thoughts. 'Need to know, I'm afraid, old boy.' Who used to talk like that? Then the penny dropped – Comfort's old boyfriend,

Oboroni! Had Peter known Oboroni in Kumasi? It was possible. Or was there someone else who talked like that? If so, Peter must have been closely involved with him to pick up and ape his mode of speech and mannerism. Then a startling thought hit Kwame: Oboroni knew Mama Kate in Kumasi, so had he become her business partner as well as her one-time entertainer?

Was Oboroni involved in the drugs cartel? It seemed both possible and impossible at the same time. If he was involved, where was he now, and what was his role? At the time he met Oboroni, Kwame had never thought that a white man could be involved in criminal activity. Weren't they rich enough already? Yet Oboroni had worked for Hanabis, a Lebanese company, and they were thought to be involved in every form of corruption and illicit money-making scheme. Could Oboroni have established a link between his Lebanese and Syrian business associates and Mama Kate's group? If so, the cartel could be much bigger than Kwame had ever suspected.

The more he thought about it the more likely it seemed to become. The Lebanese and Syrian businessmen in Ghana were primarily involved in the import and export business. On the import side, they brought into Ghana whatever they thought they could sell. On the export side, many were involved in the timber trade, shipping out both raw logs and sawn timber, while others were involved with the export of gold and diamonds. No other group could have so much knowledge of getting goods into and out of Ghana or into the UK and Europe, and no other group could have more opportunities to conceal contraband within its regular shipments.

Not everything fitted together. Kwame realised that he had only a few pieces of the jigsaw. If the Arabian businessmen were so well placed to handle exports, why were Mama Kate and Bra Yaw using young women like Akos Mary and Afriyie to bring packages to the UK? Clearly, Mama Kate and Uncle George could provide an essential distribution network through the Ghanaian diaspora in the UK but why did they need to handle part of the international trade as well? Maybe there were times when couriered airfreight was needed to speed up the business or perhaps there were other advantages in having alternative supply routes. Kwame wondered how he could find out more about the cartel. Did he want to find out more about the cartel? Couldn't it become rather dangerous to pry into its affairs, whether or not he became directly involved?

However hard he tried, Kwame could not remember Oboroni's proper name. He decided to do one thing only. In his next letter he would ask Comfort to remind him. Then he realised once again that his actions could endanger Comfort and Akosua back in Konongo and he wondered if even this simple question was a step too far. He remembered that Oboroni left Ghana abruptly after the first Rawlings coup of 4 June 1979, without giving Comfort any contact details. All she could supply was a name and that might serve no useful purpose. It might not have been a correct name or Oboroni might now use a different name, especially if he wanted to make himself hard to trace. With his usual tendency to vacillate and delay action, Kwame almost persuaded himself to drop the idea, but something urged him to follow up what he told himself was a shrewd deduction.

Kwame wrote casually in the middle of a long letter that he sometimes wondered what had become of Oboroni. He would have liked to see him while he was in England and, by the way, what was his proper name? If he ever got a chance to see him again it could only come through knowing his proper name. Kwame made no mention of Mama Kate, Bra Yaw or Peter Sarpong, Afriyie or Akos Mary. He took care to avoid hinting at any continuing connection between Oboroni and the Kumasi people. The last thing he wanted was for Comfort to start making her own enquiries.

In due course a letter came back from Comfort. Kwame had almost reached the end and was thinking that his casual question had been overlooked when he spotted a postscript added below the line of crosses from Akosua.

'His name, I think, is Crispin Russell. It was because I couldn't pronounce Crispin that I always called him Oboroni, love Comfort.'

Kwame smiled as he read these words. He knew that his people had a problem pronouncing 'crisps'. It had taken him a long time to get it right, even in England. He was not surprised that a teenager in Kumasi had given up the struggle. Now that he had the name he had to decide what to do with it. Then he noticed that Comfort had added a PPS:

'You don't think that Oboroni is mixed up in Mama Kate's business, do you?'

He smiled to himself again at the superiority of feminine intuition.

A more basic problem for Kwame was whether or not to consult Tom. Peter had stressed the need for the West African diaspora to stick together and treat all *abrofo* with suspicion. Kwame had told Tom nothing about his negotiations with Peter for obvious reasons. He had valued the close friendship that had developed during Tom's visit to Ghana but if he went into business with Peter he would be forced to distance himself from Tom and revert to their formal student-teacher relationship. Then he recalled that Peter had also lectured Akos Mary on African solidarity but that had not prevented her from seeking Tom's help when she wanted to stay behind in England. Had her feminine intuition told her that Tom was a more reliable friend than Peter? If it was true for Akos Mary, Kwame felt that it was even more true for him.

Kwame was resolved to contact Tom but it was Tom who first picked up the telephone. The university had received a communication from Kumasi suggesting some radical changes in their partnership proposal. Kwame was invited to attend a meeting at which the suggested revisions would be discussed. Kwame realised that it was an honour to be consulted in this way. It was also a daunting prospect for an undergraduate to be called before a committee of senior members. He consoled himself with the thought that Tom, at least, would be attentive to anything that he might say.

The chairman opened the meeting by summarising the situation. A proposal for a partnership agreement had been drawn up by Dr Arthur and Dr Jones, the director of the TCC at Kwame Nkrumah University of Science and Technology (KNUST) in Kumasi. This proposal had been submitted to the Overseas Development Administration (ODA) in London for preliminary appraisal and the feedback had been positive. Final approval would follow when the formal submission of the proposal came from the vice-chancellor of KNUST, after he had gained the approval of his academic board and university council. This was the document that had now arrived in draft. However, it included several new features that significantly increased the cost of the project, perhaps to a level that would not be acceptable to ODA.

Kumasi University wanted substantial funds for expenditure on related research in Ghana, more opportunities for staff to participate in research at Warwick and more opportunities for students and staff to undertake training in the UK. The chairman expressed the view that funding more research in Kumasi could be possible as costs were much lower in Ghana and modest funding could still have a useful impact. However, bringing people to Warwick, involving air fares and subsistence in the UK, would greatly swell the budget. He couldn't see how this could be done without starting all over again with the funding agency and negotiating for a project in a larger funding category. He could not say at this stage if such a funding category was available since the original project had been tailored to fit a specific call for proposals within a specified budget ceiling.

The chairman turned to Kwame to ask how he thought the changes had come about. Kwame caught Tom's eye and decided to be frank. The original proposal, he said, had been drawn up by the TCC director who was an expatriate. His primary concern was for the immediate needs of the project in purely operational terms. However, the academic board and university council, on being asked to approve the proposal, would be primarily concerned with gaining foreign funding for the university and privileges for members of staff, hence the request for funds to spend in Ghana and opportunities for staff to research and train at Warwick. Kwame added that he was sorry that this was how things stood but he hoped that those present would try to understand the needs and aspirations of people working in a poor country.

The chairman thanked Kwame for this clear explanation and said that they would try to be sympathetic in their deliberations. Some members pointed out that some modest concessions were possible within the present budget ceiling, especially if they cut down the allowance for contingencies. After some discussion of detail the chairman asked Kwame how he thought the university in Kumasi would react if they made what concessions they could within the present ODA funding limit. Kwame said that he thought that if the funding limit was explained to the vice-chancellor the revised proposal would be accepted. The Kumasi authorities would be happy that their proposed revisions had resulted in some increased benefit. 'In the last analysis we say in Ghana: a beggar has no choice.'

The chairman hastened to assure Kwame that Warwick did not consider their partners in Kumasi to be beggars. Warwick would gain substantially from the opportunities to undertake research with people long experienced in various fields of specialisation. Academically, what they proposed was a collaboration of equals, but both universities were constrained by the limitations imposed by funding bodies. The meeting agreed to resubmit the proposal to Kumasi, revised within the funding limit, and if the revisions were approved they would take the negotiations with ODA to the final stage.

As the meeting broke up, Kwame took the opportunity to ask Tom if they could have a chat about personal affairs. They met in Tom's flat a few days later. 'I suppose it's pressure of work and studies that's kept you quiet for so long,' said Tom. 'I can sympathise; you certainly have a heavy load.'

'Yes,' replied Kwame, happy to be let off with that excuse. 'I'm sorry that we haven't seen more of each other but I guess you're busy too.'

199

'Too right,' said Tom, 'but not too busy to entertain your friend Peter Sarpong.'

'Peter Sarpong! Has he been here? What did he want? I'm not sure that he's my friend,' blurted Kwame in some confusion.

'He seems to be interested in learning more about our proposed partnership agreement with Kumasi,' said Tom, 'especially in the prospect of Kumasi people coming here for training.'

'What did you tell him?' asked Kwame in some alarm.

'Only that the matter was still under negotiation and I couldn't give him any details,' replied Tom, 'but he said that he would call again later when he thought the details had been finalised.'

'Please keep on stalling him for as long as possible,' said Kwame. 'We both know what he's trying to do. I've also been talking to Peter and I now know rather more about his illicit operations.'

Kwame told Tom about his recent meeting with Peter. 'He strongly hinted that he could supply cannabis, cocaine and heroin,' said Kwame, 'and he was very keen to use my contacts at the ladies' club and the foundry school to find more helpers and more clients. He was especially keen to supply the stuff to children and teenagers in schools, youth clubs and discos.'

'Did he say how he was getting the drugs?' asked Tom.

'No, but he replied to my question about his source of supply in an unusual way.'

'How do you mean?' asked Tom.

'He said "Need to know, I'm afraid, old boy," and tapped the side of his nose just like an Englishman I knew in Kumasi.'

'So you think this Englishman is involved with the cartel, do you?' said Tom. 'It seems like a wild guess to me. It's based only on a remark that might have been mimicked after someone whom Peter might have known through his people in Kumasi. He might have picked it up from another Englishman here in England who talks in a similar manner; there are plenty of them.'

'But this man, Oboroni, knew Mama Kate,' insisted Kwame, 'and Peter and his uncle are also close to Mama Kate. Anyway, I took the opportunity to find out his name from Comfort and it's Crispin Russell.'

'If he is involved in the drugs business he could use several names,' observed Tom, 'but I guess we could try to track him down using something like telephone directories or electoral registers, if you want to take it further.'

'I don't think I do,' said Kwame. 'I'm afraid for the safety of Comfort and Akosua in Konongo.'

'Yes,' said Tom. 'Peter's gang may leave you in peace as a neutral but not if they suspect you are an enemy.'

'I suppose you're going home again during the long vacation,' said Tom.

'Yes,' said Kwame. 'I'm looking forward to it very much. What will you be doing?'

'I wanted to speak to you about that,' said Tom. 'Would you mind awfully if I came down to Kumasi again for a couple of weeks? Not on duty, I wouldn't want to tie you up again like last year, just on holiday.'

'Not at all,' said Kwame. 'I would be delighted to have you there again and I know all the friends you made in Kumasi will feel the same.'

'Shall we fly down together?'

'I'll enjoy your company and I can help you get to Kumasi again. Afriyie will be pleased you're coming.'

'I'll write to tell her right away,' said Tom.

When Peter came back for his answer he took Kwame's excuses without showing any surprise or disappointment. Knowing that Kwame always took a long time to come to a decision, Peter seemed to take the rebuff more as a postponement than a cancellation. However, he took pains to ask after Comfort and Akosua in Konongo, keeping Kwame aware of their vulnerability. As a parting gesture of goodwill Peter remarked that 'Our mutual friend Akos Mary will soon be back in Coventry.' Though filled with concern, Kwame did not risk asking for more details.

The summer term passed quickly and Kwame was into his end-of-year examinations much sooner than he would have liked. I guess it's always like this, he thought to himself. Tom was experiencing the same tumult from the other side, being suddenly weighed down with piles of papers to mark, deadlines to meet and examiners' boards to attend. He was pleased to note that Kwame had achieved a good result on his paper and he hoped that he had done equally well in his other subjects.

After the examinations came the lull of two or three weeks before the results were announced. Kwame was free of academic commitments so he decided to make one last effort to boost his building fund before he would fly home for the long vacation. There was not much extra work available at the foundry school as it was also winding down at the end of the academic year, but the ladies' club was very active with garden parties and barbecues. Kwame was also invited by some of the members to help out at private functions. At one such event, at the home of Ethel Banks, Kwame caught the faint sweet scent of what he recognised as *wee*. He suspected that Peter had not neglected the contact he had made with Ethel and he couldn't help wondering if she was sharing her restored pleasure with her friends.

It was a few days before his planned return to Ghana, when Kwame was involved in buying gifts and packing suitcases, that Akos Mary made her second appearance at his lodgings. Kwame thought to himself that if Peter Sarpong allowed the visit he must feel that he had a firm hold on the young hairdresser. Presumably, now that she had completed two successful trips for the cartel, she was firmly in their grip. Akos Mary gave Kwame a letter from Comfort and confirmed that Comfort and Akosua were well and looking forward to his homecoming. They had both had their hair restyled in his honour and Afriyie was busy making them new clothes for the holidays. Afriyie was reported to be well but she appeared to have said nothing to Akos Mary about Tom's forthcoming visit to Kumasi.

Apart from the usual pleasantries and news from home, Kwame could see no purpose in Akos Mary's visit. He asked when she was returning to Ghana and was surprised to learn that she was leaving two days ahead of his own departure with Tom. She had only been with Kwame about half an hour when Peter Sarpong came looking for her. So she's not allowed out on a very long leash, after all, thought Kwame. He still wondered why she had come but his thoughts were soon flooded again by the needs of his impending trip.

With much relief, Kwame learned of his success in the end-of-year examinations. Now he was through to the final year of his honours course. It would be the toughest year of all. Not only would he continue with studies of ever-increasing complexity but he would be required to devote much time to a special project on a topic of his own choice. He still needed to think about the topic, and to consult Tom and his other tutors, but the final decision could await his return in September. Now he could return home with his mind free of concerns about his life in Coventry.

On their journey to the airport, Kwame and Tom relived their happy experience of the year before and expected to continue to do so. However, this euphoric mood was soon to be shattered. When they presented their travel documents at passport control they were told to wait. Soon a customs official and a police officer arrived to conduct them to a part of the airport that neither had visited before. Tom later surmised that it must have been an office in the customs headquarters.

After some time a more senior officer came to speak to them. He was polite but firm. He showed them a photograph of a young woman and asked if they knew her. Both Kwame and Tom hastened to assure their interrogator that they knew the person as Akos Mary, a friend from Kumasi. Kwame added that he believed that her surname was Konadu.

'Then can you tell me why she is travelling on a passport with the name Caroline Yaa Asare?' asked the official.

Kwame looked at Tom in dismay. They both knew that Afriyie had been travelling on a false passport so it was reasonable to assume that Akos Mary would be doing the same. The official looked at his watch in a studied manner. It was clear that their flight would leave without them.

'I would advise you to cooperate with us fully and tell us all you know,' he said, 'but I will give you ten minutes to think it over.'

They were surprised to be left alone together. Tom remarked that if they were suspected of direct involvement in criminal activity they would certainly be interrogated separately. 'I suggest that we tell them all we know, which isn't much, but might be helpful to them,' he said. Kwame agreed reluctantly. He would much have preferred to keep well out of it but to refuse to cooperate would only mean extending the delay and raising suspicion of deeper involvement. 'Will you take the lead in explaining the situation?' asked Tom. Kwame nodded slowly and without enthusiasm.

'We know that some Ghanaians have been travelling from Accra to London on false passports,' said Kwame when the official returned.

'Can you give me any names?' asked the official.

'We know one man as Bra Yaw,' said Kwame. 'I believe that you know him because he was charged with an offence and imprisoned a few years ago.'

'Yes, we know him,' said the official. 'What can you tell me about Peter Sarpong?'

'Oh, he's a student at Warwick University,' interjected Tom.

'I'm more concerned about his extra-mural activities,' snapped the official, looking directly at Kwame.

'We have no definite proof,' said Kwame, 'but we suspect he's involved in importing cannabis.'

203

'I think that you had better tell me all you know, starting from the very beginning,' said the official. So Kwame began with the request he had received from Bra Yaw before his first visit to Britain: to carry a parcel of what he believed was *kenke* but might well have included something else. At the time he had refused the mission and returned a sum of money he had been given in advance. Since he had been in Coventry, he had learned that Bra Yaw made frequent trips to the UK and that his main contact in Coventry seemed to be Peter Sarpong. He also knew that Akos Mary had made two visits to Coventry and each time her movements seemed to be controlled by Peter Sarpong.

'Peter Sarpong tried to get you involved, didn't he?' persisted the official, 'What did he offer you?'

'He tried to get me to sell drugs at the places where I work,' said Kwame.

'You mean the foundry school and the ladies' club.'

'Yes,' said Kwame.

'Did you discuss only cannabis, or were other drugs on offer?'

'He suggested that later he could supply cocaine and heroin,' said Kwame in a voice that was barely audible.

'What about the young lady who left her package on the plane?' continued the interrogator. Kwame groaned; he had been hoping to keep Afriyie out of it and to judge from Tom's crestfallen countenance, so had he. 'We know her as Afriyie, but she decided not to cooperate with Peter and Bra Yaw so we felt that she was not important.'

'I'm not sure about that,' said the official. 'She boarded a plane with drugs on her person and she entered the UK on a false passport. These are both serious offences. You should advise the young lady that if she should ever return to the UK she should be carrying her own passport.'

'Does that mean that her past offences will be overlooked?' asked Tom anxiously.

'Officially, I can give no such guarantee,' replied the official, 'but if she commits no further offence we might be inclined to turn a blind eye.'

The rest of the interview was taken up with questions about Kwame's personal situation. When was he expecting to return to Coventry? How long did he have to go before the end of his course? Would he continue to work at the foundry school and the ladies' club? Was he married? Where was his wife? Did he have any children and, if so, where were they?

At length, the official indicated that the interview was at an end and Kwame could leave. Tom was asked to stay behind for a few moments but soon caught up with Kwame on his way back to the departures area. A junior official accompanied them to help in arranging seats on the next available flight. The two friends soon found themselves in the departure lounge with several hours to wait. They found comfortable seats in a quiet area and took the opportunity to review all that had happened since they arrived at the airport.

'I expect you want to hear what I was asked after you left,' said Tom.

'The thought had crossed my mind,' replied Kwame.

'In a roundabout way, they were asking me to vouch for you,' said Tom. 'I tried to give you a good character reference.'

'Thank you, but what did they need it for? They seem to know everything about me already.'

'Don't they just! They've certainly done their homework. I don't think Peter and company will be allowed to operate much longer.'

'Do you think what we told them was much help?'

'It seemed to confirm what they knew already. They must have had Peter and Bra Yaw under surveillance for some months to know all their contacts, including us, but they didn't give much away, did they?'

Kwame shook his head slowly in affirmation. 'How do you think things stand at the moment?'

'Well, the British authorities know about Peter Sarpong, Bra Yaw and Akos Mary, and suspect that they're involved in bringing drugs from Ghana for sale in the UK.'

'It's more than a suspicion. They found Afriyie's package on the plane and they must have other proof of what's going on.'

'I think they have enough evidence to arrest the small people but perhaps not enough to charge the big people. They may also want to coordinate any arrests they make with the authorities in Ghana.'

'Do you mean that Mama Kate and Uncle George could be arrested in Kumasi? I hadn't thought of that.'

'Don't they deserve it? Why do you look so worried?'

'They may have done some foolish things, but I don't want to think that I helped to put them in prison.'

'You don't seem to be much concerned about Peter Sarpong and Bra Yaw being arrested in the UK, so why are you worried about Uncle George and Mama Kate being arrested in Ghana?' asked Tom, curious about Kwame's reaction to his suggestion.

'Well,' replied Kwame, 'every Ghanaian comes to the UK to make money and everyone knows that if you make mistakes the *abrofo* will punish you.'

'But it's different in Ghana?' prompted Tom.

'Yes, at home we keep out of other people's business because we don't want to be blamed if anything bad happens to them. If people knew that I had anything to do with the arrest of Mama Kate or Uncle George I would never be forgiven.'

'Then let's hope that it will not happen,' said Tom.

'What do you think has happened to Akos Mary?' asked Kwame. 'Do you think they've arrested her?'

'Maybe not,' replied Tom. 'They seem to be monitoring what is going on but leaving the little people alone for the time being.'

'Is that because they don't yet know who the big people are?'

'Either they don't know or they don't yet have enough evidence.'

'If we see Akos Mary back in Kumasi, should we warn her not to do another trip?'

'That's up to you, but she may be tied in too firmly now to refuse further cooperation.'

'Should I have told the customs officials about my suspicions concerning Oboroni?' asked Kwame.

'Ah yes, Crispin Russell, I've been wondering about that,' said Tom, 'but I feel that your imagination may have run wild there. I don't think they'd have believed you if you had mentioned it.'

At long last they were called to board their flight. They slid down the Greenwich Meridian to be met at Accra International Airport by Comfort, Akosua and Afriyie, who had passed an anxious and uncomfortable night awaiting their delayed arrival. After a day and night resting in Accra, Kwame left with his family for Konongo and, in a change of plan, Tom took Afriyie off to Elmina, near Cape Coast, for a week in a chalet on the beach under coconut palms. Memories of the interrogation at Heathrow quickly faded, not to be revived until the two friends met again in Kumasi.

'I've kept quiet so far,' said Kwame when they were alone together, 'but shouldn't I be warning my people not to travel again?'

'Afriyie won't be travelling again for some time and I don't think Akos Mary will be free to follow your advice,' said Tom. 'As for Bra Yaw, anything you say to him will only arouse suspicion.'

'I guess you're right,' said Kwame, 'but I feel that I should do something.'

'Concentrate your energy on the building project,' advised Tom with a broad grin.

'Yes,' said Kwame. 'You must come to see it. We've raised the walls up to window level.'

Kwame knew that nothing that was within his power would ever impress Comfort but she seemed reasonably content with the amount of money he brought with him for the purchase of concrete blocks. He was shocked to find how much the price had increased since the previous year, and he realised that he could not achieve all that he had planned, but the walls were rising steadily and it was some consolation to think that each block bought in 1987 was much cheaper than it would be in 1988.

Kwame had arranged to meet the GRID project director in Tema and Tom wanted to accompany him. So a few days before Tom was scheduled to return to London, the pair made their way back to Accra and along the motorway to Tema. They were warmly greeted by Dr Jones, the former TCC director who had moved to GRID in February when the project had received government approval. 'How's the link with Warwick coming on?' he asked Tom.

'The VC added a few expensive components to your original proposal,' laughed Tom, 'but with Kwame's advice we hope that we have now reached a viable compromise.'

'I hope it comes off,' said the director, 'because I want to budget a special fund to support the work of the TCC during the second phase of EC support for GRID.'

'You know the ITTUs in Suame and Tamale,' said the director to Kwame. 'Come and tell me what you think of the Tema ITTU.' He led the way across the yard from the office block to the main workshop building. Kwame remembered how it had been the year before and he knew that GRID had only taken over in February, six months before. Much work was still in progress, machines were being installed and a foundry was being established. A client was already at work in rented accommodation with machine tools producing steel bolts and nuts. Everything was cleaner and better ordered, staff and apprentices had been recruited and the place was full of activity.

'I can see that Ghana will soon have three ITTUs,' said Kwame. 'Where will the fourth one be?'

'In Dr Acquah's home town, Cape Coast,' replied the director.

Dr Jones explained how Dr Acquah had made available to GRID a batch of machine tools donated to Ghana by the government of India. He wanted them to form the basic complement of the equipment of an ITTU in Cape Coast to serve the Central Region. GRID was negotiating to purchase a suitable building with a grant from the EC. It was planned to open the Cape Coast ITTU in the second half of 1988.

'What's next?' asked Kwame enthusiastically.

'The next two ITTUs will be at Ho in the Volta Region and Sunyani in Brong-Ahafo Region,' replied the director, 'but we don't expect to open them until 1990. By that time you'll be back with us, won't you?'

'If you'll have me,' said Kwame with a broad smile.

Tom observed that the ITTU network would succeed if enough industrialists came for advice. It was important, therefore, that the project should be well known to the general public. 'What are you doing to publicise your services?' he asked.

'We have set up a Socio-economic and Communications Division,' replied the director, 'and the communications section is making a video film and will publish a quarterly newsletter and an annual review to let people know what we are doing and how we can help them. The video film, entitled *The Secret of Wealth*, will be finished by September and we hope to have it broadcast on national television.'

'*The Secret of Wealth*,' mused Tom. 'Where did that title come from?'

'It's from *The Hidden Words* of Mirza Husayn Ali,' said the director. 'The full quotation is: *Thus it is incumbent upon everyone to engage in crafts and professions for therein lies the secret of wealth, Oh men of understanding.*'

Kwame saw Tom off at the airport and returned to Kumasi in a cheerful mood. The GRID director had promised him a job when he returned in a year's time with his BSc degree, his house was rising slowly on the hillside at Old Ahensan and there was peace in his family. For the rest of the long vacation he felt that he could enjoy the companionship of his family and friends in reasonable expectation of having the resources in hand to cover the demands that would inevitably arise. He resolved to minimise the drain on his funds by not publicising his presence and not volunteering largesse. Even though he knew that he was fated to fail, the thought could not dampen his spirits.

15

Sleuthing

The one dark cloud on Kwame's horizon was what the customs officer had called the extra-mural activities of Peter Sarpong and his helpers in Coventry. He was determined to see as little as possible of anyone involved in those pursuits and to say nothing about what had happened to him at the airport. He couldn't avoid seeing Comfort's friends, Afriyie and Akos Mary, but he would limit his conversation to social pleasantries. He thought long and hard about what to tell Comfort and decided in the end to say nothing about recent developments. In this way he held the dark clouds at bay on the horizon while he enjoyed the sunshine of the here and now. The afternoon sun shone as brightly as ever and when Comfort was ready to put her questions she surprised Kwame by coming from a new personal perspective.

'So Akos Mary visited you twice in Coventry.'

'Yes,' said Kwame. 'She brought more *kenke* for Mama Kate and Bra Yaw.'

'Are you sure you're not having an affair with her?'

Kwame didn't know what to say. Guilty or not, he felt guilty and knew that he showed it. He also knew that a denial would be taken as confirmation unless pitched exactly at the right level of tone, sincerity and brevity. There were no human rights for men in marriage; one was always guilty until proved innocent, and where was the proof? He wondered how other husbands dealt with this situation.

'No, I'm not having an affair with Akos Mary,' he said at last, feeling his way like a man on a bush path in the dark, 'but I think that Tom might have sampled the goods.'

'So he's tried them both, has he?' laughed Comfort. 'Which one will he choose finally?'

'I'm sure that his first choice is still Afriyie,' said Kwame. 'They seem to have had a good time at Elmina.'

Then Comfort asked, 'When am I going to visit you in Coventry?'

Kwame groaned; it wasn't over yet. 'I don't want you carrying *kenke* to London,' he said in a feeble attempt to parry her question with a joke.

'Wasn't I the one who stopped you carrying the *kenke*? You don't want your wife there, seeing what you get up to.'

'I would be happy for you to come. It's just that the cost of the air ticket would mean so many less building blocks for our house.'

'Don't I have any say in how our money is spent?'

Kwame knew that he was in for one of those nights. It didn't happen every month but when it did, it wasn't Christmas.

Comfort was in a much better mood a week or two later when she asked one evening, 'Do you really think that Oboroni is involved with Mama Kate's *kenke* export business?'

'It was just an idea I had after Peter Sarpong spoke just like Oboroni used to do,' said Kwame. 'You know, calling people "old boy" and such like.'

'He used to call me "old gel" sometimes,' recalled Comfort. 'It used to upset me – a teenager called old! I once kept my legs closed for a whole week because of that.'

'That should have changed his style,' laughed Kwame, 'it would change mine!'

'What does Tom think about your idea?' Comfort asked.

'He thinks that it's my imagination run wild,' said Kwame. 'He says that many Englishmen speak like that and Peter might have picked it up from another person altogether.'

'But there is a link through Mama Kate,' said Comfort thoughtfully. 'Could you mimic what Peter said for me to judge?'

'What, a mimic of a mimic, how remote is that? It can't prove anything,' Kwame protested.

'Oh, do it just for me,' said Comfort. 'I might get a feeling about it.'

'Well, Peter said "Need to know, I'm afraid, old boy," and tapped the side of his nose like this.'

'Do it again, please,' said Comfort. 'Try harder to get it right.' Kwame tried several times, but all Comfort concluded was, 'It's not much like Oboroni used to speak. I was hoping to hear his voice again.'

Kwame didn't know if he should be angry because all Comfort wanted was to recall her lover's voice, or relieved because she seemed to have reached the end of her questions. He decided on the latter; anger consumed too much energy.

* * *

Apart from interludes such as these, Kwame passed several fairly contented weeks in Konongo and the time soon arrived for his return to the UK. Once again, Comfort and Akosua travelled with him to Accra to see him off at the airport. He slept soundly through the night to arrive at Heathrow at six in the morning. He was still walking in a dream drenched in tropical sunlight when the passport control officer woke him with a start by saying, 'Mr Kwame Mainu, you have some friends waiting to see you.'

Kwame was soon back in the familiar office with the same senior customs official and two assistants. This time, however, their manner was different: friendly and almost deferential. 'Mr Mainu, we need your help with the business we discussed on your outward journey. My name is Leon Thornet and these gentlemen are officers David Barney and Jack Preece.'

'I'm pleased to meet you,' mumbled Kwame.

'Mr Mainu, can we get you some coffee or tea, would you like some breakfast?'

'I had something on the plane,' said Kwame, 'but I would like a glass of water.'

Jack Preece departed and soon returned with Kwame's order. He drained the glass in his accustomed manner and sat looking glumly at his unwanted hosts.

Officer Thornet began by recalling their previous conversation. 'You were here with Dr Arthur of Warwick University back in July. Did you have a good vacation in Ghana?'

'Thank you, yes I did,' said Kwame.

'And you have now returned fresh and reinvigorated, I hope,' continued Leon Thornet, 'ready to face the challenges of a new academic year.'

'It's an important year for me,' said Kwame. 'I will take my final degree examinations next June.'

'We appreciate that you will be very busy, but we hope that you will be able to find a little time to help us in our enquiries.'

'That will depend on what you want me to do,' said Kwame cautiously. 'I do quite a lot of work besides my studying.'

'We appreciate that too, but what we are proposing could be rather more rewarding than teaching or bartending.'

'I will try to explain why this matter is so important to us,' said officer Thornet. 'You probably know that cannabis is widely grown and smoked in your country.'

'Yes, we call it *wee*,' said Kwame.

'Well,' continued Thornet, 'some of your people have always brought it with them to the UK, but in the 1960s the trade, if I can call it that, expanded rapidly, and the trend continued through the 1970s.'

Who does he mean by 'my people', thought Kwame to himself, but he decided to keep quiet.

Thornet went on ponderously, 'Cannabis smuggling is illegal, but it wasn't our major concern until in the early 1980s West African gangs began expanding their product range. The inflow from Ghana and Nigeria started to include cocaine from Venezuela and heroin from South-east Asia. This development seems to have come about through a combining of resources of West African cannabis smugglers with established access to European markets and Lebanese, Syrian and Armenian businessmen with contacts in Asia and South America. Your friends in Coventry constitute one branch of a widespread UK distribution network that seems to be supplied by a major cartel based in Kumasi. We have been monitoring their activities since Mr Aidoo left prison in 1985. Since then, he has been coming here regularly on false passports, often with various other young men and women.'

'Why are you telling me all this?' asked Kwame. 'If you know so much, why don't you just go and arrest them?'

'That's what we plan to do, but we need to get them all, including the ones at the top,' replied Thornet. 'We suspect that there is a coordinator who spends most of his time in Britain, and we need help to identify him and obtain the necessary evidence to arrest him.'

'How do you think I can help you?' asked Kwame, feeling that he liked the situation less and less the more he heard about it.

'We feel that the present situation grew out of something that happened in Kumasi between ten and twelve years ago,' continued Thornet, 'during what you call the "era of *kalabule*", a period of much innovation in black market and criminal activity. We need help from someone who was there at the time, knows some of the key people and is steeped in Ashanti culture.'

'We say *Asante*,' said Kwame quietly.

'That's exactly what I mean,' went on Thornet enthusiastically. 'We need someone like you, an educated Asante we can trust, who can communicate clearly to us what is going on in Kumasi and here among Ghanaians in the UK.'

'Surely you have all the help you need here,' said Kwame.

'Not exactly,' continued Thornet. 'We have a *Chancellor Manuscript* situation. You know the Robert Ludlum novel don't you?' Kwame nodded, and Thornet went on, 'The black American organisation communicated in Asante dialect to confuse those who might overhear them.'

'But you must have plenty of people who speak Twi,' protested Kwame.

'It's not that easy,' said Thornet. 'Even the FBI has difficulty in recruiting reliable Twi-speaking translators. In New York last year when they were after a Ghanaian drugs gang they had to scour the city to find the people they needed to help with their investigation. But it's more than that; the cartel doesn't use everyday Twi but language that's full of archaic expressions and literary allusions. That's why we need someone like you who grew up in that culture, someone who will recognise in an instant the meaning of an old proverb or a quotation from a spider story.'

'You've really done your homework!' exclaimed Kwame, genuinely impressed.

'That's what I'm paid to do,' replied Thornet, 'but I've gone as far as I can and now I need expert help.

'I've been very frank with you,' Thornet went on. 'Now I want you to be equally frank with me. What can you tell me about your contact with business people in Kumasi, including those who are now in Coventry?'

'If I help you, won't I be putting my family in danger?' said Kwame. 'My wife and daughter are in Konongo, fifty kilometres from Kumasi, and I won't do anything that would put them in harm's way.'

'I was coming to that later,' said Thornet. 'We would be willing to bring them to Coventry to stay with you, or accommodate them in a secure location elsewhere in the UK, whichever you prefer. We would also keep your name out of any official documents and endeavour to keep your involvement secret.'

Kwame hated having to make quick decisions but he was under considerable pressure to do so now. He had little sympathy for drugs smugglers and appreciated the misery they caused. He felt that his father, who greatly respected law and order, would certainly want him to cooperate with the *abrofo* authorities. On the other hand, many modern Ghanaians looked upon people like his father as aping an alien culture with an alien value system. It was every man's duty to accumulate wealth for his family, and that was what Peter Sarpong and Bra Yaw Aidoo were doing.

As he had told Tom, Kwame was quite prepared to let Peter and Bra Yaw serve a prison sentence in England. Bra Yaw had already been inside once and had described the experience as 'not too bad'. He was let out for good conduct after serving only half his sentence. Back home in

Ghana the experience was regarded as just bad luck. But the case of Mama Kate and Uncle George was quite different. These people were his elders. It would be a great disgrace for them to be imprisoned in Ghana and the treatment would be much harsher. Kwame knew that it would also disgrace him and his family if it was known that he had contributed to their misfortune.

'I can't wait all day,' prompted Thornet.

Kwame took a deep breath and decided to be frank. 'I will help you apprehend the people here in the UK but I would much prefer not to be involved in incriminating the people I know back in Kumasi.'

'We'll agree to that for the time being,' said Thornet. 'Please tell us what you know about the background in Kumasi, omitting names or using false names for the people you don't want to incriminate.' Kwame realised that this was nothing like a cast-iron guarantee but decided to go ahead without mentioning real names.

He began by describing his market trolley business in Kumasi and how he had met a big businessman who needed large numbers of trolleys. He also related how his wife was a trader who sold shoes and collected her supplies from a market queen who imported the shoes into Ghana from the UK and other European countries. When he was coming to Britain for the first time, this market queen had given him money and sent Bra Yaw to ask him to carry a parcel of *kenke* to London. He had refused when his wife advised him that the parcel might contain *wee*.

On recent visits to Kumasi, Kwame and his wife had observed that both Peter Sarpong and Bra Yaw were building big houses and they wondered where the money was coming from. They realised that the businessman with the trolleys and the market queen were working together and that the businessman was related to Peter Sarpong. This was what Kwame knew for certain. He also suspected that Lebanese and Syrian businessmen based in Kumasi were in league with the Ghanaians but he had no direct knowledge of this.

'Do you know any Englishmen who might have been involved?' asked Thornet.

'I knew one man whom we used to call Oboroni,' said Kwame. 'He worked for a Lebanese-owned company called Hanabis and was well connected to the Arab community in Kumasi. He also knew one of the market queens.'

'Do you think that he might have brought the two groups together?' asked Thornet.

'That thought has crossed my mind,' said Kwame, and he went on to relate how the suspicion had arisen from a chance remark by Peter Sarpong.

'That's hardly firm grounds for suspicion,' said Thornet, 'but criminals do sometimes give themselves away by such small slips. Your man was certainly in the right place at the right time with the right connections. Do you know his real name?'

'He was known by the name Crispin Russell,' said Kwame.

'Did he speak Asante?' asked Thornet.

'I never heard him use the language, apart from a few simple greetings,' replied Kwame.

'This is how we think that you can help us.' It was Jack Preece who was speaking. 'Peter Sarpong seems to be the local coordinator in Coventry and there are others like him in Norwich, Oxford, Swansea and other such provincial cities. They get their instructions from someone who moves around the country, never seeming to stay in one locality for more than two or three days. He always sends instructions by telephone from a pay phone booth and all communications are in what we might call classical Asante.'

'So you want me to listen to these telephone conversations, do you?' asked Kwame.

'That's about it,' said Jack Preece. 'We monitor all Peter's calls, and those of the other local coordinators, and we have recordings of most of them for the past twelve months. In addition to helping us with translation we are hoping that you might recognise some of the voices.'

Although at first Kwame had been reluctant to get involved, he couldn't help being interested in the task that was proposed for him. It shouldn't be too difficult to understand what was being said and uncovering secrets was always fascinating. His first task was to write to Comfort inviting her to come to Coventry with Akosua. This would seem to be a perfectly natural thing to do, especially as Comfort had recently asked to visit him. His new paymasters would buy the air tickets and arrange for visas to be issued at the British High Commission in Accra. Comfort and Akosua would spend a week or two with Kwame in Coventry and then, if Kwame preferred, they would move to a secret and secure residence until the operation was completed. A school would be arranged for Akosua, now seven, and if Comfort wanted to work she would be helped to find a suitable job. Kwame would not be asked to make any move until he was sure that his family was safe.

* * *

While all the preliminary arrangements were slowly progressing, Kwame resumed his regular schedule of activities. He was now forced to spend more time on his studies but this allowed him to cut back gradually on his working commitments in anticipation of a further reduction when his investigative duties began. It was expected that his work at the foundry and ladies' club would not stop altogether, as such a complete change in his regular schedule might excite suspicion.

Kwame prepared for his new assignment by revising his knowledge of Asante folklore. He had a book of Twi proverbs collected by Peggy Appiah, the daughter of Sir Stafford Cripps and wife of Joe Appiah, an opposition politician of the Nkrumah era. This well-known work included more than a thousand proverbs with explanations in both modern Twi and English. To remind himself of the spider stories, or *anansesem*, Kwame had to rely on Rattray's *Ashanti Folktales* and a few Twi texts that he had brought with him from Ghana. He realised that he had been fortunate to have taken African Studies at university in Kumasi and to have developed the appetite to stock his personal library with published and unpublished material collected from the College of Art and National Cultural Centre. These provided invaluable information on Ashanti gold weights, *Kente* cloth patterns and *Adinkra* cloth printing symbols, including charts with diagrams and interpretations of archaic texts.

A month into the autumn term, David Barney arrived at Kwame's lodgings in an unmarked car to take Kwame to the airport to meet his wife and daughter. 'Look upon me as driver and security guard,' he joked. Kwame was impressed with the arrangements that were both efficient and inconspicuous. Comfort and Akosua were excited to be in *aburokyiri* and Akosua kept up a constant stream of comments and questions all the way from Heathrow to Coventry. On arrival, a delighted Mrs Chichester remarked that Kwame had brought some life to the house at last. For Kwame, the euphoric mood was short lived, however. That afternoon, Peter Sarpong called to welcome the new Kumasi arrivals to Coventry.

When Kwame recovered from his initial shock he recalled that Peter regarded himself as the head of the Ghanaian diaspora in Coventry. He must have heard of Comfort's visit from Akos Mary and felt that it was his duty to welcome new members of the community. At the same time he could signal to Kwame that he knew that his family was no longer in Konongo but they were still within reach of the cartel. When he had taken time to reflect on the situation, Kwame was able to convince himself that Peter could have no knowledge of his family's next destination. However, he realised that there would be only a few weeks' grace before it became known that Kwame's family was not in Coventry. It would be good if he could finish his task within that time frame.

Less than a week after Comfort and Akosua had moved on, Kwame began listening to tape recordings of the cartel's communications. The messages were mostly brief and coded. Listening first to Peter Sarpong's tapes, Kwame quickly identified Bra Yaw as 'the one who fears the worm' from the proverb 'the one bitten by a snake fears a worm', presumably because of his earlier arrest and imprisonment. Peter Sarpong was often referred to as '*osofo*' or priest, perhaps because his namesake was Bishop of Kumasi. A deal or a demand for payment was often referred to as 'a blow on the eye' from the proverb 'Blow on my eye for me, that's why two antelopes walk together.' Kwame reflected that an English equivalent might be 'You scratch my back and I'll scratch yours.'

As he listened to more and more of the tapes, Kwame found it easier to interpret them. He admired the way the language was abbreviated and rearranged to convey messages that were hidden in a literal translation. To understand it the listener needed a complete vocabulary, a good grounding in the traditional literature of Ashanti and familiarity with current affairs in Kumasi. Even the riddles of the talking drums (which ask the question, which is the older: the stream or the path that crosses it?) played a part, with the 'stream' referring to the original cannabis trade and the 'path' referring to the more recent traffic in hard drugs.

Most of the recordings related to past operations and did not yield much that was of interest to the customs officials or police. Kwame searched in vain for anything that might identify the principals or refer to future operations. Apart from Peter Sarpong and Bra Yaw he recognised none of the voices. Most of the talking was done by the coordinator, who was clearly giving instructions. He felt that he must be missing something but he couldn't figure out what. There was nothing on the recordings in English and no Twi spoken with an English accent. If an Englishman was speaking Twi he was totally fluent in the language. When Kwame received a telephone call from David Barney he was feeling guilty that he was doing little to justify his much inflated income. To his great relief, the call was not about the recordings but a summons to a clandestine meeting to discuss an interesting development.

'The police have traced a Crispin Russell that could be your old friend,' announced David, 'He was born at Lewes, East Sussex, on 21 May 1930. After attending a minor public school and Sandhurst he joined a guards regiment in 1949 and served in Korea in 1951. He was dishonourably discharged in 1953.'

'What caused his discharge?' asked Kwame.

'It's not clear at the moment but we should be able to find out from the regimental records. Anyway, he managed to get a job with a British firm of importers and exporters and was appointed West Africa Manager in 1960 with an office in Accra. He left that post in 1967 to become General Manager of Hanabis Co. Ghana Ltd. and became a partner in 1972. I think you know that company.'

'Yes,' said Kwame. 'It's a well-known Lebanese company based in Kumasi. Oboroni was working there when I first met him.'

'So it seems very likely that we have the right man,' said David Barney. 'He left Ghana in 1979, is that right?'

'Yes,' said Kwame. 'He made a quick getaway after Rawlings staged his first coup on 4 June. Do you know where he is now?'

'He bought a house in Oxfordshire in 1970,' replied David. 'There's no record of the house being resold but the present occupant is listed as Charles Richards. We don't know if that's just another name for Crispin Russell or the name of a tenant.'

'How do we find out?' asked Kwame.

'We want you to give him a buzz,' said David.

'But how can I say I got his number?' pleaded Kwame. 'He left Kumasi without leaving any contact details.'

'Isn't there any friend who might have given you the number?'

'No, and I suspect that it was quite intentional on his part not to let anyone know where he could be contacted.'

'Then can we play it another way; couldn't you pretend to be one of his associates?'

'But the cartel members all communicate in Twi, and the Oboroni I knew only spoke in English.'

'So if he replies in fluent Twi we know we have the right man.'

'That's assuming we know who's picked up the telephone. It could be one of his cartel members or any other Ghanaian or even a Lebanese who was born and raised in Ghana. Many of our people have English names and Charles Richards might be an old friend or business associate from Ghana to whom Oboroni has let his house.'

Kwame was surprised that the official couldn't come up with a better plan. He felt very uncomfortable being pushed into deciding the next move. Even if Charles Richards was Oboroni and involved in the cartel, was it likely that he would be at home to answer the telephone? Didn't the coordinator move about the country contacting his people from pay phones in public call boxes? If Oboroni was the coordinator it was unlikely that he spent much time at home. Kwame wished that he could discuss the matter with Comfort. He always felt that way where Oboroni was concerned. He was sure that Comfort would know how best to approach him now, but he neither wanted to jeopardise her safety nor do anything to reveal her former relationship.

David Barney roused Kwame from his brooding by saying, 'I guess we'd better ask the police to watch the house and try to photograph the occupant. Then we can ask you to identify him.' Kwame relaxed, his immediate burden was reduced to looking at a photograph and he couldn't see much risk in that.

'I'm sure that's the best plan,' he said, trying to keep the relief from his voice. 'I'll soon know if it's Oboroni when you show me the photograph.'

Kwame returned to his studies. It was more important than ever that he worked hard now that the end was in sight but that afternoon he was conscious of a shadow on his mind and he knew that he would have to take time to reflect upon his latest meeting with his new paymasters. So he left the laboratory early and hurried back to his room.

Why had David Barney put him in the position of suggesting their next move? Was it some sort of test? If so, how did he feel he had acquitted himself? Well, he had shown that he had some reasoning ability, that he was reasonably intelligent. He could put that on the 'strengths' side of his SWOT analysis; but what of his 'weaknesses'? Kwame feared that he had shown again his reluctance to make a quick decision on the basis of what he thought was incomplete data. How he envied Comfort her power of intuition and decisive mind! He also realised that he had revealed his basic timidity. Had he done well enough to retain his lucrative employment or had he disappointed his bosses?

Pursuing the SWOT path he came to 'opportunities'. His continuing involvement with the investigation had removed his financial worries and boosted his house-building project in Kumasi. This improved his relationship with Comfort, as did her opportunity to visit Britain. The opportunities were tangible but it was the 'threats' that concerned him most. Firstly, there was the immediate threat of the cartel discovering his involvement in the investigation. Secondly, there followed the possibility of Comfort and Akosua's hiding place being uncovered. Thirdly, if the cartel was broken up, what would happen to its members in Ghana? If they remained free they were likely to be a direct threat, and if they were imprisoned it could disgrace him in the eyes of his home community. It was difficult to see a satisfactory outcome either way.

Kwame had been forced to reduce his workload at the ladies' club and so he was free that evening. He had been asked to spend more time at the West Africa club, so that was where he headed after dinner. To his dismay Akos Mary was there, but he scarcely had time to greet her before she was swept away by an eager bunch of would-be suitors. As she disappeared into the throng her smile lingered on in his mind like the smile of the Cheshire cat. It was a triumphant smile that Kwame was given no time to decipher.

'Bees around the honey pot,' remarked Peter Sarpong as he joined Kwame at the bar. 'We're running a lottery on guessing the winner.'

'Who do you think will win?' asked Kwame, as soon as the usual greeting ritual was over.

'None of the guys here,' said Peter, 'I think her aspirations are richer and paler.'

'How do you mean?'

'Isn't she interested in your friend Dr Tom Arthur? His parents aren't short of a bob or two, as they say here.'

'No, but it will be some time before he inherits the cocoa farm and Akos is an impatient young lady.'

'Speaking of impatient young ladies, how's Comfort? I've not seen her around lately.'

'She's gone off on a sight-seeing tour with Akosua, but as far as I know they're both fine. Is Bra Yaw around?' asked Kwame.

'Not this time, the beauty queen made it all the way on her own. She's becoming quite the seasoned globe trotter.'

Kwame wondered why he had been given this information. Was Peter signalling that Akos Mary was now a trusted associate, a free agent who made her own travel arrangements? Did Bra Yaw stay behind because of suspicion that his movements were being monitored? As if in answer to this unspoken question, Peter added, 'Bra Yaw lost his uncle in Mampong and had to rush there for the funeral.'

'How's your Uncle George?'

'Oh, he's fine, still buying trolleys by the hundred. It'll be a long time before we put him in the freezer.'

A week or two later Kwame had another telephone call. This time it was Jack Preece telling him to expect to see him on his next visit to the foundry school. Fred Brown was on leave and Kwame had the use of his office so that was where he was shown the photograph. 'Yes that's Oboroni, I mean Crispin Russell,' said Kwame. 'He's put on weight and lost some hair but it's him all right.'

'Nowadays, he calls himself Charles Richards,' said Jack, 'and the fact that he's changed his name is suspicious in itself.'

'Yes, but it doesn't prove that he has any connection with the drugs cartel, does it?' groaned Kwami, fearing that whatever came next he would have a part to play.

'For us, it's a big step forward,' said Jack. 'Now we have a firm suspect and we can begin tracking his movements and monitoring his telephone calls. We know when Peter Sarpong and the other local bosses are receiving calls and if Richards is on a pay phone at those times it is likely that he is the coordinator.'

'But all the calls are in Twi and I never heard him speak Twi before he left Ghana in 1979,' protested Kwame.

'That was eight years ago; one can learn a lot in eight years,' replied Jack. Kwame was still doubtful but said nothing.

The next few weeks passed quietly by with Kwame immersed in his studies when he wasn't at the foundry school or the ladies' club. He was surprised that there were no more recordings to translate and no calls to action in respect of Oboroni. Comfort telephoned most days on what they were assured was a secure line and Kwame felt confident that his two girls were safe and well in their new life. Christmas was approaching and he looked forward to a family celebration. He knew that Akosua would be delighted with her first experience of an English Christmas. Maybe she and Comfort would see snow for the first time.

In this pleasantly settled state of mind, Kwame was reminded of the investigation only when he perused his bank statements. He hoped that even Comfort could not fail to be impressed by the balance that was accumulating and resolved to reveal all at their Christmas gathering. He was sorry that with Comfort in the UK his house in Kumasi was at a standstill, but he was excited at the speed of progress that would be possible as soon as they were back in Ghana. It seemed that there were ways to make a fortune out of drugs smuggling without running the risk of imprisonment. He was glad that he had resisted the temptation to join Peter Sarpong on the wrong side of the law.

The thought of Peter Sarpong reminded Kwame that he would soon be questioned on the whereabouts of his family. He decided to hint that he was going to spend Christmas in Ghana as Peter always did. He realised that Peter would soon find out that he was not there but the ploy should keep him in ignorance over the holiday period. When the end of term finally arrived, Kwame took a bus to the central coach station where David Barney was waiting with a car to drive him to Comfort and Akosua's secure hideaway.

16

The Okyeame

Kwame couldn't resist asking how the surveillance of Charles Richards was going. 'So far we've drawn a blank, I'm afraid,' said David. 'We've monitored several calls but we've not been able to connect him with any of them. He's been in the house when most of the calls were made. A few times he was out and about but nowhere near a telephone. However, we have noticed that he has several black friends who call on him quite frequently. That's the only possible connection that we have to the cartel.'

'Have you tried to correlate the visits with the telephone calls?' asked Kwame, 'He might be giving instructions for the calls to be made. That could explain how all the calls are made in classical Twi. Oboroni might have his own *okyeame*.'

'What's an *okyeame*?' asked David.

'It's usually translated as linguist,' said Kwame, 'but it's more than that. In Ghana, every chief has an *okyeame* through whom he speaks to visitors. The *okyeame* translates if the visitor doesn't speak Twi, but even if he does, the *okyeame* will repeat what the chief has said. The *okyeame* is the preserver and guardian of the traditional language and its culture. He knows all the proverbs and *anansesem*. In fact an *okyeame* would be the perfect person to speak all those messages you have been intercepting.'

'Then we must start trailing Richards' visitors,' said David, thinking aloud. 'Can you suggest what sort of person we should be looking for?'

'Well, he would have to be a Ghanaian,' replied Kwame, 'and not too young; an *okyeame* takes years to develop.'

'Are we sure we are looking for a man?' David asked cautiously. 'Could it be a woman?'

'I don't think any of the voices I've listened to were female and an *okyeame* is traditionally a man,' said Kwame, 'but we can never be one hundred per cent sure.'

'So basically we're looking for an older black man,' said David.

'Yes, and if you can check further, he should be a Ghanaian who has not been too long in this country.' Anticipating David's next question, Kwame continued, 'He must have spent most of his life in Ghana absorbing the culture and not too much time here forgetting it.'

Kwame had imagined that Comfort and Akosua's hideaway was in a secluded part of the countryside and he was surprised that David Barney drove into a large town and stopped outside a terraced house on a side road just off a busy shopping street. When Kwame expressed his surprise, David told him that the best place to hide was in a crowd. Kwame noticed that many of the nearby houses had BMWs and Mercedes Benz parked outside. To him that suggested Comfort and Akosua were not the only black people living in the road. They knocked on the door and were warmly welcomed by Comfort.

'Akos is still at school,' she said, 'but she finishes today at midday so we can go to meet her together; that will make her happy.'

After a quick cup of tea and a chocolate muffin David Barney took his leave to start the trailing of Oboroni's visitors. Kwame turned to embrace Comfort but she pushed him away. 'Don't think that you can wipe your mouth and continue as if nothing has happened,' she said.

'What do you mean?' blurted Kwame, fearing that the festive season might be frosty even if it didn't snow.

'You bring me to *aburokyiri* then lock me away in this bush house and you think I don't know why?'

'It's because you and Akosua could be in danger in Coventry. I explained everything to you before you came here.'

'What about the real reason? I know Akos Mary came there to see you.'

'How do you know that?' exclaimed Kwame in surprise, fearing that the cartel might have discovered the hideaway.

'Don't think that you can do just what you like behind my back,' persisted Comfort, interpreting Kwame's concern as a sure sign of guilt.

'She did come to Coventry but I only saw her once, at the West Africa club. Peter was there and she had plenty of other male companions. She didn't need me.'

Kwame wanted to find out how Comfort knew that Akos Mary had come to Coventry but he couldn't think of a way to broach the subject without restarting the row. If the information had come from a member of the cartel it would be necessary to ask for his family to be relocated. Just in case this move might become necessary he decided to telephone David Barney on the secure line while Comfort was out with Akosua on a shopping trip. As soon as he heard Kwame's anxious voice and got the gist of what he was saying, David began a profuse apology. 'I'm terribly sorry, Kwame,' he said. 'We intercepted a letter addressed to Mrs Mainu at your Coventry address and sent it on to her. You should have been informed and I will find out why the correct procedure was not followed.'

Kwame was relieved, but he felt compelled to protest about his family's mail being intercepted. 'The letter came from Ghana from a Miss Akos Mary Konadu,' said David, 'and a clerk identified the name as a member of the cartel. It was held back for further scrutiny by a senior officer before it was realised that it was a purely personal letter and passed on to Mrs Mainu.'

Akos Mary must have told Comfort that she was coming to Coventry, thought Kwame, but he said only: 'Please let me know if you redirect any other mail in this way.'

'We will; that's a promise.'

Kwame realised that the redirected letter had ruined his holiday. He wondered what exactly Akos Mary had written. Did she hint that she was having an affair with him or was it Comfort's intuition run wild? He knew that he was in for a rough time but as Comfort had prepared to give Akosua her best Christmas ever he resigned himself to being cheerful for his daughter's sake. So the little girl, now approaching her eighth birthday, collected presents from her first real Christmas tree and made repeated dashes to the window to see if snow was falling. Unfortunately, the only snow she saw was on television, but Kwame told her that she might still see the real thing in January or February. On New Year's Eve they ventured out in the cold to watch a spectacular firework display and as the New Year dawned Kwame rejoiced that 1988 would be the year of his graduation. Akosua told everyone that this year she would be eight.

Kwame tried to impress Comfort by showing her his most recent bank statement but she only complained that the money was useless as long as she had to remain in the UK.

'When can I go back and get on with my trading as well as the building?'

'As soon as they arrest the drugs cartel.'

'And when is that likely to be?'

'As soon as they identify the coordinator.'

'Is that what they call Oboroni? Are you still trying to tie him into the plot?'

'It's proving to be more difficult than we thought,' said Kwame, realising that he shouldn't reveal too much about the investigation even though he felt Comfort might be able to help.

When the end of the holiday came it was almost with relief that Kwame returned to Coventry. During his last two long vacations in Ghana he had thought that he had made some progress in understanding Comfort and satisfying her needs but his recent experience had proved that there was little improvement in their relationship. He had made the best of the holiday for Akosua's sake but otherwise for him it had been a desert without oases. Kwame couldn't take seriously the accusation that he was having an affair with Akos Mary. He felt sure that Comfort was using this as a pretext for her discontent and that her real problem lay at a deeper level. The ghost of his mother's abrupt departure returned to haunt him.

In the car on the way back to Coventry Kwame asked Jack Preece if there was any progress to report on the trailing of Charles Richards' visitors. 'We've trailed all his black visitors but none of them was reported using the telephone at the time of the coded messages,' said Jack. 'Some of our people are beginning to think that your link to Crispin Russell is too tenuous and that we are wasting resources.'

'But the fact that Charles Richards has a number of African friends must reinforce the possibility of a link,' protested Kwame.

'Oh, don't worry, we're not stopping just yet, you've convinced Leon, David and me. We intend to keep going.'

The next few weeks provided Kwame with an opportunity to study seriously and make good progress with his honours project. When Tom came into the laboratory one afternoon he told Kwame that several lecturers had commented favourably on his progress. They were particularly impressed that Kwame spent much time in the mechanical workshop making his own test apparatus. 'I learned to handle all the machine tools in the Suame ITTU workshop,' said Kwame proudly. 'Our director used to send all graduate engineers into the workshop for a year to learn practical skills with the craft apprentices. It came as quite a shock to some of them.'

'Well, it's standing you in good stead now,' said Tom. 'We appreciate engineers who are not afraid to dirty their hands.'

It had been several weeks since the two friends had had a long conversation and so they agreed to meet that evening in more relaxed surroundings. Tom suggested his flat, adding that he still had two bottles of Star beer that he had brought back from Kumasi the previous summer. Kwame had planned to start an assignment on heat transfer in cupola furnaces but the lure of the hometown brew was irresistible.

'Are you still helping the sleuths?' asked Tom, once Kwame was settled, glass in hand. Kwame took a long pull on the beer and was transported three thousand miles to the south and the sunshine. Tom knew where he had gone and followed him willingly, until at length he was ready to reply.

'I've done what I can for the sleuths, as you call them, but it doesn't seem to have helped very much.'

'So your Oboroni is not involved after all.'

'If he is, he's covered his trail very well. It's proving very difficult to connect him with Peter's activities.'

Kwame wondered how much he should tell his friend. He had not been told specifically not to talk to Tom, and Tom had been interviewed with him at his first meeting with the customs officials. He needed someone to confide in, so he decided to tell Tom more about what was going on. He related how Oboroni, alias Crispin Russell, was now thought to be using the name Charles Richards and living in Oxfordshire in a house that Crispin Russell had bought while he was still in Ghana. Charles Richards had been under observation for several weeks but could not have made any of the telephone calls that gave coded instructions in archaic Twi to Peter Sarpong and the other local bosses. However, he did have a number of regular African visitors and Kwame had suspected that one or more of them might be acting as Richards' *okyeame* or linguist.

'Yes,' said Tom. 'That would explain the fluent Twi, wouldn't it?'

'That's true, but so far they've not been able to link any of the visitors to the coded messages.'

'So there's not much for you to do these days,' said Tom. 'That's why you're putting in so many hours on your project.'

'Well, that needs to be done as well, or your lot will fail me in June.'

'There's not much doubt about you passing, my friend, only speculation about just how high you will pass. Maybe I shouldn't be telling you this, but the professor and most of the lecturers are very impressed with your work. Have you considered going on for a research degree?'

'I'm more or less committed to going back to work at GRID but it's an interesting possibility for the future if I can manage to get at least an upper second.'

After talking to Tom, Kwame was encouraged to redouble his efforts. He realised that at any time the investigation might demand more of his time and he wanted to be well ahead with his studies when that happened. Regular payments were still being made into his bank account, and he didn't need to increase his hours of working, so he had more time than he had ever had for his coursework and revision.

Kwame wondered if he should pay more visits to the West Africa club. He wanted to stay in contact with his countrymen but he was shy of Peter Sarpong asking about Comfort and Akosua. Peter must know by now that Kwame had not gone home for Christmas and answering his questions could be embarrassing. Kwame was not a natural liar and knew that he would be unconvincing when forced to tell an untruth. Nevertheless, he felt that it was his duty to call at the club. When he had summoned up sufficient courage he entered hesitantly, peering around to see if he could spot Peter before Peter spotted him. To his relief Peter was not there, and it was Bra Yaw and a group of his cronies who were propping up the bar.

'Here's someone who can tell us,' called Bra Yaw as Kwame approached.

Kwame shook each hand in turn moving from right to left. When he had completed the ritual he said, 'What can I tell you?'

'We've been arguing about the motto of Kumasi University,' said Bra Yaw. 'How would you say it in English?'

'Well, strictly it says that the knot of wisdom can be undone by a wise man,' said Kwame, 'but something like "it takes a wise man to solve a riddle" might convey the true meaning more appropriately.'

'There you are,' said one young man who had been introduced as Kofi Boateng. 'I told you that *nyansapo* was a riddle.'

'I still think that the wisdom knot is more than a riddle,' protested Bra Yaw. 'It's more like the secret of life.'

'You could be right,' said Kwame.

Kwame asked after Peter Sarpong and was told that he was well but couldn't come to the club that evening because he had business elsewhere. 'Peter said that if I saw you I should ask why you didn't go to Kumasi over Christmas as you said you would,' said Bra Yaw.

'Comfort and Akosua decided they wanted to stay here and experience an English Christmas,' said Kwame, 'so I had to stay here with them.'

'We didn't see you here in Coventry,' prompted Bra Yaw, dutifully following his instruction.

'No,' said Kwame, 'we travelled outside.'

'Have they gone back to Ghana yet?'

228

'They soon will,' said Kwame, trying to give nothing away but to say enough to stem the flow of awkward questions without giving offence.

He decided to counter attack. 'Did you come with Akos Mary this time?'

'No, she travels independently these days.'

'I heard she was here last week.'

'That's right, you just missed her.'

'What's the attraction? Does she have a new boyfriend here?'

'You know Akos Mary, She's never short of admirers.'

Kwame felt that he must call it a draw and move on. He drifted over to where Kofi Boateng was standing, glass in hand. 'It's not like the Star we get back home,' he said.

'I'm a Club man, but I know what you mean.'

'Will you soon be back on the Club?'

'Yes, this is a short visit.'

'Your first to *aburokyiri*?'

'That's right.'

'How do you like it?'

'I wish it was warmer.'

'Will you come again?'

'If I get the chance.'

Kwame realised that the new boys had been well briefed and he was unlikely to gather much information from idle chatter.

The term passed swiftly and the Easter vacation was approaching before he was contacted again by his paymasters. He was called into the foundry school office where Jack Preece was waiting with Fred Brown, who departed with a wink, closing the door softly behind him.

'Have you heard from your wife and daughter?'

'Yes, thank you, they ring almost every day.'

'Are they happy?'

'They would like to return home.'

'We are doing our best to make that possible.'

'What can I do for you now?'

'We want you to look at some photographs.' Jack Preece produced a large album from his briefcase and passed it across Fred Brown's cluttered desk to Kwame. 'These are all photographs taken of Charles Richards' visitors,' he said. 'Leon is hoping that you might be able to identify one or two of them.'

'I'll do my best,' said Kwame.

Most of the photographs seemed to have been taken outside Oboroni's house as people came and went. Some were arriving or departing on foot and others were seen getting in or out of vehicles. The photographs were obviously taken at long range with a telephoto lens but most were of good quality and facial features could be clearly seen. If Kwame knew any of the people, he felt that he would be able to recognise them.

'That's definitely Oboroni,' said Kwame, 'and I guess that's his car. He always travelled in a Mercedes Benz.'

'It's good to get a further positive identification of Crispin Russell, alias Charles Richards,' said Jack. 'We've found that he doesn't go out very often. In fact, he only went out twice during the four weeks period of the surveillance. Our man was told to photograph every coming and going but he only appears in four photographs. We're certain that he's your Oboroni but it's his visitors that we want to identify.'

Kwame turned his attention to the other photographs and slowly worked through the album from cover to cover. This was not a boring flip through a friend's holiday snaps but a serious professional undertaking for which he was being well paid. Jack Preece waited patiently, scanning Kwame's face for a hint of recognition. However, after looking at all the photographs carefully and repeatedly Kwame was forced to declare that he was unable to recognise any person, black or white, from among Charles Richards' numerous visitors. 'All I can suggest is that we let Comfort look at them,' said Kwame. 'She may recognise someone I don't know.'

Kwame gave Jack Preece a note to be sent to Comfort warning her of their intended visit at the weekend, and at noon on Saturday, after a morning session in the laboratory, Kwame met Jack for a repeat of the Christmas mystery tour. They arrived in time for the evening meal that Comfort had prepared for them. It was Jack's first chance to try fufu and groundnut soup. 'I hope you like it,' said Comfort anxiously. 'Not all *abrofo* like fufu.'

'I'll try anything when I'm hungry,' replied Jack gallantly.

Jack waited until Akosua had gone to bed before extracting the photograph album from his briefcase. He left it to Kwame to introduce the matter. 'Jack's people have been taking photographs of Oboroni's visitors and we wondered if you could recognise any of them.'

'Why should I do that?'

'Well, they want to know if he's linked to the drugs cartel.'

'You know Peter Sarpong and Bra Yaw as well as I do.'

'Yes, but he may be using others to communicate with them.'

'Other Ghanaians?'

'Ghanaians or *abrofo*, but it's the Ghanaians that you might be able to identify.'

'All right, I'll look at the photographs.'

Kwame breathed a sigh of relief as his wife pushed aside the shoe catalogues to make room on the coffee table for the bulky photograph album.

Comfort flicked quickly through the album and passed it back to Jack. 'No, there's nobody there that I recognise,' she said.

'Please take a more careful look,' pleaded Jack. 'We spent four weeks taking these photographs.'

With obvious reluctance, Comfort took back the album and went through more slowly, this time taking care to turn each page.

Kwame and Jack watched and waited. Comfort paused once or twice and Kwame noticed that each time it was a photograph of Oboroni that had caught her eye. 'You recognise Oboroni, don't you?' he prompted.

'Yes, but that's all,' she replied and handed the album back once more.

In spite of his professional training, Jack Preece could not hide his disappointment. His people had invested a good deal of time and effort in trying to identify Charles Richards' links to the drugs cartel but still they seemed to have drawn a blank.

As he left for his hotel late in the evening Kwame walked with him to his car. He wanted to try to lift Jack's spirits but not by clutching at straws. 'I'd like to take another long look at the photographs back in Coventry,' he said. Jack made a brave attempt at a smile and said that he would be there in the morning to take Kwame back to Coventry.

'Are you sure you recognised only Oboroni?' Kwame asked Comfort when he returned to the house.

'What about you? Did you recognise anybody else?'

'I'm afraid I couldn't recognise anybody except Oboroni.'

'Well, I'm the same.'

'But you knew Oboroni better than I did and you must have met more of his friends.'

'Is that what you told the *abrofo*?'

'No, of course not, but it's true isn't it?'

'Do you tell me everything about your girlfriends?'

Kwame realised that the long cold winter had not yet run its course so he decided that the day was done. He mounted the stairs with a weary tread, pulling a toothbrush from his pocket and wondering why he still bothered to paste his teeth.

On the long journey back to Coventry Kwame was lost in thought for most of the way. Something told him that Comfort had recognised someone in the photographs. Just possibly it was someone he had also met if only he could sharpen his memory. He was determined to make a further effort. At length he asked Jack Preece, 'Could I hold on to the album for a few days to study the photographs in my room?'

'I would have to get clearance from higher up, and for that I would need to give some justification,' replied Jack Preece thoughtfully. 'Why do you want to take another look?'

'I've a feeling that if I took a close look, without the pressure of someone watching and waiting, I might recognise someone I dimly remember from long ago,' said Kwame.

Back in Coventry Jack Preece made a telephone call and came back to tell Kwame that he could keep the album for three days. Kwame carried it back to his room and placed it under a bright reading lamp on the small table that served as his desk. Then he searched around for a magnifying glass that he used occasionally in his studies and drew his chair close to the table. He peered at each photograph in renewed determination to untie the *nyansapo,* the knot of wisdom. Why was that motto of Kumasi University repeating itself over and over in his head? It needed a wise man. Was he wise enough?

Kwame searched through the album from end to end looking for a clue that might remind him of some long-forgotten acquaintance. People change as they grow older, they change their hairstyles, grow beards and shave off moustaches; their hair changes to grey or white or falls out to leave a TV or a motorway. Some people suffer scarring accidents or debilitating illnesses. Some people even adopt a disguise. There are a hundred ways in which appearances can change; had he considered them all? Although he scrutinised and pondered late into the evening, Kwame seemed to be no nearer a solution than he had been in Fred Brown's office a few days earlier.

Comfort had lingered over the photographs of Oboroni. At the time Kwame had put this down to reminiscing about her old boyfriend. Now he wasn't so sure. He looked at these pictures again. There were four of them, showing Oboroni going and coming on the two outings mentioned by Jack Preece. But Comfort had not lingered over all of them, only two. Kwame noticed that in both of these photographs Oboroni was standing near his car. Was there someone else in the car? It was difficult to tell because of the light reflected on the windscreen. He peered even more intently at the indistinct image blurred and distorted

232

by the reflection. There seemed to be a person sitting in the driving seat.

Oboroni had always employed a driver in Ghana so maybe he had grown used to the convenience and also employed one in England. Kwame looked again at the photograph, peering through the magnifying glass. Yes, there was definitely a face behind the windscreen but he couldn't say if it was a white face or a black one shining in the reflected light. Was he imagining things? Was Comfort only enjoying the pictures because they were especially good likenesses of Oboroni? Or was she admiring his car and wishing she still had the comfort and status of moving wherever she wished in such luxury?

The hour was late and Kwame decided to move over to his bed and let go. He slept soundly for several hours but part of his mind never ceased its search for a solution. He was sitting under a neem tree at Suame Magazine and a Mercedes Benz saloon swept almost noiselessly off the Techiman road and onto his plot to park in front of the long neat row of market trolleys. He heard again the sweet tones of a youthful Comfort asking, 'Hey Kwame, what are you doing here?' Then fast forward to the same sweet voice saying, 'I'll pay for the trolley now and send Kofi around in the morning to pick it up.'

Kwame sat up in bed with a start, his eyes wide open but still dazzled by the bright sunlight of Ashanti, 'Kofi Adjare,' he thought, 'that explains everything!' He had not only untied the knot of wisdom, he had found the wise man!

He leapt out of bed and switched on the reading lamp. Peering again at the smudge of reflected light on the windscreen of Oboroni's car he convinced himself that the face behind the glass was that of Kofi Adjare, Oboroni's albino driver. Comfort must have seen it too. It would be natural for her to assume that Oboroni was being driven by her old friend and adviser. It would be equally natural for her not to want to incriminate him in any way. So it was not the face of Oboroni that attracted her attention but the face of Kofi Adjare. In a way, Kwame was somewhat relieved by this realisation.

Kofi Adjare would be the ideal *okyeame* for Oboroni. He was wise in the folklore of Ashanti and spoke in the poetic language of the ancestors. Any message given to him to impart would be automatically encoded in language that was almost as obscure to most modern Ghanaians as Chaucer's English would be to most modern Englishmen. Kwame felt humbled by the realisation. How could he have presumed to have unravelled the language of such a master? He realised that there must have been much that he missed in the decoding he had done for the *abrofo*. He felt that he had taken their money on false pretences, but he had linked them to Oboroni, and now he could redeem himself fully by identifying Charles Richards' linguist.

Kwame's first thought was to call Jack Preece and announce his great discovery to the world but he simultaneously realised that to do that would be to throw his whole life into turmoil. Somehow he must contain his eureka moment and resist the urge to run down the road in his pyjamas. To report Kofi Adjare to the authorities was to end all hope of rescuing his marriage. Comfort would never forgive him for causing this old man to spend his last days in a foreign jail.

Then doubts began to sweep across Kwame's mind. Could such a wise man really become mixed up in drugs smuggling? Could someone so imbued with the traditions of Ashanti and so much a contented part of that rich and ancient culture be persuaded in the evening of his life to serve the needs of avarice in a cold and distant land? The idea seemed preposterous. Yet Kofi had worked for Oboroni for several years in Ghana and no doubt a mutual respect and trust had grown up between them. Later, it seems, he had worked for Mama Kate in a similar capacity. When Oboroni needed a linguist, could Mama Kate have persuaded Kofi to make a short trip to England? Maybe he thought that he was going to work only as a driver. Perhaps that was the original intention and he was persuaded to act as a linguist after he was already here.

Did Kofi Adjare know anything about Oboroni's involvement in the drugs business? He would almost certainly know something about *wee* because that was widely used in Ghana, but did he know about the hard drugs? The more Kwame thought about it the more he felt convinced that if it was Kofi driving Oboroni's car he had been tricked into playing a part in the illicit activities. Instead of bringing the case to an end and leaving him free to concentrate on his studies, Kwame realised that his discovery, if that was what it was, had complicated his life considerably. How was he going to solve this new dilemma? What was he going to tell Jack Preece? How should he take up the matter with Comfort?

With so many urgent thoughts and questions tumbling in his mind Kwame felt a great need to share them with another person. His first thought was of Tom, but Tom, though a loyal friend, would not condone hiding information about the drugs cartel from the authorities. No, the only person in the world with whom he could discuss the whole matter was Comfort and she was not immediately available. It would require much self-control but Kwame felt that he must contain his thoughts and suspicions until he could be with Comfort during the Easter vacation. To ask to see her earlier might excite the suspicion of Jack Preece and his colleagues, and in any case he didn't want to see Comfort with a third person present.

Two days later at the foundry school Kwame handed the album back to Jack Preece with a slow sad shake of the head. 'So you made no progress even in the quiet solitude of your cubicle,' said Jack. 'I must say you rekindled my hopes.'

'What do you want me to do now?'

'I guess we must go back to the surveillance.'

'Will you bring me more photographs to look at?'

'It's probably worth one more try.'

'Well, I'm here when you need me.'

Kwame felt bad about being forced to hide important information from his employers and he was glad when the meeting was over. He tried to concentrate on his studies but thoughts of Kofi Adjare, Comfort and the investigation kept leading him astray. In spite of having ample time to attend to his coursework he knew that he was slipping behind his self-imposed schedule of revision. All his work was affected. Whereas formerly his research project had been going well, now his progress slowed almost to a halt and he was unable to generate the new ideas necessary to revive it. He realised that if his great dilemma could not be resolved soon he would be unlikely to do himself justice in the coming examinations.

Kwame also realised that at any time Jack, David and Leon might identify the linguist by another route. Perhaps they would decide to concentrate their surveillance on Oboroni's driver for reasons of their own and link him with the coded telephone calls in a way that did not require Kwame's help. Then they might be asking questions about why he had not recognised the driver, and if they suspected him of withholding information he could be facing criminal charges. Whichever way he looked the prospects seemed bleak. It was essential that he talk the whole matter over with Comfort as soon as possible.

Up to this point Kwame had not been officially informed about Comfort and Akosua's location and for some time he had been content not to know. He felt that not knowing the address increased their security because he could not divulge it accidentally. He had been more than happy to take advantage of official transport on his home visits. He had visited his family twice and even now he was not quite certain how to find them. However, he knew that they were somewhere in Nottingham and he knew the name of the road and the house number. He could take a coach or train to Nottingham and buy a street map on arrival. In the meantime, if Comfort telephoned on the secure line he would not mention his visit in case the calls were being monitored.

The journey was easier than he had expected because the address was near the city centre. When Kwame knocked on the door he was relieved for it to be opened by a surprised but smiling Comfort who told him that she had seen him through the window as he walked down the street. Akosua was at school, so after a glass of water and a cup of coffee Kwame was free to introduce the purpose of his visit. He had rehearsed it endlessly in his head but as often happened it was Comfort who took the initiative.

'Have you come about the photographs?'

'Well yes, partly.'

'I told you I didn't recognise anybody.'

'I think we both recognised Kofi Adjare.'

'You didn't tell them, did you? Please Kwame, don't involve old Kofi.'

'No, I couldn't do that, but it was Kofi wasn't it?'

So he had been right after all. It was Kofi Adjare, and Comfort had recognised him. She must have been very concerned that Kwame might also recognise Kofi and give him away to the authorities. Now it seemed she was relieved and grateful to him. At least he had opened the subject without harming their relationship; in fact he was hopeful that it was much improved.

'Do you think Kofi is deeply involved in the drugs business?' he asked.

'No, I don't think so.'

'Then why is he here helping Oboroni?'

'Isn't he just the driver?'

'No, I suspect that he's also the *okyeame* who sends out Oboroni's coded messages.'

'He could do that; he knows the old Twi.'

'But do you think that he knows that drugs are involved?'

'He might know about *wee*, everybody does, but I doubt if he knows about the others.'

'That's what I thought,' said Kwame.

Comfort managed to look relieved and concerned at the same time. 'What's going to happen to the drugs cartel?' she asked.

'Eventually the police will swoop and they'll all be arrested,' said Kwame.

'Then we must try to warn Kofi,' said Comfort. 'I really don't want anything bad to happen to him.'

'What about Oboroni, Peter and Bra Yaw,' asked Kwame, 'don't you care what happens to them?'

'Oh, they know what they're doing and the risks involved, and they're still young enough to enjoy their houses when they come out of prison.'

'Not Oboroni.'

'He's enjoyed enough already.'

'You should know.'

'How can we warn Kofi?'

'I've thought about that and I think that the best way would be to send him a coded message on one of his calls.'

'Does he ever call you?'

'No, he only calls Peter Sarpong and the other local bosses.'

'Then how will you speak to him?'

'That's the problem,' said Kwame. 'The *abrofo* monitor the calls and could probably switch me through but we can't ask for their help without telling them about Kofi, and then there'd be no point. They wouldn't agree anyway, from fear that Kofi might warn the whole cartel.'

'Is there any chance they might let Kofi off lightly if we did tell them everything?'

Kwame gave a sigh; that was the question he had hoped that Comfort would ask. 'Shall we call Jack Preece and ask him to come over tomorrow?' he suggested, as Comfort put on her coat to go to fetch Akosua from school.

'Come with me now, Akos will be pleased to see you, and we can think about it as we walk in the cool fresh air,' said Comfort. Kwame grabbed his coat and followed her out of the door, feeling happier than he had for several months past.

Jack Preece arrived late next morning and was settled with a coffee and Kit Kat before he asked why he had been called. 'It's a delicate matter,' said Kwame.

'I thought it might be.'

'We feel that a close friend may be innocently involved and we want that person protected.'

'So you did recognise someone in the photographs.'

'We don't want to say anything until we have your assurance of special treatment for our friend.'

'That's difficult. It could depend on the degree of involvement and the value of the information.'

'Let's say that it could supply the missing link.'

'Then I'll seek permission from higher authority.'

Jack Preece went out to his car to make the call and Comfort and Kwame waited anxiously. When he came back he said, 'All right, we promise to give your friend special consideration provided that the information enables us to incriminate the coordinator, your Oboroni.'

'Have you got the album with you?' asked Kwame. Jack produced the album from his voluminous briefcase. 'Look at these two photographs of Oboroni by his car,' said Kwame, 'Can you see the driver sitting in the car?'

'I can only see reflected light.'

'Look carefully.'

'If there is a driver it's a white man, not a Ghanaian.'

'It is a Ghanaian, an albino called Kofi Adjare. He used to drive Oboroni in Ghana.'

'Could he be the linguist?'

'A very fine linguist,' said Comfort, 'and a good friend.'

'What's going to happen now?' asked Kwame.

'We'll have to trail Kofi as we did the others and see if the timing of his telephone calls synchronises with the coded messages. If they do, we will have the missing link.'

'Then what?' asked Comfort.

'That will be a decision made at a higher level,' said Jack.

Jack offered to run Kwame back to Coventry and Kwame accepted. Now his mind was at rest he knew that he could return to his studies with renewed vigour. He felt that his job was done. The coordinator had been identified and the link to the regional drugs bosses had been established. He could leave the rest to the authorities. He realised that his inflated income might soon end but he could anticipate a generous bonus for his part in the successful outcome. That should enable him to complete his house. Now he had hope of repairing his marriage and a clear run through to his final degree examinations. Spring was springing and even the weather should be warm enough until he returned to the permanent heat of his homeland in July. Kwame could hear his father telling him in the words of British Prime Minister Harold MacMillan, who presided over Ghana's transition to independence in 1957, 'You've never had it so good!'

238

17

Graduation

Now Kwame could apply himself seriously to his studies with no distractions and he made good use of his time. With a much lightened working load and nothing more to do for his new employers, he was a full-time student in every sense. He spent the Easter vacation with Comfort and Akosua but put in several hours revision each day while Comfort took their daughter on minor outings around the town. One day Akosua came home very excited at having visited a children's entertainment based on the legendary figure of Robin Hood. 'He robbed the rich to feed the poor,' she cried. 'Do you know anyone like that, Daddy?'

'No,' replied Kwame, 'but I know many people who rob the poor to feed the rich.'

Later, Comfort took Kwame to task for giving his daughter this rough response to her question. 'Do you have to tell her such things at her age?'

'No, I suppose not, I'm sorry. I was thinking of the drugs cartel.'

'What about the aid agencies that support your work in Ghana, don't they take money from the rich to feed the poor?'

'Not according to Dr Schumacher, the founder of our intermediate technology movement. He said that development aid is a means of transferring money from poor people in rich countries to rich people in poor countries.'

'What did he mean by that?'

'I think he meant that many relatively poor people in countries like England pay their taxes and contribute to charitable organisations but much of the money sent to help poor countries ends up in the Swiss bank accounts of people like Nkrumah and Acheampong.'

'And Rawlings?'

'What do you think?'

Kwame completed his experimental investigations and handed in his thesis a few days ahead of schedule. His time was now clear to concentrate exclusively on revision for his final examinations. However, a telephone call from David Barney told him that he had one more meeting to attend.

'We thought you'd like to hear what's happened to your friends,' said David when they met. 'After your useful suggestion it didn't take us long to establish that Kofi Adjare was the linguist who formed the link between Crispin Russell, alias Charles Richards, and the local bosses in the drugs network. Together with the police we conducted a coordinated operation to round up all the known cartel members in the UK, including Crispin Russell and Peter Sarpong. Two days ago in Ghana, Bra Yaw Aidoo was arrested at Kotoka International Airport. No contraband was found on his person but the police established links to three other young people booked on the same flight and these were arrested on arrival in London. They were found to be in possession of false passports and packages of cocaine.'

'Has Kofi Adjare also been arrested?' asked Kwame.

'I'm afraid that was unavoidable as he played such a key role.'

'But you promised to treat him leniently.'

'He will have to give evidence in court, but if we are convinced that he was tricked into doing what he did, we will treat him as lightly as possible.'

'What does that mean in practice?'

'That's for the court to decide, but he could be given a short sentence and deported back to Ghana with a warning that he will not be permitted to return.'

'And if you think that he knew what he was doing, what then?'

'He will have to serve a longer prison sentence like the others.'

Seeing the worried look on Kwame's face David hastened to assure him that so far it seemed that Kofi had been used for his linguistic skills but not told much about what was going on. 'Would you like to see him?' he asked.

'No,' said Kwame. 'I don't want anyone who may be going back to Ghana to have any hint that I may have been involved in their bad fortune.'

'Speaking of people back in Ghana,' said David, 'I think that you ought to know what's happed there.

'I told you that Bra Yaw Aidoo was arrested in Accra. Well, it appears that your police down there found a way to persuade him to tell them all he knew. He's now incarcerated in a prison called Ussher Fort and it's my guess he'll be there for a long time. They've told us that they've arrested an *Opanin* George Debrah alias Uncle George, Madam Katherine

Agyewa alias Mama Kate and two Lebanese directors of Hanabis Ghana Ltd, Suleiman Hannah and Omar Issah. Please don't look so worried. There's no way that you can be connected to the arrests in Ghana, or the arrests here for that matter.'

'I hope you're right,' said Kwame. 'Now I must find a way to explain it all to Comfort.'

Kwame liked to brood upon his problems before taking a decision but on this occasion he was given little chance. Mrs Chichester greeted him on arrival at his lodgings by announcing that one of his lady friends was back. To his dismay he entered his room to find Akos Mary pacing about in an agitated state. Comfort was going to be very unhappy about the fate of her friend Kofi Adjare but that issue would pale into insignificance if she learned of this latest visit by Akos Mary. His first thought was to get rid of his unwanted visitor as quickly as possible but he realised immediately that she must have a reason for calling and she could be in serious trouble.

He sat her down and tried to calm her, administering the obligatory glass of water and waiting patiently while she drank. 'I need your help,' she said with a gasp.

'What's happened?'

'I was staying with Peter but he sent me away for a few days to stay with a Ghanaian family in Birmingham. When I got back I saw that the police were there searching the house and a neighbour told me that Peter had been taken away. So I ran.'

'Did the police see you?'

'No, I didn't go near enough for that.'

'Why did you come here?'

'Aren't you my friend? Where else could I go?'

Kwame felt that here was a knot of wisdom he would never be able to unravel. He had much sympathy for Akos Mary's predicament but, unlike her friend Afriyie, she had taken the decision to continue to work as a drugs courier. She had been a friend of Comfort's but was now regarded by Comfort as a rival. Kwame was not sure how Comfort would react if he tried to help Akos Mary. He could also get himself into serious trouble with the police. He could say nothing to Akos Mary about why Peter had been arrested or hint in any way that he knew anything about what had happened. He thought of asking for Tom's help but realised that he couldn't ask his friend to do anything that was illegal. It was certainly illegal to help a fugitive from justice; and that was what Akos Mary had become.

241

This moment of acute distress was brought to an abrupt end by a ring on the front door bell. He heard Mrs Chichester's voice raised in greeting and footsteps approaching the lounge. There was a burst of chatter and a child's happy shout. Then into the room came Akosua, Comfort and Jack Preece. 'I've brought your family back as quickly as I could,' announced Jack, and Akosua rushed to the rising Kwame and hugged him around his thighs, pushing him back into the chair. Comfort's gaze was riveted on Akos Mary.

Jack Preece was also quick to recognise Akos Mary. He moved to block the door and asked Mrs Chichester if he could use the telephone. If Akos Mary contemplated continuing her flight it was only a passing thought and she resigned herself to embracing Comfort and Akosua. The two women burst into a rapid conversation in Twi that Kwame was relieved to hear was good natured on both sides, while Akosua told him repeatedly that she was missing a day of school. Kwame assured her that she would be missing a few more days before he could find her a new school in Coventry.

It was not until the police arrived that Comfort realised what was happening. When the policewoman formally arrested Akos Mary, Comfort shouted at Kwame, 'How can you let them arrest my friend?' He didn't answer, knowing that there was nothing that he could do but stand with bowed head. As Akos Mary was led away she uttered one word, *oboroni*. Kwame knew that the bitter taunt was meant for him and feared that sooner or later Peter and the others would know that he was connected in some way with their ill fortune. When at length he raised his head to look at Comfort he saw the fear and anger of this realisation burning in her eyes.

Akos Mary left behind a vacuum that could transmit no sound. Although thoughts, feelings and questions were racing in every head, for a long moment they could not be shared. It was left to Akosua to restore the normal atmosphere, 'Why have they taken Auntie Akos away, Mummy?'

'You'd better ask your father,' Comfort replied coldly.

'Daddy, when we go back to Kumasi, who will do my hair?'

'We must hope it won't be too long before Auntie Akos comes back there too.'

Kwame looked pleadingly at Jack Preece but was not reassured by the look on his face.

Mrs Chichester bustled in with a tray of tea and biscuits. The interruption was just what everyone needed. Having witnessed the arrival and departure of the police, and seeing the serious countenances of Kwame and his guests, the good matron said to Akosua, 'Come and drink your orange juice with me in the kitchen. You can help me bake a nice big cake to celebrate your return to Coventry.' They departed hand in hand.

As soon as the door closed Comfort turned to Jack Preece and asked what would happen to Akos Mary.

'She will go before a magistrate in the morning charged with importing prohibited substances. It's likely that she will be remanded in custody until she can be brought to trial.'

'What can we do to help her?'

'A lawyer will be appointed to represent her and you could offer to provide evidence of previously good character.'

'What good will that do?'

'It might persuade the judge to reduce her prison sentence.'

'So she will go to prison.'

'I fear so, after all she made four visits to the UK carrying banned substances.'

'How do you know?'

'That I cannot tell you in detail, but we've been monitoring the couriers flying in from Accra since Yaw Aidoo was released from prison.'

Comfort had spoken rather roughly to Jack Preece but Kwame knew that the full venom of her snake bite would be reserved for him. He waited in acute agitation while Jack Preece took his leave. Having grasped at the last straw of seeing him to his car, Kwame re-entered the house feeling like a condemned man walking to the electric chair. But Comfort had switched to plan B. She said nothing; and as far as Kwame was concerned she remained silent for the next three days. Whatever he said to her she feigned not to hear, although she maintained normal conversation with Akosua and Mrs Chichester. Kwame mused that he was not only in Coventry, he had been sent to Coventry.

On the fourth day David Barney arrived to drive Comfort and Akosua to the airport. When Kwame expressed his surprise he was told that Mrs Mainu had telephoned to ask for transport home on the day that she returned to Coventry, so arrangements had been made accordingly. Akosua appeared to have been prepared for her abrupt departure but not for the realisation that the fact had been hidden from her father. She clung to him until the last moment and departed in tears. Comfort said nothing to Kwame, a fact that was not lost on David Barney who gazed quizzically at Kwame, perhaps expecting him to change the travel arrangements, but Kwame knew that his situation was hopeless and said nothing.

Mrs Chichester was also concerned about Kwame, the effect on him of his wife's disdain and the unscheduled loss of his family. That evening she prepared his favourite meal and when all was cleared away she offered a patient and sympathetic ear if he wanted to voice his feelings. Kwame thanked her as politely as he could in the circumstances but he knew that no *oboroni*, even one as sympathetic as Mrs Chichester, could possibly understand the feelings of total inadequacy that raged in his breast.

He had proved himself to be a negligent husband and father and an untrustworthy friend, unable adequately to support or protect his family and ready to betray his fellow countrymen. How had he come to this deplorable condition? He couldn't think of himself as a bad person and yet he must appear to many people to be unprincipled in his actions. He had tried to follow the code of behaviour that his father had taught him. Was this so much at variance with the traditional values of his culture that conflict was inevitable? Or was his downfall due to his inability to take decisive action to stop affairs drifting outside his control?

Kwame knew that he was intelligent. His progress in his studies proved that. He had also solved the problem set him by his paymasters in the drugs investigation. Yet hardly ever had he taken action by his own decision; he had every time been prepared to wait upon events. Even in his family affairs he realised that it was Comfort who suggested what they should do and he meekly concurred. So if he always went along with what others wanted, why was he guilty of getting everything wrong? He realised once again that he had yet to set himself a clear goal in life. Was this lack of direction the basis of his disgrace?

If Kwame had a long-held ambition it was to gain a university degree. His final examinations were only a few weeks away and until recently his preparations had been well up to date, but now he was plunged into such mental turmoil that he couldn't see how he could regain the tranquillity of mind necessary for success. Right now he should be revising, but how could he stop thinking of how to repair his marriage, in the short term, and in the longer term defend himself and his family from the revenge of the cartel? If he couldn't solve these problems, would his university degree be of any value?

Kwame wrestled for hours with this latest knot of wisdom. Slowly it dawned on him that this was what he always did, and usually it ended only when someone else took a decision or some unexpected event brought about a changed situation. The result may be a temporary easement but it could be part of a long-term downward slide. Maybe wrestling for too long with the knot of wisdom was not good. The *abrofo* had another knot in their culture, the Gordian knot. This knot was not unravelled but cut. That's what he must do now; find a fast and effective solution to his problem. He picked up the telephone to book a flight to Accra and a connecting flight to Kumasi.

In Konongo, three days later, he walked in on Comfort unannounced. In her astonishment she forgot her plan B until they were too far into conversation for the plan to be revived. Kwame thought that he had solved the first part of his problem. Now he must try to explain why things had turned out the way they had. So he went over recent events taking care to stress that in his dealings with the *abrofo* he never mentioned the names of people in Ghana. He was not told of the arrests until after they had taken place and he had not known that Akos Mary was in the UK until just before Comfort arrived with Jack Preece and Akosua. Akos Mary had been staying with Peter Sarpong and would have been arrested with him if she had been in the house at the time. She would have been in difficulties anyway, because she had agreed to work with the cartel and had made repeated trips to London. If she had taken the same course as Afriyie she would now be a free woman in Kumasi.

Kwame went on to explain that Bra Yaw had been arrested at Kotoka International Airport boarding a flight to London. He had been taken to Ussher Fort where he told the police about the leaders of the cartel in Kumasi. That was how Uncle George and Mama Kate came to be arrested, along with two Lebanese directors of Hanabis. It seemed that the whole cartel had been arrested and would be held in custody for a number of years.

'I hope you're right,' said Comfort, 'because if anyone has been missed you'll be in trouble.'

'There's nothing to prove that I had anything to do with their arrests.'

'Those people don't need proof, and Akos Mary clearly suspects that you were involved.'

'At least her arrest will relieve *your* suspicions,' said Kwame hopefully, but Comfort was not ready to let him off that easily.

'What's going to happen to old Kofi?'

'That depends on whether he knew what Oboroni and Peter were up to.'

'I don't think he knew about the hard drugs.'

'David Barney hinted that that was their first impression.'

'What do you think?'

'Well, I never knew him as well as you, but I would be surprised if he knew exactly what was going on.'

'I'll never forgive you, Kwame Mainu, if anything bad happens to old Kofi.'

'That's rather unfair. We agreed that Kofi was in serious trouble anyway and it was your suggestion that we report our suspicions to the authorities. He was already in too deep for us to help in any other way.'

In the deep shadows of the small room, Kwame tried in vain to read the expression on Comfort's face. He seized the opportunity of her silence to tell her about the big bonus he had been paid for helping to bring the investigation to the desired end. 'We should have enough to finish the house now,' he concluded enthusiastically.

'According to the original estimate, maybe,' she replied, 'but do you realise how fast costs are rising?'

'The money is foreign exchange, we'll get more cedis for it.'

'That will offset part of the increase.'

'Then let's press on as quickly as possible to get the work done before costs rise any further.'

'I'm not sure I want to pay for my house with blood money.'

Kwame groaned, this was what he had feared might be her reaction. 'What Peter and Bra Yaw and the others were doing was very bad; they had to be stopped,' he said.

'Yes, but if the *abrofo* didn't like what they were doing in their country they should have stopped them themselves; you didn't have to help.'

'But the *abrofo* have helped me a lot, surely I should do something to help them in return.'

'Yes, but not against your own people.'

'They are bad people. I don't consider them to be my people.'

'Then maybe Akos Mary was right, *oboroni*. Who are your people?'

Kwame tried another approach. 'Peter and his friends made a free choice; they knew the risks they were running. You stopped me from running those risks and Afriyie decided not to go on. Are you saying that you and Afriyie are the same people as Peter, and Bra Yaw?'

'Of course we're all the same people. We made different decisions; that's all.'

'Then I also made a different decision.'

'But your decision was against your own people.'

'Is Oboroni one of our people? My main task was to catch him.'

'All the others are our people.'

Kwame realised that this was an argument he could not win. He thought of asking about the police in Ghana who had arrested Bra Yaw, Uncle George and Mama Kate. Were they alienating themselves from the people? Then he realised that as an arm of government they were regarded by most people as already alienated. The people had not chosen this government, but more than that: central government itself was commonly regarded as an alien implant left over from the colonial era. Weren't the Ghanaian police only doing the bidding of their former colonial masters? He chose not to pursue the argument any further. 'What about us then?' he asked feebly.

'Look at yourself, Kwame Mainu! You're 31 years old and you still don't have a house or a good job. You've no ambition for your family. You talk about pursuing your education but you still don't have even a first degree. You can never make up your mind about anything. I'm tired of making excuses for you to my family and friends. You're a disgrace to us all. I've been talking to your mother and she says you're just like your father. He was the laughing stock of this town, an opinionated colonial gentleman who never went to church but acted as though he thought himself better and wiser than everyone else. She was forced to give up on such a useless person and I must do the same. So next time you come back, don't expect to find me waiting patiently in this hovel. I've got better things to do.'

This bitter outburst froze Kwame's brain. He rose to his feet in a wave of dizziness that was much more than he usually experienced in rising abruptly from a low stool. He groped for the door as the room swung around drunkenly. Pulling it ajar, he lurched out into the bright sunlight and stumbled across the broken ground of the compound. He was deaf to the calls of women pounding fufu and blind to the old men under the mango tree pulling pipes from open mouths as he passed. Somehow he avoided treading on infants crawling on the bare earth and passed out of the compound and onto the busy trunk road outside. Turning to the left he walked past the market square where he had pulled his trolley and listened with his father to Kofi Busia addressing the assembled citizens. Down the hill and up again he made his way past the turning he had taken so often to school. Leaving Odumase and its broken pavements behind he walked unseeing and unseen on well-worn footpaths screened from the road by tall elephant grass.

Kwame was never able to remember how far he walked that day, only that he was roused from his stupor by a violent thunderstorm. While it lasted the rain rebounded from the hard surface almost to head height, and after it had passed the steam from the road constituted a mist of equal depth. With clothes soaked through and shivering from the cold he had no option but to retrace his steps. He reached the house long after the sun had set and was met at the entrance to the compound by a distraught Akosua. 'Where have you been, Daddy, where is Mummy?' was her greeting.

Taking Akosua by the hand he led her to their room and changed quickly into dry clothes, hoping that his long exposure to wet and cold would not induce a cold or flu. 'Was Mummy here when you came from school?' he asked his daughter.

'No, I've been waiting so long.'

'Have you eaten?'

'Yes, Mrs Oppong gave me some gari and bean stew.'

'So you don't know where Mummy has gone?'

'No, shall I ask Mrs Oppong if there's any gari left?'

'Yes please, it's too late to start cooking.'

Tired out by her long anxious wait Akosua was soon asleep and Kwame was left alone to assess his new situation. He had come home in an attempt to save his marriage but losing Comfort had always been a distinct possibility. What he had not expected was to be left with Akosua. This was, he reflected ruefully, the fate that had befallen his father but at least in his case he was able-bodied. He could not be sure that the condition was permanent. Comfort might not come back to him but she might come back to reclaim her daughter. Kwame decided to wait upon events for the next two or three days before planning his next move.

Comfort did not come back. Kwame was forced to tell Akosua that he must take her back with him to England so that he could sit his final examinations. Then they would both come back to Ghana to look for Mummy. The little girl wondered why there was so much travelling and changing of plans but she was happy to go with her father now that her mother was not around. Kwame let her assume that the separation from her mother was only temporary.

Although having his daughter with him was a great responsibility, Kwame regarded it as a considerable consolation. He had always feared that to lose Comfort would entail losing Akosua as well. Now he not only enjoyed the companionship of his daughter but the necessity to constantly consider her needs kept his mind from brooding on darker thoughts. He felt that he could maintain this stability of mind long enough to get through the passage of his examinations. He expected that Mrs Chichester would give him her full support throughout this challenging period.

That was the way it turned out. Mrs Chichester, though surprised by Comfort's sudden abandonment of her family, was quite happy to assume the temporary role of surrogate mother. With the support of Mrs Chichester and with Akosua attending a local primary school, Kwame was able to resume serious preparations for his examinations. Yearnings for Comfort were never far from his thoughts but he managed to keep pushing them aside until the crisis was passed.

Three weeks after the examinations the results were posted. Kwame was happy to find that he had been awarded a degree with upper second-class honours. Tom telephoned to congratulate him and to suggest a celebratory drink in the evening. After hearing about Kwame's recent troubles, including his unscheduled trip to Kumasi, Tom said that this explained a good deal. He and his fellow lecturers had been expecting Kwame to get a first-class degree. Nevertheless, he hastened to add, the upper second-class degree still qualified him to pursue a master's or doctorate at a later date. Kwame replied that his first inclination remained to return to Ghana to work for a few years before opting for further studies.

The graduation ceremony came only two weeks after the posting of results. Kwame was impressed; in Kumasi there had been a delay of about eight months before the congregation for the conferment of degrees was held. However, after the splendour of the ceremony in Kumasi the occasion at Warwick disappointed him. Although he prized his newly gained certificate more highly, he missed the bright *Kente* robes, the drumming, horn blowing and rich cultural setting of his first congregation. He knew how proud his father would have been to see him succeed at a university in England and he hoped that in some mysterious way he could still be aware of his son's achievement. He was sorry that Comfort had not stayed on to witness his graduation but he was enthusiastically supported by Akosua who sat in the auditorium with Mrs Chichester and applauded vigorously when her father ascended the stage to receive his award.

Kwame was now intent on returning home as quickly as possible but this was not like his former departures. This time he was not scheduled to return at the end of the vacation but was leaving at the end of his course with no idea if or when he would be returning to Coventry. Fred Brown arranged a farewell lunch at the foundry school and there was a goodbye party one evening at the ladies' club. These proceedings touched him deeply; he had not realised quite how sincerely he had been befriended by these paler folk who seldom revealed their feelings. Akosua was moved to tears at seeing her father's distress and she shed tears on her own behalf when they finally took leave of Mrs Chichester. There was less emotion in saying farewell to Tom, however, as he promised to make regular visits to Ghana in connection with the link with Kumasi University.

So on a sunny day late in July 1988 Kwame Mainu BSc (Eng) flew to Accra with his eight-year-old daughter. At last, at the age of 31, he was coming home a university graduate.

18

GRID

Kwame was unsure what sort of home he was revisiting. He feared that it would no longer be run by Comfort and it might not contain Akosua, who never ceased to ask when she would see her mother again. So after briefly reporting at GRID in Tema, and arranging to start work on the first of September, he took a State Transport bus to Konongo to try to establish some order in his domestic affairs.

He found the old familiar compound almost deserted, and hailed the small geriatric band assembled under their mango tree. After the customary greetings, shaking each bony hand extended to them in strict rotation from right to left, Kwame and Akosua were invited to sit down and join the meeting. He assured the inquiring faces that he brought no trouble from the road and was assured in return that there was no trouble in Konongo. Akosua was eager to buy a soft drink so after Kwame had asked her to add two bottles of Star beer for his friends she ran off on her errand. He could see that the door and window of his room appeared to be locked, bolted and abandoned so he asked if Comfort had been there since his last visit.

After a protracted debate concerning the precise date of the visit, it was agreed that Comfort had come back once about a month ago to collect her personal belongings. The event had aroused some interest because she had been accompanied by a Lebanese man in a BMW who, she said, was giving her a lift to Kumasi. 'She seems to have found a new husband,' said one aged wag to the amusement of his companions and Kwame was forced to attempt a merry reply, but he knew that the suggestion was very unlikely. The Lebanese seldom married Ghanaians and he thought that Comfort was now too old to be taken as a girlfriend. He surmised that either she had sought help from an old acquaintance for this one mission or she was involved in providing a different service. Knowing that it was unlikely to be connected to drugs he was left speculating on its true nature. The return of Akosua with the drinks closed his opportunity for further questions.

Akosua was anxious to go on looking for her mother so Kwame decided to press on to Kumasi without even stopping to open his room. He had no idea where Comfort might have gone but he thought that Afriyie might be able to help. They hailed a Kumasi-bound one-pound, one-pound setting down passengers at the market and joined the car to Ayigya Junction where they found the seamstress at work in her kiosk. Afriyie was pleased to see her friends in spite of knowing the purpose of their visit. In answer to Akosua's urgent plea she could say only that Comfort had passed by about a month ago coming from Konongo with a Lebanese man in a BMW. She had not said where she was going but she had ordered a dress to be sewn and promised to call back to collect it. 'It's been ready for two weeks now but I know she will come for it, she always does,' said Afriyie, indicating one of her finer creations hanging on the wall of the kiosk.

Akosua was determined to wait with Afriyie for her mother to come to collect her dress so Kwame decided to lodge on the university campus with a TCC colleague and let Akosua spend the next few days at the dressmakers' kiosk. Each morning he left his excited daughter in Afriyie's care and each evening he collected his distraught offspring for a late supper and bed. Not having any other pressing business, Kwame also spent much of his time at or near the kiosk but he soon grew tired of female chatter and felt embarrassed when clients called for measuring or fitting.

After two or three days he found himself spending more time with his former colleagues at the TCC office, bringing himself up to date with project activities. What interested him most was the future relationship between the TCC and GRID. He knew that the plan was for the TCC to extend its rural industrial development projects through the network of ITTUs that GRID would establish in all ten regions. He felt that he could play a key role in coordinating the whole programme. To this end, the more he knew about current TCC operations the better.

One day at the kiosk when business was slack Afriyie asked Kwame about Akos Mary. He told her how Akos Mary had come back to England three times after her first trip with Afriyie. She had tried to stay in Coventry and find work as a hairdresser but Peter Sarpong had persuaded her to keep going back and forth. Eventually she had been arrested by the police just as Peter and Bra Yaw and many others had been and she was likely to spend a long time in prison.

'You were wise to abandon the work when you did,' he concluded.

Afriyie looked both worried and relieved at the same time. 'I warned her that was how things would end,' she said.

'Is Comfort angry with you because of Akos Mary?' asked Afriyie diffidently.

'Why do you ask that?'

'Well, she hinted to me once that she thought Akos Mary was going to England to see you.'

'Sometimes when she was in Coventry I did see her but I was not the reason for her visit.'

'Was it Tom?'

'No, I don't think that it was Tom either.'

'Akos Mary said that she was Tom's girlfriend.'

'I don't think you should believe everything that Akos Mary said.'

'Do you think that Tom still loves me?'

'I'm sure he does.'

The next evening when Kwame called at the kiosk to collect Akosua he found the little girl in tears. Even before he could ask the reason he saw that the dress was no longer hanging on the wall. 'Comfort came for the dress but didn't stay long,' said Afriyie, 'and she told Akosua that she couldn't take her with her. She refused to wait while I sent someone to call you.'

'Did she say where she was staying?'

'No.'

Now there was no reason for Akosua to spend her days at the dressmakers' kiosk but she had grown interested in the work and liked the company of Afriyie and the other apprentices, some of whom were only a few years older than herself. So Kwame let her continue to spend her days with Afriyie while he worked out what his next move should be. GRID had its headquarters in Tema but he couldn't be sure that he would be based there. The ITTU in Tamale was still expanding its activities and new ITTUs were being established in Cape Coast, Ho and Sunyani; he might be stationed in any of those towns. Wherever he was asked to go he would need to find accommodation and a school for Akosua. He would need help in running his home and looking after his daughter.

Kwame mentioned his plans and expectations to Afriyie and asked if she had any plans for her future. 'I've finished my apprenticeship here and would like to set up my own business,' she told him.

'Will that be here?'

'No, there are too many dressmakers here; I will go to a new place.'

'Where will that be?'

'Oh, it could be anywhere: Tema, Tamale, Cape Coast, Ho or Sunyani.'

'Those are all the places where I might be!'

'Why don't you help me set up my business and I'll look after your house and Akosua?'

'But I don't know yet where we will be.'

'Then you must let me know later; there's no rush.'

When Kwame had nothing to say he remained silent.

Before travelling back to Tema Kwame decided to call at his room in Konongo. He thought that there was little there that he needed but it was safer to check. Akosua might have some clothes that she would like to wear again. He turned the rusty key with some sadness. It was like opening a door into a past that had been full of expectations of happiness that would now never be fulfilled. Would life always be like that: a succession of bright hopeful mornings that never extended beyond noon, a series of exciting departures than never reached a destination? Was the only destination in life death itself? With these dark thoughts swamping his mind Kwame stepped from sunlight into shadow and peered through the gloom with rapidly dilating pupils. After a few seconds he could see that the room was bare. It was devoid of all furniture except for a small roughly made wooden stool of the type used by women when tending the cooking pot. On the stool was a once-white envelope.

Kwame blew the patina of pale-pink dust off the envelope and tore it open. It was, as he expected, a note from Comfort.

Kwame Mainu,
I'm sorry that it's the end. Don't try to find me, it won't do any good. I couldn't wait any longer. Look after Akosua.
Comfort Opokua

While it was what he had expected, its grim finality closed the lid on the coffin of his marriage. Taking his daughter by the hand he walked slowly out of the compound, leaving the door of his room ajar with the key still in the lock. It wouldn't stay unoccupied for long but he doubted if he would ever return to collect the rent.

In Tema at GRID he was greeted warmly by the director and introduced to his new colleagues, a few of whom he knew from his days at the university in Kumasi. 'I've been looking forward to getting someone who already knows the work,' said Dr Jones. 'Most of the new staff we took on last year have needed a lot of training and it will be some time before they fully understand what we are trying to do. My problem with you was to decide where to put you. I need you everywhere at once and that means that you must be based here in Tema.

'Essentially we are trying to prepare a corps of potential ITTU managers who will eventually be able to run an ITTU as an autonomous entity serving its own region. However, we can't do the training first and then think about setting up the ITTUs. The government expects the ITTUs to come into existence as quickly as possible so most of the training must be done on the job. The few of you who already understand the ITTU system, like Dan Baffour-Opoku, Dan Nyarko and Sam Sanders, will have to play a key role in training others at the same time as you gain the necessary additional experience in new situations and at new locations.'

GRID had rented a few houses and flats for senior staff and one was allocated to Kwame. Tema was a new town, rapidly expanded from a small fishing village when Kwame Nkrumah built the new harbour there in the 1960s. It was laid out by the same architect who planned Islamabad, divided originally into some eleven communities each with a similar road layout. By 1988 it had grown to be the fourth largest city in Ghana, after Accra, Kumasi and Tamale, with a population of around 100,000.

When originally constructed, most of the houses in Tema were low-cost and intended to be rented by workers at rates they could afford. By 1988, however, few workers could afford to rent these houses unless they had been fortunate enough to occupy them from the outset. Tema Development Corporation had adopted the policy of selling houses to tenants and so gradually the properties were coming into the possession of the more affluent traders and businessmen who added more rooms, installed telephones and air-conditioners and built high protective walls around the plots. This led to the situation in which improved properties with pebble-dashed walls, fresh paint and walled gardens were flanked by run-down original structures occupied by large families of labourers, small traders and unemployed people.

It was an improved house in Community 9 that was allocated to Kwame. Built originally with a hall, one bedroom, kitchen and bathroom, it had been extended to include two more bedrooms and a second bathroom. Kwame could give Akosua her own room and there was another room for Afriyie if she pursued her plan to come and keep house for them. A concrete wall topped by ornamental stonework surrounded a small garden and double ironwork gates allowed vehicular access. A primary school for Akosua was situated within easy walking distance and Tema General Hospital was not much further away. Kwame had a distance of about three kilometres to drive to GRID headquarters and the Tema ITTU, but with a project vehicle assigned to his use, his transport problems were solved.

At GRID Kwame was attached to the ITTU Operations Division headed by the chief engineer, Henry Debrah, who like Kwame was a foundry specialist. At Warwick University, Kwame had been taught the widely known undergraduate song 'You'll never go to heaven'. The verse about engineers went as follows:

Oh, you'll never go to heaven,
You'll never go to heaven,
As an engineer,
As an engineer,
Cause an engineer,
Cause an engineer,
Drinks too much beer!

Sadly this was true of Henry Debrah, but in the several years before his demons finally destroyed him Henry achieved a great deal in equipping and staffing the ITTUs in Cape Coast, Ho and Sunyani and preparing for ITTUs in Koforidua, Takoradi, Bolgatanga and Wa.

Working alongside Henry Debrah it was Kwame's responsibility to train the young men and women who would play key roles as technicians and technical instructors in the ITTUs of the future. It was intended, as far as possible, to train young people, men and women, who had recently qualified and had not grown set in the ways of traditional organisations, whether commercial enterprises, state corporations or public institutions. The ITTU was a new concept and needed a new breed of manager whose focus was always outwards towards helping its clients. It was Kwame's job to transfer the necessary technical and administrative skills while instilling this unique ethos. He would be required to do this work at the headquarters training establishment in Tema and at all locations where ITTUs already existed or where new ITTUs were to be established.

After three or four weeks in Tema Kwame felt that he and Akosua had adjusted sufficiently to their new life to consider the matter of whether Afriyie should be invited to join them. Akosua was very much in favour of this move so one Saturday morning they drove to Kumasi.

Arriving at midday, Kwame invited Afriyie to have lunch with them at the university swimming pool. After one of Mrs Dodoo's splendid meals and a bottle of Star beer Kwame asked Afriyie if she still planned to start her own dressmaking business and if Tema was a suitable location. She replied that it would depend on whether Kwame could lend her enough money to rent suitable premises and have a little capital to buy equipment and materials. He asked her how much she thought she would need. The amount she mentioned when converted into pounds was quite modest, so he readily agreed to provide these funds from the reserves that he had accumulated in Coventry.

'When can you come to Tema?'

'I've finished the apprenticeship so I can leave at any time.'

'Shouldn't you give some notice?'

'I'm not paid anything and Madam wants to take a new apprentice so I can leave at once.'

'Can Afriyie come back with us, Daddy?' Akosua asked excitedly.

'If she can be packed and ready to travel at midday tomorrow.'

'I'll be ready.'

The extension to Kwame's little Tema house was a separate structure built behind the original house and separated from it by a narrow courtyard. It consisted of two bedrooms and a bathroom with steps leading to a small walled roof garden. He allocated the rooms in the extension to Afriyie and Akosua, leaving himself the bedroom and bathroom in the original structure. The kitchen opened onto the extension, providing easy access for Afriyie to attend to her cooking duties. They would all use the hall for relaxation but Kwame was able to install a desk and bookcase at one end to constitute a small office. If he wanted to work late or had business associates visiting, the girls could conveniently retire to their rooms or enjoy the cool evening air in the roof garden.

Afriyie immediately started to look for a place to accommodate her business. She began by walking around the area noting where seamstresses were already operating and where people had built extensions to their houses or separate kiosks to accommodate informal commercial activities. When she found vacant accommodation of this sort in a suitable location she enquired about the rent and terms of tenancy. She soon learned that although the monthly rent was reasonable the landlords demanded at least three years' rent in advance. This did not surprise her, it was the same in Kumasi, and it explained why starting a small business was beyond the means of most graduating apprentices. She was glad that Kwame was prepared to finance her start in self-employment.

'How are you getting on looking for a place to start your work?' Kwame asked one evening.

'There are plenty of rooms and kiosks to rent but they all need three years' rent paid in advance.'

'Have you chosen a location yet?'

'Well, there are several seamstresses around here but I think I've found a good place in Community 8. It's near the market and a restaurant and dance hall so many people pass there.'

'Can you reach there on foot?'

'Easily, it will only take ten minutes.'

'Then let's go for it.'

The next problem was to buy sewing machines. They went to the central market on Saturday morning to see what was on offer. 'Look, only Chinese machines,' said Afriyie. 'They will be quickly spoiled by the apprentices. The old ladies were lucky; they could buy Singer machines.'

Kwame cast an engineer's eye over the machines and had to admit that they were of rather flimsy construction. They might have been suitable for occasional use by a regular housewife but not for serious commercial operation and the training of clumsy beginners. 'Let's ring Tom and ask him to send us some good heavy-duty sewing machines from England,' said Kwame. 'If he sends them by air it shouldn't take too long.'

'But I need a machine to make curtains and cushion covers for the kiosk and a few sample dresses to attract customers. I must get everything ready.'

'Maybe you can borrow or hire a machine for a few weeks.'

They soon found a sewing machine repairer who was willing to hire an old machine. Kwame asked the man what he thought of the Chinese machines. 'They don't last like the originals,' he said. 'They're always breaking down, but it's good for my business.'

Having Afriyie around revived Kwame's old problem. He had been amazed that he could survive long periods of celibacy in England but now that he was back in the torrid heat of his homeland his hormones surged with renewed vigour. He was tempted to ask Afriyie to assuage his hunger but was deterred by the thought that it might spoil his relationship with Tom. Nevertheless, he decided to discuss the matter with her and ask for her help. So late one evening after Akosua was in bed he told Afriyie how much he missed Comfort. 'It's not only Comfort, we had been arguing for a long time and the love had partly died; I need a woman.'

She didn't reply, but came to him and took his hand, pulling him gently towards his room.

'No, I'm not asking you to do it for me,' he said, 'only to help me find someone.'

'Don't you like me?'

'Of course I do, I like you very much. It's just that you're Tom's girl and I don't want to spoil it for all of us.'

'You think Tom would mind?'

'I'm sure he would; *abrofo* are like that.'

'Then I'll bring you my sister from Community 4. Can we go in the car?'

Kwame stopped the Land Rover in a small square in a maze of narrow roads. As he turned off the headlamps the surroundings disappeared from view. The darkness was pierced only by occasional lights shining dimly through wooden louvred shutters in a few of the houses. Afriyie got out of the vehicle and was immediately lost in the gloom. He strained in vain to see where she had gone. He waited, wondering what was going to happen next. He did not expect the girl to be Afriyie's full sister, or even half-sister, she was probably just a distant relative or a girl from the same village.

Did he care who she was or what she looked like? Perhaps not, all he wanted was release from this intolerable tension. Yet he trusted Afriyie to find him someone he might like. Would she be dark skinned or fair, tall or short, buxom or slender? He let his mind scan the spectrum of possibilities relishing the particular attributes of each manifestation of the female form. What would her breasts be like? Would they be *anoman* or *bintuo*? *Anoman* breasts were basically of conical form with the nipple at the apex. On some young women for a few fleeting years they jutted forward in a manner that defied the laws of gravity and structural engineering, but in most cases they folded over and hung down like Cameron Dodoo's pawpaws. *Bintuo* breasts were more hemispherical in form with the nipples at the centre. Even when they sagged the nipples stayed pointing forwards. Kwame liked to pursue this speculation and considered himself a connoisseur of form. He understood that size could be gauged empirically by remote sensing but form must be a gift of revelation: symbolising the ascent from the rational to the aesthetic. With such sweet musings the waiting passed without pain.

It was a long wait and Kwame had drifted off to sleep. He was aroused by the car door opening and Afriyie's voice asking if she had kept too long. The vehicle rocked as she climbed into the back seat of the Land Rover and another woman smelling of soap and fresh perfume climbed in beside him at the front. He turned to greet her and they shook hands but he only glimpsed her face briefly before the dim light inside the vehicle was extinguished by the closing door. 'My name is Gladys Nyarko,' she said. 'I'm sorry we delayed but I wasn't expecting to go out at this time.'

'That's all right,' said Kwame. 'I had a nap while I waited. I'm sorry to disturb you so late in the evening.'

'Oh, don't mention it. I'm always ready to help a friend of Afriyie.'

Kwame was curious to know what his new friend looked like but as she stepped into the light of the hall his first feeling was one of disappointment. Although it is said that the average woman, like the average man, does not exist, Gladys came close in almost all respects. She was neither tall nor short, neither dark nor fair, neither plump nor slim. At first he feared that she had no special feature that made her a person to remember, but as she began to engage him in conversation he noticed that she had unusually large and expressive eyes. He knew then that any man could find refreshment plunging into such deep dark pools, and he did.

The next morning the four of them had breakfast together. Gladys was busy making friends with Akosua. Afriyie told Kwame that Gladys was a hairdresser like Akos Mary, and he wouldn't have any trouble getting Akosua's hair done whenever it was needed. Gladys had finished her apprenticeship but she was still waiting for an opportunity to set up on her own. Kwame was tempted to offer to help Gladys to achieve her ambition as he was already helping Afriyie, but he decided to wait a while before committing himself to a new venture. Gladys had given him what he needed for the moment but he wasn't sure how long her spell would last.

With his domestic arrangements settled Kwame was free to concentrate on his work, and his training programme went forward smoothly. Every two or three months he rotated his young trainees through the production sections of the ITTU so that they became familiar with all the technical processes and the capabilities of all manufacturing facilities. As the technology was constantly evolving, the trainees were encouraged to devise their own solutions to the problems that arose. Gradually, as they gained experience, they were involved in helping to solve problems brought in by clients. This often entailed arranging short-term training in the ITTU, called visiting apprenticeships, and calling at client workshops to help with training, machine installations and the introduction of new products and processes.

Training a core of young engineers who were destined to extend the project in technology transfer to every region of Ghana gave Kwame a large measure of job satisfaction. He felt that he was at the heart of a programme of national importance and playing a key role in his country's development. With his savings from his work in England he could ignore for the moment the fact that his monthly salary barely covered his monthly expenditure. Absorbed in his work and with a peaceful home life, his first year at GRID passed quickly.

GRID had taken over the Tamale ITTU from the TCC in August 1987 and in April 1988 it was formally opened by Dr Francis Acquah, Minister for Industries, Science and Technology. In June 1988 the Tema ITTU also had its big day, attended by ministers, ambassadors, high commissioners and the European Community (EC) Delegate to Ghana. These grand occasions had taken place before Kwame joined the project but in December 1988 he had been present at Cape Coast to participate in Dr Acquah's last ITTU opening, this one fittingly in his home town. This completed the GRID project's first phase of activity. Now there would be a period of consolidation at Tamale, Tema and Cape Coast while preparations were made for the opening of ITTUs at Ho and Sunyani, scheduled for 1990.

The Tamale ITTU was a mature operation before GRID took over and its management presented few problems. The Tema ITTU was under the close control of the GRID project head office. It was at Cape Coast that the first instances of mismanagement arose. There, the ITTU had been pushed forward out of turn and before a specially trained manager could be provided. It had been decided to start operations by recruiting and appointing an experienced engineering workshop manager. This proved to be a great mistake, because such people were focused primarily on running their workshops at a profit rather than supporting the work of small private client workshops. Furthermore, some managers were skilful at diverting the profit into their own pockets. After only a few months it was suspected that this was happening at Cape Coast. Small client workshops were beginning to regard the ITTU as a competitor rather than an ally, and because the ITTU was much better equipped and believed to be subsidised by the government, the competition was seen as very unfair.

An enquiry proved the suspicions to be true and the first manager at Cape Coast was dismissed. As a temporary measure an experienced manager was seconded from the TCC. Kwame realised that the project faced a challenge to get young graduate engineers into key managerial positions at the earliest possible date before the new ITTUs collapsed and the concept lost credibility. In effect, his mission was to develop his own expertise and to help produce clones of himself as rapidly as possible.

Kwame pressed forward with his work with renewed vigour but it was not long before the crisis in Cape Coast returned. The manager seconded from the TCC completed his three months service and Solomon Djokoto of SRS Engineering in Kumasi also served on secondment for a similar period. Now, however, this help came to an end and another person was needed to take over. In October 1989 the director called Kwame to his office to discuss the situation.

'You know the problem, Kwame,' he began. 'We need ITTU managers who are both competent and reliable. We must have someone in charge in Cape Coast whom we can trust. I would like to send you there permanently but I'll soon need you for other duties. Dan Baffour-Opoku is in Tamale, Dan Nyarko is looking after the Tema ITTU and Sam Sanders is getting everything ready for Sunyani. What do you think of Assuah and Ghateh and the others who were here in Tema working for the Ministry before GRID took over?'

'Frankly, Doctor, I wouldn't trust most of them, they were running this place for their own benefit. Why were they kept on by GRID?'

'Dr Acquah told me he would sack them all and let us start with new people, but in the end he found that this was politically impossible. He told us that we must find them work to do where they couldn't do too much harm.'

'Well, the only one I would trust away from here is John Assuah.'

'That's what I was thinking, but I want your help to get him started.'

'How do you mean?'

'He has worked with us for 18 months and seems to understand the project and to be well motivated but I want you to hold his hand until you feel that he can manage on his own.'

'You mean transfer to Cape Coast?'

'Yes, let's hope it's only for two or three months.'

'Can I take one or two of the trainees with me? It'll be good experience for them.'

'That's what I thought you'd suggest.'

19

Cape Coast

A week later Kwame set out for Cape Coast with John Assuah and two of his trainees in a project Land Rover. Apart from attending the official opening of the ITTU the year before, it was his first visit to this former capital city of the Gold Coast colony, and now capital of the Central Region. It was often joked that Cape Coast was the education capital of Ghana, as it was the home of Ghana's third university and several good secondary schools. It was said that many people went to the Central Region to be educated but nobody stayed there afterwards; its only industry was education. Although situated between the relatively affluent Greater Accra and Ashanti Regions, Central Region remained one of the poorest in the country. This was why Dr Francis Acquah had been so anxious to introduce an ITTU to stimulate industrial development in his home region.

To reach Cape Coast from Tema it was necessary to pass Accra and this used to entail long delays, but a bypass road had recently been constructed that ran north of the capital as an extension to the Tema–Accra motorway. With the aid of this new road it was possible to travel westwards along the coast from Tema to Cape Coast, a distance of about 150 kilometres, in under three hours. This proximity enabled the director and division heads to visit Cape Coast and return the same day, a facility that had been quite impossible with commuting between Kumasi and Tamale. Kwame reflected that the same could be said in due course about establishing ITTUs in Ho and Koforidua, but today he was not planning on returning. He intended to stay in the manager's bungalow with John Assuah until his task was completed and he could leave John alone to continue the work on a permanent basis.

He was sorry to leave Akosua behind in Tema but knew that she would be well looked after by Afriyie and her education would not be further disturbed. He would let Afriyie bring Akosua to Cape Coast for a weekend or two during his posting. There were good beaches at Cape

Coast and a little further along the coast at Elmina, where Afriyie had holidayed with Tom. The little girl could swim in the sea and build sand castles to her heart's content. When tired of sand castles they could visit the historic stone castles at Cape Coast and Elmina, both of which were well preserved and open to tourists.

The Cape Coast ITTU had been started at the request of Dr Francis Acquah when he allocated a batch of machine tools donated by the government of India. With the aid of a special grant from the EC delegation in Accra it had been possible to purchase an existing building that was large enough to accommodate the ITTU. This needed a good deal of renovation before it could be brought into service but the work had been completed by the middle of 1988 and by the end of the year the ITTU had been ready for its formal opening by the minister. GRID had expected that the general poverty of the Central Region would present difficulties in generating income for the project and the corruption of the first manager had greatly exacerbated the situation. Solomon Djokoto, however, with his entrepreneurial flair, had demonstrated how the ITTU could operate viably and it was Kwame's aim to try to ensure that this became a permanent reality.

Kwame was also faced with the need to continue to develop the resources of the ITTU. Although the GRID project was well funded, the plan for the first phase of the work had not included Cape Coast. The EC funding supported the GRID headquarters operation and CIDA provided funding for the ITTUs at Tamale, Tema, Ho and Sunyani. Cape Coast was pushed forward because of the interest of Dr Acquah and the availability of machine tools from India. However, much more was needed. Several key machine tools were not included in the original donation and the foundry furnace had been irreparably damaged when dropped from a great height onto the quayside during unloading at Tema harbour. With further help from India, and also from Canada and Germany, GRID had been able to make up the full complement of machine tools, and a replacement foundry furnace had been constructed at the Tema ITTU. It was Kwame's task to finish the installations, especially in the foundry, as well as to train the manager and his staff to run the ITTU effectively.

To his relief, Kwame found that in spite of its chequered history the Cape Coast ITTU possessed some human resources of high quality. The chief technician, Kwesi Lawson, a native of the Central Region, had proved himself to be hard working, skilful and innovative. He was assisted by an English VSO, Jonathan Wilkinson, whose black-bearded countenance and tall frame concealed great technical expertise and a modest retiring nature. Together this pair had maintained solid progress in the workshops in spite of the turbulence at the management level. All technical facilities were working correctly and the first intake of apprentices was benefiting from inspired instruction.

GRID had made great efforts to gain further international support for Cape Coast. One of its successes was to persuade the British Overseas Development Administration (ODA) to finance a blacksmith-training programme. Under this scheme it was planned to bring 60 blacksmiths from villages in all parts of the Central Region and train them for three months in the repair and maintenance of the new agricultural and rural industrial machines being manufactured in Cape Coast by the ITTU and its small engineering clients. At the end of the training the blacksmiths would be given the opportunity to purchase modern tools and equipment at affordable prices on easy-payment terms.

Kwame looked forward to recruiting the first batch of ten blacksmiths and working with Lawson, Wilkinson and Assuah to get the training programme underway. He wanted the trainees to maintain contact with the ITTU and act as agents spreading its technical inputs to all parts of the region. He was determined that the blacksmith-training project should succeed and be replicated in other regions where ITTUs were in operation.

Kwame realised that the blacksmith-training programme was a good opportunity to fill the workshops with meaningful activity and put the ITTU firmly on the map. Although Cape Coast was the youngest ITTU it was being given the opportunity to pioneer this new project and he hoped that it would restore morale that had been damaged by the succession of management changes. The more he thought about the task ahead the more he felt that this was what he wanted to do. He was working at the grassroots to motivate and empower his people and promote the economic development of his country by the bottom-up approach advocated by Dr Busia and so warmly applauded by his father. He had expressed some doubts about the timeliness of this approach in his discussions with Tom but now that he was getting to grips again with the real problem he was sure that his efforts would yield tangible benefits.

If Kwame needed any extra motivation it was provided rather unexpectedly by Gladys. She had asked Afriyie if she could accompany her and Akosua when they visited Kwame in Cape Coast for the weekend. They called at the ITTU on Saturday morning when a skeleton staff on overtime was helping Lawson and Wilkinson prepare for the first influx of rural blacksmiths. After hearing about the blacksmith-training programme Gladys asked what training the ITTU was providing for women. 'We hope to train a few women blacksmiths,' said Kwame with a grin. 'We have already trained a few women welders.'

'But what about the girls who don't want to do men's work?'

'Well, we teach tie-dye and batik cloth printing and some of the ITTUs teach broadloom weaving and cotton spinning.'

'Anything else?'

'At Tema they are introducing the production of baby-weaning food from locally available raw materials, in Kumasi they have introduced machines for making gari faster and in Tamale they are improving the method of making shea butter. These activities are all done by groups of women.'

'What about honey making?'

'Yes, many women are taking up beekeeping and producing honey to feed their families and to sell.'

Gladys asked Kwame if she could stay on for a few days after Afriyie and Akosua returned to Tema. He replied that he feared she would be bored because he was compelled to spend all day at the ITTU or on trek.

'Couldn't I come with you? Maybe I could help.'

'How could you help?'

'I could tell women about the training and get more to come to the ITTU.'

'But you don't know enough about the work to do that.'

'I could soon learn; please let me learn about the women's training.'

'OK, you can attend the tie-dye and batik section for a few days and see if you like it.'

Kwame was sure that nobody in GRID would complain about the extra temporary trainee because interest and enthusiasm were valued above all else. Had he not himself benefited greatly from this attitude that had brought him promotion and overseas training opportunities beyond his qualifications and expectations? Special emphasis was also being placed on increasing training and employment opportunities for women. He recalled being told at Tema that the first two female engineering apprentices had originally been employed as cleaners. After several months of cleaning the workshops they had asked to be taken on as technical apprentices and their request had been granted. Prior to this, the recruitment of women into engineering crafts had achieved the appointment of only one female technician. Now the schoolchildren touring the Tema ITTU could see women at work alongside the men and a slow trickle of girls into engineering apprenticeships had started.

First thing on Monday morning Gladys was introduced to the tie-dye and batik section leader and left to fend for herself. The demands of work occupied Kwame throughout the day and he was only reminded of Gladys's presence when she hailed him as he boarded the Land Rover to return home in the evening. 'How did you get on?' he asked as John Assuah drove cautiously along the bare laterite track to the main road.

'I learned how to tie the cloth; it was very interesting,' she replied. 'I would like to do this work.'

'But you're a trained hairdresser.'

'There are too many hairdressers; these days, every girl is a hairdresser or a dressmaker. I want to do something new.'

'Then you'll have to complete the whole course. You can do it in Tema.'

'No, I want to do it here.'

'I may go back to Tema in a month or two.'

'Then I'll go to Tema with you.'

Kwame was not quite sure that was what he wanted, but concurred in silence.

Early in December Kwame was asked to report to the director in Tema on the progress he was making in Cape Coast. Knowing Dr Jones always asked for a written report he prepared this document and sent it on ahead to GRID headquarters. So the director was able to open the discussion with 'You seem to be just about ready to hand over to John Assuah.'

'Yes Doctor, things are moving ahead quite well.'

'What's the feeling among the clients? Have they got over the bad feelings created by the troubles?'

'Yes, they have. It was a good idea sending Solomon Djokoto there for three months. Being a private businessman himself he did much to restore the confidence of the local workshop owners.'

'Thank God for our friends at the TCC, eh? We still rely on them for experienced people. When will your young people be ready?'

'They're doing well, Doctor, especially the two I took along with me to Cape Coast.'

'Should we leave one there to help John Assuah?'

'I think that's a good idea; John would like to have the support. Will Jonathan Wilkinson also stay there?'

'He's a man we would like to have everywhere in the system, but Cape Coast must remain our priority until Ho and Sunyani are farther along.'

'Then I should return to Tema?'

'Yes, I want you to visit Cape Coast periodically to support the foundry developments but we have a new task to keep you busy here for a few weeks.'

Kwame was curious to know what the director had in mind for him and he was soon to find out. 'You've seen our video *The Secret of Wealth*, haven't you?'

'Yes, Doctor.'

'We made it in August and September 1987 with the help of a company in Accra called Televideo. Now we want to make a video about foundry developments to be used in training and to show people what we are doing. A script has been drafted, you can pick up a copy from SEACOM, I want you to check it for historical accuracy and then provide technical support throughout the filming.'

'Will we be working with Televideo again?'

'Yes; when you're satisfied with the script I want you to go to Televideo with Robert Battah, the head of SEACOM. You will be working with Beattie Canford, he's the MD at Televideo but still gets very involved in the filming and editing.'

'How long will it take?'

'That depends on Televideo, but we want to film in Tema, Suame and Tamale and it will be your responsibility to arrange the visits and ensure that there is plenty of activity to film.'

'Then I'll need to travel ahead of the film crew.'

'Work it all out with Robert and the ITTU managers.'

'Leave it to us, Doctor.'

Kwame was excited by this new challenge. He had admired *The Secret of Wealth* when he first saw it. It seemed to him to be a professional production and had been shown on Ghana Broadcasting Corporation's TV service as well as used for training and publicity at GRID. Now he had a chance to get involved in making a sequel. It would bring him into contact with many new people and new techniques. He hurried over to the building occupied by the Socioeconomic and Communications Division (SEACOM) to collect the script. Working with SEACOM was something he always wanted to do. It was staffed mainly by sociologists and journalists and produced the GRID annual review and quarterly newsletter. In the past his contact with SEACOM had been confined to handing in reports of his work. Now he was to participate fully in one of their projects.

Robert Battah was away on trek but one of his helpers soon produced a copy of the script for Kwame to take away. SEACOM had a full complement of personal computers with desk-top publishing capability. It was the first time that Kwame had been able to study such equipment close up in Ghana, although he had used PCs on his training course at Warwick. He asked if he could use one of the machines to type his suggestions for changes in the script and was told to come back the next day after he had read through the draft.

That evening after supper Kwame settled down to read the script. He had not seen such a document before with dialogue on the left and filming directions on the right. Once he had got used to terms such as 'talking head' and 'voice-over' he became absorbed in the story of grassroots foundry development in Ghana. He realised that he had lived through, and contributed to, all of the recent history. With his new knowledge gained in England he felt that he also carried the future in his head. He relished the thought of putting all this into a permanent document to guide and inspire others along the same path. At the end he couldn't see much wrong with the script; it provided a good working framework, but everything would depend upon putting the words to the right pictures. This he was sure he could do.

Gladys and Afriyie found Kwame's total absorption rather irritating. Akosua had long since gone to bed and the two young women had grown tired of their own conversation and GBC TV. They tried to rouse Kwame from his preoccupation but most of their remarks were answered with only a nod or a grunt. Was there no way they could attract his interest? They put their heads together and soon rose to take their evening showers. When they emerged they had their white bath towels hooked around their waists. Now they had Kwame's full attention!

'What have you been doing?' Afriyie asked.

'Just checking the script of a video film,' he replied.

'Well, now it's time for action!' said Gladys, and with a girl pulling on each hand he was dragged off for his bedtime shower.

Kwame was delighted by this new turn in his domestic fortunes and he was even happier when these sessions were repeated two or three times over the next few weeks. At first, Afriyie was content to play a supporting role but soon her involvement became increasingly ardent.

In spite of acute temptation, Kwame held back from trespassing on what he considered to be Tom's territory. At last, however, he could resist no more and was enticed to cross the frontier. Surprisingly, Gladys seemed as happy at this turn of events as Afriyie. It was some time before Kwame realised that the whole operation had been planned by the two women to reach just this outcome.

In parallel with these domestic diversions, Kwame was involved in producing the video. After Beattie Canford and his cameraman had completed filming the ITTU foundry in Tema, Kwame accompanied the small team to Kumasi where his old friends at Suame Magazine helped to arrange some effective shooting at the ITTU and in several private foundries. Then they moved on to Tamale where the first modern iron foundry in the north of Ghana was now in regular use at the ITTU. Kwame was happy to see that the project on which he had worked for so long was now in daily operation. They were also able to film traditional grassroots aluminium casting in progress in the private workshop of one of the ITTU trainees. This enabled the film to show one of the historical roots of the foundry industry.

Beattie, Robert and Kwame were pleased with the results of the filming. On their return to the south, Beatty invited Kwame to attend the Televideo studio in Accra to help with the editing. This was an entirely new experience for Kwame and he was fascinated by the process. Sitting beside Beattie at the editing suite he learned how to fit the pictures to the script by cutting and joining sections of what they had filmed. It was Kwame's responsibility to ensure that the film followed the script closely in presenting the correct historical sequence of developments and providing a full explanation of the technical processes. When a section of film was joined together to their mutual satisfaction, Beattie recorded the voice-over with his long-practised BBC-trained eloquence. Finally, the soundtrack was completed by adding the background music recorded during the visit to Kumasi by Koo Nimo and his band of traditional musicians.

Kwame attended several of these editing sessions, each time learning more about the technical processes involved. He also got to know Beattie's two talented sons, Pinok and Leonard. Kwame had known Pinok in Kumasi where they had both attended the mechanical engineering diploma course. With his father's help, Pinok had set up a small business involved in plastic injection moulding. He was soon making his own moulds and selling some to other enterprises. Eventually, he had developed a locally manufactured injection moulding machine and was helping other companies in and around Accra to set up in business with a full set of moulding equipment. Kwame marvelled at the progress his contemporary was making.

Leonard, an electrical engineer, was equally outstanding in his field. He was engaged in making traffic lights and installing traffic control systems. His products were in use in Kumasi and other provincial cities but not yet in the capital. He told Kwame about his efforts to break into the Accra market. This involved frequent visits to the seat of government, the Castle. He was negotiating for a contract to install traffic lights on one of Accra's main thoroughfares, Kojo Thompson Road. He was dismayed at the corruption he was encountering at all levels and had asked one of his contacts why everyone got so much involved. 'The river is flowing to the sea and we must go with it,' was the reply he received.

'And some of those guys need a new girl every night,' Leonard added with overt disapproval.

The work of editing the video eventually came to an end. Kwame felt pangs of regret that he would no longer be visiting this lively place on a regular basis. At the same time he felt a sense of real achievement in having created a permanent record of years of work that he and his colleagues had accomplished in challenging circumstances. He asked Beattie to make a copy of the videotape for him to take to the GRID project in Tema for final approval by SEACOM and the director.

As he was about to leave, an older man with a balding head came into the editing suite and was greeted by Beattie with 'Hello Professor, we weren't expecting you today.'

'How was the filming we did last week?' enquired the professor.

'Very good,' replied Beattie, and turning to Kwame he added, 'you might like to stay to see this.'

Then Beattie explained that the professor was from the University of Ghana Medical School and was studying the AIDS victims of the Krobo tribe in the Eastern Region. 'Is there AIDS in Ghana?' asked Kwame, who had previously heard of AIDS only as a disease suffered by male homosexuals and drug abusers in the USA.

'They're bringing it back to Ghana from Abidjan in the Ivory Coast,' replied the professor.

'Who are?'

'The prostitutes.'

'What prostitutes?'

271

'The Krobo girls; it's a long tradition that they go to Abidjan to make their fortunes but these days they're bringing back much more than money.'

'Are you treating them?'

'We're trying to; sometimes one or two recover when given a more nutritious diet but most are incurable at our present state of knowledge.'

Then, to Kwame's horror, Beattie started to show the video from Krobo, not on the small screen of the editing machine but projected almost life size onto the white wall of the studio. Skeletal figures lay on makeshift bamboo and grass couches as the professor and his assistants carried out routine examinations and procedures. Film shot at regular intervals of the same women showed how quickly they were deteriorating and some dropped out of the sequences as the professor and his team lost the battle to prolong their lives.

After scanning through the latest filming in more detail the professor rose, grunting his thanks, and with a grim nod back from the doorway, took his leave. Kwame sat deep in thought until Beattie roused him by asking what he knew about HIV/AIDS. 'Very little before today,' he replied. 'I didn't realise the Krobo girls consorted with homosexual men.'

'They don't,' said Beattie. 'They became infected the natural way.'

'Do normal men get it too?' asked Kwame.

'I'm afraid so,' replied Beattie. 'We filmed the first male victim in Krobo just a few weeks ago.'

'Then we're all at risk!' exclaimed Kwame.

'Not if we stay faithful to the little woman at home,' said Beattie gently. 'Other than that, we must put our faith in a condom.'

Kwame had much to think about on the drive back to Tema. He seldom remembered much of the monotonous cruise along the motorway and today he recalled nothing. What was he to make of this startling new knowledge? He had enjoyed a faithful monogamous relationship with Comfort for several years but her abrupt departure had set him on another course. He felt that he could not face the agony of another broken marriage and had resolved to remain independent, slaking his thirst from time to time as opportunity arose. Now he must review that policy. One thing was certain: he must resist the temptation to take a lady of the night, no matter how pressing his need. For the moment his needs were met by Gladys and Afriyie. Was that safe for him, for all of them? He couldn't be sure.

* * *

He was relieved of the need to make a quick decision by instructions to return to Cape Coast. He was to take over for two weeks while John Assuah went on annual leave. 'While you are there I want you to check out everything as thoroughly as possible,' said the director, 'I have confidence in the new management but once bitten, twice shy. We can't afford another scandal at *Oguah*.'

Kwame smiled; Dr Jones liked to air his knowledge of the local culture and language. 'I'm sure that John Assuah is doing a good job, Doctor, but I will look into everything carefully with Jonathan's help and bring you a report.'

Kwame was determined to spend two quiet weeks away from home to allow time to reassess his domestic life. He would miss Akosua, of course, but he wanted no visitors during this short mission. After starting her training at Cape Coast, Gladys had moved to Tema at the end of Kwame's posting. She had made good progress on the tie-dye course and was now producing lengths of cloth to her own designs and supplying them to Afriyie to make up into dresses and shirts. These innovations were creating much interest and the two women were planning a serious business venture in partnership. They felt that they could be part of the new fashion industry that was already gaining ground in the trendy youth communities of Accra and Kumasi. The close collaboration was resulting in Gladys becoming almost a permanent lodger in Kwame's Tema house. If that was not what Kwame wanted he would soon have to make his feelings known.

At the Cape Coast ITTU the work was progressing smoothly. The first batch of blacksmiths had completed training and returned to their village forges. A second class of ten rustic craftsmen had taken their place. The departing graduates had been given the option of taking away a range of modern tools and equipment on easy-payment terms. In general the blacksmiths had chosen to buy rather fewer tools than had been expected but almost all had seized the opportunity to invest in an electric welding set. This surprised the ITTU engineers as only some of the blacksmiths' villages yet had an electricity supply. However, the trainees explained that the electric welder opened up a range of lucrative new repair opportunities and even if they could not begin this work straight away they wanted to be ready when the power supply eventually reached them. It might be a long time before another opportunity arose to acquire the equipment on these easy-payment terms.

Some trained blacksmiths resolved to move their workshops to locations where electricity was already available. Unfortunately this meant that some repair services left the rural areas and moved to Cape Coast and other urban centres. This was not the intention of the ITTU programme but there was nothing that could be done to interfere with the free movement of free enterprise. Enough blacksmiths already had access to electrical power, or were anticipating its early arrival, to retain most of their operations in their original villages.

The proprietor of one industrial enterprise located quite close to the ITTU was a constant visitor. The business was a large cold store, freezing fish caught by local fishermen that was destined for delivery to markets throughout the country. The proprietor needed help in repairing his plant and installing new facilities. One day, on a visit to the ITTU, he called to Kwame, 'Weren't you working at the TCC in Kumasi?'

'Yes,' replied Kwame, 'but how do you know me?'

'You delivered bolts and nuts to our boat-building outfit in Accra.'

'Then you were with Kofifo!'

'That's right, three of us, all Kofis – hence the name of the firm.'

'You were one of our best customers; what happened to your business?'

'We kept going for several years, as you know, but eventually we couldn't get the imported diesel engines for our fishing boats and the business folded.'

'I'm very sorry to hear that. We all admired what you were doing: building ocean-going boats using local materials, except for the engines, of course.'

'That's right; with your support for the bolts and nuts and a few castings we were managing nicely. The government should have done more to support such new industries.'

'I couldn't agree more,' said Kwame.

Kwame pondered on what he had learned. The Kofifo Boatbuilding Company Ltd. had flourished from the mid-1970s making ocean-going fishing boats from the *odum* timber that was locally produced and plentiful from local sawmills. Each boat was held together by hundreds of large steel bolts and for several years these had been supplied by the Suame ITTU and its small engineering clients in Kumasi. On more than one occasion a Kofifo director had said publicly that the availability of the locally made steel bolts had made their project possible. Later, the Suame ITTU foundry began to supply bronze castings and little by little the production was becoming locally self-sufficient. However, importing diesel engines had always been problematic. Successive governments failed to issue the necessary import licences and at times the boat-builders were supplying only customers who could obtain their own engines, often with the help of a relative overseas or through the black market at extortionate prices. In those days Kwame remembered seeing long lines of large wooden hulls lying for months in the Accra boatyard waiting for engines. In the end, the three Friday men had been forced to wind up the business and go their separate ways.

If only we could have made the diesel engines as well, thought Kwame. With current foundry developments and growing strength in metal machining it shouldn't be long before this is possible. He made a mental note to study the project in detail and prepare a proposal to put to the director. He remembered the little single-cylinder Lister diesel engines he had shown Tom during their visit to Tamale: the old English machines that seemed to chug away unattended for ever. That should be our starting point, he decided; if such engines can be copied by the Chinese and the Indians, why not by the Ghanaians? Kofifo was ahead of its time and our grassroots engineers couldn't catch up fast enough, but in time we can prepare the ground for a new Kofifo to arise. With thoughts such as these Kwame turned his disappointment into positive resolve to redouble his efforts.

He tried out his idea on Jonathan Wilkinson. 'Do you think we could build a diesel engine?'

'Not here in Cape Coast.'

'No, but in Tema or Suame?'

'Maybe in Tema; I don't know what Suame can do, but isn't a diesel engine a bit ambitious? Couldn't we start with a steam engine? ITDG have a set of drawings we could use. That, I think, we might manage.'

'But a steam engine is too old-fashioned to be interesting these days. People would just see it as a sort of toy. A diesel engine would have an immediate use driving a corn mill or a cassava grater.'

'Couldn't the steam engine do the same?'

'Yes, but the people know diesel engines and how to use them; they only know steam engines from their history lessons at school.'

The two friends continued to discuss the technical and economic details for some time with the Englishman trying to see a logical progression in technology based on total local self-sufficiency and Kwame eager to keep focused on the modern world and its needs and challenges. Was he, like Kwame Nkrumah, trying to take a great leap forward that was impractical; or was Jonathan turning grassroots engineering development into a sort of white man's hobby that would never excite the interest of anyone outside the project? The two friends ended the discussion with the realisation that this was the debate that had haunted the

275

intermediate/appropriate technology movement for at least two decades. Perhaps it would only be resolved when future historians analysed developmental initiatives that had succeeded and others that had failed. Perhaps there was no theoretical or universal answer and people in different places and at different times would inevitably progress by different routes.

From speculating about what the more advanced ITTUs might do in the future, Kwame had to turn to what the Cape Coast ITTU was doing now. He had promised the director a detailed report. He decided to spend a day or two trekking in the hinterland to visit some of the trained blacksmiths in their own workshops. The Central Region is one of the smallest regions of Ghana in geographical extent and the distances were not so great as to require nights to be spent away from Cape Coast.

Kwame didn't only want to know how the blacksmiths were benefiting from the training and putting their new skills and facilities into practice, although this was important. He also wanted to get their impressions of the ITTU, how it seemed to be run, how they felt they had been treated and, above all, whether or not they felt that the project had been run for their benefit. Did they feel that anyone had been withholding any part of the overseas aid for their own benefit? Kwame's past experience in the ITTUs had taught him that illiterate rural artisans, the intended beneficiaries of most foreign-funded projects, had a nose for detecting when others were taking part of what should rightfully be theirs. While he had no intention of asking about these matters directly he knew that he could win the confidence of the artisans and that they would vent any grievances they might have.

After visiting eight of the ten blacksmiths who had undergone training at Cape Coast ITTU Kwame was satisfied that the artisans had benefited from the training and were happy with their treatment. Several mentioned that Mr Assuah, Mr Lawson and the big *oboroni* with a black beard had all been kind and helpful. Most indicated in one way or another that they had heard about foreign-funded aid projects but this was the first time that they had personally benefited from one. Kwame was relieved. This sort of feedback was the best indication that the project was being run as it should be with the focus firmly on the interests of the client. If he found nothing amiss inside the ITTU and its accounting records, he could report that the ITTU was now in good hands.

He spent the next few days with his head in the books of accounts and a pocket calculator in his hand. Although he knew that the GRID project finance officer was sending people to all the ITTUs on regular audits of accounts he also realised that there were some aspects of accounting in engineering enterprises that were best checked by an engineer. This was especially true in relation to job costing. Only an engineer could assess whether the quantities of materials or the man-hours worked were appropriate for a given job. He knew that in private workshops, for example, the proprietor would hand out electric welding rods one at a time to ensure that none was wasted or lost. In government workshops, however, a welder could be given a whole packet, with the result that one or two rods would be used on the job in hand and the rest sold in the local market or passed to the welder's self-employed brother.

Kwame had learned how to balance the books the hard way; juggling the income and expenditure of his market trolley business at Suame. Later, he had formalised his understanding on a part-time course in Coventry that he was required to undergo to qualify for membership of the Institution of Mechanical Engineers. He had somehow fitted in the classes between the foundry school and the ladies' club on long dark winter evenings. Well, the evenings were still long and dark but at least they were warm. He shivered at the thought of those winter evenings in England and gave thanks for the permanent central heating of the Central Region.

Kwame knew that many accounting irregularities were connected with purchases, especially purchases of raw materials. Traders were very seldom asked to give receipts to private buyers but government organisations always demanded them. It was common practice to make out receipts for a higher amount than the actual purchase price, with the difference going into the pockets of the manager and purchasing officer. Kwame kept himself up to date with the current market price of commonly used raw materials but he couldn't be sure about every purchase. He noted a few costly items to be checked with Lawson and Wilkinson and also in the local market but was relieved when his discreet enquiries later revealed no serious discrepancies.

He called a meeting with the accounts clerks and put to them a list of questions that he had compiled as he studied their books. Then he quizzed them about how the former manager had attempted to cover his diversion of funds and asked them if they thought that the revised regulations were making it harder for future managers to attempt the same tricks. On the whole he was satisfied with the answers he was given. He ended the session with a warning that any suspected irregularities should be reported at once to the GRID project finance officer in Tema. He knew, however, that it would be an exceptionally honourable clerk who would be prepared to report his or her manager, especially as a corrupt manager would probably ensure that his subordinates were sharing the benefit. Nevertheless, he felt that he had done all he could to check and maintain correct working. There were good people scattered throughout the project at all levels. They would not be known until they revealed themselves by their actions. Until then, one could only hope that one of them would be in the right place at the right time to blow the whistle when corruption again reared its ugly head.

Kwame returned to Tema in a contented mood. He had a good report to make to the director, having found the Cape Coast ITTU well recovered from its recent setback. He looked forward to his next assignment and speculated on what it might be. He also looked forward to being home again with Akosua and Afriyie. As for the disturbing matter of HIV/AIDS, he had decided to propose a long-term relationship to Afriyie. He had a feeling, based on recent developments, that she would agree.

As he drove his Land Rover smoothly along the motorway he felt that all was well in his small world. He could not know that shocks awaited him both at home and at work, although they would not all turn out to be bad.

20

Tom's Return

On arrival at his little house, Kwame was greeted rapturously by Akosua but rather coolly by Afriyie. Gladys was away visiting her family in the Eastern Region. Kwame spent the evening chatting and playing with Akosua. When he noticed that it was nine o'clock he said, 'It's time for bath and bed, Little One.' Akosua ran off to her shower.

'Why do you always send her to bed at a fixed time?' asked Afriyie. 'Most children are left until they fall asleep naturally.'

'It's a custom I learned in England,' explained Kwame. 'I'm sure that it's better for their health to go to bed early. There is less of a problem getting them up for school in the morning, and I'm sure they do better at school if they get enough sleep at night and don't fall asleep during classes.'

'You always want to be a modern man, don't you Kwame Mainu?' The use of his family name rang alarm bells in Kwame's head; that was how Comfort had always spoken to him when there was a serious issue on her mind.

Akosua came to kiss her father and Afriyie before running off to her room. 'When will she start to slow down?' asked Kwame jovially, hoping to lighten the atmosphere that Afriyie had created. Without answering, Afriyie handed him a letter. Immediately, Kwame knew that it was from Tom. It told Afriyie that Tom was soon to visit Ghana in connection with the partnership between Warwick and Kumasi universities and he planned to spend a few days in Tema visiting GRID. He hoped that he would have the opportunity to spend some off-duty hours with Afriyie and Kwame.

Kwame put down the letter and looked at Afriyie, sitting opposite him and desperately trying to read his thoughts. Neither spoke. This was an eventuality that both had been expecting but neither had prepared themselves to face. Always willing to put off making a decision, Kwame had hoped that the problem might fade away if he avoided thinking about it. Now the problem was coming to confront them in their own home and they had little time to decide how to approach it. Both wanted to avoid hurting the friend who had helped them so much, but neither wanted to give up their recently discovered domestic bliss.

Eventually, Afriyie could stand the strain of silence no longer. She rose and came behind Kwame's chair to embrace him and whisper in his ear, 'I love Tom, but I love you more. What can we do that won't hurt him too much?'

'I don't know,' breathed Kwame, 'but leave it with me and I'll try to work something out.'

Long after Afriyie had retired to her bed Kwame sat looking at his friend's letter. It was not a long one, only one side of A4 paper typed on a PC, as were all Tom's personal letters. He read the letter repeatedly until he almost knew it by heart. It was only then that he noticed that there were no words of endearment. It was in no sense a love letter. Did Tom always write to Afriyie in this rather formal way? How often did he write?

Kwame hurried to Afriyie's room and roused her from her slumbers. 'Can you show me Tom's last letter?' he almost shouted at the startled young woman, as she struggled to raise herself in response to his urgent demand.

'Over there in the top drawer of my dressing table,' she gasped, 'all Tom's letters are there.'

Kwame drew open the drawer and took out a small sheaf of papers. He was struck by how few they were. The last was dated nearly six months ago. 'Are you sure this is the last one?' he asked.

'Yes, I'm quite sure; he doesn't write very often.'

Kwame scanned the letter briefly; then he looked at the earlier letters. 'These are not really love letters, are they?'

'No, that's how he always writes.'

'Do you think he really loves you?'

'I used to think so, now you make me wonder.'

'If his love has cooled down we don't need to worry so much about hurting him. He may even be pleased that we have found happiness together.'

'Wouldn't that be wonderful; we could still be friends!'

'Let's hope that's how it turns out,' said Kwame, sliding under the single bed sheet beside her.

'Shall I come to your room?' asked Afriyie sleepily.

'No, I'll stay with you here.'

Next morning Kwame reported to the director on his visit to Cape Coast. As usual, Dr Jones had read his report in advance. 'You seem to have found things in good shape.'

'Yes Doctor, John Assuah has got off to a good start and Lawson and Jonathan are still doing a good job.'

'So the blacksmiths are pleased with the training programme.'

'Yes, they really value being able to add welding repairs to their range of services, but I'm sorry that a few are moving to town to get electric power.'

'That's inevitable, I'm afraid; we always have to accept a few unforeseen side effects. The migrants are by no means lost to the development process. Some may become urban-based manufacturers.'

Then the director fixed his gaze on Kwame and said quietly, 'You know I'm handing over next week, I won't be your director next time we meet.'

'I did hear something, but I didn't realise the time had come so soon.'

'Yes, I have been instructed to hand over to Dr Kofi Mensah, the co-director, on the first of April 1990.'

'Will you be leaving GRID?'

'Not immediately. I'll serve out the remaining two years of my contract as technical adviser to the project.'

'Will you still be in charge of ITTU operations?'

'Yes, but I will no longer have the last word on staff development, training, appointments and promotions. Inevitably, the new director will want to recruit and promote his own people and I'm afraid our old team from the TCC will suffer a degree of neglect.'

'How will that affect me personally?'

'That's what I want to discuss with you.'

Kwame sat intently waiting for the director to continue. 'You know all about my programme to develop a corps of effective ITTU managers. How we need a new breed of young engineering managers who are free from the constraints of traditional local workshop management practice and focused on serving the needs of their small enterprise clients.'

'Yes, Doctor.'

'Well, you have an excellent background of experience in ITTU operations, perhaps the best in the project, but to try to ensure eventual appointment as a permanent manager or a senior engineer in the ITTU Operations Division you also need an MSc.'

'Yes Doctor, I don't expect every director to value experience above formal qualifications as you often do.'

'You also know that I've been sending some of your colleagues on the MSc course in production management at the University of Cranfield. Your friend Dan Baffour-Opoku was the first to go, followed by Dan Nyarko and Sam Sanders.'

'Will I get this chance as well?'

'I've made all the arrangements. I wanted to be sure that you would get your chance before I hand over. You will be at Cranfield for a year from next October. Are you happy with that?'

'Yes Doctor, thank you very much.'

'One other thing,' continued Dr Jones. 'You know your little house was built by the Tema Development Corporation.'

'Yes.'

'Well, they have a scheme whereby their houses can be bought by tenants at very reasonable prices. I wondered if you might like to buy your house. Dr Mensah told me that it's too small for GRID to buy, so I wondered if you would like to take advantage of the opportunity.'

'But my house has been improved and extended. I thought that it was already privately owned.'

'It has a somewhat chequered history, I'm afraid. At one time it was sold fraudulently by a tenant to a private businesswoman who made the improvements, but when the TDC found out and took the matter to court she dropped her claim to the property. Apparently she is thought to own twelve properties around Tema and is under investigation by the One Man One House Committee. I don't think she'll worry about your little place.'

'Where is she now?'

'She was last rumoured to be in jail in Bombay. It seems there was something in her luggage that shouldn't have been there.'

'So the house is still owned by the TDC!'

'Yes, you won't find another bargain like this because the cost of improvements are not included in the selling price. If you want to go ahead I can initiate action before I hand over.'

'Thank you, Doctor, thank you very much, I would like that.'

'Right then, I'll set the ball rolling. Don't expect any fast action though; I'm told the process takes about a year to complete.'

Kwame stayed in his seat. He was sure the director had more to tell him. 'Your friend, Dr Tom Arthur, is paying us another visit next week. He will go on to visit our old friends at the TCC. If he agrees, I would like you to accompany him throughout his visit. It will help to keep GRID in close contact with its roots in Kumasi.'

'Keep your eyes open for any new developments that are ready for transfer to any of the ITTUs. I'm particularly interested in what they're doing in brick making, concrete roofing tiles and formulating feed for fish farming. Under the next phase of EC support we will have funds to support new developments at the TCC, and it's good that we are briefed in advance on possibilities. Please raise this issue with Sosthenes Battah, if he's back from Malawi, and see what initiatives we could coordinate with TCC and Warwick. If Sosthenes or Peter Donkor would like to come back with you and Tom, I would be happy to discuss the matter further.'

Kwame was very happy at the new prospects before him. His career seemed to be moving forward in substantial and fulfilling increments: Cape Coast, the video, Cape Coast again, the assignment with Tom and now a chance to become a Master of Science! Ever since the days when he had struggled to get into the polytechnic to begin his basic engineering training he had harboured the secret ambition to one day achieve a master's degree. Now the chance had come and he would seize it with all the ardour and serious intent that he had applied to his earlier studies. He looked forward to Tom's arrival with only a faint shadow of doubt concerning his relationship with Afriyie.

Flights from London to Accra arrive in the early evening and Kwame was there at Kotoka International Airport with Afriyie and Akosua to welcome their friend from England. As always, there was a long wait after the aircraft had landed before the passengers began to emerge from the arrivals hall. Akosua was running about, and after being retrieved several times by a vigilant Afriyie, Kwame asked her to stand still for a few moments to avoid being lost in the crowd of expectant greeters. Some travellers began to escape from the customs officials and straggle out of the arrivals hall, dragging their bulging suitcases and walking bravely forward into the throng, to be engulfed by excited friends and family. Soon they were being shepherded away by bodyguards shielding them from predatory porters and taxi drivers, the spoils of *aburokyiri* lofted high on strong shoulders.

While the joy of others is infectious it also serves to excite fear that one's own expected guest may have missed the flight or deferred their journey. Many travellers had emerged but Tom was not among them. Akosua was hopping up and down impatiently, and repeatedly asking why Uncle Tom was not coming. The main flood of emerging passengers had abated, and only a few bewildered foreigners were still stumbling out in the first stage of culture shock, when Afriyie gave a yell at spotting a familiar face. But it wasn't Tom; it was Akos Mary!

The three of them waved and shouted and Akos Mary hurried over to them. 'Tom is having trouble with the customs,' she explained hastily. 'Kwame, can you come and help?'

To his surprise, Kwame was allowed to accompany Akos Mary back into the customs hall where he was greeted by a perspiring Tom with 'Kwame, am I glad to see you!'

'What's the problem?' asked Kwame.

'It's these instruments that I've brought to help the TCC in their research,' explained Tom. 'An electric-arc spectrometer and some chemical testing equipment. The officers seem to think that they have some sinister subversive purpose. Can you explain what they are for and how they will help Ghana's technological progress?'

With a few well-chosen words in Twi, Kwame secured the release of his friend. They walked out into the Accra night which descended upon Tom like a hot wet blanket that almost made him wish to return to the air-conditioned confines of the customs hall. At the same time the familiar musty smell of the tropical evening enveloped him in happy memories of his previous visits and restored his peace of mind.

They carried their suitcases to the car park where the faithful Land Rover waited and soon the reunited party was speeding down the motorway to Tema. The vehicle was full of noisy chatter with the women in full flow in rapid Twi, Kwame and Tom in less-animated but equally earnest English, and Akosua jumping in and out of both conversations as impulse and opportunity allowed. Much to Kwame's pride, the little girl was almost as fluently bilingual as her father.

Tom had booked accommodation at a hotel but Kwame insisted that the pair stayed at his house. 'You can have Afriyie's room,' he said to Tom, 'and the three girls can share Akosua's room.'

'Yes,' said Afriyie, 'and tomorrow we'll pound you the best fufu you've ever tasted.'

'I thought you weren't supposed to taste it,' joked Tom, 'just swallow it down unchewed.'

'It's the soup that has the taste, *oboroni*,' laughed Akos Mary.

'Do you want palm nut or groundnut soup?' asked Afriyie.

'Whatever you like,' said Tom. 'I guess we'll try them all again while we're here, but please give my snails to Akos Mary, she likes them much more than I do.'

As soon as they were settled in the house, with drinks in their hands and roast groundnuts and plantain chips within easy reach, the questions started to flow. There were so many that Kwame almost suggested that they begin by drawing up an agenda. There was also the danger that the two parallel conversations started in the car might continue, with important facts and feelings being missed on both sides. So he decided to take charge by formally welcoming the visitors in English, with special congratulations to Akos Mary on regaining her freedom.

'We prayed for your early release but how did you get out so soon?' asked Afriyie.

'I'm still confused on the details,' said Akos Mary, 'I'll let Tom explain.'

'Well,' said Tom, 'where should I begin? You remember how Akos Mary was caught in your room in Coventry, Kwame? As soon as I heard of her arrest I hired a good lawyer to take up her case. He advised her to show contrition from the outset and to cooperate with the authorities. This she was happy to do and she ended up giving evidence at the trial of Peter and his collaborators in Coventry. Akos Mary was convicted of carrying narcotics to the UK and sentenced to three years imprisonment. The sentence was less than usual because of her helpful attitude. Then we began appeals for her early release on the basis of good behaviour and genuine contrition. Your friends from the customs department really helped in all this. She was released from Holloway prison a few weeks ago and here she is.'

Kwame, and he guessed, Afriyie, wanted to know more about the relationship of Akos Mary to Tom but they avoided general embarrassment by not voicing their interest at this time. Instead Kwame asked Tom about his current mission.

'It's all part of our partnership agreement with Kumasi,' he said. 'I expect to spend two days here then go up to Kumasi for about two weeks. After that, I'll spend whatever time is needed here in Tema to tie up any loose ends and then head back home. Your director suggested involving Warwick and the TCC in the second phase of the EC support for GRID and we are always keen to help spend EC money,' he ended with a broad grin.

'Yes,' said Kwame, 'the director mentioned his plans for collaboration under phase two when I met him a few days ago. It looks like an exciting opportunity to work together.'

Kwame then told his friend about his own plans. 'Since I came back I've been kept busy on some interesting assignments. We're trying to run three ITTUs and establish two more at the same time with staff

285

that's only partly trained. We're having to train the staff as we go along. I'm used as a sort of fire fighter and problem solver and I enjoy it very much. However, I will soon have to break off to do an MSc course at Cranfield.'

'Congratulations,' cried Tom. 'Well done, Kwame, I knew you'd make it onto a higher degree course! How long will you be at Cranfield?'

'Only one year,' said Kwame, delighted at his friend's response to his news.

In the course of the conversation Akosua had fallen asleep and Afriyie carried her to her bedroom. When she returned the four friends looked at one another with questions in every eye. It was Tom who broke the silence. 'I see, Afriyie, that you are staying here with Kwame, what are you doing these days?'

'Oh, I'm still sewing dresses but I now have my own business here in Tema and I look after Akosua and keep house for Kwame.'

'That reminds me,' said Akos Mary, 'you must measure me for some new dresses while I'm here.'

'I still have your measurements from before,' replied Afriyie. 'I don't need to measure you again.'

'But I lost weight in prison,' protested Akos Mary. 'You will need to take new measurements.'

'OK, but I'm sure we can fatten you up again while you're here. By the way, my hair's a mess, can you sort it out for me?'

'I'll do it for you tomorrow morning; all the boys in Tema will be chasing you.'

'I'm not sure that I want it quite that good,' said a relieved Afriyie.

Next morning, Afriyie and Akos Mary were up early preparing Ashanti breakfast of roast plantain and red bean stew with gari. By now, Tom was familiar with this fare and liked it very much. Kwame was able to get Tom to GRID well fed and on time when it opened at 7.30. Their first call was on Dr Jones, the former director and now technical adviser. He explained to Tom what he had told Kwame: that GRID would soon have funds to support the work of the TCC in Kumasi and that might include some support for the partnership with Warwick. It was up to the TCC, in consultation with Warwick, to submit proposals for projects that could be of direct interest to GRID and the new ITTUs. Much encouraged by what they heard, they moved on to meet the new director.

Dr Mensah, an agricultural economist, had been with the GRID project for two years, serving as co-director, a title that he had preferred to deputy director. There had been no plan for him to take over so early in the project but he had convinced his contacts in the Ministry of Finance and Economic Planning (MFEP) that there was a danger of the project becoming personalised to its initiator and first director and so a Ghanaian director should be appointed as early as possible. At first this proposal was resisted by Dr Francis Acquah, Secretary of State at the Ministry of Industries, Science and Technology, but with Dr Acquah's removal late in 1989 there came an opportunity to revive the matter, and the expatriate director received a letter from Dr Acquah's old enemy, Dr Oclu, Chief Director of MIST, instructing him to hand over to Dr Mensah on the first of April 1990.

The new director welcomed Tom to GRID and invited him to see whatever he wanted to see and meet as many staff members as he wished. He assured his visitor that GRID would maintain the programme initiated by his predecessor. New ITTUs at Ho and Sunyani would be opened by the end of the year and planning for the remaining ITTUs at Koforidua, Bolgatanga, Takoradi and Wa was well in hand. As few suitable buildings could be found, GRID would be involved in major construction projects, either putting up new buildings or undertaking major renovations. He was worried that not enough funding had been provided for this but he might be able to find funds from other sources.

When Tom asked about collaboration with the TCC he was told that it was intended that GRID should become self-sufficient in expertise and technical resources. It would not need a special relationship with any other institution, not even the Kwame Nkrumah University of Science and Technology, although it would maintain friendly relations with all scientific and technological institutions in the country. Tom then asked what would happen to the funding under the second phase of EC support for collaboration with the TCC. He was told that it was originally intended for this fund to support collaboration with any or all other technical institutions, not only the TCC, but it was not certain at this stage if the funding would be available for this purpose. The money was more urgently needed to finance infrastructural development within the GRID system.

The two friends left the interview in low spirits. 'It looks as if the new director wants to break the link with the TCC,' said Tom.

'Yes,' said Kwame. 'The old director hinted the other day that this might be the new policy.'

'Is there really such a need for new construction?'

'Perhaps not, but directors like big building projects.'

'Why is that?'

'I'm sure you know the reason.'

There was not much point in Tom prolonging his stay in Tema. He had seen the ITTU before. So after looking with Kwame at a few new developments he decided to move on to Kumasi the following morning. They set out early taking Akos Mary with them. By lunchtime they were again enjoying Mrs Dodoo's splendid food beside the now long-defunct swimming pool on the KNUST campus. After lunch, Akos Mary went off to visit her old colleagues at Ayigya Junction while Kwame took Tom to see the TCC director. At the close of work, Kwame took his friend to his old room at the university guesthouse.

'I think we should talk man-to-man about our girlfriends,' said Tom, after taking a long fortifying pull on a bottle of Star beer. 'I was sorry to hear about your split with Comfort. How is she doing now?'

'I've no idea. According to various witnesses, she went off with a Lebanese businessman.'

'So Afriyie is tending to your needs these days?'

'She looks after Akosua and the house.'

'Is that all? She supplies no other services?'

'It seems she thought that you had abandoned her and needed a shoulder to cry on.'

'My ardour cooled with time, it's true, but I continued to write to her.'

'Yes, but not very often.'

'True, but my affections were diverted.'

'To Akos Mary?'

'Yes.'

The two friends gazed at each other, both drawing liquid courage from the bottles in their hands. 'The last thing that I want to do is spoil our friendship,' said Tom. 'It means a great deal to me.'

'And to me.'

'So I will put my cards on the table and afterwards I hope that you will do the same.'

'I agree.'

'I have asked Akos Mary to marry me and she has agreed.'

'Congratulations – I'm really pleased, and I know that you will both be very happy.' After a pause, Kwame added, 'So Peter Sarpong was right after all.'

'How do you mean?'

'Well, he told me one day at the West Africa club when the boys were clustering around Akos Mary that he thought she was interested in a paler and richer prize.'

'The man is clever.'

'Yes, clever enough to get himself locked up for ten years.' Kwame took another pull at the bottle in his hand. He knew what was coming.

'Now it's your turn.'

'Have you heard about HIV/AIDS?'

'It's a disease among homosexuals in the USA, isn't it?'

'That's what I thought, but I learned recently that it's also here in Ghana and it affects normal people as well.'

'Is it? Does it? Now that's alarming!'

'Yes, it means that there is no longer safety in numbers but safety in staying with one woman.'

'And you've chosen Afriyie?'

'Yes.'

'Congratulations, old man! I'm really delighted for both of you.'

The two friends shook hands and hugged one another in mutual relief and joy.

There was a knock on the door and Akos Mary came in. Kwame jumped up to hug and congratulate her. Peering on tiptoe over his shoulder she said to Tom, 'So you've told him?'

'Yes, we've had a real heart-to-heart chat and Kwame's told me about Afriyie. It seems they are also intent on tying the knot.'

'That's right,' said Kwame, 'but not the knot of wisdom!'

'No,' laughed Tom. 'You told me that one is already tied and now needs a wise man to untie it.'

'I think we've both made some progress in unravelling,' said Kwame.

The next few days were spent with the TCC, looking at new projects and discussing possibilities for collaboration. Tom was again impressed by the steady progress being made under difficult circumstances. Since Dr Jones had left in 1986, the TCC had been starved of direct foreign funding support. This was inevitable because much of the support given to the TCC to support the ITTUs had moved to GRID with its much expanded ITTU programme. Dr Jones had foreseen this problem and taken what action he could to sustain his old outfit. He had helped to prepare proposals for World Bank funded rural development projects in Ghana and Malawi and for a British-funded project to develop foundry crucibles. He had also fought to ensure that financial support for the

TCC was incorporated into the second phase of the EC funding for GRID. The TCC had won the international competition to manage the World Bank project in Malawi, and the director, Sosthenes Battah, and other senior members of staff were spending long periods away. In spite of this depletion of human resources several major projects were continuing in Kumasi.

At the Suame ITTU, another World Bank funded project involved the manufacture of hundreds of intermediate transport vehicles: bicycle trailers and hand carts, for field testing in all parts of Ghana. At the old TCC workshop on the KNUST campus, equipment was being installed for a British ODA-funded project to manufacture refractory ceramic crucibles to supply local metal foundries. At a new location nearby, the manufacture of concrete roofing tiles was underway. New houses with attractive green roofs were appearing at various locations around the city. There was already a threat that local demand would outstrip the capacity of the pilot plant before local private enterprises could get into production. A race was on to train plant operators and equip local workshops.

In spite of an almost complete absence of designated foreign funding the TCC was also maintaining its farming projects. At the minimum tillage farm near Fumesua, goats and sheep were being introduced to demonstrate combined animal and crop production while at the fish-farming project the formulation of feed from locally available ingredients was being demonstrated and taught.

Tom's immediate technical interest was in the development of iron foundries. The work of the Suame ITTU, and especially of its chief technician, Edward Opare, had resulted in the establishment of a number of private foundries. Some of these used lift-out crucible furnaces: local copies of the original British furnace installed at the ITTU in 1982. Others used a locally made cupola furnace which offered the advantages of not requiring an imported crucible and burning a low-cost fuel: spent graphite electrodes from the Valco aluminium smelter at Tema. Both types of furnace were used to produce corn-mill grinding plates, by far the fastest-selling foundry product.

The cupola furnace was cheaper to operate and produced many more grinding plates at each firing. However, it was much more difficult to maintain the quality of the products, and many rejects were produced. Some defective plates were being sold, bringing the locally made product into ill repute. The Suame ITTU needed some technical help to upgrade the quality of products made by local cupola furnaces.

This was the task that Tom hoped to study during his visit to Kumasi and he spent several days at Suame working with the equipment he had brought with him from Warwick and which had excited the interest of the customs officials at Accra airport. He set about analysing the composition of the products of both crucible and cupola furnaces and comparing them with grinding plates imported from the UK, China and India. Then he changed the operating procedures of the cupola furnaces and repeated the tests.

Kwame and Edward Opare followed the work with interest and lent support in every way they could, and gradually some progress was made. However, when he had done all he could, Tom still felt that the product of the cupola furnace would always be inferior. This was because it was impossible to reduce the carbon content of the iron to the controlled level maintained in a closed crucible. He recommended that high-quality grinding plates should continue to be made in the crucible furnace, and that the scale of production should be increased, and the cost reduced, by introducing larger tilting-crucible furnaces as installed at the ITTU in Tema.

Tom's time in Kumasi seemed to pass quickly and Kwame was soon driving him back down the road to Accra. Akos Mary went with them because she and Tom were returning to England together. They had planned an early wedding but now they were considering postponing the happy day until October when Kwame, Afriyie and Akosua would be there to lend support. Akosua was already talking excitedly about the bridesmaid's dress that she wanted Afriyie to sew for her, and Kwame told Tom that he was tempted to suggest a double event.

Tom felt that there was little to be gained from a further visit to GRID and so after only one more day in Tema Kwame drove his guests back to the airport. They had left the technical equipment behind in Kumasi, so this time there was nothing to confuse the customs officials.

Akosua wanted to see the aeroplane take off and so they made their way up onto the visitors' gallery on the roof of the terminal building from where they could see the passengers board the plane. It was always a long wait but at last they were able to wave to Tom and Akos Mary as they walked out across the tarmac and climbed up the high steps. They responded to the last wave as the pair disappeared from view. Then the doors were closed and the steps were wheeled away. The engines roared, the aircraft inched forward, and as it started to roll the engine sound lessened. Now it made its long slow crawl to the end of the runway where it seemed to pause for an eternity. The watchers could see only its lights shining in the distance with one beacon flashing rhythmically. Then with another explosion of sound it moved slowly forward, gathering speed and lifting into the air as it passed opposite where the spectators were standing. The crowd gave a cheer and waved furiously although they knew their farewell would be seen by few and heard by none inside the aircraft.

Kwame hugged his family, and holding hands they walked slowly in silence back to the waiting vehicle. Parting is such sweet sorrow and nobody wanted to break the spell of the moment. Kwame reflected that his life had been transformed in the past few weeks, mostly for the better, but a dark shadow now lay over the GRID project and his place in it.

21

Assigned to Ho

Late in April 1990 Kwame reported back on his visit to Kumasi with Dr Tom Arthur. 'Why didn't Dr Arthur come back to see us again?' asked Dr Jones.

'I'm sorry, but after seeing Dr Mensah there didn't seem much possibility of collaboration between GRID and the TCC. Dr Mensah said that he would need the EC money to put up new buildings.'

'To do that he will have to persuade the EC to reallocate the funding; that may not be easy.'

'What are we to do next, Doctor?'

'For the rest of this year our focus must be firmly on Ho and Sunyani. We plan to have formal openings at Ho in August and Sunyani in December. As you will be leaving us in September, we're assigning you to Ho. Sam Sanders will continue to look after Sunyani.'

'I understand that technical support for Ho will come from the Tema ITTU.'

'That's right; and our original plan was to support Sunyani from the Suame ITTU in Kumasi, but I expect that Dr Mensah's reluctance to work with the TCC will change that arrangement.'

'But Kumasi is much nearer to Sunyani, about 130 kilometres as against 390 kilometres; it will be much more difficult if everything has to come from here in Tema.'

'Yes, it would be better to stick to our original plan, but that needn't concern you directly as your mind must be firmly focused on Ho.'

Kwame was not too sure that he wanted this new assignment. Ho was in the Volta Region which was populated mainly by people of the Ewe tribe. The Ewes had their own language and culture and had more in common with the people of Togo than with the dominant tribal group in Ghana, the Akans. During the time of Kwame Nkrumah there had been a strong political movement calling for secession of the Volta Region to Togo, but Nkrumah couldn't afford to lose one of the principal counterweights in his struggle with the Ashanti party. So the Ewes were forced to stay in Ghana and had taken their revenge by being behind every military coup in the country's short history. The mother of the present military dictator, Jerry Rawlings, was an Ewe from the Volta Region.

Kwame sat wondering how he should reply. It was the technical adviser who broke the silence with, 'Not too keen on serving in enemy territory, eh?'

'It's not that, Doctor, we're all Ghanaians these days, but I don't speak Ewe.'

'I've thought of that; Dan Ata will be your right-hand man. He's an Ewe who served the Suame ITTU for many years before coming to take over as chief technician here in Tema. You couldn't have a better man.'

'Thank you, Doctor, that's a great help, Dan's an old friend. He taught me so much about welding and steel fabrication when I started working at the Suame ITTU. With his help I'm sure we can open the ITTU on schedule.'

'Don't be overconfident; there's still a great deal to do. Keep Henry Debrah and me informed of any problems; we'll do all we can to keep you supplied from here.'

'Thank you, Doctor.'

Kwame hurried over to the workshops to tell Dan Ata the good news. Dan had lived in Ashanti for so long and spoke Twi so fluently that one easily forgot that he was from the Volta Region. Now he had a chance to work nearer to home for a few months. Kwame knew that he would be happy with his new posting. He met Dan at the entrance to the workshop, hurrying on his way out. 'Is anyone with Doctor?'

'No Dan, do you need him?'

'It's one of the new Indian lathes for Ho; there's a workhead bearing that keeps seizing. I want him to take a look at it.'

'Then let's call him now while he's free.'

Dr Jones was always ready to drop what he was doing if Dan needed help in the workshop. He knew that Dan wouldn't trouble him if he could solve the problem himself. So he walked back across the yard to the workshop flanked by the team he was sending to Ho.

The workhead cover had been removed from the offending machine and the seized bearing lay on a bench nearby. The three engineers studied the bearing seating.

'How is the bearing lubricated?'

'I can't see any oil way, Doctor.'

'There has to be one.'

'Well, there isn't.'

'We'd better drill one then. Check the drawing and see the exact location.'

'Did the manufacturer make a mistake?'

'It would seem that they still have something to learn about quality control.'

'But look, this workhead casting is not to drawing.'

'What have you found now, Dan?'

'This web is not shown on the drawing. What's it there for?'

Dan was reaching inside the machine behind the web, his long arm disappearing up to the armpit. 'Here's something else that's not on the drawing,' he muttered as he drew a well-wrapped package from deep inside the workhead.

'Ah, you've found Dr Mensah's Subaru spares have you?' said Ghateh, the former workshop supervisor, coming up quickly and taking the package from Dan Ata. 'We collected the spares from the other three lathes but we couldn't find anything in that one.'

'Wait a minute,' said Dan. 'We weren't told anything about Subaru spares.'

'No,' said Ghateh, 'but Dr Mensah asked me to collect them for him. He said that they were much cheaper in India and it was an easy way to transport them. He ordered them when he was in India negotiating for the machines.'

Kwame, Dan and Dr Jones watched Ghateh depart with his present for the director. 'I told you things might be different around here now,' said Dr Jones drily.

After making sure that Dan understood exactly what needed to be done to ensure the lubrication of the workhead bearing, the technical adviser returned to his office. Watching him go, Kwame said to Dan, 'We won't get help like that from the new director.'

'No, he's not an engineer. I'll miss Doctor; he's never too busy to lend a hand when we're in trouble.'

'I've never worked under anyone else here in Ghana, you know. He gave me my first chance in a regular job.'

'Many of us here, and in Kumasi and Tamale, could say the same.'

'How about Ho then, how do you feel about helping me with the new ITTU?'

'I'd like that; I hope you're not joking.'

'No, Doctor just told me. He wants us to work together to get the Ho ITTU ready for an opening in August.'

Kwame and Dan arranged to sit down together later in the day to plan their move to Ho in some detail. Canadian funding had provided the Ho and Sunyani ITTUs each with a heavy truck and two four-wheel-drive vehicles. These would serve to move personnel and equipment from Tema to the new locations. Ho was only about 140 kilometres from Tema and could be reached by a moderately good road in under three hours. So the logistics were not too difficult and return trips within a day were possible. Most of the machinery and equipment had arrived in Tema and was already being transported to its final destination. Dan's main task would be to complete the installation and commissioning. Kwame's main concern would be to establish a training programme for newly appointed technical staff and make preparations for the first intake of technical apprentices.

In each of the regional capitals, GRID intended to buy or lease a house to accommodate the ITTU manager, as had been done in Tamale a decade earlier. As yet no suitable accommodation had been acquired in Ho and so Kwame and Dan would stay at the catering rest house. A legacy of the Nkrumah era, catering rest houses had been established in all the regional capitals. Originally their purpose had been to accommodate government officials on trek to the regions but later they had been opened to the public to serve more or less as regular motels. They provided basic accommodation at reasonable cost to the ministries, institutions, development projects and private businesses that used their services.

Kwame and Dan moved to Ho on the following Monday. Afriyie stayed in Tema so that Akosua's schooling would not be interrupted. As the distance was not too great, either Kwame could spend the weekends in Tema or his family could join him in Ho. Essentially, his domestic arrangements would be similar to when he was in Cape Coast and, if anything, a little easier. So he experienced little personal inconvenience in concentrating his energies on his new assignment. With Dan's energetic support the work went forward smoothly.

Both in Ho and Sunyani it had been possible to find suitable existing buildings to accommodate the ITTU. However, at both locations fairly extensive adaptation and renovation had been necessary. In Ho this work was nearing completion and the installation of the major machine tools was underway. One concern was the connection of the three-phase electric power supply. Although Ho was the nearest regional capital to the great hydro-electric plant on the Volta river at Akosombo, it was poorly served with electrical power. The power lines from Akosombo ran south to serve Kaiser Engineering's Valco aluminium smelter at Tema, and branched west to supply the national capital, Accra. Ho was bypassed. Consequently, its electrical power supply had more in common with other regional capitals like Tamale and Sunyani. It was off more often than it was on. However, GRID was assured that the installation of its own step-down transformer, taking power directly from a nearby 11,000-volt line, would provide a reliable power supply for the ITTU. Needless to say, the completion of this work was eagerly awaited.

Dan worked hard at installing the machine tools but the pride that he always took in his work was sadly tarnished. The machines for Ho and Sunyani had been ordered in bulk from India and some were not to specification. Even the apprentices had laughed when the machines had been taken out of their crates at Tema. They were built neither to the correct dimensions nor to the correct quality standards. They were not even made by the manufacturer indicated in the quotation that had been originally accepted. Kwame was so shocked when he saw the machines and heard Dan's comments that he decided to try to find out what had gone wrong.

Kwame knew that the original equipment at the Suame ITTU had come from England, beginning in 1973, as reconditioned used machines. Thus he had become familiar with Colchester and Ward lathes and Elliott and Denbigh milling machines. These sturdy and reliable machines were perhaps twenty years old when they came to Ghana and they were still going strong after more than a decade in the hot and dusty conditions of Kumasi. By 1986, more than one hundred such machines had been supplied by the TCC to its clients in Suame Magazine. The Tamale and Tema ITTUs had also been supplied with some used British machines.

At the beginning of the GRID project it had been assumed that the same good used British machine tools would be supplied to the new ITTUs, but the Canadians insisted on spending their money on new equipment. They asked for detailed specifications to be drawn up and these were dutifully provided. Then the whole complement of equipment was put out to international tender and an Indian offer was accepted.

Cape Coast ITTU had been supplied with Indian machines manufactured by Hindustan Machine Tools, a high-quality manufacturer working from British drawings and specifications. Similar machines were included in the original offer for Ho and Sunyani. However, the Canadians decided to send one of their technical consultants together with Dr Mensah to

India to finalise the contract. What happened on that trip to India Kwame could only guess, but it filled him with foreboding concerning the future of the project. It was obvious that some specifications had been ignored and cheaper, poor-quality machines had been substituted for those listed in the original tender offer.

What Kwame could not understand was how the Canadian consultant had been persuaded to collude in whatever deal had been transacted, and if he had not colluded, how he could have been kept in the dark. Then there was the matter of the 'Subaru spare parts' secreted in the lathes. According to Ghateh they had been found in all four machines. Was it really auto parts or something more sinister? He recalled having been told that heroin from Asia was reaching the UK through the cartel in Kumasi. Kwame couldn't help wondering if the packages were somehow linked to the drugs smuggling. Dr Mensah had worked in Kumasi for several years before joining GRID and he sometimes asked GRID drivers to deliver packages which he said contained money to a former wife still working in that city as a secondary-school teacher. Kwame hoped that these thoughts were just his imagination running wild. He certainly had no intention of renewing his sleuthing.

Now there was nothing that Kwame or anyone else could do to improve the situation. The machines stood on the concrete floor of the ITTU, looking as ridiculous as ever, and waiting patiently to be installed. Dan and his team were working steadily down the workshop, accurately positioning each machine, checking that it was level and undistorted and bolting it to the floor. They knew that some of the machines would be next to useless; they were incapable of accommodating the usual run of work and would find only occasional use. Dan had already encountered trouble with motors overheating as well as lubrication problems while test running the machines in Tema. Kwame wondered how many other oilways had been left undrilled and made a note to inspect them all carefully as soon as he and Dan could spare the time. It would also be useful to make sure that no other packages remained inside the machines.

Until they had power in Ho there was little training that could be done on site. A few recently recruited technicians were reporting to the ITTU and Kwame was forced to arrange their transport to Tema to begin their induction. He retained one or two of the more experienced men to help Dan but Dan preferred to work with men he knew and trusted. So Kwame decided to take his trainees on a tour of the small private workshops in Ho to familiarise them with the way the ITTU was intended to support its clients. At the same time it gave him an opportunity to learn more about the environment in which the new ITTU would operate.

Ho did not have a *kokompe* or informal industrial area such as found in other Ghanaian cities. Its few industrial enterprises were scattered about the town, singly and in small groups. As such, the situation was something like Tamale when Kwame had first worked there with Frank Johnson. However, in Tamale a light industrial area had been designated with the ITTU located right at its centre and the private workshops were invited to move to new plots all around. GRID had tried to persuade the regional administration to do the same in Ho, but with everything happening on a much shorter time scale it had not been possible to run a pilot project for years in advance and prepare the ground as had been done in Tamale. In Tamale the people, led by Alhajji Issah Masters, had known of the ITTU well in advance, and awaited its opening with keen interest. In Ho the ITTU was in danger of appearing before the local community had been alerted. Kwame intended to do all he could to improve the situation by way of frequent visits to potential client workshops.

It was hard work convincing the small workshop owners that the ITTU was intended to provide them with useful services. At first, Kwame suspected that it was the fact that he was a stranger that caused the problem but when Dan Ata joined him one Saturday morning the result was much the same. He invited some of the workshop owners to visit the ITTU and see how they might benefit from training and the supply of new equipment but they continued to see the ITTU more as a potential threat than a help. Training was only useful if one had the appropriate equipment and they were convinced that the equipment would be priced beyond their means. At the same time they feared that their customers would divert their repair work to the ITTU to be undertaken on new machines at government-subsidised prices. Kwame had known about this fear earlier from his experience in other ITTUs but he had never found it so strongly or widely voiced before.

He discussed the problem with Sam Sanders the next time the two young engineers met in Tema. Sam told him that the situation was much better in Sunyani. He reminded Kwame that his old friend Kwesi Ansah had formed a strong interest group several years ago and had brought numerous rural industrial technologies to Sunyani from Kumasi with the help of the TCC and SRS Engineering. Kwesi's interest group had generated much enthusiasm for the ITTU in Sunyani and its opening later in the year was eagerly awaited. In fact, Kwesi Ansah, with the support of the TCC, had performed much the same role in Sunyani as Frank Johnson, Alhajji Issah Masters and their appropriate technology club had in Tamale. Kwame felt envious of Sam, working in such a benign environment in his mother's home region of Brong-Ahafo.

He asked Sam what he thought about the Indian machines and was not surprised to hear an echo of his own concerns. 'We expect at least two of the machines to stand idle,' said Sam. 'I know that when machines arrive later for sale to clients the ITTU managers will want first to replace the machines in their own workshops. If I'm responsible at that time I will certainly ask for them to be replaced.'

'But what if the next batch of machines is no better?' Kwame wondered aloud. 'I can't see any more used British machines being imported. That era is past.'

'Yes,' said Sam. 'The present batch of machines is from India and I heard the new director hint the other day that the next batch would come from China. He says that Dr Jones only bought British machines because he's British himself.'

'Well that's true, but we are all trained in the British system, including our clients, and we like the equipment we know, whether it's a Colchester lathe, a Lister diesel engine, a Rayleigh bicycle or a Land Rover 4WD.'

'I agree with you entirely,' said Sam.

Kwame invited Sam back to his home for lunch; he knew that Afriyie was preparing red-red and that Gladys would also be there. Sam had moved his family to Sunyani so he was glad of the chance to sample home cooking in Tema in the company of friends. Over lunch the conversation turned to Afriyie and Gladys's project of producing new-style dresses and shirts from tie-dye cloth. Sam was considering starting a tie-dye training programme in Sunyani and asked to see their set-up and samples of their products. So when the meal was over he departed in the company of the two women.

'What shall we do, Daddy?' asked Akosua.

'What would you like to do?'

'Let's go to the beach and swim in the sea.'

'OK, if you promise to be good and keep close to me.'

'You know I'm always good, Daddy.'

First they went to the seashore near to Tema where dozens of old ships were beached and rusting slowly in the warm sunshine. It was not a good place for swimming but Akosua liked to look at the massive hulls that had once proudly sailed the great oceans. She ran up and down the beach comparing and contrasting the size, shape and colour of the relics. 'Which one do you like best, Daddy? I like the white one with the green funnel.'

'I like the blue one with the yellow funnel.'

'You always pick that one, Daddy; which one do you like second best?'

'What about that little rusty one? I feel sorry for her.'

'Why do you say her? How do you know it's not a boy ship?'

'Because all ships are girls.'

'Are they, Daddy? Are they really?'

'Really, really, really!'

Later they drove along the coast in the direction of Accra. Soon they came to Navigators' Bay near Nungua, so called because a nautical college was established on the overlooking hills. Here was a good bathing beach frequented intermittently by foreign residents and an occasional tourist. One or two cars were drawn up on the grass bordering the beach but the beach itself was almost deserted. Akosua, kicking off her rubber sandals, quickly pulled her dress over her head and ran to the water's edge in the turquoise swimming costume she had concealed underneath. It took Kwame a few moments longer to get rid of his jeans and t-shirt and chase after his ten-year-old daughter in his bright red boxer shorts. The sea was calm and Akosua was a good swimmer but Kwame liked to keep as close to her as possible. An occasional bigger wave had once thrown them onto a rocky outcrop. Akosua was lucky, landing in a sandy hollow, but Kwame came down on the rocks and suffered a badly grazed chest. Now he kept well away from that end of the beach.

The sun sets quickly in the tropics and the shadow cast by the hill to the west was already gliding across the beach. Kwame called Akosua to come out of the water to dry off. They sat on the grass side by side to let the remaining sun and wind do the drying. Both sun and wind would soon be gone, the one until the morning, the other until the land had cooled. Akosua gazed straight out to sea. 'If I could see right across the water to the next land what would it be, Daddy?'

Kwame was caught out by her question. 'Well, let's see; you are looking almost due south. If you sailed in that direction on and on you would eventually come to Antarctica, where the penguins live.'

'Can we go there, Daddy? I love penguins.'

'I don't think you would like the cold. It's even colder than England!'

'But I was brave in the cold in England, wasn't I, Daddy?'

'You were brave about everything in England, Little One.'

* * *

Kwame called in at GRID before returning to Ho on the Monday morning. After reporting to the director on progress he was given instructions to prepare for the formal opening ceremony. It was to be a colourful and elaborate event with the Minister for Industries as guest of honour and numerous dignitaries including the Regional Minister, the Canadian High Commissioner and the EC Delegate. There should be a local troupe of singers and dancers in traditional costume to provide entertainment and a conducted tour of the workshops with an exhibition of the work of all the GRID ITTUs. As many clients as possible should be invited to take part in the workshop tour and exhibition.

While Kwame was talking to the director a stocky, middle-aged man with pale brown skin came into the office. 'Let me introduce Mr Hayibor; he's the new manager for the Ho ITTU,' said the director. 'Mr Hayibor, this is Mr Mainu who's getting your outfit ready for you.'

The two men greeted each other and agreed to meet briefly after Kwame had finished with the director. A few moments later Kwame was able to ask, 'What are you doing here? We need you in Ho.'

'I would like to be in Ho but I'm here with Mr Debrah for induction.'

'When will you come to Ho?'

'I should be there about a week before the opening.'

'Are you from Ho?'

'Yes I am. I was born in Tsito, I think you know it.'

'We pass there every time we drive to Ho.'

'That's right, I've spent most of my time working in or near Ho.'

'Then we'll talk a lot more when you come back.'

Kwame drove to Ho thinking about his meeting with Mr Hayibor. Why was he always suspecting things were about to go wrong? The old director, Dr Jones, had several times stressed to Kwame, and the other young graduate engineers in the project, that he wanted fresh new men to run the ITTUs, men who only knew the ITTU system. He did not want men grown set in their ways by running a commercial enterprise or government workshop for years before coming to post.

Kwame realised that he knew nothing of Mr Hayibor's background or track record but he hardly fitted the prescribed model. Far from having been through the years of training and preparation set up by the former director, he was being pitched into the job with just a few weeks' orientation. With all the difficulties already encountered in Ho, the prospects for the ITTU looked even gloomier than before. Kwame had imagined that one of his dynamic young colleagues, Dan Nyarko, Sam Sanders, or perhaps even Dan Baffour-Opoku would be assigned to Ho to sort out its teething problems and motivate its staff and clients, but now it appeared the ITTU was to be thrust into the hands of a virtual novice. If this was to be the new policy the prospects were bleak indeed.

The more Kwame thought about the work, the more the problems seemed to pile up in front of him. Yet most of the problems would ripen only in the future. They were not his immediate concern. He resolved to narrow his focus to getting the ITTU opened on schedule and then fix his mind on his next spell of training in the UK. His personal decisions could be delayed for one year at least. If he came back to find GRID in meltdown he could decide what to do at that time. In this frame of mind he rejoined Dan Ata for the last push.

Opening ceremonies were all the same. They sat like a great dark cloud on the horizon for months and months then passed in an instant flash of sunlight. Suddenly, it seemed to Kwame, the dignitaries had said their honeyed words and departed; the Ho ITTU was opened. Ho had a modern workshop with staff and even an electricity supply but it was far from having an ITTU. Yet nobody seemed to worry. Many who attended the opening ceremony would not understand the issues, but there must be some who understood but seemed not care. Kwame couldn't believe that he was the only one who cared. He hoped that some of those who appeared uncaring were only hiding their feelings, and there would be a group of concerned workers for him to join when he returned next year.

Akosua had enjoyed attending school in England and was excited at the prospect of going back for more. So Kwame decided that he would take both Akosua and Afriyie with him. With the growing shadow on his mind about the future of GRID it would be good to have the option of seeking employment in England. The more his family became used to English life the less resistance there might be to such a move. So they all packed what they needed to take with them and prepared the little Tema house to stand empty while they were away. By the time they returned Kwame hoped that the transfer of ownership from the Tema Development Corporation would be completed and for the first time in his life he would own his own home.

Afriyie was content to leave her business in Gladys's hands. Her senior apprentice would be quite able to continue the sewing and was even developing her own flair for design. Gladys would miss them but not too much because she had recently started serious courting and an early

303

wedding appeared likely. 'I may be Mrs Appiah-Mensah when you come back,' she quipped happily.

'You can be Mrs Nana Konadu Agyeman Rawlings as long as you take good care of my business,' was Afriyie's parting shot.

22

Cranfield

They were met at Heathrow Airport by Tom and Akos Mary and taken swiftly up the M1 motorway to Cranfield. Kwame was delighted to find that small but comfortable married quarters had been prepared for them and Akosua had been enrolled in the university primary school. From the twinkle in Tom's eye Kwame guessed that he had had a hand in these arrangements. Even in England, who you know can be as important as what you know, he thought to himself.

Akos Mary was telling Afriyie the arrangements she had made for them to meet regularly, and they were busy swapping addresses and telephone numbers. Akosua had turned on the television and was trying to reconnect to her favourite children's programme. Kwame smiled inwardly. His family were at home back in England almost as if they had never been away. He knew that he would have the peace of mind to concentrate on his studies. He was aware that his old director had sent many people to England for training and all had graduated successfully. He also knew of letters from Cranfield professors praising the students who had been sent from Ghana and asking for more of the same calibre. Kwame was determined to maintain the established standard.

That night, in bed with Afriyie, Kwame asked her how she felt to be back in England. 'I feel safe now that Bra Yaw and Peter Sarpong are locked away but I was afraid at the airport that they might not let me in.'

'Why was that?'

'Because of what I did last time.'

'But you never actually brought any drugs into the UK.'

'No, I guess that I never did anything bad here, except use a false passport.'

'And you won't ever do anything like that again, will you?'

'Not as long as you let me be with you.'

She turned over to sleep but Kwame's thoughts drifted on for some time. Afriyie was in most ways the ideal companion. Her demands were few and simple, she never ceased to smile and she was tender and protective towards Akosua. Yet in spite of her docile nature she could summon all the spirit he needed in their passionate moments. The thought that troubled him was that Comfort had been like that when he first took her as a girlfriend but she had gradually changed after they married. Would the same thing happen to Afriyie? He didn't think so, but could he be sure? He wouldn't have thought that it would happen to Comfort. He was very content with his present life with Afriyie and he would like to consolidate it by marrying her, but if it would change her it would be better to leave things as they stood.

Next day Kwame telephoned Tom to tell him that he had decided not to marry at this time and so a joint wedding was not in prospect. Tom was disappointed; he and Akos Mary had delayed partly in the hope of sharing the happy event with their friends, but he assured Kwame that he had no hard feelings and would go ahead with his own wedding at an early date. An invitation arrived within a few days and before the end of October Kwame took his family back to Coventry to serve as best man, maid of honour and bridesmaid.

As Akos Mary's family were far away in Ghana and of very limited means, the whole cost of the event was borne by Dr Arthur senior. He even bore the cost of bringing Mr Konadu from Cape Coast to give his daughter away as tradition required. Unfortunately, Akos Mary's mother could not be invited. Long separated from her husband and now known as Madam Florence Sims, she had recently travelled to the USA and had yet to inform her family of her current whereabouts.

Kwame was pleased to see Mrs Chichester again and so was Akosua who greeted the landlady with: 'Can I help you bake another cake to celebrate our return to Coventry like we did last time?' Mrs Chichester and Kwame exchanged a look of wonder mingled with sadness at the memory of Akos Mary's arrest, and the good matron said, 'As you're all staying with me tonight, Akosua, we will do it together in the morning.'

Kwame remembered that on the day of her arrest Akos Mary had blamed him for her bad fortune, calling him *oboroni*. He was thankful that since he met her again at Accra airport she had seemed to bear him no grudge. No doubt she had had plenty of time in prison to sort out her feelings and had come to realise that he was not directly to blame for her arrest. He hoped that she had had no opportunity to talk to Peter Sarpong while her feelings against him were high. One day he might ask her, but it was certainly not the right day today.

That night Kwame slept in his old room and his old bed. Until his recent arrival in Cranfield, almost every night of his years in England had been spent under this roof. It was a homecoming that was worthy of a fresh-baked cake. He owed a great debt of gratitude to Mrs Chichester, who had unquestioningly supported him in good times and bad. He vowed to himself that he would one day invite her to visit him in Ghana to return in small measure her tireless hospitality. In this contented frame of mind he drifted off into the familiar Coventry night.

Next morning Akosua was up early to start breaking eggs in the big bowl. Afriyie decided on a lie-in to recover from an unaccustomed quantity of alcohol consumed on the previous evening. Later, when the cake was in the oven, she planned to take Akosua on a shopping expedition with Mrs Chichester. Kwame was left to his own devices and so after some strong coffee and toast he took a stroll in the pale October sunshine down to the foundry school. He found it much as he had left it and Fred Brown was in his office. He greeted Kwame warmly but it was obvious that he had a crisis on his hands. 'We had a guest speaker lined up to give the students a talk this morning but he's just rung to say he can't make it. You wouldn't like to give them a talk instead, would you?'

'What would I talk about?'

'Oh, you know, the work you're doing in Ghana, small-scale foundry development.'

'Do you still have my slides?'

'I think I can find some.'

'They're a bit out of date but I guess they will do.'

'Then you'll do it?'

'I'll do it.'

The talk lasted about an hour followed by half an hour of questions before Fred brought the session to an end. The students returned to their regular timetable. 'You certainly fired them up,' said Fred.

'Isn't that what foundrymen do?' asked Kwame with a grin.

'No, seriously, your enthusiasm is really infectious; your people in Ghana must be very glad they have you on the team.'

'Some of my people.'

'Look, there's a fee for this talk, I want you to have it.'

'That's OK, I didn't spend much time preparing.'

'Then at least let me buy you some lunch and we can chat some more.'

Over lunch Fred returned to his pet theme. He explained that doing the same job year-in year-out it was easy to doubt whether your efforts were ever bearing fruit. It was people like Kwame who gave his life's work some meaning. 'You know, I'm really proud to have helped chaps like you to go out to promote a grassroots industrial revolution in Africa.'

'I've certainly learned most of what I know about the practical aspects of iron founding within these four walls.'

'Yes, but to put it into practice under difficult circumstances where it has never been done before is the real challenge. Your talk really brought this home to me.'

Kwame decided to try out one of his own pet themes. 'I want to have a go at building a diesel engine; what do you think?'

'Why not try a steam engine first?'

'What is it with *abrofo* engineers, and steam engines?' thought Kwame, but he explained as he had to Jonathan Wilkinson. 'We need a modern product to capture public interest. Without popular support we will only be pursuing a hobby.' He managed to avoid saying 'a white man's hobby' and continued, 'I have in mind something simple like the single-cylinder Lister.'

'Well, I'll see what I can do to help. Maybe I can find a set of drawings, and I can give you some guidelines and specifications for casting the cylinder block, but can you cope with operations like cylinder boring and crankshaft grinding?'

'Yes, we can do all that,' said Kwame.

When Kwame got back to Mrs Chichester's house he found the place deserted so he settled down to read the daily newspaper and await the return from the shopping trip. As usual, it was Akosua who dashed in first with, 'Daddy, Daddy, look at my new jeans! They're a bit long but Afriyie says I will soon grow.'

'You've been a long time, I hope the cake hasn't burnt,' said Kwame.

'No, Daddy,' said Akosua with a look of disdain at his ignorance of cake-making technology, 'we put the cooker on a timer. It will be perfect.'

And when Mrs Chichester came in with a tray of tea they all assured the little cook that it was perfect indeed.

That evening they had a telephone call from Tom and Akos Mary reporting their safe arrival in the Bahamas where they were spending their honeymoon. The next day Kwame took his family back to Cranfield to resume his studies.

After the constant turmoil of his last spell in England, Kwame was happy to settle into a dull routine. Akosua was happy at her new school and

Afriyie found a part-time job sewing alterations for a local dress shop. After the return from their honeymoon, Tom and Akos Mary often came on visits at the weekends and sometimes Kwame took his family back to Coventry. When Kwame was tied up with his studies, the two women met up on their own. Akosua sometimes slept over with friends, sometimes stayed behind with Kwame and sometimes went along with Afriyie.

True to his word, Fred Brown sent Kwame a parcel of drawings and specifications for a small diesel engine. Kwame would have liked to study them in detail right away but his coursework had to take priority. So he wrote thanking Fred and put the package safely away to be rediscovered after his return to Ghana.

In dull but peaceful routine the year slipped towards its end, but just before Christmas Kwame received a card from Dan Nyarko with a letter inside. It conveyed disturbing news from GRID. The Sunyani ITTU had been formally opened on 3 December 1990 on schedule, but at two o'clock that morning, in his house in Kumasi, Dr Jones had been attacked by five men armed with long knives and cutlasses. He had sustained a cut beside his left eye but managed to drive himself to Sunyani where he arrived with his head bandaged.

The curious thing about this raid was that it did not seem to be motivated by theft. A few things, one a gold wristwatch, were stolen but much more was smashed by the intruders rampaging through the house throwing crockery and ornaments onto the hard terrazzo floor. The aim seemed to be to inflict shock and injury. Kwesi Ansah and his interest group in Sunyani had planned an opening ceremony for the ITTU in which Dr Jones and the Canadian High Commissioner were invited to plant trees. This signal honour had not been extended to the new GRID director. Suspicion ran through the gathering that this omission was somehow connected with the brutal attack.

Kwame read this letter with a growing sense of foreboding. The suspicions that had germinated in his mind at Ho were greatly strengthened. Something was going seriously wrong with GRID. The focus was moving swiftly away from serving the community to promoting self-interest and the forces at work were prepared to resort to violence. Kwame sensed that when he returned to Tema he would be compelled to confront this issue. He wondered what stand others were taking.

It was not long before he heard that Sam Sanders was attempting to take a stand in Sunyani. He wrote to Kwame that on the whole the ITTU had got off to a good start. A full complement of apprentices had been recruited, several clients were being helped in various ways and the income earned by the workshops was building up satisfactorily. However, he had run into conflict with the new director.

Dr Mensah was a native of a small village near Duayaw-Nkwanta, not far from Sunyani. Like all successful sons, the director was building a house in his village. He placed a large order for furniture on the woodworking shop of the Sunyani ITTU and in due course the order was delivered and an invoice was sent. However, the invoice was returned cancelled and Sam Sanders was told it should not have been sent. Sam informed the GRID finance officer that he considered the order to be a private one, not an official instruction to do work on behalf of the project, as might be the case, for example, if the furniture had been intended for use in project offices. He felt that the invoice was in order and the cost of the work should be reimbursed to the ITTU.

Sam ended his letter by saying that he suspected that he might soon be removed from his post although he knew that the technical adviser, Dr Jones, was pressing hard for him to remain. So it was happening already; a direct clash was taking place between the old regime and the new. Maybe it was inevitable. The new director, being a Ghanaian, was immersed in the local community and socioeconomic environment. His prosperity was totally dependent upon what could be extracted from his current situation. He could not be expected to take the same detached view of the work as an expatriate with roots overseas in a prosperous home base. At the same time, it was a pity that so early in his administration the new director had revealed raw self-interest and a pointed disregard for the system built up by his predecessor over so many years.

With the immediate need to concentrate on his coursework at Cranfield, Kwame could not spare the time or energy to dwell on matters at home in Ghana. These issues would have to wait until later. So once he had written to Dr Jones expressing his concern over the injury, he tried to turn his attention back to his studies. However, new distractions awaited him when he met up with Tom and Akos Mary at a New Year reunion in Coventry. Akos Mary's father, Mr Konadu, had not gone back to Ghana before his visa expired and he was now an illegal immigrant making urgent demands on his daughter to sustain him.

Akos Mary seized an opportunity when they were alone to explain the situation. She had got herself a job as a hairdresser but her salary was quite small. In normal circumstances her personal income served as pocket money because it was Tom who maintained their household.

However, since her father began making his demands she had been handing over all her cash to him. Now he was complaining it was not enough and was demanding more. Akos Mary asked Kwame what she should do. She couldn't refuse to help her father but she couldn't lay hands on more money without asking Tom. She feared that Tom would not want to support an illegal immigrant and might even want to report Mr Konadu to the immigration authorities. That she could never allow; it would disgrace her for the rest of her life. She knew that Kwame would understand her dilemma. Could he help her?

Kwame gave himself time to think by asking Akos Mary about her relationship with her father. She told him that when her parents broke up neither wanted to take her with them and she was sent to live with her mother's sister who was a nurse at Korle-Bu Hospital in Accra. After that, she rarely saw her father except at an occasional funeral and he never made any contact with her. He had been brought back into her life only when Dr Arthur senior suggested that she should be given away by her father at her wedding. Of course, he jumped at the chance of a sponsored visit to the UK and probably had the intention to abscond from the outset.

Kwame saw a culture clash that threatened the foundations of his friends' marriage. He knew that he must do something, but what? 'Would your father agree to see me?' he asked. 'I'll stay on in Coventry for a few more days if a meeting is possible.'

Mr Konadu remembered Kwame from the wedding and they went dutifully through the Akan greeting ritual in a jovial mood. After the obligatory water, Kwame offered his guest beer and they continued with the usual banter about how difficult it was here in England to tell the one from the other. Kwame asked Mr Konadu about his life in Ghana and discovered that he was a self-employed trader who had tried many different lines, all with little success. Kwame decided that he was a fairly typical Ananse-trained manipulator, streetwise but not very energetic, whose one opportunity in life had come rather late. He didn't want to spoil Mr Konadu's one big chance but neither did he want to see his friends' marriage jeopardised. Realising that Akos Mary had no great emotional attachment to her father he decided to try a big bluff. If it worked it would create a win-win situation.

'So you want to stay on in England, do you?'

'That's been my lifelong ambition.'

'And now your chance has come.'

'Yes, I've waited a long time.'

311

'But you don't want to remain an illegal immigrant, always hiding from the police. You should get yourself proper papers.'

'How can I do that? I only know Akos Mary.'

'I'm afraid Akos Mary can't help you; she doesn't know the system. In fact, she is really a danger to you, being married to *oboroni*.'

'How do you mean?'

'Well, if *oboroni* finds out you're still here he will report you, and then you'll be deported back to Ghana.'

'Akos Mary wouldn't let him do that.'

'She might not be able to stop him; you know what *abrofo* are like.'

'Then what should I do?'

'You must go to London or another big city like Birmingham or Manchester. There you will soon find a large Ghanaian community, including clever lawyers who really know how to work the system. Within a few years you will be holding a British passport.'

'Will you help me to travel to London and get established there?'

'I'll make you a one-off loan provided you promise not to contact me or Akos Mary again until you're holding that British passport. If you break this promise, I'll march you to the nearest police station myself.' Kwame hoped that that would be the last he would see of Mr Konadu.

Akos Mary was overjoyed to have been relieved of her burden. Kwame knew that if Akos Mary had harboured any bad feeling towards him from the time of her arrest it was dispelled now. Tom might never know about the threat to his marriage posed by Mr Konadu but he would benefit from the outcome of Kwame's action. He was sure that Tom had often acted behind the scenes to help him in his academic career. Now he had been able to help Tom in a similar way. That's what friends are for, he mused, not only to blow on one another's eyes but also to watch one another's back.

Kwame now looked forward to a smooth run through to his final examinations in June but he wouldn't be spending all his time at Cranfield. He knew that he must undertake a project related to a current manufacturing development and he had asked to do something connected with diesel engines. He was overjoyed when he was assigned to work on a problem on the production of a new type of ductile cast iron used in making diesel engine crankshafts. He would be able to undertake much of the preparatory work at Cranfield but the field testing would take him to two or three manufacturing plants in various parts of the country.

Kwame realised that his project would not be a technical one in the narrow sense. His course dealt with the management of production, not the technology. He would not be concerned directly with the composition of the metal, pouring temperatures or the design of patterns or moulds, but rather with the optimum sequence and control of operations to ensure high quality combined with high productivity and low cost. He would model the process on a computer and experiment with changes in the production control system. Then when he and his tutor thought that he had made an improvement, he would visit the manufacturers and try the revised system in an actual production process.

Tom came over while Kwame was working on his project and made one or two useful suggestions. The work progressed well and by March Kwame's tutor was recommending that they should arrange the first phase of field testing. He suggested contacting the Ford Motor Company at Dagenham, the place where spheroidal cast iron crankshafts had first been made some forty years before. 'It will be a chance to learn more about the history of the technology,' the tutor added. 'I know you want to start ductile iron production in Ghana when you get back there.'

It was not only Kwame who was making good progress. Afriyie had become popular among the community of academic wives for adjusting old and new dresses to accommodate expanding dimensions. This was a service she was happy to provide at an affordable cost and she gained much satisfaction from seeing her clients parading ready-made garments as individually tailored and personalised gowns. When attending fitting sessions, she started wearing her own Ghanaian-style dresses in tie-dye produced by Gladys in Tema, and started to take orders, especially from the younger women who were always on the lookout for something new.

Kwame was pleased to see this additional income as otherwise he would have found it hard to support his family on a postgraduate student's grant. He still had much of his accumulated savings on deposit in a British bank but he wanted to avoid depleting this reserve. He wanted to leave untouched even the interest earned on the account if at all possible. One day, he knew not when, he might want to complete his house in Kumasi and he knew that the cost of building would be mounting year on year. Remembering how he had been pressed on this issue by Comfort he marvelled at the fact that Afriyie never mentioned building or buying a house. She had been delighted that he was able to

313

buy their little hideaway in Tema. Once again he wondered if Afriyie's attitude would change if he married her.

Akosua was proving to be an able and popular girl at school. She took advantage of most of the after-school activities, whether they involved sport, music or arts and crafts. Everything seemed to interest her. 'What will I be when I grow up?' she repeatedly asked Kwame.

'You must do whatever interests you the most,' was his standard reply.

'But I want to be an engineer like you, or a doctor, or an actress, or an athlete; oh I don't know!'

'You have plenty of time to make up your mind,' was Kwame's usual attempt at a closing remark but it seldom satisfied his daughter.

'I'm eleven years old, don't you know, •you must help me decide,' she would say with a pout and a stamp of her foot that shook her budding breasts.

Kwame had been raised by his father to believe that one should be free to make one's own personal decisions on the important matters in life. Of first priority were the choice of a career and the choice of a partner. In the old days, he realised, these matters were often dictated by parents but he wanted to be a modern parent and let Akosua make her own choices. He knew that her present demands for his help would probably fade away over the next few years and he might soon be faced with a need to apply the brakes if he thought that she was heading in the wrong direction. At the same time he realised that many communities in Asia and Africa still believed in imposing parental choice, and espoused the benefits of that system.

Young people often make mistakes; maybe he had done so himself in marrying Comfort. He also recalled how Joe Appiah, that wily old politician, had once told him that his son, a Cambridge double first and professor of philosophy at Harvard University, had asked his parents to choose him a wife, being firmly convinced that this was the best system. Well, he thought to himself at last, I will monitor Akosua's progress, give her as much freedom of choice as possible but try to be ready to answer her call for help if it continues.

At Dagenham, Kwame spent most of his time working with a small technical management team of production engineers and planners. He demonstrated his computer model and explained the changes he was proposing. Then he spent a few days working out the practical details involved in setting up a trial run on an auxiliary production line used intermittently for small runs of specialised components.

As he moved around the plant Kwame became aware of many black faces among the production workers and he wondered if any of them came from Ghana. During the lunch break he wandered into the main works canteen and sat down at a table ringed with black faces but with one vacant place. 'That's Kwame's place,' shouted a chorus of angry voices.

'That's right, I'm Kwame,' said Kwame with a grin, but he stood up to let the resident Kwame claim his home territory. After putting down his plate the resident greeted Kwame in Twi and the two Saturday men moved over to a vacant table.

'You're new to this place, aren't you?'

'Yes, I'm just on a visit from Cranfield University.'

'So that's why you're walking around with the big men.'

'Are they big men? They're production engineers.'

'Why don't you eat with the big men?'

'I've already eaten in the senior staff canteen, I wanted to meet someone from home.'

'Where are you from in Ghana?'

'From Konongo, and you?'

'I'm originally from Takoradi but my parents are now in Accra.'

'How long have you been in this country?'

'About six years.'

'How long have you been working at this place?'

'About a year and a half.'

It wasn't long before the conversation grew more friendly and the two Kwames agreed to meet up for a drink in the evening. Kwame found that Kwame Darkwa was similarly situated to Issac Owusu, the Birmingham-based bicycle maker, although he had not been in the UK so long. He was by no means satisfied with his lot. Working as a cleaner on the shop floor, he earned just enough to maintain himself in England but not enough to go home to Ghana, even on a visit. He felt trapped in a cold and alien environment. Once again Kwame felt sorry for his unskilled and semi-skilled compatriots who made such great efforts to escape overseas. If they kept within the confines of the law they would never return and build their big houses. If they engaged in illegal activities they were risking being detained for long periods at Her Majesty's pleasure. Neither route offered any guarantee of success. This was the reality that was forever hidden from the next generation of aspirants back home.

At the first trial, Kwame's modified production system seemed to work well but the good results could not be repeated on the next day or on the day after. Kwame realised that he must return to Cranfield and do more work before his system would be ready for further testing. That evening he rang Tom to cry on his shoulder.

After listening patiently to all the details Tom replied reassuringly, 'It's always like that Kwame. The first test always goes well. It's beginner's luck or nature's way of encouraging us. Then we are forced to do the real work and thoroughly understand what is happening. Sometimes it takes a long time to repeat the success of that first trial. But after that every test runs like clockwork. Now you must work hard to iron out all the bugs. I know you can do it. I will be there at the weekend to lend a hand.'

On the Saturday morning the two engineers pored over Kwame's software program and the detailed notes from the test runs. Why did it work on the model but not on the real production system? What feature had Kwame failed to model accurately? Most mystifying of all, why had it worked well the first time? It would seem that the clue might lie in detecting some special feature of the first test run, although Tom warned that he had often wasted much valuable time on such wild-goose chases. Could the temperature have been lower; had the system not fully warmed up? The recorded data did not show any differences of temperature and, in any case, they made a cold start on the second and third days as well. Was there any residual contamination from a previous production run? That seemed more likely as this could not have been recorded in Kwame's notes and it would have been removed by the first test and not present in the subsequent tests.

They decided to call the Ford engineers and ask them for details of the previous production run. A cheery voice told them, 'We've been wondering about that; the previous run used an alloy with a higher chromium content but everything was thoroughly cleaned afterwards and, in any case, your system balanced that up, didn't it?'

'Yes it did,' replied Kwame, 'but I'd be obliged if you would fax me the details.' When the fax came through they went over the details once more but again they drew a blank. They decided to break off for a while and have some lunch.

When they came back the telephone was ringing. It was Kwame Darkwa. Kwame had forgotten that they had swapped telephone numbers. After the usual greetings, Kwame Darkwa said, 'I heard your test didn't go too well and I wondered if we had messed it up.'

'How could you have messed it up?'

'Well, we're not supposed to wear jewellery on our job but you know the Nigerian guys, they don't take any notice of what the bosses say.'

'No I guess not, but how does that affect my tests?'

'Well, before you came, our team was told to clean up the plant. They told us to be very thorough and do a special job.'

'Yes.'

'He lost his neck chain, didn't he?'

'Who did?'

'The Nigerian guy.'

'Where did he lose it?'

'It must have been lost in your test plant.'

'What was it made of?'

'That new metal, like silver but not so heavy.'

'Titanium?'

'That's it.'

Kwame thanked his new friend and told him that he would soon ring him back. He couldn't wait to share the news with Tom. 'There was probably some extra titanium in the first test run, could that have affected the result?'

'It might have done; how much titanium?'

'A man's neck-chain's worth.'

'How much is that?'

'I don't know; let's go to a jeweller's and find out.'

Tom drove them into Bedford and they soon found an H. Samuel store. 'I'm relying on you to pick out what a Nigerian man might like to wear,' said Tom.

'It will be quite big and showy,' said Kwame with a grin. He picked out what he thought might be appropriate and asked a sales assistant if he might see it.

Removing the neck chain from the glass case, the sales assistant asked, 'Are you interested in buying it for yourself or for a friend?'

'Neither,' said Kwame. 'I want you to weigh it.' Without further comment the neck chain was placed on a small weighing scale and the digital display turned to give Kwame a clear view. He jotted the figure in his notebook.

'Will there be anything else?' enquired the patient assistant.

'Let's get some little presents for the girls,' said Tom and selected three small charm bracelets for Akos Mary, Afriyie and Akosua. 'It will reward them for their patience and compensate them for our neglect,' he added cheerfully.

Now they could calculate the approximate additional content of titanium in the batch of cast iron processed in Kwame's first test run.

It was quite small but the two engineers knew that very small changes in minor alloying elements could produce significantly different results. They tried the new data in Kwame's computer model and the output was satisfactory but that proved nothing because his model had worked equally well with the original composition. Even if they had found the practical answer to the problem, Kwame would still have to revise his model to make it sensitive to the change.

Kwame was anxious not to expose his new friend, Kwame Darkwa, to any recriminations, either from his employer or from his workmates, so he decided to say nothing about the lost neck chain. When he telephoned the Dagenham engineers on the following Monday morning he said only that he had found an error in the titanium content and that it should be marginally increased. He was promised that the test would be repeated the next day and, much to his relief, he learned later that all had gone well. His subsequent visits to two other manufacturers served only to confirm the result. With a little more help from Tom he found the error in his model and corrected it. His tutor was pleased with Kwame's work and proposed that they should prepare a joint publication for a leading foundry technology journal.

In June 1991 Kwame was awarded his MSc in Production Management and made plans to return with his family to Ghana. All three expressed some reluctance to go; they had all enjoyed their stay at Cranfield, but all understood that even if they stayed in England they would need to start a new life somewhere else. Tom and Akos Mary said that they were sad that their friends were leaving but they would visit Ghana as often as they could. Kwame took the opportunity to suggest to Tom that on one of his future visits he might consider bringing Mrs Chichester along as Kwame's guest. Tom said that it was a nice idea and he would bear it in mind. Akos Mary gave Afriyie a list of dresses to be sewn and sent to her by parcel post, adding that if she decided to include any *kenke* she should make sure that it was the genuine article.

Akosua joked that she didn't know if she wanted to go back to Ghana with Kwame and Afriyie or stay in England with Uncle Tom and Auntie Akos. Tom laughed and said that he was sure that Akosua would soon be old enough to travel on her own and she was welcome to come to England on holiday whenever she wanted a break from Dad. Kwame said that he now knew where to send Akosua when he grew tired of having her around. With such banter they parted once more at the airport and Kwame braced himself to meet whatever storms awaited him in Tema.

23

Goodbye to GRID

When he returned to GRID at the end of June 1991, Kwame was expecting to meet a changed situation but the degree of change still took him by surprise. The GRID headquarters building had been extended to provide the new director with an impressive new suite of offices. Whereas Dr Jones had used an existing office and kept his door open to all comers, the new director was now hidden away behind two closed doors with an outer office and secretaries and clerks to control access. The suite was completed by a well-appointed waiting room for visitors and an office for the Canadian consultant who had accompanied Dr Mensah to India to conclude the purchase of machine tools for Ho and Sunyani.

The old director's office had a ceiling fan, louvred windows, a tiled floor and standard furniture like all the other senior staff offices. Now, Dr Mensah sat in an air-conditioned cubicle with thick carpeting, heavy curtains and plush furniture. Kwame realised that a considerable amount of project money had been spent on enhancing the personal comfort and status of the director, an extravagance that would never have been countenanced under the old regime, either at the TCC or at GRID.

More important than changes in accommodation were the changes in management style. Twice a day when in Tema, Dr Jones walked around the ITTU workshops. With an eye for detail, he would call for the correction of faults and suggest improvements in equipment and technique with particular emphasis on the safety of workers. Advice would be given on current technical problems and all staff and apprentices had an opportunity to bring their ideas or grievances directly to the boss. He called for written reports on all aspects of the work and insisted that all important communications should be in writing. He never failed to send a written reply, whether commenting on a technical report or replying to a request, so there was a permanent record of every decision that was taken and the reason for taking it.

320

The new director was not an engineer. He seldom visited the ITTU workshops. When he did, he did not understand all he saw, seldom pointed out any faults and gave no advice on technical problems. Kwame was told that when at first he was brought written reports he waved them away with the remark, 'Let's have a chat.' Now Kwame found that most of the senior staff had stopped writing reports, although a few were still being prepared for the technical adviser and for publication by SEACOM. Kwame wondered if the same approach was being taken to the preparation of statutory records of the project, including financial accounts, and then he remembered what he had been told had happened during the time he had been in Cape Coast.

In October 1989, shortly after the departure of Dr Francis Acquah and a few months before the change of director, the GRID project had been investigated by the Audit Commission, a government agency set up to investigate corruption in public service. This investigation had been initiated in response to a petition signed by a number of junior and middle-level staff of the Tema ITTU who had been employed at the workshop before the founding of the GRID project. This was the group that Dr Francis Acquah had tried in vain to sack. No doubt, they felt that they had been demoted by the new regime. However, although this group had signed the petition, it was generally suspected that the document had been drafted for them by the then co-director, Dr Mensah.

The Audit Commission made a thorough investigation of all the financial and administrative records of the project since its inception in February 1987. The final report stated that hard documentary evidence had been found to refute all of the charges made in the petition and the auditors praised GRID for keeping such comprehensive records. With this ringing endorsement of the management of the project the new director was able to take over in April 1990 with a completely clean sheet. He could expect several years to pass before the Audit Commission was likely to turn its attention again in the direction of GRID. It was under cover of this sanctification that much routine reporting was now being neglected. Kwame suspected that people who avoided leaving a paper trail might have something to hide.

He found Dr Jones in his old office. The door was still open. After receiving hearty congratulations on the award of his master's degree Kwame expressed his sympathy for the assault on the morning of the opening of the Sunyani ITTU. 'We were all so ashamed that such a thing could happen in Ghana.'

'Oh, it's forgotten now, everyone was very kind, and the tree is thriving.'

Then Kwame remarked on the changes that were taking place.

'Yes Kwame, things are rather different around here now. It's getting more and more difficult to keep the work on track.'

'How long will you stay on?'

'My contract ends next July; I've just one year more to serve.'

'Many of us will be sad to see you go, Doctor.'

'Some changes are necessary, and my departure may be one of them. The new director has his own ideas on how to run the project, and I realise that the administration needs to be brought more in line with the ambient ethos, but I hope that people like you will try to keep reminding the director about service to the community.'

'But there aren't enough of us and we aren't in senior positions.'

'Well, let's keep on trying for another year at least.'

Kwame next found Dan Nyarko, still serving as the manager of the Tema ITTU. He asked how the ITTUs were faring. Dan told him that Tema and Tamale continued to progress reasonably well and Cape Coast was still doing well with the blacksmith-training programme. Of the new ITTUs, Sunyani had made an excellent start under Sam Sanders' energetic leadership but Sam had now been recalled to Tema and was complaining of having nothing to do. Meanwhile more permanent staff had been taken on in Sunyani, seriously inflating the running costs, and the performance had declined markedly. 'What do they need the extra staff for?' asked Kwame.

'I guess the director is under pressure to find jobs for his people – what do you think? The same thing is happening in Ho,' continued Dan.

'Ho is the big disappointment of the project so far. It still has no apprentices under training after a year in operation, it is generating very little income and the manager is floundering. He told me that he has no funds to employ apprentices, but I pointed out to him that he has recruited far too many permanent staff in senior posts that serve no real purpose. That is his real problem. It's the same thing that's happening in Sunyani now Sam has left, but I guess in Ho it's the manager's friends who are being given the jobs. However, some people think that it's a pay-off for Dr Oclu at MIST and Miss Spence at the Ministry of Finance and Economic Planning (MFEP) for their support in removing Dr Jones.'

'Is Dr Oclu also from Ho?'

'He's from Tsito, the same as Hayibor, the Ho ITTU manager. Maybe Hayibor is related to Oclu and that's how he came to be appointed in the first place.'

'What about Miss Spence?'

'She's also from the Volta Region but I'm not sure which part.'

'At least Sam recruited a full complement of apprentices; are they still there?'

'Yes, so far. I think Dr Jones wants to send Sam back to Sunyani to try to sort things out but the director won't agree. Maybe we can persuade the director to send you back to Ho instead. I know how you love the place,' Dan added with a grin.

'At least you have a good job to do here in Tema,' said Kwame.

'Yes, I enjoy the work here but I don't know how long it will last.'

'What do you mean?'

'Well, all of us who've been specially trained to be ITTU managers are regarded as Dr Jones' people. Dr Mensah seems to want to replace us all with new recruits.'

'Why should he want to do that?'

'I'm sure you know why. It gives him a chance to provide more jobs for his friends and eliminates any opposition to the changes he wants to make in the way the ITTUs operate.'

'What is Dr Jones working on these days?'

'He's trying to support Henry Debrah in getting the Takoradi ITTU started and later this year he'll be going to Zimbabwe to help with an ITDG project in Harare.'

'How long will he be away?'

'Only about a month, leaving in the middle of October, but before that he'll be temporarily in charge again here; the director is taking his annual leave overseas in July.'

July in southern Ghana is usually cloudy and overcast with only light rain. It is usually the coolest part of the year. This year, however, the major rainy season held on longer than usual with heavy downpours. Many of the rivers were swollen and burst their banks. The road to Cape Coast in the Central Region was particularly badly affected, with deep flooding in places, but a steady flow of traffic from GRID to the Cape Coast and Takoradi ITTUs needed to be maintained and the Land Rovers and heavy trucks were still getting through.

Robert Battah, head of SEACOM, suffered with eye trouble and often combined visits to the Cape Coast ITTU with visits to an eye clinic run by a foreign church mission. Having an appointment with the eye clinic, he planned a trip to Cape Coast in the SEACOM Land Rover.

This vehicle had an experienced driver, Sammy Dzadake, who was one of the most jovial and popular employees of the project.

Robert and Sammy set out on the morning of 15 July together with Robert's wife. At Winneba they stopped to give a lift to a woman whom Robert recognised as another patient of the eye clinic. Motoring on, they came to where the road crossed the Nakwa River but on this day the river was overflowing the road with a strong cross-current. Sammy, with characteristic faith in the strength of his Land Rover, drove firmly forward but the vehicle was swept off the road and into deep water by a flash flood. Robert managed to escape and cling to an overhanging branch of a tree. The other three travellers drowned. Robert returned to Tema in a police car to report the tragic event. The whole project was deeply shocked.

On that day, 15 July 1991, the Accra weather station recorded rainfall of 128 millimetres, with 120 millimetres falling in just two hours. This quite exceptional inundation was what took the lives of three people. The next day the vehicle was pulled from the river and the three trapped bodies were removed. The stranger was taken away to be buried by her family in Winneba. Robert and GRID were left with responsibility for the other two. Kwame guessed that this was a time when Dr Jones wished that he had not been left in charge. Two funerals needed to be arranged at short notice.

Both the deceased were natives of the Volta Region. Robert's wife came from Ho and Sammy came from the nearby hometown of the Battah family, Tsito. Sammy's modest funeral was held on the first Saturday, followed a week later by a rather more elaborate ceremony in Ho. Dr Mensah returned from leave just in time to attend the second funeral. Waiting for the funerals to come had extended the dark period for the whole staff. Morale fell to an all-time low from which it was likely to take a long time to recover. To Kwame it seemed that even the elements were conspiring to defeat the project.

Kwame knew that Dan Nyarko and Sam Sanders were worried about the future of GRID and so he was not surprised when they invited him to a meeting to explore their options. It was already clear to all three that their future prospects in the project were bleak. Kwame asked about Dan Baffour-Opoku whom they all regarded as the senior member of their group of young graduates trained to run the ITTUs.

'Haven't you heard?' said Dan Nyarko. 'He's applied for the post of deputy director when Dr Jones leaves next year.'

'Good!' said Kwame, 'I hope he gets it; at least we will have an engineer helping to guide the project.'

'But do you think the director will agree to appoint Dan?' asked Sam Sanders.

'It's the GRID project board that makes senior appointments, not only the director,' said Dan Nyarko.

'Yes, but with the director and the chairman both coming from Sunyani everyone expects the director to get his way. He won't want one of Dr Jones' protégés as his deputy. Unless,' Sam added as an afterthought, 'he can win him over to his side.'

The three agreed that much of their own fate would hang upon the fate of Dan Baffour-Opoku. If Dan was appointed deputy director and proved to be effective in keeping the project on course they could all expect some meaningful involvement in the work. On the other hand, if Dan failed to be appointed, or was appointed but meekly followed the new line, they could all expect to leave the project at an early date. In that case they should all consider their options.

'I've already started to build my own foundry,' said Dan. 'With luck, by next year I could leave to run it full-time.'

'I'm more interested in an academic career,' said Sam. 'I think I might apply for a lectureship at KNUST in Kumasi.' They both looked at Kwame.

'I'm not sure what I will do,' he said. 'I'll begin to look around now I know what you both have in mind.'

In considering his future beyond GRID Kwame's thoughts turned to his house in Kumasi. He decided to talk it over with Afriyie. 'I'm thinking about moving to Kumasi next year,' he told her, 'what do you think about that?'

'Are you thinking of sending Akosua to St Louis'?'

'Yes, but as St Louis' is a boarding school she could still go there even if we stay here in Tema.'

'Then why move to Kumasi?'

'It would give me a chance to finish my house.'

'Would you live in it?'

'Of course!'

'Where would I live?'

'With me of course.'

'What, in Comfort's house? I couldn't do that.'

'Why do you think of it as Comfort's house?'

'You were building it for her, weren't you?'

'Well, yes.'

'And she told you exactly what she wanted?'

'That's right.'

'Then the house is for Comfort.'

Kwame had not expected this problem. He had always regarded Afriyie as gentle and pliable. Now she had shown her hard core for the first time. He wondered why the women in his life had this proud attitude towards houses. Fortunately, he thought, the building is by no means finished. If I offer to make extensive alterations maybe she will agree to live there. So he said to her, 'Next time we're in Kumasi, let's go and look at the house and you can show me any changes that you would like to make.'

'I don't want to change Comfort's house.'

'But Comfort doesn't need it any more.'

'How do you know what Comfort needs?'

'Doesn't she have a rich Lebanese boyfriend to look after her?'

'I don't think so; she's in England.'

'How do you know that?'

'I got a letter from her last week.'

'Why didn't you tell me?'

'She asked me not to.'

Kwame had learned so much from this short conversation that he didn't know which aspect to dwell on first. He knew that Afriyie and Comfort had been close friends but he hadn't realised that they had kept in touch. Maybe Afriyie sensed that Comfort might need the Kumasi house sometime in the future and she didn't want to be accused of stealing her house as well as her husband. After all, it was much easier to get a new husband than a new house. Anyway, it seemed that Afriyie couldn't be persuaded to cooperate in any plan to alter or complete the house, and that created a range of new problems. Kwame thought that, after paying for his Tema house, he had just sufficient funds to finish the half-built house in Kumasi, but he knew that he didn't have enough to start again on a fresh plot, especially as the cost of building plots had escalated since he acquired the land at Old Ahensan in 1986.

As far as his financial situation was concerned Kwame had relaxed for the past three years, believing that his capital resources would be sufficient to support his building programme whenever he decided on reactivation. Now, at a stroke, he was thrust back to the situation in 1986 where if he bought a plot of land he could not be sure if or when he could complete the building. His chance to earn a large sum of money had been a unique opportunity. It was unlikely that a similar chance would recur. So once again he was back to wondering what he should do to get money to satisfy the needs of his family. Once again the temptation to live and work overseas pressed upon his mind. He had returned to Ghana to play his part in what Fred Brown had called the grassroots industrial revolution. With that opportunity now fading fast, the lure of *aburokyiri* shone brighter again.

He wished that he could talk the whole issue through with Sam and Dan but Dr Jones had seized an opportunity to send Sam back to Sunyani and Dan to Ho. Kwame had temporarily taken over Dan's place in Tema. Now the technical adviser had left for Zimbabwe and it was likely that Kwame's two mates would be recalled to Tema. He might soon have an opportunity to talk to them again.

What should he make of the new attitude displayed by Afriyie? He had decided against marriage in the hope of avoiding such a change in attitude but it was still happening. If it wasn't marriage, what was it that caused this deterioration in his relationships? Had he given the impression to Afriyie that even if they weren't married they were in a stable long-term relationship and this was enough to embolden her? When you loved someone you wanted them to feel secure, yet it seemed that it was security that changed them into someone you couldn't love. Why was life so complicated? Should he do something to make Afriyie feel less secure before her transformation became irreversible?

He asked Afriyie about her business and her partnership with Gladys. She told him that Gladys had looked after things quite well while she was away. Now Gladys had finished her training at the ITTU and had joined the business full-time. Their dresses and shirts were still growing in popularity and the future looked bright. 'Can you rely on Gladys now she's married?' asked Kwame. 'What if she wants to start a family?'

'I don't think she will stop the business. Her husband is only a labourer at the steelworks; she needs the money.'

'I saw one of your apprentices at the ITTU the other day; are you having her trained there?'

'You mean Mary Bansah, yes, she's finished her apprenticeship with me but I'm keeping her on as an assistant seamstress. I thought it would be good for her to learn the tie-dye to keep it going if Gladys leaves.'

'So you're not completely sure about Gladys.'

'You know how it is; people can disappoint you at any time.'

* * *

327

After the technical adviser returned from Zimbabwe in November Kwame sensed that a major disagreement had arisen between the old and new directors. He learned that Dr Mensah had succeeded with the help of his contacts in the Ministry of Finance and Economic Planning (MFEP) to convert the fund for supporting collaborating institutions into a building fund. Then he had searched for a major building project and had hit upon the idea of establishing a Centre for Engineering Design on the Tema compound. He announced the project to the staff just before the return of his predecessor.

Dan Nyarko told Kwame that Dr Jones was opposed to the idea and had made his position clear to the director and the GRID project board, as well as to Henry Debrah, Dan Baffour-Opoku and the other senior engineers. He felt that Ghana might benefit from the establishment of a centre for engineering design but GRID did not possess the expertise to carry it through. In any case it was no part of the project's original objectives and would divert energy and resources away from developing the ITTUs. If a centre for engineering design was to be established, it should be at the School of Engineering at KNUST in Kumasi. The ITTUs would be able to draw upon its expertise through the TCC. He argued that the issue was of national significance and as such it should not be decided in isolation within GRID. He suggested that a committee of experts, including representatives from MIST, CSIR and KNUST should examine the proposal in detail and advise the government accordingly.

Kwame knew that Dr Mensah would not be happy to hear this criticism of his proposal and suspected that he would press ahead anyway, ignoring the advice of his predecessor. The contractor who had worked on the refurbishment of the Ho ITTU building was calling regularly at GRID. He was clearly pressing for the award of the new contract in spite of complaining openly about the size of the commission he had been forced to pay to secure the work in Ho. Kwame could imagine the amount of money that was to be made from the award of the far bigger contract to build the engineering design centre. The issue was too big to be spoiled by the susceptibilities of a foreigner.

When Dr Jones was preparing to leave in June 1992, Kwame read the technical adviser's final report with interest. The current performance of the ITTUs under GRID was compared to the record of the Suame ITTU in its early days. Only the ITTUs at Tamale and Tema showed any promise of reaching the level of performance achieved at Suame in the period 1982 to 1986. The main problem with the GRID ITTUs was identified as over-staffing. Too many permanent staff were being appointed instead of relying on a few highly skilled instructors supported by teams of apprentices. As a result, the training output was low, money was being wasted on unnecessary salaries and client enterprises were not benefiting in the way intended. The report concluded that the ITTUs were failing to develop their full potential because the focus on the client was no longer there; the memory of Suame had been lost.

After the departure of Dr Jones, Dan Nyarko, Sam Sanders and Kwame Mainu carried on with whatever duties were assigned to them and waited to see what would happen. They had plenty of time on their hands in which to meet and consult together. There was a brief period of expectation when Dan Baffour-Opoku was appointed deputy director but he soon gave up the struggle to get the project back on course and meekly endorsed every move proposed by Dr Mensah.

Now began an exodus of some of the most senior and experienced staff. Much to everyone's surprise one of the first to leave was the finance officer. It had seemed to many observers that the lady had been willing to turn a blind eye to the director's neglect of standard accounting procedures, but she told Kwame later when he met her in Accra that she could no longer stomach what was going on. Another lady who left early was Yvonne Walter-Brice, head of the Rural Industries Division (RID), who had done much to promote the small-scale textile industry. When Kwame asked her why she had decided to leave she replied simply that Dr Jones had left first.

One division head who soldiered on was Henry Debrah, Chief Engineer and head of the ITTU Operations Division. Always a heavy drinker, poor Henry's addiction increased to the point where Kwame suspected it was unlikely that he could ever get another job at senior management level. Always in debt, the director had little problem in moulding his allegiance. The younger engineers looked to him to keep technical issues in focus when important decisions were being taken, but like the deputy director he was overwhelmed by the aura of absolute power assumed by Dr Mensah.

All decisions were now being taken by one man, often without any pretence at consultation. He had cultivated strong political support in key ministries and it was rumoured that his contacts extended all the way to the wife of the head of state. Under the new regime GRID had been converted from a democracy into a dictatorship, with the GRID project board serving only to rubber stamp the actions of the director. People opposed to these developments began to feel that any serious challenge to the regime would have to wait upon a change in the national government, and in the New Year of 1993 that possibility seemed many years away.

Some political progress was being made at the international level. At the meeting in Paris in July 1989 of the leaders of the Group of Seven industrialised nations, President François Mitterrand, had been delegated to tell the Ghanaian dictator Jerry Rawlings to institute steps to return Ghana to democracy. When summoned to Paris with his secretary for finance, Dr Kwesi Botchwey, Rawlings lost his temper at a press conference following his meeting with the president of France but was persuaded to accept economic and political reality. A constituent assembly was convened to draft a new democratic constitution. At the end of 1992 the first national election in more than 13 years had returned Rawlings to power as elected president for a four-year term. If the former flight lieutenant respected the new constitution he could serve only two four-year terms. Thus many Ghanaians began to focus their hopes on the year 2000 as the time when a real change of regime might be possible. But in 1993 that was still seven years away, far too long for young and energetic people to wait.

It was not long before Sam and Dan activated their escape plans and handed in their notice. In three months they would both be gone. Dan had decided to jump into full-time self-employment as managing director of his Danco Foundry Ltd. and Sam had gained an appointment as lecturer in mechanical engineering at the KNUST in Kumasi. Kwame did not relish being cast in the role of a rat leaving a sinking ship but that was how he felt.

For the past 12 years Kwame had been associated with the development of the ITTU network. Starting at Suame in Kumasi in August 1980 he had later served a long spell at Tamale, then, more recently, at Tema, Cape Coast and Ho. He was convinced that the ITTU concept was sound and offered an effective mechanism for transferring technology to small-scale urban and rural enterprises. As such, it could play a vital role in the bottom-up economic development of Ghana. But an ITTU was much more than bricks and mortar and machine tools; it was a human organism, earnest, sensitive and responsive to the needs of its clients. Without people long trained, experienced and motivated to serve

330

the needs of their clients the ITTUs would fail. Yet these very people were being driven out of GRID to be replaced by untrained sycophants. Operational efficiency was being subordinated to gaining the spoils of nepotism; providing benefits for insiders was replacing service to the community. It was time for Kwame to do what he always hated to do: take an important decision.

He carefully considered his options. They were clearly divided into two groups: what he could do in Ghana and what he could do overseas. He decided to consider the domestic options first. He had returned home hoping to continue his work in grassroots industrial development and he wanted to try to continue this effort if any possibility existed. Firstly, could he follow the lead of either of his two friends? The idea of applying to work back at the university in Kumasi was attractive in many ways. He was less interested in lecturing than the possibility of working for his old outfit, the TCC. However, he knew that the centre was now poorly funded and seldom had openings for new recruits. If he opted for a lecturing post it would give him some time to pursue his other interests but he really wanted to work full-time on development issues.

Dan had been working on his foundry for some time and was now ready to try to earn a living from his own business. Kwame knew that he didn't have time to start a similar foundry project from scratch, but Dan might be interested in a partnership, especially with one who could contribute a substantial capital investment. It was an exciting possibility. The two friends would be working in the light industrial area and would be interacting with other small enterprises in many ways. With their broad knowledge of the needs of small workshops and the services that could supply them, they could act as a catalyst for development in much the same way as an ITTU, if on a rather smaller scale. Here was the germ of quite an exciting idea but Dan might feel that his foundry was too small to support two full-time directors, and Kwame didn't want to put his friend in the embarrassing position of having to turn him down.

Did he really need to be in partnership with Dan? Could he start a new development project without the need to establish his own foundry or workshop? After all, he had sold many market trolleys without having his own workshop. He could invite Dan, and perhaps Sam also, to be involved as part-time helpers. With Dan in Tema and Sam in Kumasi they could do something really useful. He would need to set up a new agency, perhaps a non-governmental organisation, an NGO, and he would need to write some project proposals to attract overseas aid funding.

331

He had his savings to tide him over until new money came in. He decided to invite his two friends to discuss his ideas in more detail.

Dan and Sam greeted his proposal with enthusiasm. 'So you would base yourself in Tema and run the new project on a full-time basis, and Sam and I would help part-time to implement the work programme in Kumasi and Tema,' said Dan.

'Yes,' replied Kwame, 'and we could easily cover Accra from here as well.'

'But what exactly could we do?' asked Sam.

'I've been thinking about that,' said Kwame. 'I think that we should start by looking for gaps in what the GRID ITTUs are doing and try to fill them.'

'How do you mean?'

'Well, you know that the final year apprentices are sent on six-month attachments to private workshops to give them experience of how small enterprises are run.' Dan and Sam nodded. 'Dr Mensah is dropping the scheme, to shorten the period of apprenticeship and save money. If we could raise funding, we could sponsor the attachments. I've even thought of a name for it. I want to call it our Suame Scholarship Scheme.'

'Would all ITTU apprentices be included in the scheme?'

'Of course!'

'What else could we do?' asked Sam.

'How about a survey of engineering workshops to identify the needs that aren't already being served?' suggested Dan.

'Yes,' said Kwame. 'If we start with that we don't need to be too specific about our other services until the survey is complete. We will have time to think things through carefully.'

'But we know of one pressing need already,' said Dan. 'The TCC used to import a lot of good used machines and tools from England and sell them to small enterprises at prices they could afford. When GRID started, Dr Jones continued this scheme but now they only intend to bring in new machines from India and China and the prices are likely to be unaffordable.'

'I agree,' said Kwame. 'We should try to restore the importing of used machine tools and equipment right away.'

The three friends then turned to more practical matters. 'How will you support yourself until we get some aid funding from overseas?' asked Dan.

'I have a little money saved,' replied Kwame, 'enough to buy a vehicle and keep me going for a year or so.'

'If it goes beyond that, and my foundry does well,' said Dan, 'I'll try to give you some help, especially if funding support is in prospect.'

'What will we call the new outfit?' asked Sam. 'How about "Appropriate Technology Ghana" or "AT Ghana"?'

So it was all agreed, and on the following day Kwame Mainu handed in his letter of resignation.

24

AT Ghana

Early in 1993, at the approach of his thirty-sixth birthday, Kwame was back on his own as he had been in Suame Magazine twenty years before. He had succeeded then and he was confident that he could succeed again. However, it gave him a strange feeling to be without a regular job after so many years of employment at the TCC and GRID. He began at once to take steps to establish Appropriate Technology Ghana.

Firstly, he registered his new NGO with the Registrar of Companies as a not-for-profit company limited by guarantee. Then at the Department of Social Welfare he registered AT Ghana as a charity devoted to promoting new small enterprises and employment opportunities. Finally, he registered the company as an employer with the Department of Inland Revenue and the Department of Social Security. Now he had created a new enterprise that could operate legally in Ghana and be recognised as an NGO both domestically and internationally. He hurried to the bank to open a local cedi account and a foreign currency account, designated in pounds sterling, making initial deposits from his own resources as a loan to the new company.

He was glad that he had applied to Ghana Telecom for a telephone when he had first taken residence in the Tema house, otherwise he might have waited two years for a telephone for the business. However, he decided to buy one of the new mobile telephones as a back-up. It could only be used in or near Accra, Tema and Kumasi, with a long silent stretch between Accra and Kumasi, but he expected as time went by that the coverage would be extended.

To give himself mobility in all parts of the country he placed an order for a short-wheelbase Land Rover with a turbo-diesel engine and waited impatiently for its delivery. Kwame couldn't imagine himself driving anything else. The TCC had always used Land Rovers and some were still operating after almost 20 years. GRID had started in 1987 with a fleet of Land Rovers but the new director was now importing

Japanese vehicles, much to the dismay of some ITTU managers who were disappointed not to be provided with the long-trusted 'original'. Kwame was free to make his own choice and he was still convinced by the slogan: 'Land Rover first – because Land Rovers last!'

Kwame's most serious task in those early days of self-employment was proposal writing. He decided to make his central appeal to the British ODA for a project to undertake a survey of engineering enterprises in Ghana. He called this effort the Technology and Enterprise Development (TED) project. The objective was to determine the most pressing needs of the small engineering enterprises and then devise a range of services to supply them. The initial proposal was well received but ODA wanted some changes to meet their standard procedures and Kwame sensed that the period of negotiation could be quite protracted.

He also expected to be able to gain funding support from some British and international NGOs. His first move was to write to ITDG for a list of NGOs with an interest in helping small enterprises and promoting informal training and rural development. When the list came to hand he sent his proposal for the Suame Scholarship Scheme to several of them. Much to his delight he had an early reply from the Abolish Hunger Foundation sending him the funds that he needed for the first year's programme and inviting him to apply again next year. Now he had the beginnings of a work programme. The funding would barely cover direct costs, leaving very little to help towards administration and overheads, but almost from the outset AT Ghana could claim to be doing something useful.

Kwame prepared letters to be sent to all ITTU managers, offering to arrange workshop attachments for final-year apprentices and to bear all the costs of transport and subsistence. Although many workshops run by past and current clients of the ITTUs were prepared to offer free accommodation for the apprentices on attachment, Kwame decided to provide a small sum to compensate the proprietors for expenses incurred in connection with accommodation, training materials and tool breakages. This created a fund of goodwill for the scheme and helped it to get off to a flying start. In the first year most apprentices were attached to workshops in Kumasi, including SRS Engineering and enterprises at Suame Magazine.

Much to Kwame's dismay, Dr Mensah prevented the GRID ITTU managers from replying to his letter on the grounds that it should only have been sent to him. So in 1993 only Suame ITTU participated. After consulting Dan and Sam, Kwame decided to make up the number by sponsoring a few final-year apprentices from private workshops. The experience was deemed to be useful because it enabled the apprentices to learn skills that could not be provided by their permanent masters and would expose them to the manufacture of a wider range of products.

Kwame wrote to Fred Brown to tell him of his new project and ask him to look out for used equipment that might be useful in small enterprises in Ghana. It was not long before he heard of a donation of tools from a workshop that was closing down. Kwame decided to use his own resources to transport the consignment to Ghana. He could recover the cost of transport from the selling price which he judged would still be affordable. This gave AT Ghana another line of activity. Kwame sent lists of the tools to Dan and Sam for circulation to workshops in Tema, Accra and Kumasi.

Tom also greeted Kwame's new venture with enthusiasm. He offered to help in inspecting engineering equipment before purchase or shipment and in making small purchases needed to maintain the work programme. He also offered to seek donations of equipment and to accumulate small items such as thread-cutting taps and dies to carry down with him on his periodical visits. He asked for a list of requirements from Dan Nyarko's foundry in the hope of helping that project to flourish.

The three founding members of AT Ghana decided to invite others to join their company. The first, Dan Baffour-Opoku, reluctantly declined the invitation on the grounds that it was incompatible with his position as deputy director of GRID. 'I suppose that means that Dr Mensah won't let him,' observed Dan Nyarko. A more enthusiastic response was received from the staff of the TCC where Sosthenes Battah, Edward Opare, Mike Boakye, now in charge of beekeeping, and Don Degbor, in charge of ceramics and refractories, all agreed to join. This gave AT Ghana a significantly broader reach in terms of technical expertise.

Although Kwame had no regular income, and sooner or later this issue would need to be seriously addressed, he very much enjoyed this initial period of pioneering effort. From a secure base in his own small house he was reaching out to provide useful services to engineering enterprises in Ghana's three main industrial centres of Tema, Accra and Kumasi. Dan's foundry was rapidly gaining strength and would soon provide AT Ghana with a valuable technical base and training centre from which it could offer a range of additional services. Already Dan had offered rent-free workshop accommodation to a young man who had completed his apprenticeship at the Tema ITTU. Equipped with a small centre lathe imported with AT Ghana's first batch of used machine tools, a new venture in self-employment was given a starter home.

Kwame arranged to visit Kumasi to discuss progress with Sam Sanders and to strengthen AT Ghana's links with the TCC. However, he had a more pressing personal reason for the journey. As he had told Afriyie, he wanted Akosua to attend St Louis Secondary School.

St Louis Secondary School in Kumasi was widely regarded as one of the best girls' schools in the country. It was situated on the Accra to Kumasi road just inside the city boundary. Belonging to the Roman Catholic Church, its counterpart school for boys in Kumasi was named after the *Asantehene*: Opoku-Ware. Given a free choice, Kwame would not have chosen to send his daughter to a religious school but he wasn't given a free choice.

If Akosua had not been so attractive he might have risked a co-educational state school, but as she had inherited the handsome features of her parents he considered it essential to try to protect her from the predatory interest of male teachers. So he felt compelled to send her to a single-gender school where there was strict discipline and mostly female teachers. The only such schools with good academic records were private schools run by religious organisations. However, believing as his father did, that everyone should be free to choose his own religion when mature enough to make a rational judgement, he was confident that Akosua would weigh any indoctrination objectively and would not be easily brainwashed. He was forced to admit that in the last analysis he would rather deal with a Catholic daughter than a teenage pregnancy, although he realised there could be no absolute guarantee that he wouldn't end up with both.

Kwame had written to the headmistress and received an invitation to bring Akosua on a visit to the school. So setting out at dawn on the appointed day they arrived in Kumasi at the appointed hour and turned right into the school compound. The low-rise buildings were hidden from the road by a line of trees and they found that the whole compound was quite heavily wooded. Trees with red and yellow blossom lined the roads and adorned grassy areas between the buildings. At first sight, it seemed a pleasant environment in which to pass one's years of education.

They hurried into the administration building and announced themselves to the head's secretary. After a short delay they were invited into the presence of the big lady. Kwame was relieved to find that he was not confronting a nun. After the usual greetings the headmistress asked Akosua about her schooling to date. She explained that she had started school in Konongo, then went to a school in Nottingham, England, then after a few days back in Konongo she had attended school in Coventry, then school in Tema for two years, then a year at Cranfield, England, and for the past year and a half she had been back at school in Tema.

'Mr Mainu, it's seems that your daughter has had very unstable schooling up to this time.'

'That's why I want her to come here, to give her some stability.'

'She's just thirteen, is that right?'

'Yes, her birthday was on 16 February.'

'She's the right age to start here in September. Is she taking the common entrance examination in Tema?'

'Yes, she may have had unstable schooling, but she's very bright.'

'Every parent thinks that they have produced a genius. I hope that in your case you are right. We will give Akosua a little test now and if she passes that, and the common entrance examination in May, she can have a place in September.'

'Thank you,' said Kwame, thankful that he had been asked nothing about his religious beliefs.

Kwame asked if they could take a look around the school and the headmistress asked her secretary to arrange for a sixth former to serve as their guide. Akosua was taken away to undergo her unexpected testing and Kwame was left with the *Daily Graphic* and *Ghanaian Times* to await her return. Since becoming an avid reader of the *Independent* during his time in England, Kwame had come to regard Ghanaian newspapers as very light on content and devoid of objective analysis. During the next half hour he read the two on hand repeatedly from cover to cover, searching in vain for something that he might have missed. The experience did nothing to change his opinion, and he grew more and more impatient for the return of his daughter.

Akosua returned with the secretary, smiling and signalling discreetly to her father with the thumbs-up sign she had learned in England. The secretary assured Kwame that their guide would soon come to take them on their tour of the school. When the girl arrived Kwame realised why teachers were prepared to work for such low salaries. Then he switched back abruptly to anxious parent mode as it dawned on him that he was seeking to protect Akosua from just such wayward thoughts. 'Are most of your teachers women?' he asked in what he hoped was an off-hand manner.

'Oh yes,' replied his tormentor, 'except for Father Ambrose, who teaches RE and a few technical specialists who come in part-time.'

Kwame reflected gloomily that they were unlikely to need a part-time instructor in foundry technology.

They were shown around the classrooms and laboratories. In some rooms where classes were in progress they were able to watch for a few minutes through windows providing a view from the corridor. As Kwame expected, the discipline was strict. Akosua was less pleased; she was used to a much less constrained situation, both at the school in Tema and in Cranfield. At the Tema school, the children were often left unsupervised, either because of staff shortages or because teachers had failed to report for duty. In Cranfield, Akosua had experienced the relaxed discipline of contemporary education in England. Either way, Kwame reflected, she had not become accustomed to the strict discipline that he remembered from his own schooldays. She would have to learn to accept it if she enrolled at St Louis.

They were then led across to the dormitory blocks. These seemed to both father and daughter to be Spartan in the extreme. The space allocated to each girl was only just enough to accommodate a narrow bed and a cupboard with two drawers. 'Where will I put all my things?' asked Akosua, and Kwame told her that she would have to leave most of her things at home.

'After all,' he added, 'you'll be wearing school uniform most of the time.'

'That's right,' said the girl guide. 'We all had to get used to leaving our pretty things behind.'

Then Kwame remembered how all the girls at university in Kumasi dressed as though entering a fashion parade. It must be due to the feeling of happy release that comes after spending five or six years in school uniform, he thought.

Their guide asked if they would like to see the dining room. 'It's time for first sitting,' she said. 'You'll see what we are expected to survive on. Most of us bring food from home to keep going.' The food didn't seem too bad to Kwame but he guessed that it could become monotonous if repeated too regularly.

Akosua showed more concern. 'Will you bring me plenty of food, Dad, when you come to visit?'

'It looks as if I'll have to,' said Dad, reflecting ruefully that a secondary school girl might not have a Daddy any more.

Walking back to the administration building their path crossed that

339

of a matronly white woman in nurse's uniform. She paused to greet the visitors and introduced herself as Dorothy Irvine, the school nurse.

Kwame said that he was pleased to see that there were medical services on site if the girls fell ill while at school. 'That's a big relief for parents,' he said. Then he asked about the most common health problems.

'Well, apart from malaria, which is always with us, the biggest problem is stomach ulcers.'

'Stomach ulcers!' said Kwame, 'How is that?'

'You parents are to blame. You raise your children on hot peppery food and they find the school food too bland. So you give them red pepper powder and *shito* to bring to school and they add some to every meal. The result is stomach ulcers!'

'Thanks for the warning,' said Kwame. 'We'll see that Akosua's pepper is strictly rationed.'

As he drove on into Kumasi to visit the TCC Kwame pondered on what he'd been told. He had already been wondering about stomach ulcers, not for Akosua but for himself. Just as the nurse had said, he had grown to like strong pepper in early childhood and the predilection had not abated. In fact, like most men he suspected, he had tended to like his food even hotter as the years passed. But recently he had been experiencing some acute abdominal pains an hour or two after meals and he already suspected that it might be a stomach ulcer. Now, after listening to the nurse, he felt that he had no excuse not to consult a doctor.

When they reached Ayigya junction, Akosua asked if she could visit Afriyie's old workplace where she knew most of the girl apprentices. Kwame agreed so long as she promised not to wander about. 'Stay with your friends and I'll pick you up later,' he said. She got down from the vehicle and then Kwame turned left into the campus and parked outside the TCC. Edward Opare worked at Suame so Kwame did not expect to see him, and Sosthenes Battah, the director, was tied up with a visitor, but Mike Boakye and Don Degbor were eager to talk about the new project.

Kwame told them how things were going towards raising money to support a broader work programme and they were interested in knowing if there would be work for them to do. 'After we have completed at least part of the survey of engineering enterprises,' said Kwame, 'I expect that we will sponsor some short training courses here at the university and we'll need help in organisation.'

'Won't Sam Sanders look after all that?' asked Mike.

'Being an engineer, employed in the School of Engineering, he'll have

340

a lot to do on the technical side,' said Kwame, 'determining the course content, briefing the lecturers, preparing materials and coordinating the classes, but there will also be a lot to do arranging accommodation, catering and transport. I hope you'll both be able to help with that.'

While they were talking, Sosthenes Battah came in with Sam Sanders. Kwame took the opportunity to ask the TCC director how the World Bank project was going in Malawi.

'We've introduced all the small industry technologies that were proposed in the tender document and Solomon Djokoto is there finishing some of the installations,' he said, 'but the people seem to be very lazy and not very interested in working to earn a living. They seem to be much the same to us as we Ghanaians seem to be to Europeans. I keep recognising in myself the same frustration that I saw in Dr Jones when I first knew him.'

'Well, Dr Jones overcame his frustration,' said Kwame. 'I guess you'll overcome yours.'

'I don't need to,' laughed the TCC director, 'I've finished my work there now.'

'How is GRID now Dr Jones is gone?' asked Sosthenes.

'Don't ask me,' said Kwame, 'it will take too long to answer.'

'It's that bad, is it?' said Mike. 'Are other people leaving?'

'So far they've lost the finance officer, Mrs Walter-Brice, the Head of RID, Dan Nyarko, Sam and myself,' said Kwame. 'I don't know how many have left from the technical and junior staff.'

'It's more difficult for those people to find new jobs,' interjected Sam, 'but I know that several are looking for new opportunities.'

'What about Dan Baffour-Opoku?' asked Sosthenes. 'I thought he was unhappy with the way things were going.'

'He's now deputy director and seems to accept the situation for the moment but I have a suspicion that he's only waiting for the right opportunity to come along.'

'What sort of opportunity?' asked Don.

'You know, a job paid in foreign exchange with a UN agency or an international NGO.'

After a pause, Mike said slowly, 'That's what we'd all like: a job with a hard currency salary.'

'At least you're on university salary scales,' said Kwame. 'GRID isn't on them any more.'

'I thought when GRID started Dr Jones insisted on university salary scales so that GRID staff could move more easily back into the university system when the project finished.'

'That was the original idea,' said Kwame, 'but the new director accepted lower salary scales in his negotiations with the government to convert GRID from a project into a permanent institution.'

'And Dr Mensah was always criticising Dr Jones for not looking after the interests of the Ghanaian staff,' said Sosthenes. 'What about the scheme to help you all get your own cars?'

'Don't ask me again,' said Kwame. 'Dr Jones held a meeting with the EC people, the Canadians and the Germans to discuss bringing in small affordable Russian-made Lada cars for sale to the senior staff on hire purchase terms, but the new director has dropped the idea.'

'Well, he already has a Mercedes Benz and a Subaru; I guess he doesn't need another car,' said Don.

'But none of the other senior staff has their own car,' said Kwame, 'and most of them were looking forward to benefiting from the scheme.'

'Then it's no wonder people are leaving,' concluded Don.

'I didn't come here to talk about GRID, I want to discuss ideas for new project proposals for AT Ghana,' said Kwame. 'I have an idea that the International Labour Organisation (ILO), or another of the UN agencies, might be interested in a project to increase awareness that careers in engineering are open to women as well as men. I want to find more women who have already been trained in one of the engineering crafts. We know a few but we need more.'

'What do you have in mind?' asked Sosthenes.

'Well, we can help them with training and equipment, and perhaps workshop accommodation, and then use them as role models. We might attract some publicity to the cause by holding a seminar in Accra and inviting some prominent people to speak. Some of the women could tell their own stories and that might encourage others. Also, most master craftsmen are reluctant to take female apprentices; we might do something to break down barriers and increase opportunities.'

'I think that's a very good idea,' said Sosthenes. 'Here in Kumasi we seem to be behind both Tema and Tamale in recruiting women engineers but I feel that we should try to do more.'

'I don't remember seeing any women technicians or apprentices at Suame or at SRS Engineering or anywhere else in Kumasi,' said Kwame. 'Do you know of any?'

'I'm afraid not,' said Sosthenes, 'but you could check at Kumasi Polytechnic and Kumasi Technical Institute (KTI) to see if they've trained any women technicians.'

Kwame took Sam with him to pick up Akosua from the dressmakers' kiosk at Ayigya Junction and then drove into town. He didn't think there was much chance of tracing any women engineering technicians at the polytechnic but he decided to call at KTI, a relatively new and progressive institution supported by the Canadian International Development Agency (CIDA). They were lucky to find the deputy principal in his office. After explaining his mission, Kwame was told that one female student had attended a course in welding. Consulting his records the deputy principal said, 'Yes here she is; her name is Akosua Akomwa.'

'Where is she now?' asked Kwame.

'She had a small workshop on the ring road before you reach the Sunyani circle; maybe she's still there.'

Kwame decided to drive there right away. It wasn't too far and there were still two hours before sunset. Akosua kept telling him that if one Akosua could be an engineer she was sure another one could. When he reached the stretch of road to which he had been directed, Kwame stopped the car and Sam got down to ask some passers-by and wayside traders if they knew of a woman welder. They were soon directed to a small wooden shack a short way off on the other side of the road. Sam walked across, and Kwame parked the car near the shack, getting down with Akosua. A small human form was crouched on the ground intent on work that generated bright flashes of violet light. Even Akosua Mainu knew that that signified an electric-arc welder was in use.

Kwame told Akosua not to look directly at the flashes of violet light and she noticed that the welder was wearing a face mask with a dark glass to protect her eyes. After a few moments Kumasi's only female welder noticed that she had company and stood up, removing her mask. Kwame had seldom seen a grown woman of such small stature. Akosua at 13 was already taller and heavier, although it was clear from her mature figure that the little artisan was perhaps a decade older. What she lacked in stature she made up in spirit and it soon became clear to Kwame and Sam how this woman had pioneered a career in a man's world.

When she heard about AT Ghana and the new project Akomwa said that she was eager to take advantage of any scheme to help women engineers. She was trying to make a living in Kumasi but faced so much competition that it was very difficult. All her competitors were men and many people believed that only men could do the work. She would like to move her business to somewhere where there was less competition and perhaps where women artisans were becoming accepted. Kwame explained that working with the Suame ITTU he had been helping young people to make their own products rather than rely on people bringing them repair work. He suggested that Akomwa might succeed better if she too made her own product. She thought that was a good idea but what should she make?

Kwame told her that he could help her get some ideas for her own products by sponsoring her for six months training at a workshop where all the effort was devoted to manufacturing. He would suggest SRS Engineering here in Kumasi or the Redeemer Machinery and Tools Works in Tema. He and Sam outlined briefly what each enterprise was making. Akomwa was delighted at the offer and, saying that she was tired of Kumasi, she opted for a new life in Tema. So Kwame promised to arrange a Suame scholarship at Kofi Asiamah's progressive workshop on the same light industrial estate as Dan Nyarko's Danco Foundry. He and Sam were sure that she would be welcome there because Kofi Asiamah was an enlightened master craftsman who already had two young women apprentices in his workshop and had eagerly agreed to participate in the new scheme.

Kwame and Sam were very pleased with their afternoon's work. They had managed to weave together several strands of their new project and arranged a demonstration that could serve to promote any or all of them. They had extended the application of the Suame Scholarship Scheme, built upon their contacts with the light industries of Tema and, most significantly, found a way to further the cause of women in engineering. They felt confident that when they saw initiatives of this sort the international aid agencies would be interested in supporting AT Ghana.

Kwame dropped Sam at his house near the university campus. It was only then that he realised he had not stopped for lunch. The pains were starting again. He knew that he must eat. 'Did you have any lunch?' he asked Akosua.

'Yes, I had some gari and bean stew with the girls at the kiosk,' she replied, 'but I'm hungry again now.'

'Let's hurry to the senior staff club for some supper,' he said. 'We're staying on the campus in a guest house tonight.'

'Are you a good man, Daddy?'

'Oh, I'm Daddy again now, am I? This morning I was Dad.'

'That was in front of the big girl, Daddy. I was shy to use the diminutive at secondary school.'

'And I'm impressed with your English.'

'You haven't answered my question, Daddy.'

'One mustn't make self-judgements but I try to be a good man.'

'Akomwa said you were a good man, and Uncle Sam.'

'Well, I guess she doesn't get help very often.'

'Is she coming to work in Tema?'

'Yes, I think so.'

'That's good; I like her.'

At supper they both concentrated on their food but Akosua couldn't keep silent for long. 'Why is she so small, Daddy?'

'Who, darling?'

'Akomwa of course.'

'Maybe her family was very poor and couldn't feed her well when she was young.'

'Is that what they call kwashiorkor?'

'Yes, lack of protein causes stunted growth, or kwashiorkor, but we can't be sure that was Akomwa's problem. She may just be small because her parents are small.'

'Do you know that kwashiorkor is a Ghanaian word?'

'Yes.'

'It's not a Twi word though.'

'No, it's from the Ga language that they use in Accra.'

'That's right Daddy, we learned it at school.'

'So you might be a doctor, after all, or a nurse like Mrs Irvine.'

'Oh, I hope I don't get stomach ulcers.'

'I hope you don't.'

After Akosua had subsided into sleep, Kwame sat brooding for some time. The work had got off to a good start but would he be fit enough to sustain it? He had worked at GRID for several years without needing to see Dr Kwapong, a friend of Dr Mensah, who was retained to provide medical services for employees of the project. Now he had left GRID he would have to consult the doctor as a private patient. Until then, he must be careful not to miss a meal, cut down as far as possible on pepper, and maybe even give up his occasional bottle of Star beer.

'Life is so full of sacrifices,' he muttered to himself with a sigh.

25

Women in Engineering

Kwame knew that he liked women. It was more than sexual attraction. He admired their intuition and their determination to succeed in the face of enormous difficulties. He appreciated that the lot of the weaker sex in Africa was very hard and not getting much easier, even in this enlightened age. He knew enough to understand that most of the hard work on which the economy depended, especially in the agricultural sector, was done by women.

In some ways the women of his country were emancipated. The constitution guaranteed them equal voting rights, and equal rights to education and healthcare. However, they often lost out because of poverty. Poor families still gave priority to sons when paying fees for schooling or medical services or providing their offspring with a start in life. As a result, women had fewer opportunities in education and fewer chances to set up in self-employment, other than on the smallest micro-scale as petty traders. Most women, especially in the rural areas, were still condemned to the drudgery of home and farm.

In informal industrial areas, such as Suame Magazine, thousands of young men were given the opportunity to learn a skilled trade. Later, many of them were helped by family or friends to establish their own small workshops. It was this activity that the ITTUs were set up to promote and modernise. But women were largely excluded from the system. There were many women to be seen in the *kokompe* but they were itinerant purveyors of food and iced water, and sales assistants in spare-parts stores. During his years working with the Suame ITTU, Kwame could not recall seeing or hearing of a single woman artisan or apprentice in any of the engineering trades.

In Tamale, much to his surprise, one or two young women had applied to train as welders or machinists but it was not until he came to Tema and the GRID project that Kwame became aware of a determined attempt by a few enlightened engineers to actively promote the involvement of women in engineering. It was Dan Nyarko and Kofi Asiamah who took the lead. As manager of the Tema ITTU, Dan was able to recruit a female technician to lead the welding and steel fabrication section. Then he instituted an active campaign to attract girls as well as boys into craft apprenticeships. He invited local schools to bring their children on tours of the ITTU and girls often expressed their surprise and delight at seeing women engaged in the work. One by one the girls applied to join, and the Tema ITTU built up its contingent of female apprentices.

Kofi Asiamah already had one girl apprentice, his niece Edna Okai. He asked for her to complete her training at the Tema ITTU to extend her range of skills, and Dan Nyarko readily agreed. Edna was already more than semi-skilled and from the outset she did much to encourage her sister apprentices. It was the beginning of an alliance between Kofi and Dan that was to become the backbone of the cause. It was with this in mind that Kwame had been confident in offering Akosua Akomwa a Suame scholarship at Kofi's Redeemer Works in Tema. Since the time of Edna Okai, further progress had been made and there were now several young women who had completed their apprenticeships and were looking for an opportunity to establish their own workshops.

Kwame decided to recruit one of these trained technicians to help with AT Ghana's Women in Engineering project. By this time, Edna Okai had chosen to take her skills to Canada and was no longer available, so Kwame approached Hilda Kwaaku, a graduate of the Tamale ITTU. Hilda had already decided to try to establish her own workshop in Tema where she judged the conditions to be more advantageous. She had been promised starter accommodation in another Tema light engineering workshop, Entesel Ltd. Kwame offered her a modest salary to work for AT Ghana part-time, leaving her much time free to develop her own business. He also promised to supply her with a small lathe and a few other tools from the first shipment of used tools from England. This was an offer she readily accepted.

Hilda's first task was to make all necessary arrangements for Akomwa's attachment to Kofi Asiama's workshop. This was an easy introduction to the work because Kofi was an enthusiastic collaborator. In a few days Akomwa was resident in Tema and beginning her visiting apprenticeship. Kwame now had two women engineers actively involved in his new project and he was ready to begin to search in earnest for international funding support. He circulated his proposal among the agencies he knew were active in Ghana. Then he relaxed for a few days to attend to personal matters while he waited for a response.

Kwame had had very little contact with the medical profession since the days in Konongo when he had made repeated appeals on behalf of his disabled father for treatment on credit and time to settle the bills. He had come across the Hippocratic Oath rather late in life and it came as a surprise to learn that doctors were supposed to put the needs of the patient before their own avarice. He knew that most students applying to enter university put medicine as their first choice because it was widely known that it commanded the highest salaries. He was also aware that many families with an ailing elder relative were ruined financially by the high cost of medical care followed by the further expense of the funeral. So like most of his countrymen Kwame had put off consulting a doctor for as long as possible.

The abdominal pains had been growing more acute and more frequent. He could procrastinate no longer. So he telephoned Dr Kwapong and made an appointment for the next day. This was Kwame's first visit to the clinic but he was not surprised to find that it was newly built on a grand scale. A large car park extended in front of its dazzling white walls but the only other car was a new Mercedes Benz coupe. Was this an indication that business was bad or business was good? Kwame hurried in through the double doors into a large waiting room, devoid of people. His footsteps echoed as he walked across to the reception desk and gently roused the receptionist from her slumbers. 'Mr Mainu?' she yawned. 'Go right in; Dr Kwapong is expecting you.' She indicated a door on a corridor to her right.

Kwame had met Dr Kwapong only once before. He was a short slim man with horn-rimmed glasses who hastened Kwame into a chair beside his desk to lessen his physical dominance. After the usual greetings and noting Kwame's name the doctor asked, 'Now what's the problem? If it's something nasty picked up from the girls, don't worry, I have all the latest treatments from London.'

Kwame was somewhat taken aback by this overture and could only assume it was intended to put at ease patients with a sexually transmitted disease. He imagined that many of the big men, who were wealthy enough to afford the doctor's services, often brought this problem to him. He wondered how the doctor would deal with the problem of HIV/AIDS. The professor he met at Televideo had told him that there was no known cure – not even in London.

Kwame made an effort to reply in the same vein, 'Not this time, doctor, but I'll bear it in mind. No, my problem is a little higher up.'

'In your stomach?'

348

'Yes, just here.' Kwame indicated an area just below his breastbone.

'When do you get these pains?'

'Usually an hour or two after meals and sometimes in the night.'

'Please lie on the couch and I'll have a closer look.'

After Kwame was settled horizontally with bared stomach the doctor continued, 'Is it here?'

'No.'

'Here?'

'Yes that's it, *agyei!*'

'Well it's not appendicitis. I think you know what it is.'

'I suspect it may be a stomach ulcer.'

'You're not being treated for arthritis or rheumatism, are you?'

'No.'

'Then I would like to do a test for *Helicobacter pylori*. Have you been taking any antibiotics recently, say in the last four weeks?'

'No, Doctor.'

'Any other medications?'

'None at all.'

'Then I can do the test today if you have the time.'

'Yes, I want to sort it out as soon as possible.'

'Of course! Please wait outside while I get set up.'

Kwame went back to the waiting room where the receptionist had resumed her slumbers. At least here the reading material is a little more to my liking, he thought, recalling his wait at St Louis in Kumasi. He reached for a copy of the *Economist* and settled back for a long read, but a nurse came to call him much sooner than he expected. The more interesting the reading material, the shorter the wait, he said to himself; I think I'll call it Mainu's Law. Kwame looked at the nurse and then glanced back at the dormant receptionist. Dr Kwapong certainly has an eye for the girls, he thought, I wonder if he sometimes has to self-medicate. Then recalling his mind to his own problem he followed the swaying hips back into the consulting room.

Dr Kwapong took two samples of Kwame's breath. He was reminded of the test for drink-drivers in England. Then he was asked by the nurse to drink a foul-tasting concoction that he was told was c-urea. After a short interval, two more breath samples were taken. 'We'll have to send these off to Accra for analysis,' said Dr Kwapong. 'We'll have the results within a few days. I'll give you a ring. If the result confirms my diagnosis, we can start the treatment right away.'

'How long will it take?'

'I employ a one-week triple-therapy regimen.'

'Will that cure the problem?'

'The treatment is said to be effective in about ninety per cent of cases. I expect it will clear up the present problem if, as I think, we've caught it in time, but it's once bitten twice shy with gastric ulcers, I'm afraid. You must eliminate the irritants that brought about the first one.'

'Does that mean no more pepper?'

'I'm afraid so, and it's best to cut out alcohol as well. It's good you're not a smoker or you'd need to stop that as well.'

'Are there any pleasures I don't have to forgo?'

'Only one!'

On the way out the receptionist was wide awake. The nurse slipped her a note. 'We will require a deposit, Mr Mainu,' said the receptionist with well-rehearsed authority. 'There's the consultation, the fee for the test, including the analytical services at the laboratory in Accra, the nurse's fee, plus overheads and tax.' She mentioned a substantial sum.

'You don't charge for the car park then,' said Kwame with a grin.

'No, that's provided free for the convenience of patients,' she replied, trying to suppress an answering smile. 'By the way, Dr Kwapong has asked me to inform you that this will be the cost of your treatment if the test results are positive.' She scribbled on an invoice pad, tore off the top leaf and passed it to Kwame. He decided to look at it later. It was bad enough having a stomach ulcer; he didn't want to add a heart problem.

A few days later the telephone rang and Kwame learned that he could start the treatment. He was given three boxes of tablets to be taken twice a day for seven days. Dr Kwapong explained that one was a proton pump inhibitor, to lessen the production of gastric acid, and the other two were antibacterial drugs to eradicate the *H. pylori*. He was warned to report any side-effects that he might experience such as nausea, vomiting, abdominal pains, flatulence, diarrhoea, constipation, headache and dizziness. Kwame felt that the cure might be worse than the disease and started the treatment in some trepidation, but he was relieved to find as the days passed that these horrors did not appear. At the end of the treatment his bank balance was a good deal lighter but he was assured that his immediate health problem had been solved. Dr Kwapong advised him to come back at once if any symptoms recurred and otherwise to call back for a check-up in one month.

Giving up pepper presented Kwame with some serious problems. It wasn't only that he had to overcome his own cravings. The food was prepared for the whole family and Afriyie and Akosua would not want to give up their pepper. They didn't have stomach ulcers – yet. It didn't seem to Kwame to be practical to prepare two separate soups: one for him, and one for the rest of the family and any guests who might be dining with them. Could he negotiate a compromise? He decided to discuss the matter with Afriyie.

It was only in relation to the Kumasi house that Kwame had found Afriyie to be at all unreasonable. On the matter of his food, and his health, she was both sympathetic and practical. 'I really don't mind preparing soup for you separately,' she assured him. 'My sister in Kukurantumi has to do the same for her husband; he has the same problem.'

'But I will see and smell your soup, it will be torture for me,' he complained. 'Couldn't we all have the same but with only a little pepper?' Then he told Afriyie what he had learned at St Louis' school. 'It would be good for Akosua to cut down on pepper. I don't want her to get stomach ulcers at school like some of the other girls.'

The telephone rang and Kwame picked up the receiver to hear a voice from the past. It was Robert Earl, the engineer who had arranged his first training course at the foundry in Coventry. Thinking that it must be an international call he said, 'Robert, how good to hear from you, where are you now?'

'I'm in Accra with the ILO, when can you come to see us?'

'Have you seen our proposal?'

'Yes, that's why I'm ringing; we're very interested.'

'Will tomorrow morning at ten be OK?'

'We'll see you then.'

The next day Kwame drove to Accra, taking Dan and Hilda with him. They found the office near the beach in a large area arrayed with what in colonial days had been intended to be temporary wooden buildings, constructed on the pattern of army barracks. Originally occupied by government ministries, the offices had become available for other purposes as one ministry after another succeeded in erecting its own multi-storey concrete buildings on the landward side of the coast road. Several development agencies, domestic as well as international, had established offices in the vacated buildings to be in close proximity to the ministries with which they interacted.

Kwame introduced Dan and Hilda to Robert Earl, recalling how it was Robert who met him at Heathrow airport on his first visit to the UK and got him started on his first foundry training programme. 'You were working with ITDG in those days; how did you come to be with the ILO?' asked Kwame.

'It's a long story,' said Robert. 'You've probably heard it from others, but ITDG changed the emphasis of their work in the 1980s from developing technologies for Third World countries to undertaking socioeconomic studies and trying to influence policy makers and governments. They also transferred more of their work overseas to country offices. In short, there was much less work for technical people and we all began to leave. Now there's only Bob Spencer left at the Rugby headquarters.'

'I suppose his technical enquiry service will never end,' said Kwame. 'Not as long as ODA keep funding it.'

Dan asked Robert about the ILO.

'It's one of the oldest of the United Nations agencies,' said Robert, 'a living reminder of the earlier League of Nations from before the Second World War, and it still has its headquarters in Geneva. It has the objective of increasing employment opportunities and improving the lot of workers generally.'

'And that includes helping women in Ghana to become more involved in engineering, does it?' asked Kwame.

'Yes, I'm very interested in your new project and the ideas you have for increasing employment opportunities for women. That's one of our priority areas just now.'

Kwame told Robert how Dan had established his own foundry and Dan invited him to visit on his next trip to Tema. 'Yes, I'll be coming soon to see what you're all up to,' said Robert, 'and I guess that Hilda is looking after your women's project.'

'We'll show you the Redeemer workshop where we already have some girls under training,' said Hilda. Kwame smiled inwardly; Hilda would be a great success, she had already multiplied Akomwa into a plurality, but then he remembered Kofi Asiamah's other female apprentices and realised that she had not unduly distorted the truth.

When Robert Earl came to Tema a few days later he said that he was very impressed with Dan's foundry, especially the quality of the castings. He was equally impressed with the quality of the aluminium-spinning lathes and large bench saws that he saw under construction at the Redeemer Works. He told Kwame, Dan and Kofi that in Rugby they had been really proud of their association with the TCC, and

Ghana generally, because they saw projects pursued for many years until they became a reality. So often in other countries they had been involved with projects that were abandoned after just a few years with no lasting benefit. In his view the TCC and now GRID had established a long history of successful technology transfer that had no equal in any other African country. Now it was the turn of the three Tema engineers to feel proud of their country's achievement and their part in it.

Kwame took the party back to his house for cool drinks and a detailed discussion of the Women in Engineering proposal. He explained to Robert that they wanted to try to find and register all the trained women artisans and all the female apprentices still under training. They would assess each person's situation and determine what help was needed to promote their career. It might be more specialised technical training, supply of tools and equipment, help with workshop accommodation, a working capital loan to purchase materials, advice on choice of products or services, marketing, supply of technical drawings and specifications, and so on, or any combination of these things.

After a period of, say, six months, when the register was complete they would hold a seminar in Accra to which they would invite government ministers, heads of technical institutions and representatives of foreign funding agencies and industrial development projects as well as all the known women artisans and apprentices and their workshop masters. AT Ghana would present a report of their findings, and guest speakers would be invited to make presentations, but the central feature would be short talks by some of the women artisans and an appeal from them for more help in providing more opportunities for girls to enter the engineering crafts, gain formal sector employment or set up in self-employment.

Robert asked Kwame and Dan why they had left GRID and why they felt that AT Ghana was needed to initiate the project. 'Couldn't GRID or the TCC do it?' he asked.

Kwame answered that four members of the TCC, including the director, were members of AT Ghana and would be helping but unfortunately there were very few women engineers in Kumasi and the present search would be concentrated mainly in Accra and Tema. As for GRID, one reason for Dan and Kwame leaving was the increasing neglect of apprentice training, especially the support given to ex-apprentices. AT Ghana aimed to fill some of the gaps left by changes in the way that GRID was operating. Kwame mentioned the Suame Scholarship Scheme as an example. He explained that although it was primarily intended to sponsor final-year ITTU apprentices on industrial attachments, the Abolish Hunger

353

Foundation had agreed that the benefits could be extended to apprentices in private workshops with particular emphasis on providing support for young women. It was under this scheme that Akosua Akomwa was being sponsored for six months at Redeemer.

Robert then asked if AT Ghana had the resources to undertake the survey. Kwame agreed that AT Ghana was a young and small organisation but he felt that the survey wouldn't be beyond their capabilities. As former ITTU managers, Kwame, Dan and Sam knew most of the engineering enterprises in Tema, Accra, Kumasi, Cape Coast, Tamale, Sunyani and Ho. They knew that very few enterprises employed female technicians or enrolled girls as apprentices. They could easily trace the few women trained at the local polytechnics and technical institutes, as they had in the case of Akomwa.

Hilda, an ex-apprentice of the Tamale ITTU, knew personally all the young women who had been trained at the Tema and Tamale ITTUs and all the current apprentices. Making enquiries of these contacts may turn up a few more useful leads but the task was not expected to be an extensive one. 'If we need more help I'm sure some of my sisters will be willing to join in,' said Hilda. Once again Kwame gave her silent thanks for saying the right thing at the right time.

The discussion ended with Robert promising to recommend the funding of the project. As the funds required were small it should take only a few days to receive formal approval from Geneva. Watching Robert drive away towards the motorway in a cloud of red dust, Kwame said to his companions, 'It looks as though we might have found a role for AT Ghana.'

'Yes,' said Dan thoughtfully, 'there's a lot of interest in what we want to do, but we need a bigger project and more substantial funding support to sustain us in the longer term.'

'That will come,' said Kwame. 'This small start will get us established with some regular activity and the serious support will follow in time.'

Although the Women in Engineering project was soon approved there was a problem in releasing funds. Robert asked Kwame if AT Ghana could pre-finance the activity and with help from Dan this was arranged. Then Hilda began her survey in Tema and Accra and later extended it to the other main regional centres. Kwame analysed the reports she brought back from interviews with the female apprentices and technicians and began to draft a report to be presented at the seminar.

A few weeks later the first consignment of used machines and tools arrived from the UK. After clearing the goods from Tema port, Kwame and Dan set selling prices that would recover the shipping costs and administrative expenses. Then they tried to allocate the items fairly to the many workshops that had requested supplies. There was not nearly enough to meet the demand so priority was given to supplying newly qualified apprentices. Hilda became the proud owner of a small bench lathe that she installed at the Entesel workshop. Now she would have some self-generated income to supplement her modest AT Ghana salary.

At work, Hilda always wore blue denim overalls and the heavy safety boots she had been allocated on a short training course in Canada. In a situation in which most apprentices wore only rubber sandals the boots were a much prized possession. It was these boots that brought her to Kwame's house one evening with a curious problem.

Kwame had often wondered why Hilda had no husband or boyfriend. Although strongly built as befitted her occupation, she was not unattractive. She told Kwame that she had met a man she liked and they went out together a few times. Then one day she invited him to visit her at home for a meal. After eating, they were relaxing with a drink when the boyfriend noticed the heavy boots. He jumped up saying he must leave at once as he feared getting involved with a woman with a husband in the army! Poor Hilda tried in vain to convince the man that the boots were her own, that she wore them at work, but he couldn't imagine anyone but a soldier wearing such boots.

Kwame thought that the solution was easy. 'You should leave your boots and overalls at the workshop to put on when you arrive in the morning and take them off before going home in the evening.'

Hilda looked doubtful, 'Don't you think they will be stolen?'

'Then you need to keep them in a locker,' said Kwame. 'We'll see if we can find you one.' He feared that the boots had cost Hilda one opportunity for romance but following his advice she should be more successful next time fortune smiled on her.

The Women in Engineering seminar was held at the British Council hall in Accra in July 1993 and was a big success. All the dignitaries who had been invited put in an appearance and some made encouraging speeches. The young women bravely told their stories and were well received. Several engineering employers who were present promised to recruit men and women on an equal basis. The media gave the event good coverage. Many more people would now be aware of the injustice of the present system and many more people would now be willing to promote equal opportunities for women in engineering. Kwame, Dan,

Kofi Asiamah, and especially Hilda, were delighted with what had been achieved. They felt that their infant AT Ghana had been given a suitable outdooring – the traditional ceremony for introducing a newborn infant to the community.

Early in September 1993 Kwame and Afriyie took Akosua to Kumasi to continue her education at St Louis Secondary School. Akosua was excited to be starting a new life and only a little concerned about being away from her family. For several years past she had been forced to live without one parent or the other, and Kwame felt that she was as well prepared as most young people to start a semi-independent existence. He and Afriyie promised to come to Kumasi every few weeks to take Akosua out of school for a weekend and restock her food supplies. However, Kwame warned his daughter that her pepper supply would be strictly rationed.

Over the next few months life for Kwame and his family fell into a regular routine. Every two or three weeks Kwame or Afriyie visited Akosua and took her out of school for the weekend, returning her on Sunday afternoon with a bulging bag of food. Akosua came home to Tema for the Christmas holidays. Kwame celebrated his thirty-seventh birthday quietly in Kumasi with his two girls on 2 March and shortly afterwards Akosua came home to Tema for the Easter break. After two terms of this new regime, Akosua said that she was happy with the amount of time that she could spend with Kwame and Afriyie but she wished that she could also see her mother sometimes. Kwame wondered why Comfort took no interest in her daughter but he remembered how it was left to him to re-establish links with his own mother.

Life and work in Tema seemed to be going smoothly for Kwame but he couldn't prevent dark thoughts returning to haunt him from time to time, especially now that Akosua was not there to fill his idle moments with animated chatter. Ever since his return from Coventry in 1988 Kwame had tried to forget about his compatriots languishing in gaol. He was much less concerned about Peter Sarpong in an English prison than he was about Uncle George, Mama Kate and Bra Yaw imprisoned in Ghana. When he failed to prevent his mind dwelling on the matter it was the fate of the two older prisoners that distressed him most. In his darker moments he couldn't help wondering how long Uncle George and Mama Kate could survive in the harsh conditions that he assumed existed in his country's penal institutions.

At the time of the arrests Kwame had been worried that Peter would suspect he had played a part in their downfall. He even feared that Akos Mary might have had an opportunity to speak to Peter after her arrest, while she was still angry with him. It was unlikely, he felt, that the police would have allowed them to communicate after their arrests but the slight possibility still troubled him. However, as the years passed these fears had subsided and Kwame had become more at ease with his conscience.

It was Kofi Boateng who revived Kwame's fears. When he first saw him standing at the door of his Tema house one Sunday afternoon in May, Kwame had difficulty in recalling where he had seen him before. Then he remembered that Kofi was one of the suspected drugs couriers whom he had met at the West Africa club in Coventry. It was Kofi who had been arguing with Bra Yaw about the meaning of *nyansapo* when Kwame had been asked to adjudicate. More importantly, he recalled that Kofi was a Club man and was glad that he had some of the Accra brew in his refrigerator.

Kwame realised that he had given no thought to whether Kofi Boateng had been arrested with the other cartel members or whether he was still at liberty. It was possible that Kofi had served a short sentence somewhere before regaining his freedom; it was, after all, more than five years since the arrests. Kofi's reappearance brought many questions flooding into Kwame's mind but he knew that none of them could be asked directly. So after the usual extensive greetings and the offer and acceptance of Club beer, he began by asking, 'What have you been doing since we met in Coventry?'

'It was only a short visit; I came back to my work in Kumasi.'

'What do you do?'

'I used to help Uncle George with his market trolley business.'

'You're not still doing that work?'

'I did for a while, even after Uncle George was arrested, but now he's dead, the business has stopped.'

'Uncle George dead! When did that happen?'

'Two months ago in Nsawam prison.'

So what Kwame had dreaded in his darkest foreboding had happened. The old man had not been able to withstand the rigours of imprisonment and like Kwame Nkrumah's arch rival, Dr J.B. Danquah, he had passed away in the medium security prison in Nsawam. Once again a tumult of questions threatened to overwhelm Kwame's mind and once again none of them could be voiced openly. For some moments his mental floundering came up with no safe utterance.

357

He was rescued by the arrival of Afriyie. 'Did I hear that someone has died?' she asked. 'When will the funeral come on?'

'It's Uncle George,' said Kwame, passing on the other question to be answered by his visitor.

'We held the funeral in Kumasi last month,' said Kofi. 'Peter couldn't come down so the family went ahead with the funeral as soon as they recovered the body.'

'What a pity we couldn't go,' said Afriyie.

Kwame introduced Kofi Boateng to Afriyie. Afriyie was sure she had met Kofi before but she couldn't remember where. 'Maybe it was at Mama Kate's,' she suggested. 'I made her a dress once.'

'It's possible, I often used to go there on errands for Uncle George,' replied Kofi.

Then Afriyie asked, 'Peter is his heir, isn't he?'

'Yes, he should get all Uncle George's property, but it will be difficult for him to claim his inheritance.'

'How do you mean?'

'You know how it is; those on the spot can usually make the first grab.'

Kofi drained his glass and stood up. Kwame hadn't expected his visitor to leave so abruptly but he was relieved that almost nothing had been said about how or why Mama Kate, Uncle George and Peter Sarpong had been detained. He rose to follow Kofi to the door and walked with him in the bright sunlight across the small front garden to the ironwork gate.

Inside the gate Kofi paused and turned to Kwame. 'I have a message from Mama Kate,' he said. 'She sends you her greetings and hopes that you will call in to see her next time you're in Kumasi.'

Kwame's brain raced to formulate a suitable response, but before he could speak Kofi was through the gate and striding away down the narrow street between the rows of workers' low-cost houses and the assorted vehicles that all but completely obstructed the pathway.

If Kwame had needed a trigger to restart his stomach ulcers he believed that he had one now. So Mama Kate was back in Kumasi and apparently a free woman! How had that happened? What did it mean for Kwame and his family? Kofi had made no direct threat but did the message from Mama Kate imply a veiled one? If Mama Kate was re-established as the Kejetia shoe queen she would wield much power and authority. If his former benefactor was now his enemy his fears were well founded. It was ironic that at a time when he was doing all he could to empower disadvantaged women, one woman who had grown too big and powerful had become a potential threat to the whole enterprise.

Once again Kwame was forced to consider the safety of himself and his family. Would they be safe if they stayed in Ghana? Would they be safer if they returned to England? This renewed concern would now dominate his thoughts and revive in urgent form the old dilemma about where to spend his life and fulfil his destiny.

26

Destiny Deferred

Shortly after Kofi Boateng's visit Kwame received the good news that his proposal for the Technology and Enterprise Development project had been accepted for funding by the Overseas Development Administration (ODA) in London. If the news had come through a few weeks earlier Kwame would have been overjoyed. Now, he wondered if he would be able to stay on long enough to see the project implemented.

The TED project promised to maintain AT Ghana in business for the next three years with Kwame employed full-time as chief executive. The salary was modest in international terms but paid in hard currency and far above the salary he had been getting at GRID. It would meet his immediate needs and enable him to start replenishing his building fund. The project would also provide funds with which to pay his colleagues' fees and expenses for undertaking the survey of engineering enterprises and later to meet the costs of mounting short training courses at the university in Kumasi. In addition, AT Ghana would receive a second Land Rover, a personal computer and two laptops. These facilities would support the survey by allowing data to be collected, stored and analysed efficiently.

With the promise of these new resources Kwame and Dan Nyarko rented a room in a new building in the light-industrial area in Tema and established a head office for AT Ghana. Sam Sanders' office at the university would provide a base for operations in Kumasi. Kwame and Dan had already developed an extensive questionnaire to be used on the survey and with enough suitably qualified engineers already recruited the fieldwork could begin right away. The full input from the ODA would not come to hand for two or three months but Kwame decided to get the project off to a flying start.

Making all the necessary preparations for the new project tied Kwame to Tema for a few weeks and it was left to Afriyie to visit Akosua in Kumasi. It was possible to take a State Transport bus from Tema directly to Kumasi and so Afriyie did not have to change transport in Accra. Kwame dropped her at the Tema bus station. Although he did his best not to pass on his worries, he told Afriyie that Mama Kate was back in Kumasi and she might make a few discreet enquiries to see how things stood. Afriyie said that she would stay on a few days beyond the weekend to look up some old friends in the trading community. She promised not to ask direct questions but to listen carefully to the current rumours. Kwame was content; it was often said that there were no rumours in Ghana.

In spite of having plenty to do Kwame could not help looking forward to Afriyie's return. He met her at the Tema station at the appointed time and she reported on Akosua's welfare on the ride back to the house. Kwame was happy that his daughter was in good health and still enjoying the challenge of secondary school. It wasn't until after his supper of red-red and pineapple that Afriyie began to relate the more serious business.

'It's true Mama Kate is back in her old place at Kejetia,' she began, 'and people are saying that it's someone high in the government who got her released from prison.'

Kwame groaned; this seemed to be the limiting factor in all his endeavours. It was high-level patronage that was rumoured to be abetting the corruption and mismanagement at GRID and now it seemed that the same powers had released a convicted drugs trader. Then the idea struck him that his troubles stemmed not from two separate sources but from one and the same. However, he couldn't be sure if it was just that corruption was widespread in the system or whether the people who had taken over GRID were in some way linked more directly to the Kumasi drugs cartel.

He remembered reading in the Kumasi press that heroin had been found in the luggage of some members of the head of state's party on a visit to the USA. At the time he had dismissed this as malicious gossip spread by the political opposition. Now he wasn't so sure. The GRID director who was known to have friends in high places had spent several years working in Kumasi before coming to Tema. He regularly sent packages, which were said to contain money, to a former wife still living there. Were the mysterious packages found in the Indian lathes intended for transport to Kumasi and perhaps for onward transmission to the UK or USA? Was this the hidden reason for the GRID director's interest in importing machines from Asia? Kwame couldn't be sure if this was deductive reasoning or merely paranoia, but could he afford to take a chance? The sort of people who had resorted to violence against Dr

Jones, a foreigner, over a commemorative tree planting would not hesitate to use violence against a Ghanaian suspected of betraying his own people. He felt forced to assume that his own safety, and that of his family, was dependent upon a change of regime, and that couldn't occur before the year 2000, at the earliest.

Kwame's meditation on this disturbing theme was interrupted when Afriyie added, 'Comfort isn't happy.'

'Comfort, did you see Comfort?'

'Yes, she came to the house of one of my friends.'

'Why isn't she happy?'

'It seems that while Mama Kate was in prison, Comfort took over the shoe trade, importing from England.'

'She wanted to be the new shoe queen, did she?'

'That's what Mama Kate seems to think; she's very angry with Comfort.'

'Has Comfort been to see Akosua?'

'No, but I tried to persuade her to go; I think she might.'

'What did she say?'

'She asked if you would go to see her.'

'What did you say?'

'I said that I would ask you but I wasn't sure you would agree.'

'Where is she staying?'

'She has a house in Nhyiasu.'

At first Kwame could see no point in going to see Comfort. It was she who had walked out on him, and now that he had reconstructed a happy family life he didn't want the revival of old feelings to bring complications. On the other hand, Comfort had been a source of much inside information in the past and she might be able to tell him if he was now in any danger from the cartel. He had been told that she seemed to have fallen out with Mama Kate but Mama Kate had been out of the system for several years. Comfort might know the feelings of some of Mama Kate's collaborators who had maintained their freedom. She might know something from her Lebanese contacts. Of one thing Kwame was sure: Comfort would not be part of any conspiracy against him, so he saw no trap in her request for a meeting.

When Kwame went to Kumasi a few weeks later it was to work out with Sam Sanders how the survey would be conducted at Suame Magazine and in other parts of the town. Sam had arranged with Edward Opare and Solomon Djokoto to do the necessary fieldwork. With the TCC and its people knowing almost every engineering enterprise in the city, it was felt that the work in Kumasi would be the easiest part of the project. Kwame soon realised that he could leave the work in the safe hands of his colleagues and with time to spare his thoughts turned to the possibility of meeting Comfort. At last he resolved to take the plunge and drove his Land Rover up the hill to Nhyiasu, the garden of the Garden City.

Nhyiasu was the most beautiful part of Kumasi. In colonial times it was where the British administrators built their houses and their golf course. Off wide tree-lined streets with tree-lined drives these large colonial residences enjoyed the cool breezes and dark shade that Europeans found essential in the days before air-conditioning. Now the foreign administrators were long gone save for the managers of the Kumasi branches of Barclays and Standard Chartered banks and the managing directors of Kumasi's two breweries. Most of the houses were occupied by the more successful Ghanaian and Lebanese businessmen and a few big women traders, transport operators and hoteliers. Comfort had certainly come a long way in the past six years to have joined this affluent community.

Kwame knocked on the front door of the house, still not entirely sure that he wanted Comfort to be in. She wasn't. A maid informed him that Madam had not returned from the market but she was expected soon and he could wait if he wished. He was left seated in a large comfortable armchair with the obligatory glass of water, feeling that he needed something stronger.

The crunch of tyres on the gravel drive brought him to the window in time to observe the arrival of a BMW saloon. The driver got out and quickly opened the rear door. With rather less agility but perhaps a little more dignity than he remembered, a rather larger Comfort emerged from the air-conditioned cubicle of the car to hurry into the air-conditioned expanses of her mansion. Kwame stood transfixed. It was not the sight of his long-lost wife that astonished him; it was the identity of her driver. Comfort was being chauffeured by her old friend, the albino *okyeame*, Kofi Adjare.

Having already seen the Land Rover in the drive, Comfort expressed no surprise at finding Kwame in her lounge. The greetings were rather cool and awkward. Kwame was forced to turn down the offer of a Star beer on the grounds of his stomach ulcer so Comfort told her maid to bring tea. She expressed her concern for Kwame's ill health and hoped that it would not recur. Kwame asked how she was keeping and she replied that health-wise she was fine but these days she had to watch

363

her weight. Kwame said that her enhanced stature suited her status as a market queen but he saw at once that he had touched on a raw nerve. They sipped tea in silence for what seemed like a long time. 'You've certainly got the big house you always wanted,' he said at last.

'Yes, this is a nice place. Would you like me to show you around?'

'Lead on,' he said, putting down his cup.

House tours did not usually interest Kwame but he trailed around trying to make the right remarks in an attempt to break the ice and steer the conversation round to more serious matters. It was a large and comfortable house in a large and well-manicured garden and he felt that it must fulfil every part of even Comfort's exacting expectations. He wondered how it was that Comfort had succeeded where his mother had failed. 'It's a lot bigger and more elaborate than the little house we were building at Old Ahensan,' he said.

'Yes, that's what I wanted to talk to you about. Let's sit in the garden for a while and discuss it.'

'I've not done much to it since you left,' said Kwame.

'I don't think you've done anything, have you?'

'Well, no; there didn't seem to be much point.'

'Would you let me complete it?'

'Of course; it was for you anyway, but why do you want it? I thought you didn't want a house paid for with blood money.'

'I didn't want you to complete it with your blood money. My money is different. I want to rent the house to the university for staff accommodation. These days they're very short of living quarters and they're paying good rents for houses near to the campus.'

'Yes, I hear that some professors are ignoring the rules and staying on the campus after they have finished building their own houses with loans from the university.'

'They're better off letting their houses to the university than living in them.'

'It's the government's money, so nobody cares.'

Kwame was aware of Comfort's gaze. She stared unblinking for some moments before saying, 'Of course, I'll pay you for the land and the construction so far.'

'No need,' he said, 'it was for you anyway.' He knew that Afriyie had no interest in the house.

'Thank you,' she said quietly. She stood up, 'Let's go back in and have some dinner; you can still take fufu, can't you?'

'Yes,' he replied, 'but I'm not supposed to take pepper.'

It was a good meal and afterwards they relaxed with some soft drinks. He was offered a choice of four or five different beverages. In spite of the scarcities it seemed to Kwame that Nhyiasu people could get everything they needed from their foreign exchange shop. No Henry Ford syndrome here, he thought, recalling Tom's remark about only having Coca Cola to drink on that hot and dusty afternoon in Suame Magazine.

He decided to risk plunging into the more serious issues that were weighing on his mind. 'So you're not happy about the return of Mama Kate.'

'Is that what Afriyie told you?'

'Well yes, but I can imagine it's true.'

'We weren't expecting her back so soon.'

'How will it affect your business?'

'I was doing very well importing and selling the shoes. Now she will take over most of the business again.'

'So that's why you're moving into property.'

'That's a business where nobody can be queen, not even Mama Kate.'

'How did she get out?'

'Mama Kate? Oh, it was Uncle George's death that helped her.'

'How do you mean?'

'They say that her friends petitioned the government, saying that the same thing could happen to Mama Kate if she wasn't released.'

'That was enough?'

'Mama Kate had been a big supporter of Nana Konadu's 31 December Women's Movement and so she was well known in high places. It seems that efforts had been made to get her released earlier but it was decided to wait until the international interest had subsided.'

'So here in Ghana it's only Bra Yaw who's inside now,' mused Kwame.

'I expect he will also be out soon. The Lebanese guys at Hanabis, Omar and Suleiman, were released last year.'

'Ah yes, I'd forgotten about your Arab friends. That must have cost them.'

'I'm telling you.'

'Weren't there three directors at Hanabis? What happened to the other one?'

'Oh, Bachir Abizaid never returned after he left with the others in June 1979.'

'Do you think he's still linked to Hanabis or the drugs cartel?'

'Probably, but he's not in Ghana.'

With Comfort speaking so freely, Kwame was tempted to probe further. 'Are your Lebanese friends still helping you?'

'I needed their help at first. I had my rainy day savings, thanks to Oboroni, but I needed much more to start importing, especially foreign exchange. Now I've finished repaying the loans and I hope I've finished with them for good. They're back with Mama Kate and the drugs and I never wanted anything to do with that, as you know.'

'Yes, I'm glad you stopped me that time when Bra Yaw brought me the *kenke*.'

'Was it *kenke*? That's a very old trick. They've come up with some better ideas these days.'

'How do you mean?'

'I hear that they now conceal cocaine in babies' diapers, shoes and traditional soap, *alata samina*. Some women are hiding blocks of cocaine in their ornate hair-dos and a lot goes in hollowed-out wood carvings. The cleverest idea I've heard so far is to hide packets of cocaine inside the shells of live snails.'

'Doesn't it kill the snails?'

'Apparently not, but they're to be eaten anyway.'

'Do the snails die happy or is it the people who eat them who get the benefit?'

'Don't ask me, I haven't tried them.'

Kwame changed the topic, 'How did you like being the temporary shoe queen?'

'I always envied Mama Kate's power to control so much business and so many young men and women, but I couldn't do what she did.'

'How do you mean?'

'I had too much sympathy for the young women who struggled to get a start in the business as I had struggled. I gave many of them shoes on credit and I didn't used force to get my money back.'

'What about the boys?'

'I didn't need them for strong-arm work and I've enjoyed too much sophisticated romance to be content with clumsy toy boys.'

Kwame wondered if she counted him among her sophisticated lovers. He surmised that for the young people of Kejetia the substitution of Comfort for Mama Kate must have brought a welcome lightening of their burdens. If there were any democracy in the system he suspected that Comfort would be elected shoe queen by a large majority. He wondered if Mama Kate would also want to take back the driver she had inherited from Oboroni. 'Will you let Kofi go back to working for Mama Kate?'

'Oh, you saw him driving me home, did you?'

'I didn't know he was back in Ghana.'

'They kept him locked up for four years and then sent him home.'

'And you took pity on him.'

'His former employers were in gaol.'

'Mama Kate will want him back though, won't she?'

'Perhaps, but he won't be much use to the cartel now. I'm hoping that I can keep him out of all that.'

'Good luck!' Kwame changed the subject again. 'Did Afriyie tell you that Akosua was at St Louis?'

'Yes, I'm not very happy about that.'

'Why not?'

'Well, if the cartel wanted to move against you she could be an obvious target, alone here in Kumasi.'

'Do you know of any threat like that?'

'No, nothing for certain, but it's always at the back of my mind.'

'Mine too; could you help keep a look-out for us? Would you visit Akosua sometimes? I know she would like that.'

'Yes, now that we've had this chat I think I would like to.'

'Do you think the cartel suspects my involvement in their troubles?'

'I don't think so, but it's possible.'

'Why do you think Kofi Boateng brought me an invitation to visit Mama Kate?'

'I think they still want to recruit you as a courier.'

'But I wouldn't agree.'

'You might if they were holding Akosua.'

'I know you can't ask directly, but has Kofi dropped any hint that the cartel might threaten me or Akosua?'

'You know Kofi; he says very little, and what he does say is hard to understand.'

'You're telling me! But you've picked up no clue?'

'He did speak of you once, or rather of your father.'

'What did he say?'

'He told me that in his youth one of his brothers worked at a Lebanese sawmill and your father used to come to look at the machines.'

'Did he say anything else?'

'He said your father's accident removed a tripping stone from the path of the sawmill owners.'

'Is that all?'

'He added one of his obscure proverbs, something about when you lift a stone you must watch out for what is underneath.'

'It sounds to me as though he suspects that the sawmill owners had something to do with Dad's accident and that I might be seeking revenge.'

'Whatever he suspects, I think he'll keep it to himself.'

'I wish I could be sure.'

After a long pause Kwame continued, 'Do you think that Peter Sarpong might want to take revenge against me over the death of Uncle George?'

'He might, but he's not in charge. The big people take a more practical view of things. As I was telling you, they would try to use you to promote their business.'

'Why do you say that?'

'They're losing more couriers these days. More are being arrested at the airport because the *abrofo* are getting better at finding the drugs. Some of the women are dying when condoms burst in their stomach and the publicity is causing more problems. People are less willing to be couriers. Someone like you, who might get through several times before arousing suspicion, would be worth a fortune to the cartel.'

'I'm certainly not swallowing any condoms.'

'No, you wouldn't need to do that.'

Kwame returned to Tema with a heavy heart. He had not been reassured by what Comfort had told him. Sooner or later, he felt, the cartel would begin to suspect him and when they did it made little difference if they threatened him with violence or tried to coerce him into cooperating with them. He didn't want to take that risk, for himself or for Akosua. With uncharacteristic resolve he decided to plan his escape.

Having put so much time and effort into starting AT Ghana, Kwame wanted to do all he could to ensure its continued success. He discussed the matter with Dan Nyarko who couldn't understand why Kwame wanted to hand over his role as chief executive but nevertheless promised to give the matter some thought. A few days later he was back with a suggestion. 'Do you know that Dr Jones is still in Ghana?' he asked Kwame.

'No, what's he doing?'

'He's staying with a friend in Accra and doing some freelance consulting.'

'Are you suggesting that he might like to run AT Ghana?'

'We could ask him, couldn't we?'

'Let's go and see him.'

Dr Jones was pleased to see two of his GRID engineering protégés. He explained that since he had left GRID he had looked around for another project to promote grassroots industrial development but so far he had found no long-term employment. When he was told about AT Ghana he tried to persuade Kwame to stay on as executive director. 'You're doing exactly what needs to be done and nobody is better qualified to make a real impact than you, Dan and Sam. You three between you have more expertise than all that is left in the GRID project, and you have devised an appropriate vehicle for putting that expertise to work. It is far better that you young Ghanaian engineers carry the work forward than that it should revert to an ageing expatriate.'

'But Dan and Sam will stay on to continue the work,' said Kwame. 'It's only I who must leave. Dan will run the programme in Tema and Accra, and Sam will look after Kumasi. We also have Edward Opare, Solomon Djokoto and Albert Ansah signed up to help with the survey. We need you to coordinate the activity and handle the relationship with ODA. That wouldn't take up all your time; you'd still have time to do other freelance work.'

'It's a tempting proposition,' said Dr Jones. 'I'll give it some thought and let you know.'

Kwame's next problem was how to plan his departure without attracting attention. First, he asked Afriyie if she wanted to come with him and Akosua or stay behind in Ghana. 'I want to come with you,' she said, 'but how long will we be away?'

'I suspect that Akosua and I must stay away for a long time, at least six years, but I think that you could come back on visits from time to time.'

'Would we be in Coventry or Cranfield?'

'We might be in Coventry; I could apply for a post at Warwick University. I'm sure Tom would help me and you would be near Akos Mary.'

'That would be nice.'

'Don't set your mind on it, though. We might need to go somewhere where we aren't known and couldn't be traced.'

Kwame's biggest problem was how to bring Akosua from Kumasi to Kotoka International Airport. In his disturbed state of mind the very name of the airport symbolised for Kwame the threat of violent retribution. Kotoka had been one of the generals who had overthrown Kwame Nkrumah in 1966 and been killed in a failed counter-coup a year later. His statue now brooded over the approach to the airport at the point where he had fallen, a grim reminder of the fury of those who felt themselves betrayed. Kwame didn't know if he was under observation from the cartel but it was safer to assume that he was. For this reason he didn't want to fetch Akosua himself or to involve Afriyie. He decided to ask Comfort to help. He was relieved to learn that she had already started visiting their daughter at St Louis School.

Kwame knew that British Airways flew from Accra to London late in the evenings of Sundays and Wednesdays. He chose a Wednesday because the roads would be busier and there would be more people around in the town and at the airport. On his next visit to Accra he called at the British Airways office on the corner of Kojo Thompson Road and Tudu Road and bought one child's and two adults' tickets to travel to London on Wednesday 27 July 1994.

In the afternoon of the appointed day, Comfort drove herself to St Louis' and took Akosua out of school on the pretext of an urgent visit to the dentist. They drove back into town but instead of turning left towards Nhyiasu they turned right and headed for Kumasi airport. Soon they were flying south-east towards a rendezvous with Kwame and Afriyie at the airport in Accra. There they waited for a few anxious hours until the flight to London was called for boarding after 11 pm. Comfort stayed with them until it was time for the travellers to go through passport control into the departure lounge. Akosua was sad to leave her mother so soon after their reunion, but Comfort promised that if they could not come back to Ghana she would visit them in England when she came to negotiate her shoe purchases.

Soon after they were seated on the aircraft Akosua and Afriyie were sleeping soundly, but Kwame's attempt to join them in blissful oblivion was frustrated by thoughts that refused to be suppressed. It was the matter that always troubled him. Had he taken that last fateful decision or had it been taken for him? It was the conversation with Comfort that had provided the final push. She was the one who had suggested the possible threat to Akosua, left alone at school in Kumasi.

Just as when he left GRID he couldn't help feeling like a traitor. He had abandoned the task he had set himself after many years of soul searching: to strive for the economic development of his country. He was little better than the thousands who ran away at the first opportunity to make their fortune in a richer country where life was easier; selfishly pursuing their own interest and giving little thought to the needs of their country and its impoverished people. His father would not have approved of his action.

But didn't he have a good reason for abandoning his homeland? If he thought that he and his loved ones were safe he wouldn't now be running away. Perhaps he should be gentler in his self-criticism. He hadn't given up without a struggle. What had forced him to abandon his mission was what the *abrofo* called illegality. If there had been no drugs smuggling, if there had been no corruption and nepotism, and if the political system had not largely condoned these socially corrosive activities, he and his comrades could have carried their work forward for as long as they had strength. Who knows what might then have been achieved in realising the ambitions of Kofi Busia and Fritz Schumacher.

He was sure now that the approach adopted by the TCC had been the right one. In the days before GRID had lost the memory of Suame the ITTUs had helped to create hundreds of new small enterprises and thousands of jobs. If this effort had been vigorously spread throughout the country, still firmly linked to its roots in Kumasi, it could not have failed to raise the economy from the grassroots.

He had not been alone in the struggle. A highly skilled corps of well-motivated people had been assembled and prepared to undertake the task, but all had been forced to abandon the effort by either leaving the project or joining the sycophants. Kwame hoped and expected that many of those left behind would continue to do all they could in their dispersed stations but they had been denied the opportunity to combine their efforts in a coordinated programme. One generation with good intentions had failed to realise its aspirations. He could only hope that another would arise with equal resolve in a more favourable political and social climate.

Kwame recalled his father telling him about the excitement and expectation that accompanied the birth of independent Ghana in 1957. The first British colony in Africa to be free had possessed great human, natural and financial resources, and a democratic system of government. There seemed to be nothing that it could not achieve. Yet his father had died of a broken heart, hastened to his grave by the overthrow of Kofi Busia in 1972. Why couldn't Ghana make democracy work and enjoy a government that could be held accountable for its actions? One after another the dictators had come and gone, enriching their families but impoverishing the nation.

Was Ghana any better off in 1994 than in 1957? True, there had not been a coup since the last day of 1981; after five military coups in the previous sixteen years the nation had grown weary of these upheavals. The present military dictator now claimed to be an elected president.

According to his own constitution, he could serve no more than two four-year terms. If he could be persuaded or compelled to adhere to what he had signed, Flight Lieutenant Jerry John Rawlings could be ousted in the year 2000. So, thought Kwame, Ghana must look to the new millennium for a chance to fulfil the promise of the 1950s.

The thought of the new millennium excited him. Maybe his exile need not be open-ended. If democracy could be restored, corruption suppressed and the rule of law enforced, a day would come when he could return, confident in the knowledge that his work could be resumed. How long would that take? Perhaps a decade; it was a long sentence, but not unendurable, even for a man who could no longer take pepper! He was, after all, only 37, just four days older than his country.

It was then that Kwame noticed that Akosua was no longer sleeping. She was holding him in the same steady speculative gaze that Comfort had used before offering to pay for the house.

'Will you buy me some new dresses to wear in England?'

'Afriyie has brought your pretty things from Tema, do you need any more?'

'Mummy says I should ask you to buy me new ones because the other girls will laugh at me in those old things.'

'Well, Mummy knows what's fashionable, especially shoes. Has she given you some to wear in England?'

'No Daddy, she said there was no point in sending shoes back to England.'

'Then what's in the big suitcase you brought from Kumasi? You had no home clothes at St Louis, did you?'

'No Daddy, but the big case isn't for me. Mummy said I should give it to Auntie Akos Mary when she meets us at the airport.'

'Akos Mary must be missing Ghanaian food; yearning for yams, plantain and stuff like that. Afriyie is also taking her some.'

'But do you know what Mummy said Auntie Akos misses most of all?'

'No, what is that?'

'Snails, Daddy, and they're still alive inside the case!'

Glossary

AT Ghana	Appropriate Technology Ghana
BRI	Building Research Institute
CFA	*Communaute Financiere Africaine* The CFA franc is the currency used in 8 West African francophone countries, including Togo, Cote d'Ivoire and Burkina Faso, all bordering Ghana. The currency was tied to the French Frank during the time of the story (It is now tied to the Euro) and so was regarded by Ghanaians as a 'hard currency', much sounder than the Ghanaian cedi. 'CFA' has stood for somewhat different words in the past. The words have been changed, but the CFA has been retained because it is strongly identified with the currency in West and Central Africa and in international trade.
CIDA	Canadian International Development Agency
CSIR	Council for Scientific and Industrial Research
DAPIT	Development and Application of Intermediate Technology
EC	European Community (from July 1987 to November 1993)
EEC	European Economic Community (until July 1987)
GRID	Ghana Regional Industrial Development
ILO	International Labour Organisation
IMF	International Monetary Fund
ITDG	Intermediate Technology Development Group
ITTU	Industrial Technology Transfer Unit
KTI	Kumasi Technical Institute
KNUST	Kwame Nkrumah University of Science and Technology (from 1966 to the early 1980s the 'Kwame Nkrumah' was dropped and the initials were UST)
MBA	Master of Business Administration
MFEP	Ministry of Finance and Economic Planning
MIST	Ministry of Industries, Science and Technology

373

NCWD   National Council on Women and Development
NGO   Non-Governmental Organisation
ODA   Overseas Development Administration
PCU   Plant Construction Unit (of TCC)
RID   Rural Industries Division (of GRID)
SEACOM   Socioeconomic and Communications Division (of GRID)
TCC   Technology Consultancy Centre
TDC   Tema Development Corporation
TED   Technology and Enterprise Development
USAID   United States Agency for International Development
UST   University of Science and Technology (KNUST in Kumasi
          was called UST from 1966 until the early 1980s when the
          name 'Kwame Nkrumah' was restored. However, 'UST'
          continues to be used occasionally for brevity.)
VSO   Voluntary Service Overseas